FALLS THE SHADOW

SHADOW

EMANUEL LITVINOFF

STEIN AND DAY/*Publishers*/New York

The publishers wish to thank Atheneum Publishers
for permission to use an extract from *Language and
Silence* by George Steiner.

The author is much indebted to *The Defense of
"Obedience to Superior Orders" in International Law*
by Professor Yoram Dinstein; A. W. Sijthoff-Leyden;
Dachau—the Official History by Paul Berben; the
Norfolk Press, London. Mrs. Wichman of the
Wiener Library, London, was most helpful.

FIRST STEIN AND DAY PAPERBACK EDITION 1984
Falls the Shadow was first published
in the United States of America in hardcover
in 1983 by Stein and Day/*Publishers*
Copyright © 1983 by Emanuel Litvinoff
All rights reserved, Stein and Day, Incorporated
Printed in the United States of America

STEIN AND DAY/*Publishers*
Scarborough House
Briarcliff Manor, N.Y. 10510
ISBN: 0-8128-8084-6

1

SUNDAY MORNING, beginning of another working day.

Neat in his navy blue alpaca suit, eyes hidden behind smoked glasses, sixty-seven-year-old Avram Benamir emerged from his apartment block on Blumenthal Street, Tel Aviv, and started the engine of his black Peugeot. A man stepped out of the shrubbery in the forecourt of the building carrying a British Airways canvas holdall. As Benamir reversed before moving into the stream of traffic, the man produced a gun out of his bag and fired through the windscreen. The black Peugeot rolled back out of control until it crashed into the car parked behind.

For some moments the scene froze. A terrified woman clutched her child; pale and dazed, the gunman stared at the round bullet hole in the shattered windscreen; passing pedestrians turned sharply, arrested by shock. Traffic halted. People emerged on balconies and peered into the street. Someone started to shriek.

Holding his airways bag in one hand and the gun in the other, the pale assailant remained motionless, central figure in a melodramatic tableau. The sun glinted on the barrel of his weapon. Suddenly an elderly woman ran out of the apartment block, her cries disrupting the unnatural quiet. She pulled open the car's door, stared in horrified incredulity and began a shrill ululation of demented grief.

Soon the first faint siren was heard, taken up from different directions, coming closer, moving in fast and menacingly.

For Amos Shomron, a senior investigation officer of the Tel Aviv police, the morning began with a phone call about the domestic crisis that had been going on for nearly a week. "What's Leah trying to do to me?" groaned his brother-in-law. Sleep-fuddled Shomron fumbled with the receiver. "What time is it, Berl?"

"Nearly six-thirty. I haven't closed my eyes all night. How can my wife walk out at a time like this?"

Berl had a knack for stating the obvious. Answers were not required, nor was Shomron in a condition to give them. Not before a drink of strong coffee and the first cigarette.

Deborah, sleeping naked beside him, stretched and yawned. "I wish they'd make it up," she said. "We'd have some peace in the mornings."

Putting on her horn-rimmed glasses, she got up, opened the slats of the blind to let the sunshine in, then unrolled the raffia mat to do her morning exercises. Amos listened to Berl's monologue and watched the rhythmic movement of slender, deep-tanned legs. Her thighs, she claimed, were disfigured by something called cellulite. She did bust-tightening exercises and punished the muscles of her trim waist. Physical fitness was a new obsession. Every evening after finishing work on the magazine she hurried to the Gordon pool overlooking the sea shore and swam her twenty lengths. Linus Pauling had converted her to the supreme benefits of vitamin C; she also swallowed tablets of ginseng and brewers' yeast. It had something to do with her "self-image." At thirty-one, after twelve years of marriage and two children, she'd begun to grumble about feeling caged. If he wasn't so sure of her he'd worry that she was working up to infidelity.

They'd met one freezing night in January during some army maneuvers in Sinai—Deborah huddled inside a shapeless greatcoat, a disconsolate nineteen-year-old army conscript homesick for the comforts of middle-class Tel Aviv, himself a twenty-three-year-old reserve tank officer involved at the time with a cool, hard-edged blonde law student named Shulamit Fenster. He had no intimation then that the brief encounter was destined to be momentous. A week later they went to

5

a concert at the Mann Auditorium and it hit him, the shock of love. He felt it coming in the silence when the restless audience stilled and the soloist opened the first movement of Schumann's Concerto for Piano and Orchestra in A minor. Deborah leaned forward with grave intensity, a lock of rich brown hair falling across her cheek, her eyes shining, and as he watched her the music caught him under the ribs and his heart pressed against his breast-bone in a sudden fullness of emotion.

His brother-in-law's voice continued in plangent complaint. That marriage had been in trouble for years. It had something to do with his sister's failure to get pregnant—Berl's low sperm count, according to her. She had no inhibitions about discussing it openly in the family. "What are families for?" she demanded. Viewed from the perspective of his profession, the family was the breeding ground of jealousy, betrayal and violence, physical or psychological, if not both.

"She can at least see me before I go to the airport," entreated Berl.

"Sure, I understand," Shomron said resignedly. "Look, I'll put her on to you."

He got out of bed, unplugged the phone and, stepping over Deborah's Yoga-twisted body, went into the next room. "Berl's on the line, Leah," he said, reconnecting the instrument. "He wants to talk to you."

The springs of the couch squealed as his sister flung over to face the wall. "Tell him I've got nothing to say."

"Don't be obstinate, Leah. The man's flying to Paris this morning."

"So when he goes I'll move back into the flat. You can tell him that."

Shomron shook his head in exasperation. "Listen," he remonstrated, "what harm is it if he wants to have a dialogue with some Palestinian Arab intellectuals?"

Leah sat up abruptly. "What intellectuals? Killers, assassins of schoolchildren. He runs after people no one in the country would talk to. Paris, Milan, Vienna, God knows where. Berl Reznikov, a one-man peace movement on a university lecturer's salary. It's losing us all our friends."

Anguished noises came from the telephone receiver.

"She's exaggerating, Berl, don't take it to heart," Shomron soothed and hung up. Leah's sulks were famous in the family, but this was ridiculous. Not enough she should nurse a grievance over his alleged spermal deficiency, politics also had to be brought into it.

"Why are we such a quarrelsome tribe?" he soliloquised during breakfast. A simple difference of opinion is not enough, we have to start a new faction, a personal vendetta, a blood feud. The Hasidim have divided into rival dynasties because two hundred years ago in the shtetl a couple of ancestors quarrelled over some Talmudic sentence. The first kibbutznik to commit the sin of owning a private radio was driven out of the communal Garden of Eden. As for our politicians, they stone their opponents like religious zealots pelting car drivers who violate the Sabbath."

"Did they throw a stone in Moshe Dayan's eye?" eagerly enquired Noam, aged nine.

"Orit, if you don't eat your egg I'll never speak to you again," Deborah scolded their eleven-year-old daughter. "Leah and Berl are not fighting over politics," she declared flatly.

Shomron heaped some cottage cheese over a slice of bread and spread honey on top. "Neither are the politicians," he said, taking a huge bite.

Leah appeared at the door in her kimono, puffy-eyed and aggrieved. She drew up a chair and poured a cup of coffee. "The phone's ringing, can't you hear it? If it's that husband of mine again, say I've already left."

"One day he'll stop caring," Shomron flung over his shoulder as he went to take the call. The speaker was Gabriel Cohen, his deputy. Gaby, about to leave for the District Court to give evidence in a drugs case, was ringing through about a shooting in Blumenthal Street, near the Municipality. One man killed.

A sudden burst of laughter came from the breakfast table—Leah doing one of her comic acts to amuse the kids. Shomron put down the phone and closed the door as though to segregate his family from the violence of the outside world.

"I've only got the bare details," Cohen resumed with professional aplomb, "but it sounds fairly straightforward, a routine homicide."

8

Shromron smiled. Young Gaby was impersonating the hard-bitten cop. Nothing was ever routine. Crime had its roots in fantasy, in the psychic undergrowth where men conceal their illicit greeds, passions, perversities. He felt suddenly buoyant and energetic, brimming with curiosity.

Murder. An interesting way to start the week.

In a country alert to terrorism the machinery of counter-violence moves fast. When he arrived the street was already cordoned off. A fleet of police cars, an ambulance and a mobile laboratory stood by, red lights pulsating, and the area swarmed with blue-uniformed figures, one of them conducting a staccato conversation by short-wave radio with central headquarters. Onlookers strained against the barriers watching with morbid curiosity as one of the policemen rested a drawing board on his left forearm and sketched the scene of the crime, and a photographer prowled around the victim's car. Snap! The view through the shattered windscreen. Snap! A shot of the interior where the dead man lay, head lolling, dentures exposed in clowning grimace. Snap! Close-up of face showing the bloody cavity made by the bullet when it smashed through the dark lens of the glasses into the right eye. Snap! Snap! Angles of the street, sun and shadow, figures transfixed. The photographer adjusted his camera and focused on two men in quiet conversation, one, Gillon Romm, a tall senior police officer of massive build, the other pale, slight, his head absently

9

inclined in the attitude of someone waylaid by a stranger seeking directions but too preoccupied with his own affairs to pay much attention.

An eyewitness? More likely the man at the centre of the affair, the assailant himself, Shomron concluded, noting the bemusement, the glazed exhaustion, tell-tale symptoms of shock. Gillon met Shomron's eyes, nodded briefly. He was following routine procedure, conducting an on-the-spot-interrogation. Many an involuntary confession was elicited in that traumatic interval when a suspect's mind groped to recover sanity—unless sanity was absent in the first place, or the killer was a trained assassin.

Two officers disentangled the corpse from the driver's seat, its head shrouded, and carried it on a stretcher into the lab. Dr. Buchner, the pathologist, glanced up from his work as Shomron entered. A small, ruddy man with a bald sunburnt scalp, he pointed at the massive laceration around the cadaver's eye cavity and said in a brisk, cheerful voice: "Nasty, isn't it? The bullet ripped through the anterior fossa and penetrated the cerebellum diagonally at an angle of roughly fifteen degrees. He died instantly. I'll carry out a full autopsy when we take him over to the Institute."

Shomron's glance slowly traversed the portly body, assessing age, social status, personality. A vague resemblance to Kissinger, perhaps, a common enough type among Tel Aviv businessmen. Dark, well-pressed suit, white shirt marked by a livid trickle of blood on the collar, blue tie with subdued red stripes, small feet shod in soft gleaming leather. The face was flaccid, nose short and rather broad, round skull covered in a distinguished thatch of silver hair. The dead man had a small prim mouth and wore a gold wedding band on the third finger of his left hand. The total impression was of a tidy, conventional, fussy individual, an elderly Middle European of comfortable means.

On a sudden intuition, Shomron lifted the corpse's right arm, pushed up the sleeve of its jacket and unbuttoned the shirt cuff. Neatly stencilled in the forearm was the number of a concentration camp inmate.

"You see this, doctor?" he asked.

Dr. Buchner snapped off his rubber gloves and shrugged. "Shall I show you mine?"

Yes, of course, the stigma was unremarkable. Stroll along any beach on a Sabbath afternoon, wander into the communal dining-room of a kibbutz or glance at the outstretched arm of a veteran bus-driver as he took your fare; an elderly woman weighing vegetables in the central market, the scientist in his antiseptic laboratory, a gathering of Yiddish writers memorializing the death of their murdered language—the brand was everywhere, burned into the flesh and the mind, so familiar it no longer merited comment. Survivors.

The still nameless corpse had acquired a generic identity. He saw him among the living cadavers pressed against the wire of their charnel house prison, blinking in dazed disbelief at the liberating soldiers of an Allied army. Slow recuperation in some displaced person's camp, then the last migration from the continent of death, creeping through mountain passes, smuggled at night across hostile frontiers, trekking towards the warm Mediterranean and the Jewish refugee boats that defied the British naval blockade guarding the forbidden shores of Palestine.

Searching through the dead man's pockets, he extracted a wallet, keys, fountain pen, monogrammed handkerchief, a small bottle of pills. "Digitalis," said Dr. Buchner. It figured. The driving license was made out in the name of Avram Benamir. He'd lived right there in the street, killed on his own doorstep.

Shomron paused in the corridor outside Benamir's apartment listening to the muted sounds of grief. The bell was answered by a stout Yemenite woman, swarthy as a desert Arab, her head covered in a cotton kerchief. She stood kneading her hands in her apron, moisture glistening in the cavities of her blunt nostrils.

The apartment's hall led into a room crowded with neighbors, their low distressed voices providing a background chorus to the guttural sobbing of an elderly woman.

"*Adoni,*" said the Yemenite, "who are you? Why have you come here?"

"Police." Shomron produced his identification. She stared at it with the uncomprehending gaze of an illiterate and hurriedly explained that she was the house cleaner. "Tell me what happened this morning?" he said.

"Something terrible!" Tears spurted from her red-rimmed eyes. "Someone shot Mr. Benamir."

"I know that," he said gently. "Were you here when it happened?"

"When I come the Madame gives me coffee. We didn't hear the shot because of the radio, only the bang-crash of the auto. Madame ran to the balcony to look and was screaming. She run downstairs. In the street I saw the man holding the gun."

"Did you recognize him? Have you seen him before?"

"Never!" She shuddered. "But his face, I cannot forget it. Evil! Why did he shot poor Mr. Benamir, an old gentleman who never in his life done harm?"

"We'll find out." Shomron edged past and entered the living room. It gave off an unaired whiff of closeted lives—massive funereal furnishings in polished mahogany and hide upholstery, velvet drapes of imperial red, the dull sheen of glazed green plant pots that could have come from the foyer of some old Viennese hotel. The curtains were drawn, mirrors shrouded to prevent the ghost of the deceased taking fright at its own reflection. Two aged men, one wearing a black homburg, the other a skullcap, rocked backwards and forwards facing the wall and muttering prayers. Each paroxysm from the weeping figure in the center of the group brought a reprise from the women clustered around her. Communal grief, profound, exorbitant, ritualistically exclusive.

As disembodied, for all the attention he got, as the departed object of this mourning, Shomron

13

wandered over to the sideboard and glanced at the display of family photographs. One early snapshot showed the dead man and his wife, judging by their shabbiness and the imprint of hunger on their gaunt features newly arrived in the country. Benamir looked startled and uneasy as though the camera had caught him unawares. A reticent background figure in other snapshots, his face so artistically obscured in a studio portrait as to be barely recognizable, he seemed to have disliked being photographed. The pictures accelerated the passage of time—Mrs. Benamir with one child, then two, then making a matronly appearance with two sturdy boys and an adolescent girl, wedding photographs of a daughter, a son, photos of grandchildren. Occupying pride of place in the center of the sideboard was a silver framed picture of a young soldier in battle fatigues. The image was blurred, evidently extracted and enlarged from a group snapshot for part of a disconnected arm rested on the youngster's shoulder. He had been captured in a carefree mood, grinning into the camera lens.

As surely as if he saw the fatal wound, Shomron knew that the boy in the silver frame was dead.

A ring at the doorbell made him turn. The Yemenite servant admitted a trim young police-woman, a sergeant, her navy-blue and white hat perched far back on her dark curly head. She was accompanied by a male civilian. Shomron intercepted them in the hall and introduced himself.

"This gentleman is the family doctor," said the sergeant.

"Epstein," the doctor said, offering a limp handshake. He looked depressed. In any circumstances, death was a professional failure. "How is she, the widow?"

"Very distressed, of course."

"Of course. What a tragedy! Such nice, quiet people. I've known them for twenty years. Why did such a thing happen?"

"We're making enquiries," was Shomron's neutral reply.

In the sitting room the bereaved woman inconsolably moaned that she wanted to die. Dr. Epstein picked up his bag. He could deal with that. "I'll put her to sleep," he said decisively.

Shomron turned to the policewoman. "What's your name, sergeant?"

"Zina Kogan, sir."

"I think it would be good to ask the people to leave. The woman has a daughter. She should be called. Stay around and see what you can find out."

Sergeant Kogan gave a capable nod: she had an unmistakable air of authority, cool eyes, a resolute, ambitious jaw. Shomron smiled. He appreciated women like that. Too much, perhaps.

Downstairs, the crowd around the barriers had grown, private tragedy turned to public spectacle. Next it would feed the insatiable appetite for newspaper sensation and finally be excreted into the national statistics of crime, and forgotten.

He found Gillon Romm and the prisoner huddled together in the police van. Manacled wrists hanging between his knees, the latter stared

15

unresponsively at the floor. "Why did you do it?" Gillon was saying. "What did you have against that man?" Sweat dripped from the prisoner's lowered face on to his shackled hands, but he remained silent. Shomron quietly withdrew. His presence was not required. Something about Gillon—his huge athletic frame, his rumbling voice and jovial laugh, the strong, good-guy personality reminiscent of the hero in a Hollywood western who stands rock solid in defense of the weak and helpless—all these reassuring qualities encouraged confession even in the most taciturn.

The time was still barely eight-thirty when he parked his car outside the Motzkin Street entrance of Tel Aviv police headquarters. A procession of orthodox Jews sweltering in long black gaberdine and large-brimmed black hats marched up and down in the fierce sunshine protesting against an autopsy due to be made on an old woman found dead in suspicious circumstances. Cutting up dead people, probing into their visceral mysteries, was a *Chilul ha-Shem,* a desecration of the Name, just another of the unholy practices of the usurping Zionist State that blasphemously sought to anticipate the coming of the Messiah. One flushed, angelic youth with long flaxen side-curls and eyes of blazing innocence prayed aggressively into Shomron's ear.

Shomron wiped the holy spittle from his cheek and took the lift to his office on the third floor. It was hot and humid: his secretary had forgotten to switch on the air-conditioner. Brushing away a large fly that insisted on grazing the damp roots of his hair, he settled down to deal with the neat pile of papers deposited on the desk. An internal memo gave details of a protection racket in Jaffa. Car thefts, robbery with violence, a syndicate selling carrion as kosher meat, prostitution, rape, drug-dealing—he sometimes thought of routine police work as picking lice out of the fur of a dirty animal.

The phone rang. "Amos, what can you tell me about the murder this morning in Blumenthal Street?"

Shomron recognized the voice. Dov Yudkin, free-lance crime reporter, zealous, shrewd and persistent. He had to be or he'd go a long time between meals.

"Who said there's been a murder, Dov?"

"All right, what can you tell me about the *killing* in Blumenthal Street?"

"A man is being held for questioning."

"Can you add a little detail to that? Who is he, what's the victim's name, what are the circumstances?"

"All in good time, Dov. It's too early."

"I could go around to the house and talk to the relatives."

Shomron's tone hardened. "Don't waste your time. Our people won't let you in."

"O.K., I'll come back on that later. What about the Jaffa protection racket? I have it on reliable information that the Yemenite Mafia is running it."

"Dov, it's not my case. I wouldn't know."

"Sealed lips. All right, Amos, I've got plenty of sources. By the way," Yudkin added insinuatingly, "I hear your brother-in-law is off to have a secret meeting with the PLO in Paris?"

"Goodbye, Dov," Shomron said coldly. Click. News got around fast. Berl was still somewhere in the air, flying over the Greek islands towards mission impossible, but the back-biting had already begun.

During the next hour or so the telephone hardly stopped ringing. For quite a few reporters, impatient of the circumlocutions of the Press Department, Amos Shomron was the horse's mouth, one of them, anyway. Their importunities were not unwelcome: information is by no means a one-way traffic. If the police are seen as an organized army of the law, investigative journalists are its guerrillas, able to move freely, operating behind the lines, raiding deep into enemy territory. Shomron disclosed what he could disclose, picked up a few random leads into the byways of the underworld, entered one or two appointments in his desk diary. Suddenly, glancing at his wristwatch, he saw that he had to hurry for his meeting with Lipkin.

Lipkin was in diamonds. That meant he carried a small wash-leather bag filled with tiny grey unpolished stones about his shaggy person and did swift, mysterious deals in the shallow reaches of Tel Aviv's diamond bourse. It brought him into contact with an ambiguous population of drifters, wide-boys and *luftmenschen* of all kinds. More to the point, through the operation of random chance Lipkin was one of Amos Shomron's most valued informers. Hauled in by the police net in an investigation of a smuggling racket with ramifications in New York, Amsterdam and London's Hatton Garden, Louis Lipkin proved to be small but valuable fry, a scavenger fish which swam in the wake of the great predators of the deep, gobbling up whatever nourishing fragments floated from their masticating jaws. To gain sympathy he began to tell Shomron the traumatic experiences of his life. Shomron was reminded of the delinquents' song to Officer Krupke in *West Side Story,* only instead of pleading a deprived childhood Lipkin's appeal for mercy was based on the scarring effects of the mid-century Jewish experience in Europe. It was, indeed, a hell of a story, but no worse than one could hear from almost anybody over forty-five stopped in an Israeli street. Lipkin, a repository of folk wisdom, remarked: "Ach! The younger generation. I could wring more tears from a stone." He had the watery blue eyes of that Tel Aviv rarity, a Jewish drunkard, and a glint of shrewdness showed when he said: "If you're Amos Shomron, I knew your father." He said it as if that practically made him a relative. Shomron did not know his father, whom he had last seen early in 1946 at the age of two and could not remember at all. Shomron's father, a young man of twenty-four, was sent to Europe to help in the smuggling of Jews to Palestine and fell victim to a Russian bullet. "Among his helpers was a certain person, Louis

Lipkin," said Lipkin. He wangled food, transport, forged papers, medicines, bribed officials, traded in black market currencies. So his life hadn't been all bad, after all. "Can't we strike a bargain, good for me and good for you also?" he argued with all the old skill he must have used in helping Shomron's father, if indeed he did help Shomron's father. They struck a bargain.

Which involved meeting at intervals by arrangement in various locations. This time it was in Beth Hatefutsoth, The Museum of the Diaspora, located near Gate Two on the campus of Tel Aviv University in Ramat Aviv. Shomron caught sight of Lipkin's short scarecrow figure browsing among a small display of Hebrew amulets. Shabby he might be, but not a careless dresser. Whatever the heat he sported a bow tie, his sweat-stained trilby hat was adjusted at a rakish angle over the right eye and his wrinkled baggy trousers, three inches short in the leg, were securely suspended by elastic braces. The threadbare coat he wore billowed out when it caught the wind, propelling him in a series of gusts along the pavement. Deliberately antediluvian, Shomron had concluded. Eccentricity disarmed suspicion and in Lipkin's trade that could be a positive safeguard of health.

"This is a good place," the informer confided, moistly pressing his hand. "The air-conditioning, beautiful. And you can learn something new every time. Do you know what that is?"

"An eighteenth century Persian amulet," said Shomron, reading the label.

"Yes, but what is it for?"

20

"An amulet, to bring good luck, of course."

A party of American tourists approached. Lipkin hitched up his shoulders, twitching an invisible scholastic gown, and said in a loud voice: "I'm an expert on such things. It was made to protect a pregnant lady from the demon Lilith who copulates but cannot give birth. Inscribed are the names of three angels. If you study the Kabbala you know they have the power to prevent Lilith breathing poison into the womb. Don't laugh, young man, even today there are sophisticated ladies, rich Americans from Fifth Avenue, who wear this between their breasts." The tourists loitered. Lipkin gave a satisfied nod: he'd succeeded in generating interest. "Maybe it's a little old-fashioned to believe in the Evil Eye," he conceded, "but who can tell for sure? And an amulet is still a beautiful ornament. For a few dollars, I know a place in Tel Aviv where you can get copies better than the original. Silver on copper. In real silver, a bit more expensive."

Shomron had already begun to walk away. Lipkin left a business card on the showcase and hurried after him.

"I should charge a fee," he said. "People come from all over the world, and where's the guide? They are entitled."

"I'm also entitled," Shomron said dourly. "What have you got?"

"Something sensational." The informer rotated his head in all directions. "I'll give you a name, Rivka Kloster."

"Tell me more about her."

"A handsome woman. If she was younger, a beauty queen."

"Is she in your line of business?"

"Diamonds? Ach, a depressed industry. In something much more flourishing."

"Heroin."

"Don't ask me. Look into it."

"Is she a dealer, Louis?"

"Amos, I have enough trouble sleeping already. You know these *chevra*. For them to break somebody's leg is just a pastime. And would I be so lucky? They'd put me in small pieces down the toilet. I wouldn't be the first. Where there's no body there's no crime. It shouldn't be necessary to tell this to a detective."

"Would I let them do that to you, Louis, a man who knew my father? This Rivka Kloster is a dealer, yes?"

Lipkin's tongue itched. The struggle to resist temperation was lost. Leaning closer, he breathed: "One of the biggest . . . To say more is to sign my own death warrant."

"You'll live to be a hundred and twenty," promised Shomron. "Let me run you back into town. Don't worry, we'll take a roundabout route."

Stepping from the cool, museum interior into the fierce, white sunshine of the campus, he hustled Lipkin over to his parked Volvo. In this hot little capsule of steel, he drove from Ramat Aviv to the sea road, pulled up at a quiet spot near the beach and put the pressure on. Drug dealers were rogue human phagocytes, the enemy in the bloodstream. And the gangsters were winning. Intelligence, vital in any war, was hard to come by and Lipkin might provide a small but useful breakthrough.

"If something comes from this, there should be a big reward for me," Lipkin said, always the opportunist.

"Don't think you've invented the bicycle," Shomron growled. "Most of what you told me is stuff we already know."

It had been a good day. Tidy up a few things back in the office and perhaps he would be able to get away early. However, as soon as he arrived he found a message from Gillon Romm asking him to ring urgently. It couldn't be the Blumenthal Street affair. Surely that was cut and dried. But it wasn't.

"I think we'll have to call this Operation Kafka," Gillon's voice boomed down the line. "There's something weird here. How soon can you come over?"

"Tomorrow morning?"

"What's wrong with now?"

So much for good intentions, Shomron told himself, replacing the receiver and dialing another number.

"You've caught me with my mouth full," Deborah said in a muffled voice. "It's a madhouse here today. I'm eating a herring and cumcumber sandwich, crumbs all over the typewriter. What is it, Amos?"

"It'll ruin your diet," he teased.

"No time to worry about that, little one. There's a story to write." The brisk and playful tone meant he'd got her in a good mood. At work the mother of his children underwent a regression to girlhood. The flush in her cheeks owed less to cosmetics, she moved again with that gauche eagerness that had first captivated him, a flirtatious exuberance lightened the timbre of her voice.

"You sound excited. Writing something special?"

"Specialissimo! Hold on a minute, the photographer's arrived. This is a double page spread with pictures."

Perched on the edge of his desk, Shomron shifted impatiently and glanced at his watch. A neat, darkly pretty police girl came into the room, smiled, and stood on tiptoes to reach for a file on a high shelf. Her skirt rode up, taut over her rounded buttocks, and showed a shapely length of leg. He sighed. She looked nineteen. Now that he was nearing forty, the girls in the service seemed to get younger and more seductive every day.

Deborah came back on the line trailing a laugh. "Sure, Noah, I'll pose for your center-fold any time. . . . Are you still there, Amos?"

"Just about," Shomron gruffly conceded, his glance lingering on the object of his middle-aged lust. They exchanged smiles as she brushed past him on the way to the door. Little minx. He recognized the perfume, Chutzpah.

"Noah's brought in some fabulous pix," said

24

Deborah. "I'm doing a feature on a new arrival from Russia, a sort of female Solzhenitsyn. You've never heard anything so horrifying as the way women were treated in those Soviet prison camps."

"Darling, I'm sure it was ghastly."

"It was not only the hunger, the Arctic cold and the savage hard labor. They were raped by everyone, male prisoners, guards, criminals, young boys, gangs of them. But worst of all was to be deprived of their femininity. They were turned into beasts of burden, soaked in filth, not women at all but un-men."

She spoke with bitter indignation, with horrified intensity, as if not Stalin but the entire race of men were somehow responsible. "Dreadful," Shomron muttered.

"Well," said Deborah, resuming her wifely manner, "why have you rung?"

"Darling, it's about the theater tonight."

Ominously: "Oh, yes."

"Can we call it off?"

"Call it off! I shall do nothing of the sort. I've been looking forward to it for over a week."

"Well, you'd better go on your own. I may be late."

"Fuck! Not again. Why?"

"There's a bit of a balagan here. I'll get there as soon as possible."

Speaking slowly and deliberately, Deborah said: "Amos, I am not going to the theater alone."

Those nerves that are fretted by the abrasions

of marriage began to quiver in Shomron. As though they were in the same room, he saw her eyes turn narrow and cold, her lips grow taut. It presaged one of those moods in which they became lethally formal and polite, a condition that lasted until one or another contrived an accidental touching in bed and the hostility dissolved in a torrid bout of lovemaking.

"I'm sorry, but I have to do my job," he said.

"Of course," she said. There was a silence.

"I'll do my best to make it on time," he reluctantly added after a while.

Deborah hung up. It was the equivalent of turning her back on him. He listened to the high-pitched buzz of the disconnected phone then gave a wry shrug and replaced the receiver.

"Wedded bliss," he said to the empty room.

The Gordon pool was uncomfortably crowded. Deborah emerged from the women's changing room into the white glare of late afternoon sunshine and steered delicately through a congestion of deckchairs, striped towels, rubber mattresses and raffia mats, the sprawled, perspiring masses of broiling flesh, to her usual corner near the toddler's pool. The cement paving was so hot it scorched the soles of her feet. Almost at the same moment, Noah came out of the men's dressing room in dark glasses, slack hairy belly hanging over his brief trunks, and stopped to pick up a couple of deckchairs before following her. Nurit and Esther and Drora, Ruthi, Phyllis, Shulamit and all the usual crowd were already encamped there with children, water-wings, sun lotion, cigarettes, magazines.

Bare arms were lifted lazily in greeting. Meeting so frequently, they spoke in shorthand, perfunctorily, with quick smiles and wordless gestures, preserving their energy for gossip and yelling at the kids. Noah got some reserved and guarded attention, quickly withdrawn. He had taken to tagging along after Deborah these past couple of weeks and his intrusion created a certain restraint. Maybe they were having a thing, the others wondered. Or, inseparable from his Nikon which he frequently aimed at the sexier looking females around, maybe he only hung around to take pictures.

"Well, I've got to do my stint," said Deborah, glancing at her digital watch and adjusting her bathing cap and water goggles. Some near-naked teenage boys and girls, brown, slender and smooth-skinned, were jostling and laughing on the high board. She watched them twist and flail in the sun, splattering her face with rainbow spray as they struck the water, then entered the pool herself with a clean purposeful dive. Gliding to the surface, and pausing only momentarily to relish the sensual coolness of the salt water on her burning skin, she joined the serious swimmers, the "keep fitniks," who ploughed relentlessly up and down the pool again and again, scattering the more casual bathers who floated into their path. Thirty lengths today, ten each of breast-stroke,

27

back-stroke and Australian crawl; twenty minutes of intense physical activity in which her mind could relax into free-floating meditation.

In rhythm with her breath, her first thoughts reviewed the day. It had been full and satisfying. She'd stopped off at school to see Noam's teacher. They discussed his mathematical precocity, the frustrations of an over-gifted child, and arranged for him to have special coaching. An agreeable problem for a proud mother to have. And work had gone well. All those chaotic notes on that amazing Russian woman had somehow arranged themselves into a clear, compelling narrative, and excitement surged through her as the shape of it emerged on the typewriter. But perhaps it took more out of her than she'd realized. That bitchy, niggling argument with Amos. It wasn't as though he could interrupt an important investigation just to get to the theater on time. She was married to a police officer, not a business executive.

Yet it wasn't only nervous fatigue. Just recently—quite suddenly in fact—a disturbing awareness had come to her that the juice of their marriage was drying up. After all, twelve years was a long time. Sometimes more than a week would pass before they made love and she had the feeling while they were doing so that Amos fondled her the way he might handle the controls of his car, instinctively moving the right gears, responding to the familiar rhythm of the engine. He seemed to have drifted into an absent sensuality quite different from the sharp, hungry intensities of sexual desire. Once this became lodged in her mind, her own responses turned sluggish and she had to resort to the pathetic female strategies of fake orgasm, saucy lingerie. She began to look at herself with critical disfavor. Although her figure had actually improved after the birth of the children—Amos said she became sexier—her bust had undeniably lost its firmness. Now she detected a thickening around the waist, an unattractive softness in her thighs, the beginning of bum-sag. So she'd begun to take herself in hand—exercise charts, dieting, swallowing vitamins, cutting out cigarettes, spending more than she could afford on creams, lotions, cosmetics, hairdressing. And nursing resentment, a nagging sense of rejection. Why did women always think the fault must be theirs when their husbands went cool on them?

Panting from her exertions, she pulled herself out of the water and vigorously shook out her long brown hair. Noah was waiting with the towel. Wrapping it around her, he took advantage of the concealment it offered to press his pelvis up against her, and with a sudden throbbing of lust she felt the stiffness of his prick against her cleft.

"For God's sake, Noah!" she muttered furiously, trying to push him away.

Noah grinned and continued to hold her close. He was nearly fifty, a swarthy, blunt-featured Iraqi Jew, married, with five grown-up sons and daughters and four grandchildren. His skin was coarse and pitted, his wiry black hair grey-white at the temples, and his middle-aged body, short in the legs, had passed the point of mere flabbiness and was turning to obesity. Yet, improbably, unwillingly, his crude, powerful masculinity evoked in her an erotic response that had long been missing from her marriage bed.

He must sense that, of course. Talking about a woman they knew who came to one of their dinner parties, Amos had said: "Vera's become available." It happened at a certain stage in marriage, he explained, and a man could tell it immediately. Was it so with her? She'd worked with Noah on stories on and off for about three years without anything more complicated than the kind of jocular flirtation people went in for, but recently he'd begun to play it for real.

Noah said: "Too many witnesses, eh?" and relinquished her. He slipped into the water to douse his rod, splashed about a bit and waved as she turned away to rejoin her friends. They seemed so languid and relaxed, smoothing suntan oil on their deep-tanned limbs, strolling over to the refreshment kiosk for cold drinks and ice-cream for the children. Yet theirs was a deceptive tranquillity, as the peace of the sultry afternoon was deceptive. A Phantom bomber ripped through the deep blue of the sky and they interrupted their conversation until its reverberations died. Two of these young women, still in their twenties, were war widows; and thinking of their dead husbands they thought of their sons, as Deborah thought of her own little mathematician whose every birthday brought dread closer. And not only their sons. Deborah had never quite recovered from that appalling March day in 1978 when thirteen Arabs landed in rubber dinghies on an Israeli beach near the main Haifa–Tel Aviv highway, massacred thirty-four men, women and children and left seventy-two others wounded. She had wanted to flee the country, join thousands of other Israelis who drove taxis in New York, opened boutiques, art galleries, or joined symphony orchestras, drama groups and universities in Paris, London, California. All her life there'd been wars, atrocities. She longed to be able to look into the future without fear, to be free of rival chauvinisms, the pervading atmosphere of hate, the endless and futile discussions about the how and why of peace. But she'd said nothing to Amos. For him leaving Israel would have been cowardly, an act of desertion. He'd be shocked and appalled that she could even consider it.

The sun burnt through her closed eyelids: dark colors of the spectrum. Deborah drifted into drowsiness, voices receding in a blur of sleep from which she suddenly awoke refreshed and cheerful although it could only have lasted two or three minutes. Noah's shadow fell across her legs. "Come and have a beer," he proposed, a neanderthal figure looming against the sky.

She sat up briskly. There were things to do before going to the theater—shopping, feeding the kids and getting them to bed, the usual household chores.

31

"Sorry," she said, "I'm on a tight schedule."

"I'll squeeze in somewhere," he grinned, stroking her bare stomach with his horny foot. Noah's courtship was notoriously lacking in finesse. If nothing else, that alone would inhibit her from adultery.

In the changing room, Phyllis joined her. A sturdy English woman with assertive blue eyes and a strong jaw, she'd run off to Israel years before with the son of a Jewish property tycoon. Before long he returned to Hampstead Garden Suburb; she remained, discarding husbands but never Israel. In former days she might have been an empire builder, a missionary to the heathens, or joined a wagon train en route to the American Wild West. Instead, speaking an oddly fluent and strident Hebrew, Phyllis cleared stones in a frontier kibbutz, pioneered a settlement in Sinai, did medical work among Christian Arabs crossing at the "good neighbor fence" on the Lebanese border.

They left together. The lilac dusk of early evening blew in from the sea. Neon lights flashed red, blue and emerald along Dizengoff. Garrulous crowds clustered around fast-food restaurants, boutiques and discotheques, and behind the noise of swift-moving traffic Deborah sensed with a shiver of anticipation the quickening beat of approaching night. In that she had not changed since she was sixteen. Night was the magical transformation of the city into a place of unexpected and dangerous meetings, of sudden encounters with destiny, a place where life took on intensity.

Phyllis disrupted her mood. "Tel Aviv gets worse and worse," she decided, glancing at the passing procession of soldiers of both sexes out on the town, overfed American tourists, the girls in tight, crotch-revealing jeans and flowing hair, young coxcombs swaying their narrow hips to the music of transistor radios. Idlers sprawled at pavement cafe tables. A mendicant sidled up demanding alms with a mixture of arrogance and servility.

"If they'd have a goya in Gush Emunim, I'd join one of their settlements in Samaria. They're the only pioneers left in this country," she said.

"Oh, Phyllis! You can't be serious," exclaimed Deborah. "I did an article on them once. Born-again Jews, they come with their Brooklyn accents, bible in hand, to reclaim the land God gave them four thousand years ago. And God help anyone who tries to stop them, Arab or Jew!"

"Well, here's a Christian who believes they're right," asserted Phyllis.

The noise of gun battle greeted her when she arrived home. In the darkness of the living room, the children were watching a Hollywood western on Jordanian TV, the sound at full volume. There were groans when she switched on the lights and turned down the set. Ignoring protests, she said: "I'm going to make supper now and I want you both to get ready for bed."

She found Leah in the kitchen drinking a cup of coffee, adding the stub of yet another cigarette to an overfilled ashtray. Vestiges of a crying jag

33

smeared her unhappy eyes and she was still in her dressing gown. Depositing the shopping bag on the table, Deborah said accusingly: "Haven't you even been out today?"

"Berl phoned from Paris. We had a row," was the sullen reply.

"It must have been expensive."

Deborah heated some chicken soup, cleared the table and put out cheese, yoghurt, pickled herring, sliced hard-boiled eggs, and a salad of tomatoes, olives and avocado prepared that morning before she left for work, all the while paying distracted attention to her sister-in-law's sardonic commentary on the blight that had settled on her life. In comparison Deborah's own dissatisfactions seemed trivial.

"How many people do you know who are completely happy, Leah?" she demanded. The question was equally addressed to herself. How lucky they were compared to her female Solzhenitsyn for whom an extra piece of sour bread, a few more shreds of stewed fish, had provided gleams of brightness in the frozen darkness of Siberia.

"That's what I keep asking myself," said Leah. "We're born, we marry, we have kids, we die. If it stops being fun, then what's the point?"

The children were splashing about under the shower in the bathroom. Nine-year-old Noam touched one of his sister's swelling nipples.

"You're growing bosoms," he said in awe. "Soon you'll be old enough to have babies."

Orit pushed his hand away. "I'm never going to

34

have babies," she emphatically declared. "At least, not till I'm very old."

When Deborah was getting ready for the theater, Leah appeared and leaned against the lintel of the bedroom door, a cigarette drooping from the corner of her mouth in a pose of weary cynicism.

"How would it be, Deb, if I go out one night and get myself impregnated by some random stallion picked up on the street?"

Deborah carefully smoothed her lipstick before replying. "Yes, Leah," she said in a judicious tone, "but what else would you pick up?"

All dressed and ready to go, she phoned Amos at the office to find out why he was late. Someone said he was out on a case. "Damn!" she said, and hurried out to get a taxi.

2

THE DISTRICT Police Station at 14 Rehov Harakevet is a big rambling building set around three sides of a large courtyard. By the standards of Tel Aviv, a sprawling city sprung out of nowhere (witness the famous 1909 photograph by Abraham Soskin of the first hundred or so settlers standing on the empty sand dunes casting lots for building sites), it was of moderate antiquity. An indistinct blob near the right-hand edge of Soskin's picture is a seven-year-old boy who later became Gillon Romm's father, too young of course to have acquired a piece of the future city. Yet an ironic coincidence connected that boy with the building on Rehov Harakevet of which his own son was to become the commander. Rounded up with other young Jews during an outbreak of communal strife in the time of the British Mandate, he had spent four nights below ground in one of the building's two prison cells.

Gillon's latest prisoner now occupied his father's old cell, the other holding two Arabs arrested for stealing materials from a construction site. They were small, dark, hook-nosed men with black malignant eyes and greasy hair like Mexican bandits. The newcomer's arrival provided a diversion. They stood at the bars of their cage watching him surrender his tie, belt and shoelaces before being led into the cell next door and released from his handcuffs. Waiting until the elderly turnkey had gone back to the gloomy vestibule and immersed himself in a newspaper, one of the Arabs called softly through the bars: *"Salaam Aleikem,"* and asked in bad Hebrew for a cigarette. There was no response. Breaking off to urinate in the sanitary hole, he returned and tried again, in English. "Psst! effendi, you got tobacco? . . . Where from you come? You Jew, *Yahudi?"*

The newcomer remained deaf to the importunate voice. As though entranced, his gaze travelled over blank grey walls, the stone passage, the barred light that came through a window grille. You could see that he couldn't make sense of it. He looked down at his own body as if to convince himself that he was there, in the flesh, that the experience was not a dream. He seemed unable to fit himself into the unfamiliar space. A regular wrongdoer, a petty crook used to going in and out of clink, sizes up a new cell pretty quickly and settles in like a commuter taking his seat in a railway carriage. The Blumenthal Street killer reacted like a sleeper who awakes to find that everything has become terrifyingly strange, who cannot be sure he is who he is, and suffers a desolating loss of identity.

After a while, the guard appeared with some food, a kind of bean pudding and a dry hunk of bread.

"How long will they keep me here?" asked the prisoner in a dazed voice. The eyes of a sleep-walker looked out at him from the officer's bored exhausted face. "Don't you understand English? Can I speak to someone in authority?"

"It's all right," came the indifferent reply.

"I must have a pen and paper, somewhere to write. It's very important."

The guard turned his back and walked stiffly away. In the next cell the Arabs hungrily spooned up their food. The dungeon silence closed in on the prisoner. He settled down to wait, hopelessly, trapped in that vacuum in which time has no measurement, therefore no meaning.

High above ground in the station commander's office, Gillon Romm, handsome proconsular head framed by the sun-filled window, gave a massive shrug and said: "I think we've got hold of a nut. Did he kill the man? Yes, freely admitted. He had to do it. For what reason? All will be revealed at the proper time. When will that be? At the trial. For the rest it is strictly rank, name and number, like a soldier captured by the enemy."

Gillon lifted a white cloth on the desk, uncovering the prisoner's personal effects—a British passport, keys, travellers' cheques, leather wallet, small pocket diary and ball-point pen, some loose coins, an SN 9mm Israeli army pistol.

Shomron took up the passport. It was made out in the name of Frank Sinclair, journalist, born 17 June 1932 in Prague. Judging from the photo, one of those dim representations produced in a coin-operated kiosk and no more reliable than a police mug shot as a guide to character, Frank Sinclair, like his victim, gave the impression of mistrusting the camera. He stared out of the picture as if startled, discovered in a shameful act, poised for flight. Turning the pages, Shomron noted that the passport holder had visited Germany and Austria several times, Czechoslovakia twice. There was no previous record of a visit to Israel.

"Anything useful in the diary?" he asked.

"Shopping lists, book titles, travel details, memory joggers. There are a few British names and addresses which may be helpful. He records that he arrived here on a British Airways flight on the thirtieth of April, booked in at Pension Rosenfeld in Hayarkon Street and spent sixty-seven shekels on bread, cheese and fruit."

Gillon stuffed the bowl of the large curved meerschaum he favored, lit it, and filled the air with narcotic fumes of sweet tobacco. Feet on the desk, he relaxed into a meditative soliloquy.

42

"This is, or appears to be, a premeditated killing. The killer arrives three weeks ago. How does he pass his time? One assumes that he had to get hold of a gun—airport security would have made it impossible for him to bring one into the country. Unless an accomplice exists, the weapon had to be bought or stolen. What else does he do? The diary tells us nothing. One gets a picture of a man wandering the streets aimlessly, returning to his rented room to eat his bread and fruit, reading a book, waiting. I turn to Saturday, the twenty-second of May. What goes on in his mind the day before he sets out to kill? Doubt, last minute fears, a crisis of conscience? There is a single line entry. "Be in bed by ten. Take two Mogadon." He instructed himself to get a sound night's sleep. That's all. Here," he passed the diary over, "see for yourself."

Shomron spent some minutes going through the small green book. Apart from the meticulous recording of domestic expenditure and other practical details, the owner's social life seemed blank —no luncheons, dinners, parties, no visits to theaters or concert halls, no countryside excursions. At regular two-week intervals, always on Friday, the symbol X was entered. Sex, perhaps, but if so no indication with whom. The diary gave Sinclair's address as 157a Belsize Close, London NW3.

An episode from his past rose up in Shomron's mind. He knew the location, an area of large shabby rooming houses in London's Swiss Cottage. In his student days, after the Six Day War

43

when the PLO launched its terrorist attacks against Israeli diplomats and overseas legations, he had spent some months as a security guard at the Embassy in Kensington. The desperate mission became a sentimental education. All that training in fast shooting, unarmed combat, dismantling explosive devices, in penetrating apparently harmless disguises to unmask arsonist or assassin, had gone unused. But, as usual, he'd fallen in love. The girl was supple in sex, Irish, an ex-ballerina lamed by an ankle injury. They lived in adjoining furnished rooms in a house in Belsize Park owned by Hasenklug, a psychiatrist who collected erotic art. She had the narrow elongated face of a Modigliani and long black silky hair parted in the center which he first saw from the street one summer afternoon hanging from an upstairs window to dry in the sun. How easily he burned in those youthful days. She was not pretty but the hair ignited a romantic flame. Hasenklug showed him the painting he'd made of her stretched naked on a couch draped in red velvet. For this she had lived rent free a whole month, she told Shomron. The picture was a flagrant imitation of Goya's *The Naked Maja,* coarsened by lechery's hairy paw, and Shomron in his youth blazed with a fierce, chivalric indignation that his silken-haired princess had been so wantonly exploited.

Her name was Aileen and they soon became lovers. In retrospect, it seemed to him that never before or since had he known such exorbitant and tireless and consuming lust, nor a woman so versatile in giving pleasure. Aileen made his blood sing, quickened all his responses. Afterwards, ravenously hungry, they would go to a restaurant in neighboring Finchley Road and gorge themselves on rich Hungarian, Viennese or German dishes, sitting among uprooted Central Europeans who still after thirty years retained a culinary nostalgia for their former homelands.

But they also came for fellowship, a bit of human warmth, these aging exiles. They sat a long time sipping the dregs of their coffee, eavesdropping on neighboring laughter, engaging in one-sided banter with surly waitresses, anything to delay the moment of return to the tenements of loneliness. Could Sinclair have been one of them? Fleetingly recalling those vanished faces, Shomron re-examined the passport photograph. It struck a dim chord, but that was all. Only Aileen emerged with distracting clarity from that twilit limbo and in the end the affair had turned out badly. Bitterness and betrayal. He shrugged the thought away. That part of it he'd rather not remember.

"The diary keeps its secrets," he remarked dryly. "What's known about the victim?"

"Sergeant Kogan is writing her report. I'll ask her to come in." Gillon spoke into the intercom. "Send Zina along," he said. Glancing at his watch, he added: "I'll have to rush. There's a meeting in Jerusalem with the Attorney-General. You're not in a hurry, are you? This might take a bit of time."

45

"We're going to the theater tonight."

"Ah, well, Deborah's a very understanding woman," Gillon cheerfully declared. After a while there was a knock at the door. "Come in!" he called, swivelling around in his chair. Walking crisply and erect, Sergeant Zina Kogan entered and stood to attention before her commander.

"You sent for me, sir."

"Yes, can you give Captain Shomron here a brief run-through of the information we have on Benamir, the man who was shot this morning."

"I'll have the full report ready in half an hour," the Sergeant said.

"The gist of it will do for now."

A hint of disapproval registered in the young woman's steadfast gaze. In a brisk, impersonal tone, she said: "I spoke to the daughter, Mrs. Fink, the family doctor, a next-door neighbor and the house cleaner. Mrs. Fink told me that her parents arrived in the country early in 1947. Her father fought in the War of Independence. He opened a printing and bookbinding business and built it up to a small factory employing twenty workers. He was a quiet person, well respected, a good family man who had no enemies. She said she couldn't understand why anyone should want to do him harm. The doctor is also puzzled. Model citizens. The eldest son, a boy of nineteen, was killed in the Six Day War. Another son, an electronics engineer in the defense industry, is on an official visit to the United States. A telegram has been sent asking him to come home immediately."

"Thank you, sergeant," said Gillon. "Is that enough for you to begin with, Amos?"

Shomron spread his upturned palms in a gesture of resignation. It would have to do. "Any chance of Sergeant Kogan staying with the case?" he asked.

"Sorry, she's too busy," said Gillon. "We've got a heavy juvenile case load."

"I've always wanted to work in homicide, sir. I'll make time," Zina Kogan said quickly, an ambitious gleam in her eyes.

Big Daddy was cross. He fixed her with a baleful stare but she unflinchingly stood her ground. "All right, go and finish your report," he growled. "I'll think about it."

Shomron watched her as she smartly about-turned and marched out of the office. "It wouldn't be for long. We need a woman on the case and she's a bright girl," he said.

"Bright!" Gillon grinned. "That kid intends to go right to the top—and God help you if you get in her way." He knocked the ash from his pipe, stood up and stretched mightily, his powerful arms almost reaching the ceiling.

"O.K., I'll leave you to it," he said, yawning. "Don't lean too hard on the guy, will you?"

When the prisoner entered the interrogation room, Shomron was standing by the window looking out at the street and smoking a cigarette with studied informality.

"Please sit down," he called over his shoulder and took his time before strolling across to perch

47

on the edge of the desk, pretending an affability he was far from feeling as he scrutinized his adversary. If he succeeded in making the theater on time, which was now doubtful, he'd have to forego stopping off at home to shower and change.

Until one looked more closely, Frank Sinclair, journalist, born 1932 in Prague, appeared much younger than fifty. Underneath the physical signs of aging he retained an adolescent awkwardness. He was a thin, grey, diffident man with a high, smooth forehead, pinched nostrils and a tight, narrow mouth. Unhappiness lurked in the face like an incurable disease and his posture, crouching in the chair, was watchful and defensive. Shomron was reminded of those reclusive individuals who wander in public gardens carrying stale crusts in paper bags to feed the birds. You make a remark about the weather and they shift away. One day they are found dead behind the drawn curtains of their dusty rooms. No one has noticed their absence.

"I suppose you don't speak Hebrew, do you, Mr. Sinclair?" he began pleasantly.

Frank Sinclair shook his head.

"Well, it's not easy. There are people who've lived here twenty years and still break their teeth on it. Let me introduce myself. My name is Shomron, regional investigator. Would you like to tell me what happened this morning?"

"I have already explained to your colleague that at this stage I have nothing to say," Sinclair replied, speaking English with the precise articulation acquired in language classes.

"Yes, I know. But having had time to consider, I thought you might change your mind. In your own best interests."

The prisoner obstinately averted his head.

"After all, what do you gain by remaining silent? If you fire a bullet into a man's face there must be an explanation," Shomron pointed out dryly.

"I'm not ready to give it now." The thin mouth twitched. "When I am it will astound you."

"Why?"

"You will see."

"How long do I have to wait?"

"Until the trial. I intend to conduct my own defense. To prepare the case I need writing materials and a quiet place to work." Sinclair had suddenly become animated. "The men in the next cell insist on pestering me with questions. I would also be grateful for the help of an Israeli lawyer to explain your legal procedures." The prospect of the trial obviously excited him. A feverish glow had entered his eyes and a rush of adrenalin was making it difficult for him to keep still. "How soon do you think it will be before the case comes to court?" he went on eagerly. "I could be ready in a week or so."

"It would speed up things if you gave us a full statement."

"And if not?"

Shomron shrugged. "We'll bring you before

the magistrate and ask him to remand you in custody while we complete our investigations. That could take a long time."

"But why? You arrested me at the scene of the shooting. There are witnesses who saw me fire. Surely you have enough evidence to bring an indictment."

"Mr. Sinclair, you sound like counsel for the prosecution," Shomron said in mock dismay. "But for us it's not so simple. We are interested in finding out the truth, in justice. Anyone can see you're not a violent man. If you can convince us of your innocence, if for example you acted in self-defense, or the gun was accidentally discharged, or your mind was disturbed, it's possible that a trial can be avoided."

His calculation proved correct. A look of consternation spread over Sinclair's face. "This is moral blackmail!" he burst out, trembling with indignation. "You are threatening to certify me insane. Give me any test you like, I'll prove that I'm not!" Staring at Shomron with agonized defiance, he said: "Very well, you demand a statement. Here it is! I came here to kill the man you call Avram Benamir and I did it, deliberately, in cold blood. There, does that satisfy you?"

Shomron gazed at him dispassionately. He stood up, wandered thoughtfully to the other side of the desk, settled into the swivel chair and studied his fingernails, then looked up sharply. "What do you mean 'the man we call Avram Benamir'? Are you saying he's really somebody else?"

50

Silence.

"Is that what this is all about? Not satisfied just with killing the man, you want to expose him, destroy his reputation, with maximum publicity. What can he have done to make you hate him so much, I wonder?"

"Don't speculate," muttered Sinclair. "You will never guess."

The strain of the day had taken its toll. A slime of perspiration coated the greenish pallor of his skin and his eyes swam with tears of exhaustion. Time, thought Shomron, for a change of tack.

"According to your passport you're a journalist," he said. "Do you work for a newspaper?"

"No."

"Freelance?" Again there was silence. Shomron rapped out a rapid series of questions. "When did you leave Prague? When did you settle in England? Do you have British nationality? Do you have relatives here? Are you married?"

"Captain Shomron," Sinclair interrupted tersely, "my work, where I live, my nationality, how I conduct my life, is no business of the Israeli police. Outside this case nothing about me is your concern."

"That's where you're wrong. You came here and committed an act of homicide. Everything about you is now our concern. Why do you resent us so much? Have you got something against the State of Israel?"

A faint flush mounted the prisoner's cheeks. "Israel means nothing to me," he sullenly declared.

"Then what makes you so angry?"

"Angry!" Sinclair gave an agonized laugh. "If you must know, I pity this country. I pity the people in it, every one of them! You call it a state, I call it a ghetto. You are surrounded by enemies, fifty to one, and wrapping yourselves in a flag of independence won't save you!"

So he cared. The rage, the despairing rhetoric, betrayed a grinding anxiety. Despite his cadaverous Gentile features, the schooled precision of his spoken English, Frank Sinclair was a Central European Jew—ergo, concluded Shomron, a victim. There lay the source of his desolation, and there perhaps the motive for his murderous act, some real or imagined grievance burning like a slow fuse through the years.

"Did you know that Benamir was a concentration camp survivor?"

The unexpected question struck with the velocity of a rifle bullet. Sinclair flinched at the shock. Without giving him time to recover, Shomron commanded: "Pull up your sleeve!" The other drew back. Leaning across the desk, Shomron grabbed his wrist and bared the forearm.

The number.

"So that's it," Shomron said quietly. "Where were you, in Auschwitz?"

Sinclair massaged his arm as though the pain of the tattoo was still fresh and looked at his interrogator with an expression that may have been in his eyes when the sinister brand was imprinted.

"Dachau." He pronounced it like an obscenity.

"And you knew Benamir there. You don't have to reply if you don't want to. The answer can be read in your eyes. Tell me," said Shomron, his voice charged with bitterness, "was he one of the Jewish camp police, a kapo?"

No reply.

"A bad one, a cannibal rat fattening on the misery of his terrified victims."

Again there was no reply.

Shomron nodded grimly. One of the things that rankled with his generation was that there had been Jews like that, men who befouled their human image. And cases of delayed vengeance had occurred, kapos recognized in the street, kicked and trampled to death. Shomron had found his bearings: he knew in which direction to go.

Deborah, wearing the green dress he had bought for her thirty-first birthday, was standing in the midst of a chattering group near the bar, sipping an orange juice.

As always when he saw her away from home and children, in unfamiliar surroundings, and especially when she talked and laughed with that eager gregarious animation, a tremor touched his heart, a disturbing sense of strangeness, a renewal.

He stood in the doorway, waiting. In a moment she would turn, responding to some psychic link. She turned, transmitting a long, cool look across the noisy, smoke-filled room.

"At least you made it in time for the interval," she remarked with barbed amusement when he navigated through the crowd and arrived at her side, falling in love again. She was wearing her contact lenses and her mascara'd eyes, their lids embellished with green eye-shadow, showed glints of gold in the brown and lustrous irises. A beautiful, ripe and supple woman: how lucky he was. And at the same time he felt a sharp and unpredictable apprehension.

He smiled apologetically. "I came as soon as I could."

"O.K." She patted his arm, a truce, and after greetings all around the conversation picked up again. They were talking politics, not theater, and principally personalities, family gossip touched with malice about Ezer and Arik, Shimon and Yitzhak, Begin of course, and the shrewd and tricky Dayan, too famous in the world at large for first name intimacies: brittle talk of intrigue, folly, betrayal, political seduction that seemed to Shomron to overlay a haunting sense of loss.

It must be his melancholy temperament, he decided, noting the zest with which Deborah entered this social game. Glum husband, vivid wife. No wonder the friends they had moved over to her side of the bed.

"Hi, Amos!" someone called, Benno Rizkin, a short chunky American Israeli in a pink shirt unbuttoned to the midriff to expose a large medallion on his hairy chest. Rizkin owned a nightclub in Jaffa, a jewelry boutique in the Dan Hotel, and a luxury villa for weekends by the golf course in Caesaria. Tonight, judging by his proprietorial hand around her slender waist, he also owned a tall sunburnt blonde with big, blue, vacant eyes and stupendous breasts that bounced under the clinging chiffon when he propelled her over.

"This is Marilyn, my new vocalist," Rizkin said. "Terrific, a new Peggy Lee. Listen, why don't you and Debbie come over to the club after the show."

"We'd love that," said Deborah. "Wouldn't we, Amos?"

Amos wouldn't. The notion induced a faint nausea. Overcrowded, smoky, tourist-infested, earsplittingly noisy, expensive, Rizkin's bit of tourist Jaffa, Sheba's Cave, was conceived as a kind of Solomonic period Montmartre with young Arab waiters done up as Nubian slaves. On the infrequent occasions when Amos had been there (always in the line of duty) he'd come away with a bad dose of misanthropy. Feeling uxorious as he did, he would have much preferred to hurry home to bed with his wife after the theater. But being wrong-footed by turning up late, he did not insist.

The interval bell went. Entering the drama

when it was half-way through gave him an odd feeling of intrusion, as though unlike the rest of the audience he had no business being there. "A week later, evening," said the programme. Five people sat in a city apartment, one an old, shabby man sunk in senile meditation. He took no direct part in the conversation and was ignored but while the others laughed, boasted, indulged in amorous skirmishes, he spoke meanderingly of a dead woman he had loved (wife, mistress, mother?), of hunger and revolution, a house destroyed by fire, a world gone. Who was he? What circumstances had brought these people together? A large picture window looked out on impenetrable darkness. As the play proceeded, the light in the room slowly began to fade and the darkness outside was lit by flames.

Shomron's thoughts wandered. A Friday evening at the family dinner table and much the usual mix of guests—Deborah's editor and her heart specialist husband, old Greengold the retired engineer, the Jerusalem lawyer Fuchs with his smart American wife, his third matrimony, and Shomron's sister Leah sparring as usual with Berl. "My peacenik at any price," she calls him and Berl grimaces as though the joke gives him heartburn. He'd come back from another abortive "peace conference." The Palestinians had failed to turn up, a pan-Arab meeting had re-dedicated itself to *Jihad,* holy war, Israeli zealots threatened to resist eviction from their illegal West Bank settlements with guns—and Leah's famished womb rejected his sperm. Life for Berl had been an intractable struggle against encroaching darkness ever since his return from battle in Sinai where the desert smouldered with burning tanks and incinerated human flesh. "Our love affair with violence is over," he said. "It felt good to be able to defend ourselves, but five times in a single generation has solved nothing. There has to be another way."

Pity it's not a comedy, Shomron thought, reluctantly returning his attention to the happenings on stage, in full darkness now except for the reflected glow of the fire raging outside. The curtain descended, actors took their bows and the house lights came on. Everyone looked relieved that the cultural ordeal was over and they could relax over a good meal.

"We won't stay long," he warned Deborah, driving in the car to Jaffa.

She gave him a long-suffering look. "For God's sake, Amos, we're supposed to be having fun. I need it. This is a very harrowing story I've been working on."

"I know," he said.

"You should see this woman. You should listen to the things she told me. She showed me a photo of herself before they arrested her—a pretty round-faced student of nineteen. There isn't a tooth left in her head. Her skin sticks to her bones. She looks like one of those Egyptian mummies unwrapped after four thousand years." Deborah stared miserably out of the car window. "But you know what? When I was writing it up it excited me. Listening to her was horrifying, yet as I started to type out the story I actually felt a kind of elation."

"Professionalism," murmured Shomron.

"So we tell ourselves. Remember that naked child running along the road in Vietnam, her body burning with napalm. 'My God!' somebody said, 'what a picture,' and he filmed it. They put it in magazines all over the affluent world next to advertisements for limousines and Paris perfumes. Professionalism."

"It was the most effective anti-war picture ever taken," Shomron said. He glanced quickly at her severe profile and squeezed her knee. "You're depressed by that lousy play. Don't think about it now. Enjoy yourself. I promise not to keep looking at my watch."

The lights of Jaffa's tourist quarter glimmered on the black Mediterranean. Warm breezes floated through the starry night and the sound of disco music reverberated from Sheba's Cave. Israel's Costa del Sol. Running the car off the road until the front wheels bit into sand, he said: "Let's stroll along the beach before we face the crowd." Deborah took off her high-heeled shoes. They walked in silence until they reached the water's edge and then he kissed her.

"You are romantic suddenly," she said, oddly embarrassed.

"I've been wanting to do it all evening," he solemnly confessed. "I want you to know that whatever happens you're my anchor, my hold on everything that gives life meaning."

Deborah looked at him. "Amos, there's not going to be another war?"

"That's Israel for you. A man wants to make love to his wife so she leaps to the conclusion that there must be a national crisis."

"Oh, well," she laughed, "if that's all it is, I'm not getting lumps of tar on my bum by doing it here. Let's go inside, I'm hungry."

"What's been keeping you guys so long?" Rizkin yelled above the noise, throwing out his stubby arms in extravagant welcome. He had to yell to be heard. The Cave was doing great business, not a vacant stool in the place. "Come to my table, the cabaret is about to begin." His arm commandeered Deborah's waist as he led them to a booth already occupied by the bosomy Marilyn and two other people. One was a youngish saturnine man with narrow cheeks and a thin, scarlet mouth, his eyes half-closed against the curling smoke of a long cigar. The other was a pleasant-looking woman in early middle-age, comfortably fleshed, with a dimpled smile and the healthy complexion of a milkmaid. The man was raffishly stylish, the woman matronly dignified, an incongruous pair.

Rizkin's introduction was brief yet expansive. "Deborah and Amos, Rivka and Sydney, me and Marilyn making up the six." His shrewd little eyes twinkled roguishly and he made it sound like the preliminary to a group orgy. Nubian slaves brought platters of chicken and rice, chilled bottles of Israeli champagne, orange slices marinated in brandy. Marilyn did not join the feast. "I've got to get ready for my cabaret spot," she announced, disappearing into a dazzling smile. This left some moments of awkwardness among the four strangers that even their host seemed at a loss to disperse.

"So you're a detective," Sydney began, fastidiously picking at his food.

"The best," boasted Rizkin on Shomron's behalf, laying a hand on his shoulder. "He's got eyes like a lie detector."

"Great. They tell me a lot of police work is done by machine now, computers, electronic bugging devices, miniature cameras."

"Is that so?" Shomron said politely.

In the brief silence that followed, Sydney's amiable companion was heard discussing children and other womanly matters with Deborah. "I have a son in the Hebrew University and next year my daughter has to go into the army. I'm already looking forward to being a grandmother," she declared with a wry shrug.

"Oh, surely you're too young," objected Deborah.

"And sexy," said Rizkin, completing the obligatory response. He turned back to Shomron. "Tell me, Amos, are you working on the Blumenthal Street murder?"

"What murder, Benno?"

"The one I read about in the afternoon paper.

Some old guy shot down by a gunman as he got into his car."

The melodramatic description of diffident, unworldly Frank Sinclair as "a gunman" had a jarring effect. Shomron shrugged. "I haven't seen the paper yet." Bored and irritated, he resisted glancing at his watch. Rizkin he could put up with, but there was something about the dark, smooth Sydney that aroused an instinctive antipathy. As if to confirm this dislike, the latter brought up a notorious case of police corruption. It concerned a man sentenced to life imprisonment for murdering a girl soldier. After six years in which he vainly protested his innocence, a retired police officer came forward with startling allegations that torture, sleep deprivation and enforced starvation had been used to extort a confession from the convicted man. A filmed reconstruction of the crime had been faked and used in evidence. Although the Attorney-General reopened the case and ordered a new trial which resulted in the prisoner's acquittal, although he had no personal connection with the event, the shame still rankled with Shomron. It was peculiarly humiliating that Jews who had themselves endured a history of torture could inflict torture on others, and it was abominable that the torturers were policemen in a country that offered refuge to all Jewish victims of persecution. But he wore the same uniform, he was spattered with the filth of it, and he did not relish this sly reminder.

"You seem to have made quite a study of that affair," Shomron said, unable to disguise his hostility. "What do you do for a living?"

Rizkin answered for him. "Sydney's an international wheeler-dealer."

"Movies," the other corrected. "I'm putting together a TV spectacular on terror. The Libyan Connection." He extracted a cigar from a moroccan case, clipped it and smiled thinly. "Have you had any experience?"

"Of what?"

"Counter-espionage, seek and destroy missions—" he lowered his voice—"there's a whisper that the Mossad has infiltrated agents into Gaddafy's group of PLO advisers. Is it true?"

A hard gleam entered Shomron's eyes: he did not take lightly to being treated like a fool. Even Rizkin looked uneasy. "Come on, Sydney," he protested. "That's top secret stuff."

Sydney's companion, Rivka, who appeared to have the knack of following another's conversation while simultaneously holding her own, leaned over and said with an unexpected note of asperity: "That's Sydney's idea of a joke. Take no notice," and Sydney went silent as though throttled by a strong grip.

Shomron regarded her with interest. He had wondered about the relationship. She did not have the look of a woman who would need the services of a hired stud. Nor for all his slick grooming did Sydney come across like a gigolo. Yet the impression of sexual partnership came through in glances of habitual intimacy, in small, unobtrusive gestures.

"Are you also in movies?" he asked.

In reply, she held up a shapely hand to display a fortune in rings. "Diamonds. My late husband left me shares in De Beers."

Just then the canned music abruptly stopped. A spotlight was switched on signalling the start of the cabaret and Rizkin stepped up to the microphone to announce the acts. Shomron took the opportunity to sneak out. He smoked a cigarette. He strolled among tourists of every nation shopping for souvenirs. Simmering pleasantly with lust, he stared at long-legged girls in light summer dresses. When his return could no longer be delayed, he re-entered the Cave. Glittering Marilyn, who had changed into a tight sequinned gown of transparent black, caressed the microphone with her tiny, breathless voice.

Rivka murmured to him as he resumed his place: "You're very naughty. You missed the folk-dancing."

Deborah said: "You cheated."

"I've so enjoyed meeting you both," said Rivka. "You must come to dinner. Soon."

She fished a card out of her handbag and passed it over. The name in small neat letters read: "Rivka Kloster."

Shomron slipped the card into his pocket. The mystery of coincidence—or was it? He looked up and met her eyes. She smiled with engaging candor.

Lipkin, he thought, and the tape of his memory played back the conversation. Is she in diamonds? ... something more flourishing ... heroin, a dealer, the biggest ...

"Thank you," he said. "I'm sure we will meet again."

"It's really too hot to make love this time of the year," Deborah said contentedly, when it was all over. The sheets were tangled up at the bottom of the bed. Slippery with sweat, they rolled apart. "I'm going to shower even if it does wake the kids," she said.

"It'll wake Leah, which will be worse," he said. "Besides, I'll soon feel sexy again."

"Boaster." Deborah reached across him for the cigarettes.

"No." He held her captive, her small breasts pressed against his chest. "Besides, you've given up smoking."

With typical illogicality, she protested: "Just because I want one cigarette it doesn't mean I haven't given up smoking." Sitting on the side of the bed puffing away, she said: "Married sex isn't too bad. It's the first twelve years that are hard." Shomron grunted. "I wonder," she went on, "what Mrs. Kloster sees in that creep?"

Shomron wondered about several things, but he was too sleepy to think about them.

"My father used to say, 'Everything we were, everything we believed, that is all on the other side of the grave. We're not the same people. Palestine was a new beginning,'" said Benamir's daughter. "Why is it necessary to go into my father's background forty years ago?"

She was a tall rangy woman with a bad complexion and startling blue eyes that met Shomron's suspiciously.

"The man we're holding may have been in Dachau at the same time," he said.

She stared, outraged. "Is that a reason for killing him?"

"We're just looking for connections. It's a matter of routine."

"Well, I can't help you. I don't even know that my father was in Dachau. My parents preferred not to say much about the past. It was too painful to talk about. Also, they wanted to protect us from the horror of it. Life is bitter enough without putting such a burden on children."

She compressed her lips against an onrush of tears, no doubt thinking of the tragedy that had just befallen her own. Shomron waited for the spasm of grief to pass.

"Weren't you curious to know more?" he persisted.

"It was discouraged. Both of them had lost everybody. In my mother's case, not only her parents and all her relatives but also her husband and little boy. She was married in Budapest at eighteen. My father met her in a refugee camp at a place called Bad Reichenhall, on the Austrian frontier. Misery brought them together. Who is this man?"

she demanded harshly. "What have we done that he should bring such a misfortune to us?"

"We're doing our best to find out."

"But you must know something about . . ." Benamir's daughter began then stopped abruptly. "Mama! I thought you were asleep. What are you doing out of bed?" she cried in a shocked voice.

Mrs. Benamir stood in the doorway leaning against the lintel, her short grey hair unkempt, a robe thrown over her nightdress.

"Yael," she said, bemused, "who is this gentleman? What have you done with the children?"

Her daughter jumped up and led her to the sofa. "Imma, darling! How are you feeling?" Turning to Shomron, she muttered: "The doctor said she'd be out for forty-eight hours."

"I feel old." Mrs. Benamir made fluttering, helpless gestures with her hands. "I feel so tired. Are the children in school?"

"Yes, Mama. I'll call Dr. Epstein. He'll come and give you another sedative."

"No, Yael, leave him in peace. Do I have so many more days that I can afford to sleep so much?"

She was stronger than her daughter thought, Shomron noted. Having been raised by an early widowed mother, he did not undervalue the fortitude and resilience of women.

"Is Shulamit still here?" she asked.

"Yes, Mama. She's in the kitchen."

"Ask her to bring some coffee." When they were alone, she said to Shomron: "Who are you, young man?"

66

He hesitated, then quietly replied. "A police investigator. I'm sorry to intrude on your sorrow but there are things we need to know."

Mrs. Benamir looked through and beyond him, her grieving eyes puzzled and accusing. "Many times in my life I have asked, Is there a God? Where is He? How can He allow people to suffer, to be destroyed? For what? If God exists, what is He doing when innocent human beings are slaughtered by monsters?" With sudden violence, beating her breast and staring directly at Shomron, she cried: "This is what I ask myself! This is what I demand to know!"

Shomron nodded silently. In his profession it was a familiar cry, an outraged protest at the absence of divine justice, wrenched out of torment and despair. All one could do was act as a lightning rod until the frenzy passed.

"My husband believes very much in God," Mrs. Benamir proceeded in a sunken voice. "He is not a religious man, but for him there is no doubt at all. If you want to know if God exists, you only have to look at the Jewish people and there's the proof. Isn't that so, Yael?" she asked as her daughter re-entered the room. "Didn't Abba always tell us that?"

Yael forced a smile and stroked the older woman's face. "Yes, Mama, he did."

"You see, young man, these things meant nothing to me, nothing. We were Hungarians. Did you know that Jews were settled in Hungary even before the Magyars? My father was a great patriot.

His family owned a large paper mill and many of them intermarried. I have many Christian cousins there even today. Of course, the regime of Admiral Horthy was antisemitic and when the war came we were treated badly. But we were spared the worst. It's strange to think of it now, but life went on almost like normal. You went to the theater, you gave dinner parties, in the summer you had picnics in the countryside. Then in the spring of 1944 the Nazi army occupied Hungary and everything changed."

The Yemenite servant brought in a tray of coffee and Mrs. Benamir thanked her absently, her thoughts entangled in the barbed and lacerating past. Yet she seemed to be retreating into it wilfully. The past at least was over and the bruised soul had survived. Only the present was still unendurable.

"Everything changed," she said sombrely. "There was an underground Jewish rescue committee and my husband thought we should ask them to smuggle us into Switzerland, but father said let us hold on because the war will soon end. The Red Army was advancing and the Americans and British were getting ready to start a second front. They used to quarrel about it. When we were ordered to put on the yellow star I had a terrible premonition that nothing could save us. It was too late, Eichmann had come to Budapest. I was twenty-three years old. I had a child of four. I loved my husband, my parents, my aunts and uncles, my cousins. I loved Budapest, my country, the Hungarian language. Even with all the suffering, life was beautiful. And then the sun fell out of the sky. The deportations began. They couldn't hurry us to death fast enough."

Mrs. Benamir's daughter watched her mother anxiously. Handing her a cup of coffee, she said: "Don't talk anymore, Imma, it upsets you."

The cup trembled in the widow's hand, slopping its contents into the saucer. Carefully, she placed it on the low table.

"You want to know something, Yael? For months, for years, I do not speak about it, but there is not one single day when it is out of my mind." She stared into her daughter's appalled eyes. It was now a conversation from which Shomron was excluded. "Yes, it's on the other side of the grave, like your father says. And where am I? One morning I went out to look for food—a few potatoes, some cabbage leaves. When I came back the street was empty, they were all gone. On the floor near the cot was my baby's shoe—" Her voice broke—"just one small shoe. I ran to the station like a mad person. I went up to a Nazi officer and cried out, "Please you've taken my family, I want to join them." He said, "Don't distress yourself, you'll go on the next train," and he took me to a railway shed. There were some Jewish girls there under guard. I never saw my child or my family again. We were sent to Ravensbruck women's concentration camp. They were all taken to Auschwitz."

Yael moved swiftly and put her arms around

her. "I wish you hadn't come," she told Shomron bitterly. "Can't you see what this is doing to my mother?"

Entrapped in her memories, Mrs. Benamir seemed unaware both of Shomron's guarded interest and her daughter's agitation. The room had become full of ghosts.

"I was a lost creature. I had no feeling, my heart was burnt to a cinder. We who survived were things, not people. We were not dead and not alive. Everything was darkness. Then gradually I became aware that there was someone at my side—Avram. We were now in the DP camp. Avram didn't speak much; he was just there, but it was enough to bring me back to life. The pain began again: that was the first sign. It was summertime, birds and flowers and sunshine, unbearable. After we were married, they asked us where we wished to go. 'We can send you back to Budapest,' they said. The thought made me shudder. I wanted to go as far away from Europe as possible, America, maybe. Avram took me aside. He said we must go to Palestine. 'But why?' I asked him. 'I was brought up to be a Hungarian girl. I have never been to a synagogue. I know nothing of Jewish life.' Avram said he would teach me. It was God's will that the Jews should come back to their Promised Land, and even though it was hard to understand, that was why these terrible things had happened. He told me about Judaism and taught me a little Hebrew, as much as he knew himself. So we came. It wasn't easy, the struggle to come here. The British navy stopped our boat and interned us in Cyprus. More guards, more barbed wire. But Avram was right. It was a new beginning."

And the threshold of other tragedies. Mrs. Benamir relapsed into an exhausted silence. Despite the heat infiltrating the apartment, a chill sensation prickled Shomron's skin. He sipped his lukewarm coffee despondently. Never had duty been more disagreeable. With enormous hesitation, he asked: "Did your husband ever talk about his experiences in—" and was struck down in mid-sentence by a look of pure hatred from Yael's blue expressive eyes. He had made an enemy.

With infinite weariness, the widow answered: "Do you think he could tell me anything I had not seen myself? Anything at all?"

She offered him her suffering face and his nerve failed.

"Don't go," Yael ordered in a hard voice. "I'm putting my mother to bed and I want to speak to you before you leave."

He stood up when she strode back into the room. There was an Amazonian quality about her, her tallness, the fury of her compressed lips, the blaze of a scorching contempt.

"My father was murdered," she said with icy clarity. "Nothing can in the slightest degree justify this brutal crime. Don't ever suggest it."

Shomron made a formal and evasive response: it was not an undertaking he was in a position to give. He wished to God that he had been able to.

3

"It's Dov Yudkin again," said his secretary. "He insists it's urgent."

Shomron gestured impatiently. The crime reporter's persistence got on his nerves. "Tell him when I have a statement to make he'll be the first to know."

She relayed the message: it was not well received. "There's no need to be offensive, Mr. Yudkin," the girl said sharply, red spots appearing in her cheeks. "Will you repeat that again without the insults . . . I see, just a moment." Placing a hand over the mouthpiece, she said: "He wants to know if you have any comment on the report that a terrorist group called the Tishrin Commando has claimed responsibility for killing Benamir."

"What?" Shomron spun around and grabbed the phone. "Is this a stunt of yours, Dov?"

Yudkin was hurt. "I'm a reputable journalist, Amos. The report was broadcast by Beirut Radio a few minutes ago."

"What exactly did it say?"

"I've written it down somewhere. Hold on a minute while I find it."

Drumming impatiently on the desk, Shomron listened to the shuffling of disordered papers and a distant altercation between the crime reporter and a woman as to which was responsible for mislaying the vital document.

"Got it!" Yudkin exclaimed a trifle breathlessly. "Are you holding on to your seat?"

"Dov, don't play games with me."

"I wouldn't do that, Amos, you're too big a boy, but listen to this!" Yudkin began reading with relish. "Responsibility for the assassination yesterday morning in Tel Aviv of the Israeli military scientist Yuval Benamir is claimed in a communiqué issued by a Palestinian guerilla group, the Tishrin Commando. The Commando, who have adopted the title of the Syrian army newspaper *Tishrin,* is a splinter group of the PLO who have declared their intention of seeking out and killing prominent Israeli and Zionist military experts. A PLO spokesman has denied that there is any foundation to the claim."

"There's your answer," said Shomron, suppressing a vague disquiet.

"What makes you so sure it isn't true, Amos?"

"The victim's name is Avram, not Yuval. He was not a scientist. Besides, you know as well as I do that rival PLO groups are always claiming to have carried out operations inside Israel."

"You definitely rule it out?"

"Definitely."

"Then why are you so secretive about the identity of the killer?"

"Secrecy has nothing to do with it. We're following normal procedure."

Yudkin grumbled: "I've heard that before. Can you at least disclose his nationality? Is he an Arab?"

"No."

"An Israeli?"

Reluctantly, Shomron admitted he was not. Dov Yudkin was on to that like a flash. The terrorist international—Japanese, Germans, Cubans, Scandinavians, any of that false passport brigade could have been enlisted as hit men.

"But not Jews, Dov."

The crime reporter disagreed. He reminded Shomron that a former Israeli paratrooper and a kibbutznik were serving long prison sentences for transmitting military, political and economic information to Syrian intelligence and conspiring to plant explosives in Israel on behalf of the PLO. Traitors for a cause, a perversity not unknown among Jews.

Shomron returned to the task of compiling his notes. After a minute or two he threw down his pen, unable to concentrate. The Tishrin Commando. That he'd never heard of the group meant little; it was not improbable that Syrian intelligence had set up a special team of trained assassins to kill Israeli defense experts. Or that, despite denials, the Palestine Liberation Organization had itself formed such a team. Or Libya's Gaddafy. The formation and re-formation of Arab murder squads was a prolific industry that constantly required updating by Israel's intelligence specialists.

But the notion that Frank Sinclair, a Jewish paranoiac, had been enlisted by them was, to say the least, unlikely. And what would be the point of choosing as victim an elderly obscure Israeli citizen? Added to that was the confusion of names. Yuval?

Suddenly he recalled the picture of two boys among the framed snapshots on the Benamir's sideboard, one a young soldier killed in battle. What of the other, now a man in his thirties? Could it be . . .

Shaking his head as if to dispel an unwelcome notion, Shomron dialed an unlisted number. "Extension five," he said.

In a quiet book-lined room, more like a private apartment than an office in the Jerusalem government complex known as the Kirya, a neat grey-haired man lifted the telephone. Not until he heard the caller's code did he speak. Shomron came straight to the point. "Do you know of a scientist named Yuval Benamir?"

Instead of a direct reply, the grey-haired man said: "We have already monitored the Beirut report."

"But does such a man exist?"

"What is the purpose of your enquiry?"

"To check (a) if there is such a person, and (b) if he's related to a homicide victim whose case I am investigating."

"We know about the case," the man commented in the tone of one who knew everything and disclosed nothing.

Containing his exasperation, Shomron said in a patient voice: "I'm trying to find out what connection if any exists between a sixty-seven-year-old printer and bookbinder and someone who appears to be the target for a highly specialized group of assassins."

What he meant was that he was groping for reality in a fog of mystification; among people who were not what they appeared to be, who went to tortuous lengths to mask their true objectives, whose methods were subtle, devious, perverse and deadly. He was chasing phantoms, and all the attributes of a disordered dream were there—bodiless voices, a vague and menacing organization, the baffling confusion of identities.

In Jerusalem, the grey-haired man smiled faintly. His face was shrewd, deeply seamed, melancholy. He was skilled in deciphering the silences between words, the thoughts that speech disguised. As he listened, his hand rested on the manilla cover of a secret dossier. Imprinted on it was the name "Benamir, Yuval."

"I'm sorry, this is not a matter that can be discussed over the telephone," he murmured. "Shalom."

Fuming, Shomron sent for Zina Kogan. "In your report yesterday you wrote that Benamir's son was on an official mission in America and had been cabled to return home immediately," he said the moment she appeared.

"Yes, sir," she replied, adding with brisk efficiency: "The cable was sent at eleven-forty a.m. His sister was uncertain of his precise whereabouts so she addressed it care of the Israeli Embassy in Washington."

"Do you know his first name?"

Sergeant Kogan touched the back of her hair, an uncharacteristic feminine gesture of nervousness. Her voice lost assurance, she took pride in her efficiency.

"I . . . I never thought to ask."

"You should have," Shomron growled. "Check if the man's already arrived. If not, when he's due."

To ease his impatience while waiting, he searched through the phone book. No Yuval Benamir listed. There couldn't be a stricter blackout of information for the chief of Shin Beth, even his telephone number and address were classified. Zina returned in a fluster and blurted out that according to El Al no Benamir appeared on passenger lists of flights from New York.

"Have you tried the Washington embassy?" he asked with heavy sarcasm. "This is homicide, sergeant, the big league. Links in five continents. If there's any problem put them through to me," he yelled after her as she exited with as much of a flounce as her tight, uniform skirt permitted.

The phone on his desk had made only the faintest whirr when he seized it. A diplomatic voice politely repeated that the Washington Embassy had made no flight reservation to Israel for anyone named Benamir.

"Who am I speaking to, the security officer?" A discreet cough travelled half way across the globe. "This is Tel Aviv police headquarters," Shomron snapped. "I'll ask you one simple question. Have you been told to make any special reservation, for anybody, under any name at all?"

Again a cautious hesitation. "We've made a reservation, yes. I don't think I should say more. Flight LY002 from Kennedy. It left at eighteen hundred hours New York time."

"When is it due here?"

"At ten-fifteen."

Shomron hung up and looked at his watch. If he hurried there was just enough time to meet the plane.

The busiest airport in the Middle East was as stiff with security as if a major terrorist attack was expected. To the sunburnt tourists in the departure lounge and the pale newcomers in Arrivals, soldiers armed with Uzzi machine guns were to be expected in an airport where Japanese "tourists" had once whipped out guns and grenades and massacred a group of Christian pilgrims returning home. But the trained eye detected more than the uniforms. Youngsters of both sexes, indistinguishable in dress from others, moved among the crowds just a little overcasually. One noticed that they were oddly uninterested in the tannoy announcements of impending flights. Their hands were unencumbered by packages, they were very fit, and there were a lot of them. Also, strategically placed men murmured into short wave radios, and some of the duty-free shop assistants were good at detecting more than the color of your money.

In Arrivals, chanting Hasidim in wide, fur-trimmed hats, beards and long coats flying, whirled around an ancient rabbi in God-intoxicated dance, but even these did not escape attention. After all, terrorists had been known to masquerade as priests and nuns, and quite an armory could be concealed under the gabardine of a devout-looking Jew.

Nor did Shomron escape suspicion. The man who scrutinized his pass at the VIP lounge left nothing to chance. "This doesn't look like you," he remarked, suspiciously examining the I.D. photo and running an expert eye over his slim lightly-clad form checking for the bulge of a concealed weapon.

"Maybe it was taken on an off day," Shomron answered sourly, lifting his arms high as if inviting a body search. The man must be new. Airport security usually recognized him on sight.

Inside, he blinked at the battery of photographers, TV cameras, radio engineers and reporters. A table was laid out with cocktail sandwiches, orange juice and wine. The VIPs had standing room only. Shomron recognized among them two or three government ministers and the general who had led his division across the Suez Canal into Egypt in the war of October 1973. Some reception committee! Who were they meeting, a second Einstein?

The clear voice of a female announcer cut through the noise and there was a rush for the tarmac. A file of passengers descended from an El Al Boeing 747, half-blinded by the dazzle of sunlight. Shomron was puzzled by their appearance. One man proved to be the focus of all the excitement. He stood with a strained smile enduring the embraces of the famous while cameras clicked and microphones were thrust at his white, drawn face.

"It's Rozinov," said a reporter. "Don't you recognize him? The famous Prisoner of Zion. The Russians exchanged him for one of their spies caught in America."

It explained everything—the dazed look of the newcomers, a certain awkward provincialism as though they were inhabitants of the past suddenly transported into a bewildering future. The plane had brought Soviet immigrants who had drawn winning tickets in the lottery for freedom; and freedom has its dangers, like learning to fly. Shomron rejoiced for them, but wasted no more time and went straight to the airport security office.

Restless images flickered on a battery of closed-circuit television screens, the operator zooming in to examine an individual here and there in greater detail. The Chief Security Officer occupied the driving seat of his formidably efficient machine at a desk in an inner room. "Come on, Amos," he called cheerfully. They knew each other well. "Have you met David?" The fair, blue-eyed, scholarly man indicated stood up and gave him a firm handshake.

"Yes," Shomrom said in surprise. "It must be, what, fifteen years."

He had come to the front door of the Israeli Embassy in Palace Green, Kensington to confront the pale, diffident English student who had turned up on a bicycle, carrying a rucksack, a dubious caller. Radical opinion was beginning to swing against Israel in those tense post-Six Day War times throughout the Western world and a boy called Danny the Red brought Gaulist France to the brink of revolution. Shomron was astonished to be addressed in fluent Hebrew, elegantly phrased, even more so when the visitor turned out to be vice-consul of Israel in the Hague on a cycling holiday in England. For three nights he slept on a borrowed mattress in Shomron's Belsize Park bed-sit, evading personal confidences, disappearing mysteriously. Then one summer day shortly afterwards, Shomron was detailed to keep an appointment outside a certain cafe in Rome's Piazza Navone to hand over a locked briefcase. At the precise moment of his arrival a car drew up. Out of it stepped a fair-haired young man wearing the uniform of a British army captain—David Lester. Before he had recovered from his astonishment, the car, the briefcase and the "captain" vanished into the Roman traffic. Not only that but into total obscurity. Until an article signed "David Lester" appeared in an Israeli newspaper tracing the persistence of Hebrew words in the criminal argot of the Dutch underworld; and later still a Hebrew translation of classical Arabic poetry was published: translator, "David Lester."

This versatile linguist contemplated Shomron with quizzical amusement. "I seem to recall an Irish girl, Aileen, a dancer with beautiful black hair. Whatever happened to her?"

Shomron shrugged and tapped his breast. "Locked up in here."

Sabra brevity: there was no need to say more. David nodded in sympathy, but the preliminaries were over. With an abrupt change of tone, he said: "Have you come to meet Yuval Benamir?"

"Yes."

"The plane is slightly overdue. You know, we're very concerned about the murder of his father."

"We in this case, I suppose, being the Mossad?"

David Lester fixed him with a luminous and penetrating gaze that gave nothing away. "You're holding a suspect. What have you found out from him?"

"That he's a British subject of Czech origin and the two men were both imprisoned in Dachau."

"His motive?"

"Revenge, I think."

"The Beirut Radio report suggests that it may have been political."

"Too clumsy, too amateurish. And Arab terrorists are trained in the best universities not to hang around waiting to be picked up by the Iraeli police."

The irony was ignored. "We take it very seriously."

"So I see. This airport is under maximum security. What I don't understand is why."

An exchange of glances took place between Lester and the Chief of Security. Shomron experienced a rush of resentment. They were carrying the intelligence principle "need to know" to a ridiculous extreme, as if the police and security were sealed off in separate compartments; as if he was not to be trusted.

He said: "I'm the investigating officer in this case. Don't you think I ought to be told what's going on?"

David Lester stretched his long legs, lounging in the chair. With his blond, clean-cut good looks, the casual elegance of his open-necked khaki shirt and crisply ironed slacks, his blue, appraising stare, he looked very cool, very British. He even spoke Hebrew with a cut-glass English accent.

"There's nothing personal about this," he declared mildly. "In your work, investigating a murder, newspaper publicity is inevitable. In ours it is impermissible. We have very good reason for wanting to keep Mr. Benamir out of the news."

"That will be difficult. The airport is swarming with reporters."

The other laughed. "Yes, and it nearly gave us heart failure. We hadn't counted on Prisoner of

Zion Rozinov arriving at such an inconvenient moment."

"I promise not to produce Mr. Benamir at a press conference," Shomron said sarcastically, controlling his anger. "But he is essential to my enquiries. If you insist on withholding information about him I shall have to get it elsewhere."

The confrontation had reached deadlock. David Lester considered, came to a decision. Rising abruptly, he said: "Just a minute, I'll make a phone call." When the door closed behind him, the Chief of Security blew out a long breath. "Amos, it's not easy," he said, producing a pack of cigarettes and handing one over.

"It's ridiculous to make such a fetish of secrecy!" Shomron fumed. "The man's father has been shot dead. Even if he's the most important scientist in the world, you can't protect him from that."

"I think," the Chief of Security began, but the thought remained unfinished, certain things being better left unsaid. He pulled absently at his hairy nostrils, smiled, and made an excuse to leave the office. In a fit of mild paranoia, Shomron noted that not a scrap of paper was left out on the polished desk, everything securely locked away from the danger of prying eyes. It seemed appropriate that the place had no window, that people and events were viewed there through cold, electronic eyes.

David Lester apologized on his return for having taken so long. A whimsical politeness: he'd only been gone a few minutes.

"I've been asked to explain why this affair is serious for us," he said, and gave a deprecating smile as if to suggest that his own role was insignificant, a kind of junior spokesman. "Yuval is an electronics engineer, the sort of fellow who's described by people who know more about these things than I do as an innovator of genius, perhaps the most brilliant of his generation." His eyes registered amusement at the hyperbolic excesses of such praise. "Anyway, he's obviously pretty hot stuff. He does secret work and our experts regard him as irreplaceable. The Tishrin Commando business came as a disagreeable shock because, you know, it blows his cover. Also, we can't discount the possibility that his father's assassination was indeed a blunder and someone was really after Yuval."

Shomron said: "I'm convinced it's sheer coincidence."

"You're probably right." Lester shrugged. "But until we're sure, we can't take any chances."

"Am I allowed to know what work he does?"

"Hm!" Lester studied the ceiling before coming to a decision. "I'm probably exceeding my brief. Let me put it this way, he's a scientific polymath, a problem solver. The technicalities are beyond my arts graduate mind, but I'm told that certain things that happened in the early days of the Yom Kippur War—you were in it, of course, so you'll know what I mean—will never recur. That's one problem solved. Yuval is perfecting a device to neutralize a whole range of weapons."

"Until someone on the other side perfects a device to neutralize the device," Shomron could not forbear to comment. Like his brother-in-law, Berl, he had no confidence in the protection provided by military technology.

"As in the war against crime, outright victory is impossible. The best one can hope for is to stay a little bit ahead. The narrow margin of survival." David Lester spread his hands and Shomron nodded bleakly. On that they were in agreement.

The intercom buzzed.

"Let's go," Lester said laconically. "He's landed."

They joined the others grouped around the TV screens. A Boeing 747 jumbo jet taxied to a halt. Motorized steps were driven over and connected. Two men descended from the forward exit of the aircraft, glanced keenly around and gave a hand signal. Three others then came down the steps and the five people entered a car which swiftly bore them the short distance to the special security entrance of the air terminal, monitored by the cameras all the way.

As the group entered the building, Shomron had no difficulty in identifying Yuval Benamir. He bore a strong resemblance to his mother, the same high cheekbones, deep-set eyes and small curved nose, and he moved with the dazed incomprehension of someone newly afflicted by grief.

"I'd like to speak to him alone," he said to Lester.

"Not for long," the other reluctantly conceded. "The car is waiting to take us to Jerusalem."

Shomron took the scientist by the arm and

steered him into the inner office. He closed the door.

"Are you all right?" he asked. "Would you like something to drink?"

"No, I'm just tired. I didn't sleep on the plane." Yuval spoke with an effort; he seemed to have difficulty in focusing his attention. "If you're here to debrief me, I must ask to be excused. I'll need a day or two to get myself together."

"No, that's not why I'm here. I'm from the police. I'm investigating your father's death."

The scientist, struggling for composure, turned his head away.

"Did he . . . suffer much? In her telegram, my sister didn't . . . there were no details."

"No, it was instantaneous. I doubt if he had time to realize what was happening."

"How could he know? They were after me. That's what makes it so hard to take."

"It had nothing to do with you. I'm sure of that."

"Yes it has. There are reasons. You wouldn't understand. This murder is a message to me, a warning. I have a wife and children. They are saying if we can't get at you we'll strike at your family. Your father is only the first."

Yuval Benamir, his struggle for self-control lost, was swept by a spasm of incoherent grief.

Shomron laid a comforting hand on his shoulder. "Please believe me!" he urged. "You have no reason to blame yourself. It had no connection with you or your work. Try to put out of your mind the idea that you were in any way responsible. Here, drink this, it will do you good."

90

He took out the silver hip-flask of brandy he kept for emergencies and poured a medicinal dose into the screw-cap. Benamir obediently swallowed it. He tried to smile. "Do you have a cigarette? I gave up smoking, so I never carry them."

"My wife does the same. She usually ends up smoking more," said Shomron, relieved at the easing of tension. He produced a packet of Sheraton and they both lit up. He needed it too. The treacherous minefield of the past was still to be negotiated. "Tell me," he said carefully, "what was your father's original family name?"

"Bindermann. He took a Hebrew surname after the State was established."

"The man we're holding in connection with this crime was a fellow prisoner of his in Dachau. Did your father ever mention having made an enemy in the camp?"

Yuval Benamir looked horrified. "He had no enemies! That's what makes his death so meaningless."

"Did he ever tell you about his experiences in Dachau?"

"No, he said nothing to me about it."

"Isn't that unusual? Survivors usually have a compulsion to speak about such things."

The scientist stared at the glowing tip of his cigarette, reluctant to venture into forbidden terrain. A family taboo was about to be broken.

"My father's silence was terrifying," he said at last. "I knew only too well what he left unsaid. Who in this country doesn't know? Yet it hurt that he kept it to himself. There can't have been a

91

single day when he didn't think about it, but he wanted to spare us the pain. Silence was his strength: I respected him for it. He told us only one thing, over and over. Israel is the redemption. That is why we are here, because of all that happened. My brother died for that belief and that is what I work for."

Shomron observed a brief pause in token respect for these sentiments. He did not himself care for the notion that six million Jews were required to be done to death as part of some mystical act of national redemption. The epidemic of cruelty that raged throughout the planet in this most murderous of centuries should have laid to rest that intolerable myth.

"Perhaps," he probed, "your father might have found writing about it easier than talking. Could he have kept a diary or some kind of notebook dealing with his experiences?"

"I know of no such document."

Yet the possibility that one existed could not be dismissed. If Avram Benamir had indeed paid a shameful price for his survival, at what sacrifice of principle or conscience had he done so? Silence might be strength: it was also concealment. It is not easy to resist the compulsion to unburden oneself of a secret guilt—to a lover, a friend, a priest, or by a written confession hidden in a locked drawer.

"Why are you going on about the concentration camp?" the scientist burst out, his anguish reviving. "It's unnecessary to drag all that up! I know why my father died! I could write the formula for his murder on a single sheet of paper."

At this point, without warning, the door opened and David Lester stepped into the room. Behind him, neat and anonymous in their dark business suits, stood two of the bodyguards who had supervised Yuval Benamir's safe return from America.

"It's time for us to go," Lester said.

Yuval Benamir ignored him. "Whatever you do," he said in quiet desperation to Shomron, "please respect my father's good name."

"It's all right, Yuval. We won't let it happen," said David Lester. "Please wait outside for me, I'll join you in a moment."

He closed the door and turned to Shomron.

"When I get to Jerusalem," he said with finality, "I'll recommend to my people that we take over the investigation of this case."

"You have no grounds for doing that. National security is not involved."

"I think it is—and not just because of the PLO. Let me explain something with which I'm sure you're already familiar. Yuval Benamir has a vital role in our defense industry. When we deal with someone of that importance we leave nothing to chance. We know everything about him, and about his friends and family. Of course, that includes his father. Some of the details are vague. An Austrian Jew, a concentration camp survivor, he was brought here with other DPs from a place called Bad Reichenhall. Maybe he did something discreditable in the camps. A frightened man clinging desperately to life, who are we to judge? But it's over, it's done with. The man is dead. We have to think of his son, and where his son is concerned so is our national security."

Shomron obstinately shook his head. "I'm as much concerned about security as you are," he argued tenaciously. "If the circumstances justify it, we'll keep it out of the press. But this is a clear case of civilian homicide and I'll do everything I can to oppose it being taken out of the hands of the police."

David Lester shrugged and gave a slight smile. "I can't stop you," he said.

The tone was regretful. The smile was the smile of a victor.

"Simmer down, Amos, I've already heard the news," Gillon Romm said calmly, pausing to take a large gulp of ice-cold beer. His huge wrestler's torso threatened to collapse the flimsy deck-chair as he lay reclining in the noon heat. "Why don't you strip off and have a swim. There's a spare pair of trunks in my locker."

Shomron let out a sigh of exasperation and impatiently shook his head. The fresh shirt he'd put on that morning was already damp with perspiration, less because of the heat than from the sweat of anxiety. Nearby, mummified by the dehydrating rays of many fierce suns, a grave and solitary old man held a pocket radio to his ear and listened to the midday news, taking the pulse of the sick world. For Shomron the shock headlines

94

were a goad, reminding him how swiftly events moved into the past. He was wasting time. Half the day already lost, and here he was chasing after Gillon who with aristocratic disdain had taken himself off in the middle of a crisis to relax for an hour at the Ramat Aviv country club.

"Yes, they wasted no time in telling me," said Gillon. "I was already out of the building on my way here when the front desk came chasing after me. Top priority call. What could it be, I wondered, a national emergency? I raced to the phone and that's all it was."

"That's all!" Shomron stared. "You didn't agree?"

"I make a point of not quarrelling on the telephone," Gillon replied ambiguously. He gave Shomron a curious look. "Amos, I'm a bit worried about you. You seem all screwed up about this."

The remark was not unjustified. There were particulars about the case that Shomron found peculiarly repugnant. It opened wounds. The contemplation of the horrors it evoked had driven people to madness, suicide. The nearest he could get to understanding his own motivation was the experience of combat. However frightened one was, however sickened by the squalor of war, when a decisive battle loomed an instinct to press forward overcame reluctance. You were all screwed up but you had to be in it.

That morning before leaving for work Shomron had gone into his study, opened the book *Language and Silence* by George Steiner, and re-read this searing paragraph:

In the Gestapo cellars, stenographers (usually women) took down carefully the noises of fear and agony wrenched, burnt or beaten out of the human voice. The tortures and experiments carried out on live human beings at Belsen and Matthausen were exactly recorded. The regulations governing the number of blows to be meted out on the flogging blocks at Dachau were set down in writing. When Polish rabbis were compelled to shovel out open latrines with their hands and mouths, there were German officers there to record the fact, to photograph it, and to label the photographs. When the SS élite guard separated mothers and children at the entrance to the death camps, they did not proceed in silence. They proclaimed the imminent horrors in loud jeers: *"Heida, heida, juchheisassa, Scheissjuden in den Schornstein!"*

He was one of a generation, imbued with the spirit of self-reliance, which had found these things incomprehensible. How could the Jews of Europe have allowed themselves to be slaughtered with scarcely any resistance? The Warsaw Ghetto Rising, yes, the doomed breakout from the death-camp of Treblinka, the young partisans in the forests of Lithuania. But it was not enough. The thought had filled them with pity and shame. Many saw only meekness and timidity in the two-thousand-year history of the Diaspora and rejected it, looking to the example of their biblical Hebrew ancestors for inspiration instead. The days before the Six Day War turned them into Jews again. Suddenly enemy armies were massed along their borders and the threat of annihilation revived. Standing crowded on their narrow strip of land, backs to the sea, outnumbered and alone, they heard the barking of guard dogs, the suffocating cries of men, women and children choking on the fumes of Zyklon B, saw again the heaps of wasted cadavers, the queues of naked victims shivering on the edge of blood-soaked ditches awaiting their turn to be machine-gunned. But they were the generation of post-Auschwitz Jews. It must never, never happen again. So they primed their ammunition and fought as Jews had not fought since they were scattered throughout the world by Babylonian cohorts and Roman legions.

And still the past remained unexorcised. Psychologists noted that the children of holocaust survivors relive in nightmares the experiences of their parents. Even if amnesia was possible, it would be rejected. The Jews cling to their history. Children who have scarcely learned to read remember the names of tyrants who afflicted their forbears thousands of years before, names carved on stone in long-forgotten tombs. It was as though they had devised a mnemonic for survival, for nations that forget their history soon disappear.

Shielding his eyes from the glare, Shomron glanced towards the shallow end of the pool, watching laughing young mothers playing with their children in the water, bright drops splashing in the sunshine. The sight had become unbearably poignant.

"Justice is not the first priority of the security service, and I think it should be in this case," he said with an effort.

Gillon stood up and plunged into the pool, his swift brown body gliding under water to break surface with a brisk shake of the head at the far side. Swimming back leisurely, he said: "I can't see how Mossad can be kept out of the investigation. So far we haven't even got a statement out of the prisoner and your idea that Benamir was a villainous Jewish camp policeman is pure speculation. Has a reply come in from Interpol yet?"

"The telex only went off yesterday."

Throwing a towel over his shoulder, Gillon strolled towards the changing room. Shomron stood for a moment gazing after him, then hurried to his car and drove back to the office.

"Urgent you reply to my XTA 124 immediately," he scribbled on a pad and sent it to the telex machine. An hour later he confronted Frank Sinclair in the interrogation room of the Abu Kabir remand prison in Jaffa.

"Do you think we'll get any summer at all this year, George?"

Detective Inspector Willis stood looking disconsolately out of the rain-streaked window of the Interpol room at New Scotland Yard on a typically wet morning in June, rattling the loose change in his trouser pocket.

"Good for the garden, sir," the sergeant replied. A staccato clicking came from the telex. He left the desk and ripped out the message. "Tel Aviv," he said.

"I bet they're not short of sunshine there," grumbled Willis. "What is it?"

"They're asking for an urgent reply to their XTA 124."

The Detective Inspector frowned. "I don't recall anything from them, not just recently."

His subordinate opened the register and glanced at the entries. "Yes, here it is. Came in yesterday."

"Yesterday! Sunday?"

"Yes, sir. The duty officer took it." The sergeant examined the signature. "Bill Simpson. He was on this Sunday."

Unhooking a clip from the wall board, he leafed through a sheaf of messages and extracted one. "Here it is, XTA 124. Information required concerning a homicide suspect, Frank Sinclair, British national, of 157a Belsize Close, London NW3."

The Detective Inspector gave a short laugh. "Sinclair, must be columns of them on file. O.K., we'll see if we've got anything on him. And tell the local police to send a man around to the address." From the corridor came the welcome rattle of the mid-morning tea-trolley. Just the right pick-me-up for a cheerless day. "I know they're in a hurry," said Willis, grinning, "but it can wait until after our elevenses."

After their elevenses other, more important, matters came up—an FBI tip-off that an international drug-smuggling gang was about to fly into

Heathrow with a consignment of heroin; a warning from Rome about a team of Libyan assassins; some business involving the snatching of a child from its mother by an estranged Australian husband who had already fled the United Kingdom; these and one or two other things delayed response to the Tel Aviv request.

It was while they were snatching five minutes from the hectic day for another cup of tea and a quiet smoke, shortly after six that evening, that Detective Inspector Willis suddenly tapped his forehead and said: "George, didn't we have to do something urgent for the Israelis?"

"That's right, sir. They want the gen on a homicide suspect."

"Christ! so they do. Well, if the man's got a record that'll be easy. Otherwise it's got to wait till tomorrow."

"I'll check," said George, stubbing out his cigarette and leaving to consult the computerized records. Very soon he returned carrying a sheet of paper.

"We're in luck on this one, sir," he said. "Special Branch opened a file on Sinclair. He's a Bush House BBC man, travelled quite a bit to Berlin, Vienna and Prague. You remember the umbrella assassination of that Bulgarian broadcaster? Quite a few Bush House people were checked out afterwards."

"Did Special Branch come up with anything on him?"

"Nothing at all."

"O.K.," Willis shrugged. "We'll pass on what we've got."

The sergeant sat down at the telex and tapped out the following message:

Re your XTA 124. Frank Sinclair, formerly Franz Slonimsky, born in Prague, Czechoslovakia, June 17, 1932. Brought to UK in November 1945, age 13, one of a group of child refugees liberated from concentration camp Dachau. From February 1950 to July 1952 served with Allied Military Government in Berlin. Graduated BA London University, September 1954. Became naturalized British subject February 18, 1955. Employed by Jewish Welfare Board, London, until 1975, then joined the German Section of the BBC Overseas Service, Bush House, where he is presently employed as a writer on Current Affairs. Sinclair is unmarried. Has occupied his present address, 157a Belsize Park Close, London NW3 for the past 15 years. No criminal record.

The telex arrived at the Motzkin Street headquarters of the Tel Aviv police at eight-twenty p.m. local time. Shomron was no longer at his desk. For in the interval since he'd sent his request to Interpol the killing of Avram Benamir had acquired a frightening significance.

4

DRIVING TO ABU Kabir, a donkey cart piled with scrap slowed their car to a crawl in one of the narrow streets of old Jaffa. Here little had changed since the days when it was still an Arab town. The clang of metal sounded from a cavernous workshop where sweating dark-skinned men hammered rods of sizzling iron in the blue-white glare of oxy-acetylene torches. Washing dried in the sun. Women in bright North African cotton, their heads modestly covered, gossiped, scrubbed, shrieked at half-naked children playing in the dust, or stood with sloe-eyed fatalism outside their dilapidated old stone houses. The wailing of Oriental music came from a small cafe.

"Adoni, pull around the corner, we're in a

hurry!" Shomron yelled out of the car window. The old rag-and-bone man yelled back at him in a mixture of Arabic and Hebrew, cursing his immoderate haste, his affluence, his lack of respect for age and his arrogant Ashkenazi lordliness over the misfortunes of poverty.

Sergeant Zina Kogan compressed her lips in disapproval. "You get a lot of juvenile crime in these Moroccan districts," she said, speaking as an expert, and delivered herself of a series of sociological clichés about "the other Israel," Jews from Arabic countries, their profligate fertility, lack of hygiene, primitive habits and educational backwardness.

Jewish racists never ceased to dismay Shomron. At one time it threw him into a rage. When he was a schoolboy he overheard a neighbor bewailing that her daughter wanted to marry a *shvartser*. "Such a beautiful girl, so blonde, and she goes with a black man." The "black" in question was a saffron-colored Jew from the Yemen. The woman herself had been a victim of racial persecution, fleeing Nazi Germany in 1938 after the *Kristallnacht* burning of synagogues and vandalizing of Jewish shops. Looking with her German eye at the Jewish inhabitants of Palestine, they must have seemed a mongrel mixture of breeds, almost as varied as the entire human species. Bloodlines of three continents had filtered into the veins of the scattered Israelites, so that when the collisions of history brought them unexpectedly face to face again they stared at one another's unfamiliar features aghast; narrow-eyed Tartars, fair-haired Visigoths, long-nosed, olive-skinned Spaniards, kinky-haired Assyrians with bold, curved beaks, small agile men from the fringes of Sahara, Romans of patrician bearing. "Is this also a Jew?" they asked themselves. Tribal differences, alien habits, strange tongues, held together by the rituals of a common religion and a common history of persecution. It had bruised his youthful idealism to discover that even among these, some, carriers of the virus of xenophobia, could despise others for the color of their skins.

Stalled in a Jaffa alleyway, he listened to pretty, public-spirited Zina Kogan, whose Polish great-grandfather had drained mosquito-infested swamps to build a socialist Jewish homeland, and knew that if he drew her attention to the offensive overtones of her remarks she would be hurt and indignant. She had not meant it that way.

His thoughts shifted to the refrigerated corpse in the police morgue, if his suspicion proved correct, a Jew who had made of himself an ersatz Nazi, who looked at his own people and was able to separate himself from their humanity. Emaciated, running with sores, stinking of dysentery, did he persuade himself that they deserved to die, inevitable losers in the struggle that rewarded the strong and ruthless with survival?

A perverted Darwinism: the meek shall be disinherited of life.

Erlich, the governor of Abu Kabir, moving stiffly

from an old war wound, stood up to greet them on their arrival with all the hospitality of a veteran kibbutznik. He sat them down in his comfortable office and ordered up glasses of tea, his weather-beaten face wrinkled in an inscrutable smile. There was more than formality in the invitation: he had obviously something else on his mind.

"I know, I know!" he said, waving away Shomron's impatience. "The rumor got here ahead of you. Take a drink of tea, no one will snatch your Englishman from under our eyes."

"How has he been behaving?" Shomron asked.

"A model prisoner, a gentleman, but full of surprises. He requested a private cell, writing materials and a copy of Volume IV of *Laws of the State of Israel* dealing with the punishment of Nazis and Nazi collaborators. I was not able to oblige him with any of these requests."

"Did he explain why he wanted the law book?"

"Not directly."

Shomron put down his glass and stared. "What do you mean, not directly?"

The prison governor gazed steadily at him from under bushy eyebrows. "Is it your impression that this man is sane?" he asked abruptly.

"That's not a question I can answer. Diminished responsibility is possible. But you obviously do believe he's mad. What has he said to give you that impression?"

"To me? Nothing at all."

"Have you been monitoring his behavior?"

"I think there is somebody here you should talk to," Erlich replied mysteriously. He looked at Ser-

108

geant Kogan. "It might be better if you saw him alone."

"Zina, please wait outside," said Shomron.

"Yes, captain," the girl said stiffly. She got up with some violence and straightened her hat, pausing at the door to ask: "Will you still want me to be present for the interrogation?"

"Why not? We're still friends," Shomron humored her, exchanging a grin of masculine complicity with the governor. "A very keen young officer," he explained. "This is her first experience of a homicide investigation. Now, what is this all about?"

Erlich plucked absently at a hairy nostril, prolonging the suspense. "It's a very strange story," he said. "You must prepare yourself."

"I'm sitting on the edge of my chair."

"Good." The prison governor pressed a buzzer on his desk. "We're ready, send him in," he said quietly.

A man in his early twenties came slouching through the door. His appearance was ostentatiously disrespectful—longish, greasy, unkempt hair, faded jeans so tight they showed the bulge of his crotch; a sweat-stained shirt unbuttoned to the navel exposed a thin hairy chest with an outsize Magen David hanging from a chain, cuban-heeled shoes and rings like knuckle-dusters on his tobacco-stained fingers. There were pouches under his eyes and his hollow cheeks were pitted and unshaven. A surly, unsavory young hood, a small-time gangster.

Shomron recognized him immediately. Police

109

Sergeant Motti Rubin, undercover Drugs Squad officer, working on a street assignment.

"Well, Motti, this is a surprise," he commented.

Police Sergeant Rubin gave a crooked smile. "I was playing drums at a jazz party. We were raided by the fuzz. They caught me with cannabis and pulled me in."

He lit up a Gauloise and spread himself in a chair, one arm negligently draped over the back. Six months immersion in the drug scene had transformed the clear-eyed, alert, prize-winning graduate of the police college into a dissolute physical wreck. He'd need a strict regimen of diet, exercise and medical supervision to repair the damage. But he was on his way up. Motti got results.

"By the way," he said, "I tuned in to some gossip about your friend Lipkin, the diamond merchant. The word's got around that he's a grass. I tried to turn it off. He's just a nosey old bastard, I said. Still, you best tell him to lay low."

Shomron glowered. "I'll skin alive anybody who lays a finger on him," he said through clenched teeth. He had a wry affection for Lipkin, felt responsible for him. Lipkin was not just an informer: Lipkin had known his father. That almost made him a relative.

"Tell Captain Shomron about the Englishman," Erlich prompted.

"Yeah, well—" Motti Rubin flicked ash from his Gauloise on to the floor and blew out a cloud of pungent smoke—"I was shoved in this cell around three a.m. Two other guys were there, both asleep, I thought. One was a drunk snoring his head off. It was bloody hot last night, a real *khamsin*. I lay sweating on my bunk, gasping like a fish and thinking there must be an easier way of making a living. Then this guy got up to have a piss. I asked him what he was in for. "I don't speak Hebrew," he said in English, so I turned on my side and shut up. I guess I must have dozed a bit. A noise woke me up, it was the Englishman. It sounded as if he was praying."

Disposing of his cigarette by dropping it on the floor and grinding it under a high cuban heel, Motti Rubin asked the governor for a drink of water. His ringed fingers clicked on the glass as he drank thirstily, wiping his lips with the back of his hand and resuming.

"His voice was low, but I could hear almost every word. It wasn't prayer at all, he was making a speech. I took a peep over the edge of the bunk. The guy lay on his back, eyes closed, and he had a look of tremendous concentration on his face. 'I am not a murderer,' he was saying. 'Violence is abhorrent to me. If I lean towards any religion at all it is to the Buddhist belief that all life, even that of the smallest insect, is sacred. Yet there are forms of life that are not sacred, disease bacilli, locust plagues, vermin.'" Rubin looked at Shomron and grinned. "I could give you the whole megilla—I've got pretty good recall—but it would take too long. There was more of that sort of philosophy. The guy's a highly educated man."

111

"Okay, Motti," Shomron said dryly. "You can summarize."

"Get to the bit you told me," urged the prison governor.

"Well, then he started talking about the law to punish Nazis and their collaborators for acts of genocide and crimes against the Jewish people. 'I take my stand on that law,' he said. 'The man committed genocide against Jews. He was a Nazi officer. That's why I killed him.'"

Shomron glanced up sharply, sure he had misheard. "Say that again."

"He said he killed him because he was a Nazi officer."

The prison governor shook his grizzled head in bemusement. "Incredible, isn't it?" he exclaimed.

"What were his actual words?" Shomron leaned forward and gazed tensely into Rubin's face.

"His actual words." Rubin closed his eyes and concentrated. "His actual words were these: 'I shot the man you call Avram Benamir to death. It was not murder but an act of justice. In 1945, when I last saw him, Benamir was a Nazi officer. He sent thousands of Jews to their death. For that crime I executed him.'"

There was a stunned silence.

"It gave me a jolt, I can tell you," the young police sergeant said. Fumbling in the pocket of his shirt, he extracted another cigarette from the crumpled blue packet of Gauloise, lit it and inhaled deeply. "I took another peep at him. He caught me at it and stared, a look of absolute terror. 'Stop fucking muttering and let a fellow sleep,' I said, you know, just to make him think I hadn't heard. In the morning when we slopped out I made myself known to the warder and came up here to report."

"This is ridiculous, impossible," Shomron told himself in dazed disbelief. He recreated the scene in the cell. Three a.m., dead of night. Motti is brought in, abruptly transported from the high decible gaiety of a jazz party. The disorientating effects of prison atmosphere—dim, grainy light, stone corridors, caves of shadow, an eerie silence broken only by solitary footsteps. Through iron bars, glimpses of figures abandoned in sleep. The stench of human excrement. In the bleak cell, lit by a single low-watt bulb, Motti climbs into his metal bunk. "I guess I must have dozed a bit," he said. Perhaps he'd slept more deeply than he thought; perhaps he woke up drowsy and confused and his mind distorted what it heard.

"You were caught with cannabis," he said, launching a sharp attack as if interrogating a suspect. "Had you been smoking the stuff?"

Motti was taken aback. "Well, a few puffs, maybe. You know how it goes when you're playing jazz at these gigs. Somebody rolls a joint, passes it around . . ."

"What about drink?"

Motti briskly waved the suggestion away. "I never touch booze. A beer or two, that's all."

"That's all!" Shomron jeered. "Let me put it to

you that you were in no condition to be clear about what happened. You were high on dope, you had a beer or two or maybe three or four, you'd been playing drums at a hectic party and the adrenalin was pumping. Then you were arrested, shoved into jail and you came down fast. Mental and physical fatigue, clapped out. According to you, it was bloody hot last night, a *khamsin*. I can nail that, for one. The temperature last night was moderate for the time of the year. There was no *khamsin*."

"Hey, Captain, you're running ahead of yourself!" Motti Rubin was ironically amused. Pointing a derogatory finger at his disreputable appearance, he said: "This is not me. These are my working clothes. I'm supposed to be fairly good at my job. That means I don't let myself get carried away—just enough to make a convincing impression, that's all. If you like, I'll demonstrate how to smoke marijuana and not get stoned."

Shomron was suitably discomfited: the reprimand was justified. He apologized but continued tenaciously: "The point I'm making is that in those circumstances, at that time of night, under the influence of shock at what you heard, your recollection may be inaccurate in one small but vital detail. There are reasons to assume that the man Sinclair shot was a kapo, or that Sinclair believes he was. A kapo can be described as a Nazi collaborator. Are you absolutely sure you didn't mishear that word? Instead of 'Nazi officer,' could he in fact have said, 'when I last saw Benamir, he was a Nazi collaborator?'"

"Hm!" Motti Rubin showed signs of indecision. He bit thoughtfully at his thumbnail, stared out of the window, uneasily changed his position in the chair. "Well," he eventually concluded, "I thought I was sure but you've planted a doubt. The guy's voice was very low. If I had to swear on oath . . . O.K., the word could have been 'collaborator.'"

The prison governor said: "Let's hope so. For my part, I think we're dealing with madness. *Rabboine shel Oilom,* Father of the Universe! Imagine the trauma if it really turned out that a Nazi criminal has been living in Israel for thirty-five years!"

"These proceedings are of course hush-hush," Shomron warned Sergeant Kogan while waiting for the prisoner to be brought.

She smoothed her skirt and nodded primly. "I understand that, Captain."

"Good."

The silence grew awkward. He glanced at his watch, tapped his foot, smiled, and suddenly asked if she was married.

"Divorced," she said with a wry lift of the shoulders, smiling in return.

"I'm sorry."

She shrugged again. "It was one of those things. We met in the youth movement. He became a steward in El Al and travelled a lot. That's the way it worked out, only absence made the heart grow fonder. I found it easy to like him when he was away in New York."

"Marriages have been known to work better that way," Shomron declared.

Their glances interlocked and a current of complicity was transmitted, eye to eye, generating a response in his loins. It was immediately succeeded by a vague embarrassment. He was only making conversation to fend off anxiety. Absurd that he should be so keyed up, almost dreading the imminent encounter with Sinclair.

Restlessly, he stood up and walked to the window, gazing down at the sun-baked street, then returned to the desk and drank some water to ease the dryness of his throat.

The knock made him start. "Come in," he called and Sinclair's grey presence infiltrated the room.

"Wait outside," Shomron told the escorting officer and signalled the prisoner to take the chair facing the desk. Sinclair inclined his head, distantly polite, showing no interest in his surroundings.

Much could be learned about a man from the way he reacted to loss of liberty, in Shomron's experience. The least badly affected were habitual criminals for whom jail was a normal professional hazard. Men who sacrificed their freedom for a cause were contemptuous of captivity and tempered by it, becoming more dangerous. Frank Sinclair was more difficult to categorize. There was a surprised elation in his manner. His eyes were visionary, intense yet unfocused, as if he beheld an unfolding dream. It was a look of fanaticism. One almost expected him to burst out with a prophetic message.

The moment this occurred to him, Shomron knew he had stumbled on the key. Governor Erlich was right: they were dealing with a mind beyond the reach of reason. In the clinical sense Sinclair was not insane, no more so than any zealot who is convinced he is in exclusive possession of the truth, or a mystic who strives for levitation. Madness is a surrender of responsibility and Sinclair had not surrendered it. On the contrary, he had made it the center of his existence. The knowledge increased Shomron's dread; the unnerving suspicion came that here was someone who had chosen his own form of martyrdom. He decided to put the suspicion to the test.

"Did you have a good night?" he began.

Sinclair gazed down at his folded hands. "I have no complaints," he said.

"Aren't you worried about what is going to happen to you?"

"It's not important."

"Why not? How old are you, fifty? Surely there are things you want to do with your life?"

It took some time for the other to respond. It was as though he was receiving the interrogation on a defective circuit, as though he inhabited a different dimension of reality.

"There's no point in trying to explain. You wouldn't understand," he replied, still without raising his eyes.

"He thinks we're too stupid," said Shomron in a calculated aside to Zina Kogan. "Rough and ready Israelis, incapable of understanding such a sensitive European intellectual."

"Oh, no! Not at all." Sinclair looked up with a start as if he had only just become aware of his surroundings. He glanced with some embarrassment at the policewoman. "I don't like talking about myself. You must respect my desire for privacy."

"The moment you pulled that trigger you forfeited all right to privacy," Shomron informed him in severe official tones. "Why are you so indifferent to the consequences? Is it because you believe you've fulfilled your mission?"

"There is still the trial."

"And after that nothing else matters, is that what you're saying? We don't have the death penalty here, but for some people life imprisonment can be worse than death."

"Maybe I am already dead," Sinclair said.

Sergeant Kogan's pen froze in her hand. Recovering, she bent her dark head over the notebook and painstakingly recorded the chilling utterance. It would, Shomron thought, provide a field day for examining psychiatrists. Was it meant literally, as a metaphor, or as a philosophical observation? He had the notion that Sinclair was not exploring Cartesian doubt, denying Descartes' celebrated principle: "I think, therefore I am." He was voicing the pessimism of a morbid personality, someone whose own encounter with death had been so close and searing as to forever affect his ability to re-enter life.

"It seems that you were talking in your sleep last night," he said, abruptly changing direction. "Did you know that?"

"Are you referring to the spy you put into my cell?" Sinclair replied coldly.

Shomron brushed the accusation aside. "Were you conscious of what you said?"

"I was not asleep."

"Then perhaps you'll be good enough to confirm what the witness heard. He told us you quoted the Israeli law on genocide and claimed that you were justified in killing Benamir because he collaborated in the Nazi murder of Jews."

Sinclair shook his head in emphatic denial. "I did not say that." He maintained a momentary silence before going on. "There are certain things I did not wish to reveal before my trial. As a result of what happened in the cell last night, I've decided to make one brief statement. Please don't try to cross-examine me on it, you will be wasting your time.

"Take this down," Sinclair said to Zina Kogan, speaking with quiet deliberation. "The man known in Israel as Avram Benamir was Ulrich Walther Kampfmann, Oberleutnant in Himmler's SS. He selected Jews in Dachau for extermination. Kampfmann was a Nazi war criminal."

5

SHOMRON GOT out of the car and stretched his cramped limbs, breathing in the sweetish stench of piety from the old monastery next door to the Arab mansion in Salaheddin Street that housed the Ministry of Justice. They'd left Tel Aviv in broad daylight but in the hurried drive up from the foothills twilight descended, then the abrupt dark as if a giant hand had snuffed out the sun. Gillon Romm locked the car and joined him. They spoke into the entry-phone, watched by the eye of a closed-circuit TV camera. Across the street, behind the plate glass window of a used car showroom, an Arab sales-man stared rigidly with the narrowed gaze of a marksman taking aim. Shomron experienced a prickling at the nape of his neck: he did not feel at ease in East Jerusalem at the best of times.

The Ministry had closed down for the day, abandoned to the security staff and a few solitary officials working under hooded lights in otherwise empty rooms. In the vestibule of the Attorney-General's chambers, Gillon and Shomron talked in hushed tones like visitors to a sickroom. They had arrived in response to an urgent summons and the prognosis was grave.

"The Attorney-General is ready for you," announced the male receptionist in a subdued though ceremonious voice, ushering them into the Presence.

Professor Yoram Halevi, Israel's chief law officer, was a tall saturnine man in his early forties. Formal and precise in speech and manner, he had inherited the haughtiness and melancholy features of distant forbears driven from Spain by the Inquisition, one of whom must surely have been a hanging judge himself. The Professor was not alone. "You know Colonel Lester, of course," he said. A slender figure in uniform rose from the depths of an armchair and advanced into the light. The smile was boyish and engaging, but Shomron immediately realized that he'd been outmaneuvered. This was going to be a trial and he had no doubt who stood in the dock.

"Well, gentlemen, let us begin," said the Attorney-General, erect and magisterial in his chair. "Until two hours ago I knew nothing about this case. The bare facts, I am told, are as follows. Early on Sunday morning a man was shot to death as he was leaving his home in Tel Aviv for his place of business. The assailant, apprehended at the scene of the shooting, arrived in Israel two weeks ago on a British passport. He refused to make a statement, declared his intention to conduct his own defense and insisted that he would only disclose his motive when brought to trial. Early this morning, Beirut Radio broadcast a report that an Arab murder squad had claimed responsibility for the killing and described the victim as 'the Israeli military scientist, Yuval Benamir,' who in reality is the dead man's son. In another unexpected development, the detained man was overheard to say that his victim was a former SS officer and war criminal. He repeated this allegation to Captain Shomron. Is that correct?"

Shomron nodded. "In my opinion . . ." he began nervously.

"At this stage, opinions are not relevant," interrupted the Attorney-General. "In your investigations, what have you learned about the shooting victim?"

With stiff composure, he waited while Shomron undid the combination lock on his briefcase and took out a folder containing notes. His hands shook and it filled him with chagrin. Then as he read the report of his conversations with Avram Benamir's widow and her daughter, recalling their grief and the bitterness of their exchanges, an unprofessional tremor entered his voice. David Lester leaned forward with an expression of concern, a sympathetic listener who found the lines difficult to follow. Gillon Romm stared at the ceiling. The Attorney-General unfolded a spotless handkerchief and painstakingly polished his rimless spectacles.

"Of course," he concluded lamely, "this was only a preliminary enquiry."

"Yes, yes! Is there anything known about Sinclair's background?"

Apart from the Interpol report, which Shomron had found waiting for him on his return to the office from Abu Kabir, practically nothing. Except opinions. And opinions were unwelcome. It felt like another failure.

"What about his politics? I take it," the Professor dryly remarked, "that he's not a Zionist."

Shomron hesitated. "He told me Israel means nothing to him. Israel is a ghetto outnumbered fifty to one by enemies and unlikely to survive."

"Did you report that?" Gillon asked, frowning.

"I didn't consider it relevant."

The same gloomy thought must have occurred to everyone in the room at some time or another, but it would now be chalked up as incriminating evidence supporting the theory of a terrorist assassination.

"I think we can take it that we're dealing with an anti-Zionist," the Attorney-General ruled.

"Not necessarily," Shomron argued tiredly. "We hear that sort of thing even from people who claim to be our friends. Sinclair is a holocaust survivor. Not the kind of experience to generate optimism. Paradoxically, I believe it shows concern. He's frightened for us."

"It should have been reported," insisted Gillon.

"It is certainly relevant," said the Attorney-General. He bent his severe countenance toward David Lester. "Can you add anything *material* to all this, Colonel?"

"One or two additional facts," was Lester's understated reply. His youthful face had the bright, eager and guileless look of a top-of-the-form pupil modestly taking his place in front of the class. The Mossad had done its homework. It had tracked down the DP card for rations and accommodation issued at Bad Reichenhall to Avram Bindermann, who later became Benamir. It located a former member of the camp administration, now an official in the Ministry of Finance, who recalled Bindermann as someone who went out of his way to persuade inmates to settle in Palestine rather than return to their former homes or emigrate to America. From army records, Mossad obtained details of Benamir's military service in the 1948 War of Independence; nothing glorious—he had been neither fit enough nor young enough for battle duties—but he'd dug roads and built defenses and spent nights standing guard in those crucial months when the survival of the newly-born State hung in the balance.

"I'm not here to vindicate a dead man's reputation," David Lester said, speaking with quiet urgency. "Nor are we only concerned with the possible threat to the life of one of our most valued scientists. Yuval Benamir is a sensitive, highly strung man already under tremendous strain. An ugly public scandal, however unjustified, will make it intolerable for him to carry on his work, work vital for our national security."

Professor Yoram Halevi, Attorney-General, carefully adjusted his spectacles the better to stare into his sharp, well-ordered mind. One could almost see the pieces of a puzzle clicking into place as he lightly tapped his fingertips against the hard bone of his lofty forehead. At last he was ready to speak.

"Gentlemen," he said, "let us dispose in the first place of the allegation that the victim of yesterday's homicide in Tel Aviv was a Nazi officer and war criminal who successfully concealed himself in Israel for thirty-five years in the guise of an Israeli-Jewish businessman. This is the most improbable story I have ever heard. As a young man, the subject of my doctoral thesis was the nature of war crimes and their prosecution under international law. I learned many extraordinary things in the course of my researches.

"In the closing period of the Second World War, the Nazis established a highly efficient, richly subsidized escape organization. It provided false identities, money, clothes and secret travel routes to South America, Arab countries and other places. Many Nazis were able to settle in the United States with forged documents that represented them as refugees from Hitler or as people

128

uprooted by the Nazi invasion of their native lands. Moreover, countless Nazis were able to remain in Germany by adopting new identities and disappearing into the general population. Given these various possibilities, what kind of insanity would lead a Nazi war criminal to choose Israel of all places as a suitable hiding place? Every day of his life he would fear to venture into the street in case he was recognized and torn to pieces. One incautious word could lead to self-betrayal. The judgment of Solomon could not devise a more agonizing retribution for such an individual.

"Now consider what we know of Avram Benamir. Here is a man who arrives with survivors of the holocaust at a camp for Jewish DPs. Millions of hungry, desperate people, slave laborers, refugees of all kinds, were chaotically adrift in liberated Europe. Some tried to pass themselves off as Jews in the hope that Jewish relief organizations would provide them with food and shelter. The Jewish DP camps, struggling to feed and accommodate the thousands upon thousands of survivors, were compelled to try and distinguish those who genuinely were Jews from those who pretended to be. Rough and ready tests were devised—some rudimentary knowledge of Jewish religion or customs, a few words of Yiddish, the names of famous Jews. Who is Herzl, or Weizmann? You say you come from such and such a town. Do you know where the synagogue is, the Jewish market place? Avram Benamir had more than a rudimentary knowledge of the Jewish religion. He spoke some Hebrew. Far from being reluctant to come to the Yishuv, then still Palestine, he persuaded his young wife to go there with him when she had it in mind to emigrate to America. He argued that because of all they had gone through, Palestine was the only place for Jews. He preached the same message to others: "Palestine is the new beginning," scarcely, one would think, the sentiments of an SS officer who had sought the total extermination of the Jewish people. So Avram Benamir and his wife arrived here after much travail along with many other penniless immigrants to find a country in turmoil—riots, howling mobs, knives flashing, vehicles ambushed, houses burning. Their story merges with our history. The Yishuv was on the brink; either independence or annihilation. Avram Benamir shouldered a rifle along with our parents. And when it was all over, he went to work and raised a family, imbuing his children with a deep love of Israel. One son is killed in battle, another is vitally involved in building our defenses. There are grandchildren, the future of the nation . . ."

The Attorney-General had lost his judicial calm. It wouldn't do. Closing his eyes, he pressed a finger hard against the center of his forehead as if to check the uncontrolled rush of rhetoric. When he resumed, his tone was scrupulous and dry, his face expressionless.

"For the present, I don't intend to enter into the credibility of the claim that this man was a victim of an Arab terrorist assassination. Too little is

130

known about the background of his assailant. What we are given to understand is that Sinclair is determined to denounce him in open court as a Nazi murderer. I am concerned about the consequences if this should happen. There are disturbing parallels with the Kastner affair of 1953. Rudolf Kastner, you may recall, was a member of the Budapest Rescue Committee during the German occupation of Hungary and a prominent leader of the Hungarian Jewish community. This inevitably involved him in dealings with Eichmann. Kastner survived the war and settled in Israel, where he became a senior official of the Jewish Agency. In 1953, as a result of an article by a certain Malkhiel Grunwald published here in a Yiddish newspaper, Kastner sued for libel in the district court of Tel Aviv. Not only did he lose the case, the judge denounced him as a Nazi collaborator who had sold his soul to the devil. The judgment was reversed on appeal and Kastner was exonerated. But it came too late. Kastner had already been shot dead on a street in Tel Aviv by an unknown assassin."

Shomron's glance collided with that of Gillon Romm. A persistent rumor existed that Kastner's assassin had been a former agent of Israel's Secret Service. They both looked at David Lester. No reaction. It all happened long before his time, long before any of them had been old enough to comprehend the spine-shuddering shock of Kastner's violent death in the public street, the guilt and bitterness it revived.

"It is difficult to speak with exactitude about this traumatic episode," Professor Yoram Halevi said, frowning in an effort to achieve the necessary verbal precision. "There is a sense in which one would have to say that Kastner was already dead before he was shot. We are dealing in terrifying moral ambiguities. Men in his position were forced into an impossible dilemma: should they collaborate with the Nazis in the hope of saving some lives, and if so confront the appalling choice of which to save? There can be no end to the debate: each of us has a different answer. Kastner may not have sold his soul, or the price he exacted for it may have been heroic, but once the accusation was made it destroyed him. In this land of survivors, each of whom has brought with him the ghosts of those who perished, the multitude he could not, did not, save, whose lives he is accused of bartering away in return for the immunity of others, rose up against him. There was no corner where he could hide, no place but the grave left for him."

Shomron shifted his weight. He disliked being lectured to.

"Yet even the grave has not ended his ignominy. The Eichmann Trial had a cathartic effect upon this nation. The sovereign Jewish people, risen from the ashes, passed judgment not on one criminal alone but on Hitler, Nazism and the entire Thousand Year Reich. In symbolic value, in the reassertion of human justice, it had deeper resonance than the Nuremberg Trials. But Kastner was ours, our torment, our compromise, our monstrous dream. The shame lingers; our enemies have made of Kastner a symbol of Jewish infamy, an obscene caricature that enables them to gloat over our grief and present us as a people more degraded and vile even than those who devised and operated the vast factories of death.

"Israel emerged from the Holocaust and is defined in relation to that catastrophe. Others may wish to relegate it to the past, we cannot. Hurrying into the future, the shadow overtakes us. Imagine the bitterness that would flow out of old wounds in a trial of the nature contemplated by Sinclair. Eichmann and Kastner were able to confront their accusers, not so Avram Benamir. There is no way in which this dead man can vindicate his reputation. Diseased imaginations will fill in lacunae in his biography, suspicion will linger. The story will fly around the world—New York, London, Paris, Rome, Moscow, the Arab capitals. 'Maybe there's something in it, imagine, a Nazi war criminal accepted for over thirty-five years as a model Israeli citizen!' Just think of the consequences for his widow, his children and grandchildren. They would be destroyed by rumor. How could they go on living here? Or anywhere except as fugitives moving from place to place, changing their names, existing in constant dread of exposure?"

The rhetorical question reverberated in the silence that followed. From the street outside came the grumble of passing traffic. Despite air-conditioning, the heat in the room was oppressive. The heat and the nightmare. Each of them, Shomron thought, might have put it differently, with less forensic skill, but they would have arrived at the same haunting conclusion. A miasmic depression clung to his spirits. It had been a long, emotionally exhausting day and no good could come of it. Damn Sinclair!

Severe and tight-lipped, the Attorney-General pushed back from the desk and cleared his throat, ready to announce a decision. They all became still.

"There are two immediate alternatives that occur to me," he said in his precise, clipped voice. "The first is *nolle prosecui,* to stay proceedings in the public interest. The second, in view of the security implications raised by the Beirut Radio report of Arab terrorist involvement, is to arrange for Mr. Sinclair to be tried in camera by a military court." Professor Halevi allowed himself a grim smile. "I propose to do neither. *Nolle prosecui* sets a man who has committed homicide at liberty. Also, it does not prevent Mr. Sinclair from finding another way to advertise his charges against the unfortunate victim. Trial by military court can be held in reserve. It is imperative that certain questions be answered first. Police investigations have attracted undesirable public notice," he said, glancing at Shomron with a strong hint of reproof. "For the time being, therefore, my office will undertake enquiries. In the meantime, the district magistrate will be requested to order that the prisoner be remanded in custody for fifteen days and

134

given a psychiatric examination. He will be transferred to a high security prison and kept in solitary confinement."

As they left the Ministry of Justice, Gillon said with a sidelong glance: "It's a sticky case, Amos. I'm glad to be rid of it for a while."

The case is not rid of me, Shomron thought. In the darkness of his mind a shutter clicked open and for an instant he saw the small boy in the Warsaw Ghetto, arms upraised in terror before the gun of the German soldier who had caught him with stolen potatoes hidden in his ragged coat.

He stopped on the pavement gazing absently at the street. An Arab in a keffiyeh brushed against him, one eye milky with blindness, the other glittering in his dark, weather-beaten face. A service was in progress in the church beside the Ministry. Liturgical voices lingering in the sultry night, the languid flow of people making for the Old City bazaars, and the halo of light that rose above towers, minarets and cupolas, created a deceptive tranquillity that veiled the malignant enmities lurking in dark corners of the four-thousand-year-old, bitterly contested city.

"Who said Jerusalem is the end of the road?" he asked.

Gillon gave him a quizzical look.

"On that morbid note, let's go home and get to bed," Shomron said, entering the car for the winding descent to Tel Aviv.

The children were still awake when he arrived

limp from the journey. Hoarse staccato voices, wailing sirens, the screech of skidding tyres followed him up the three flights of stairs to his own apartment, and when he let himself in a car chase in the streets of San Francisco was playing to the vacant living room. Grumbling under his breath, he switched it off. Deborah appeared from the kitchen, wiping her hands. She had that look about her.

"I'm glad you've come," she said. "Say good-night to the kids, there's something I've got to tell you."

"Is it about Leah?"

"Leah's moved back to her own place. We've got other problems besides Leah. Hurry up! I'll have your supper on the table."

"Can't I shower first?"

Deborah raised her eyes to heaven and sighed. "Shower! Amos, let it wait, I want to talk." About to re-enter the kitchen, she added in warning: "Be careful what you say to Orit."

"Why? What is it?"

"Shush!" she hissed. "I'll explain."

"School trouble," he thought to himself resignedly. Or a tantrum over having her own room, the growing pains of incipient adolescence. Ever since the tiny swelling of her breasts, Orit had become moody and capricious.

Noam was sitting up in bed, engrossed in a book.

"You should be asleep, young man," Shomron said with mock severity, bending down to kiss his damp, curly head. "What are you reading, the

Bible? Don't tell me we're going to have a rabbi in the family."

The small boy gazed up at him, a troubled look in his luminously intelligent dark eyes. "Abba," he said, "would Abraham have slayed Isaac with his knife and burned him on the altar to God if the angel of the Lord didn't call out from the sky to stop him?"

Shomron's heart ached. "It's just a story, son. You mustn't think it really happened."

"Yes, but the places in the story are real—Beersheba and Kiryat Arba and Hebron. And Abraham was real. If he wasn't real we wouldn't be here. He was our forefather."

"He lived a long, long time ago. We don't know very much about him, so the people who wrote the Bible made up legends."

Shomron sat on the side of the bed, his arm around his son, and spoke of primitive beliefs in dark and vengeful gods, of ancient fertility rites that required the sacrifice of human lives. In a flash of inspiration, he interpreted the parable of Abraham's readiness to offer up his son's life and the angel's last minute reprieve as a message from God that such barbarous practices were to be discontinued.

"It was God's way of saying, 'This is how things used to be but now it will stop forever.' And since then it doesn't happen any more," he lied, hoping to exorcise terror from a nine-year-old's dreams. Life would teach him differently.

Noam's winged mind had already hopped on to

137

another twig. "A man on television said the world began by *accident*. Does that mean God made a *mistake,* like he wasn't *looking* when it happened?"

Shomron picked up the Bible and replaced it on the bookshelf. "I'll think about that, son. You go to sleep now."

"Mummy hasn't kissed me goodnight yet," Noam grumbled, snuggling down and rubbing his favorite velvet cloth against his soft mouth.

Closing the door quietly, Shomron went to wash his hands.

"You can't come in, I'm having a bath!" yelled Orit. That was another new development in his relations with his budding daughter. She'd become shy of allowing him to see her naked.

"Well, be quick about it," he answered sternly. "It's nearly ten o'clock."

Orit came out in a white bathrobe, thin and lithe, with Deborah's huge, dark, melancholy eyes. He gathered her up in his arms and carried her into the children's room. Noam was already fast asleep, one arm outflung, an absorbed expression on his dreaming face.

"Turn around, Abba, I'm going to put on my nightdress," Orit commanded.

When she was tucked up in bed, he held her hand and told her another story about Fischel, the Donkey, who wanted to be an opera singer. Orit preferred her stories to be funny. She was one of those grave little girls who easily explode into laughter. When her giggling subsided, Shomron asked lightly: "Anything interesting happen today, monkey?"

"Our class went to the Planetarium in a special coach," she said. "Did you know there's a hundred billion stars in the Milky Way?"

"The Milky Way. Isn't that the name of a dairy? Or a chocolate bar?"

Another burst of merriment.

"All right, sweetheart, that's enough for tonight," he said, kissing her.

Just as he was about to switch off the light, the child said in a muffled voice: "I had blood in my knickers today. Did Imma tell you?"

He stood stock still, his hand frozen on the light switch. "I haven't had a chance to talk to Imma yet," he said huskily.

"It's because I'm growing up," Orit explained in a solemn tone. "We learned about it at school."

Shomron retraced his steps and awkwardly embraced her, trying not to make too much of it, show too much emotion. "This is an important day, little one," he said. "I'll have to buy you a nice present."

"A bicycle?" Orit eagerly suggested.

"We'll see," he temporized.

Deborah was seated at the kitchen table over a cup of coffee, staring into the smoke of a smoldering cigarette. He lowered himself into a chair, looking dazed, and began picking at his food.

"I gather you've been informed," was her wry comment.

"Are you sure there isn't some mistake? After all, the child's not yet twelve."

"No, it's definitely the curse. A woman already, poor little thing." Deborah blew a reflective smoke ring and gave a rueful laugh. "Nature is preparing us to be grandparents—probably before I'm forty."

She shook her head with a kind of impatience and got up abruptly to wash the dishes, a tall, handsome, energetic woman who had reached a point in her life when she was going to make things happen.

"As long as there isn't another war," she said in a determined undertone. "I can stand anything but another war."

They were making love in a gentle companiable way when the phone rang. At first Shomron didn't hear. They'd switched off the instrument so as not to be disturbed and its distant sound was drowned by the racket of the bedroom's old-fashioned air-conditioner.

"The phone's ringing," Deborah said languorously after he'd climaxed. His head lay between her breasts and their limbs were still entwined. She ran her fingertips along the ridge of his spine. "Don't you think you'd better see who it is?"

"No." He rolled over and glanced at his watch. "At midnight it usually means trouble."

"It's probably your lonely little sister," she said. "Or Berl phoning from Paris to tell us he's signed over the West Bank to Yasir Arafat."

The ringing persisted. Shomron flung out of bed, tripping over his shoes in the darkness, and took the call in his study.

"Who is it?" he asked curtly.

"Motti." The voice spoke close to the mouth-piece against a cacophonous background of rock music and inebriate hilarity. "Sergeant Rubin. Listen, I've got bad news for you. Your friend Lipkin has been in an accident."

It took a moment for Shomron to react.

"Did you hear me?" Rubin turned away to deal with an interruption. "Hey, bugger off! I'm talking to my girl."

"How did it happen?" Shomron demanded, deadly quiet.

"He got hit by a car."

"Bad?"

Rubin didn't know the details. "You know he drinks. It could have been a genuine accident."

"Motti, who was driving?"

"I don't know that either. Not yet."

"Find out, Motti," Shomron said through gritted teeth. "I want the name of the bastard."

The stirrings of panic he'd been suppressing all day clawed at his stomach. Hunting feverishly through the directory, he rang three different hospitals. Lines were engaged, calls went unanswered for nerve-stretching minutes, indifferent night-time voices procrastinated. "Lipkin!" he found himself yelling. "A small man, about sixty." There was never a shortage of traffic accidents in the hustling streets of Tel Aviv with its devil-may-

141

care drivers. Beilinson Hospital in Petah Tiqva checked the identity of an elderly male run over by a truck; but it was in Weizmann Street's Ichelov Hospital that he finally located Lipkin. He'd been picked up outside the Diamond Bourse, victim of a hit-and-run driver. Multiple injuries. Condition critical.

Shomron came back to the bedroom and switched on the light. Deborah stared at his taut, white face. "Amos, what's happened?" she asked, scared.

He told her.

"How awful! He's the man who knew your father."

She had never met Lipkin, knew nothing about Amos's professional connection with the man, only that he was fond of Lipkin, told amusing stories about him, that the funny little diamond merchant was someone he cared about because he provided a link with the father Amos himself had last seen at the age of two. She did not know that Amos had put Lipkin in danger, promised him protection. There were things about his work he did not talk about.

Amos stood in the light of the lamp, naked, arms hanging limply by his side in an attitude of defeat. He had suffered a crippling blow: she could see that.

Slowly, he began to dress.

A hospital porter went by at the double wheeling a sick man into the emergency room. Shomron caught a glimpse of his florid face gasping for air. An ambulance swung out of the courtyard, sirens screeching. Behind a screen, cries of pain, quiet voices, the clink of metal instruments, an aseptic smell of disaster. A woman sat on the bench in muted dread, crumpling a handkerchief.

Waiting in an agony of suspense as random casualties were rushed into the brightly lit surgery, he still experienced the soldier's secret guilt at getting through unharmed; and the fear. For him, too, the time would come—the sudden spasm of the heart, cerebral hemorrhage, a spiralling fall into the dark.

"Are you the person asking about Mr. Lipkin?" enquired the doctor, a young, fresh-complexioned man with a hint of Slav in his broad cheekbones. He spoke fluent Hebrew with a Russian accent. "Is he a relative?"

Shomron produced his official ID and the other's eyes contracted warily.

"Ah, police. I'm sorry, you can't question him. He's very ill and still unconscious."

"He's a friend," Shomron said. "How bad is it?"

"Fractured pelvis, internal injuries, heavy loss of blood, concussion. We've only carried out preliminary tests so far. Fortunately, there's no spinal damage, but at that age . . ."

The doctor's shrug was fatalistic, offering only a fragile thread of hope. He seemed impatient, anxious to get on with more pressing duties, and Shomron fought down an unreasoning anger.

"I want to see him," he said.

"It would be best to leave it for a day or so. Perhaps tomorrow."

"I'd rather do so now."

The young Russian stiffened at the sharpness of his tone, undergoing a rebellion against a lifetime's training of obedience to police authority. "Very well, sir. If you insist," he said, mockingly deferential, and led him in silence along the corridor, up a stone flight of stairs, through a hushed and dim-lit ward where a night-duty nurse sat writing at a table, into a small annexe. Unobtrusively, he signalled the nurse who got up quickly and followed them.

The inert figure lying on the bed behind a screen bore no relation to the Lipkin Shomron knew. Connected by tubes and wires to drip feeds and monitoring machines, he seemed less a functioning human being than a breathing specimen subjected to some weird laboratory experiment. Dark stubble showed on the waxy skin of his face and his closed eyelids had the final appearance of death. The doctor studied minute oscillations on various instruments; the nurse stood by, a severe guardian angel, watching Shomron as though he was a body snatcher. And Shomron was engulfed by a surge of despair. There was nothing he could do, nothing.

Lipkin's veined, brown-speckled hand lay exposed on the white sheet. Impulsively, he held it. There was no response to his pressure.

"I think the patient should be left now," said the doctor, making an entry in the case history.

Shomron hesitated: it was like running away. "I don't like the idea of him being on his own," he said. "He needs to be kept under constant observation."

"We know how to run a hospital," the Russian reprimanded him, meaning "don't patronize me because I got my training in the Soviet Union." Downstairs again, he broke a frosty silence to add: "There are some valuables. They were put into the safe. Perhaps they should be in police custody."

The antagonism was ridiculous, Shomron thought, but he had only himself to blame. It had been a long, exhausting day. He felt shaken and depleted, overwrought.

"I'm sorry if I sounded officious," he muttered. "I didn't mean to interfere. The man means a lot to me. I feel responsible . . ."

The doctor frowned. His gaze became professional and he nodded to himself as though confirming a silent diagnosis.

"When did you hear about this?" he enquired.

"Less than an hour ago."

"Well, it's understandable. This time of the night, a sudden shock. But you don't have to worry, we're doing the best that is possible." His bleeper began its clamor, summoning him to Emergency.

Shomron waited in the small staff room, smoking a furtive cigarette, glancing aimlessly at the notice board. Someone wanted to sell a car. Announcements of lectures, theater visits, apartment exchanges. On the table, among other journals, a copy of Deborah's magazine lay open at her article about the female Solzhenitsyn. The young Russian doctor must have been reading it.

"My wife wrote this," he said when the doctor returned.

"Really!" The other was impressed. He smiled for the first time. "She has great insight, your wife. Is she from Russia herself? No? Then it is even more impressive." He brought out a small greasy wash-leather bag.

Lipkin's diamonds. His stock-in-trade, his portable means of security. "More than once, diamonds saved my life," Lipkin used to say. Shomron's hand shook as he signed the receipt.

"I'll leave my telephone number. Please, if there's any development . . ." he began but was interrupted by the bustling arrival of the small, sprightly, hyper-active pathologist, Dr. Buchner.

"What a coincidence! Just the man I want to see!" he greeted Shomron. "Are you investigating a crime?"

"No, I've been visiting a friend. And you?"

"Insomnia, my dear. Workaholism. Besides, I have an interesting case of poisoning. A man, a wife, and a lover who knows a little too much about toxic substances. I am preparing a report which will no doubt find its way into your pigeon hole. If Dr. Zitofsky will excuse us, we will drink some vile coffee from the dispenser and talk."

The young doctor said hurriedly: "I have to go anyway. Patients to see," and fled.

Dr. Buchner filled two cartons with a thin, brown liquid, wryly sipped a mouthful, pronounced: "Cold!" and set it down with a shudder. "I have been instructed to release the body of Avram Benamir for burial," he said. "There are rumors. I read the papers. What is going on?"

"Rumors?" Shomron temporized.

"Dov Yudkin, the crime reporter, came to see me. He thinks there is a conspiracy of silence."

"So what did he want from you?"

"A very curious piece of information." The little doctor leaned forward, his eyes sharp under their bushy brows. "He asked if the corpse is circumcized."

Shomron's skin prickled. "And is it?"

"An extraordinary thing, I couldn't remember. A Jew: one takes it for granted. I actually had to look again."

"Yes?"

"Ach! Just like anybody else. Now it is my turn to be curious. Why did he ask such a question?"

Why, indeed? Only five or six people knew of Sinclair's bizarre allegation and they all understood the need for secrecy. Had Yudkin ferreted out information from an unknown source?

"Dov Yudkin is given to sensational speculation. Didn't he explain himself?"

"You are being evasive." Dr. Buchner waggled a stern forefinger. "There is a mystery here. First I read about a terrorist assassination, then along comes a clever reporter looking for a foreskin that shouldn't be there. I am a colleague, a man of discretion. In my long life I have kept more secrets than you will ever know. What is the truth?"

"A subject for metaphysical disputation."

"A scientist is more concerned with pragmatism, my dear. For example, the intervention of a gentleman whose business is intelligence."

"David Lester?"

"Precisely. He gave the order for the release of the body."

If Shomron had not been so low-spirited; if it had not been that unguarded hour of the night when vigilance slips from the drowsy mind; if the events of the day had not left a residue of bitterness, anxiety and frustration, he would have used his practised formulae of concealment, governed by the principle of "need to know." Pathologist Dr. Buchner's business was autopsies, forensic medicine, not what an obsessive suspect had spoken in the darkness of his cell, the haunting image of evil disgorged by his disordered imagination, the unpragmatism of irrational motivation.

"You can trust me," urged Dr. Buchner in the warm encouraging tones of an understanding physician. And Shomron succumbed to temptation. The confidences of the confessional: it would make him feel better. For it was disturbing how much pain came out as he spoke; an inexplicable sense of personal involvement, the exposure of an inner wound.

When he'd finished, the doctor sat for a while with eyes closed, stroking an imaginary beard.

Then he reopened his eyes, nodded briskly, and said: "It's not inconceivable."

Shomron stared. "You can't be serious?"

"Perfectly." Dr. Buchner drew up his chair so that they were very close. "Look, my dear, I will give you an example. You are an officer in a defeated army that has butchered the civilian population. You are on the run from retribution. If the victors capture you they will shoot you out of hand. Where do you hide?"

"Please tell me."

"The country is swarming with refugees, untold thousands of them. You take off your uniform, bury it, dress yourself in rags and disappear in the crowds. A drop in the ocean, who will look for you there?"

"But at the first opportunity you will go off alone and seek refuge with friends. There is the risk that someone will recognize you. You don't know the language and customs."

"Also true," conceded Dr. Buchner.

"We'll never know one way or the other," Shomron said. He drank his bitter coffee, thinking the night was half over, it was time to go, and he didn't feel better, after all.

Dr. Buchner remained contemplative. "The SS, an extraordinary organization, a black brotherhood . . ." he mused, adding inconsequentially: "According to the biographer Joachim Fest, Hitler did not know who was his grandfather. There was a legend that he may have been a Jew named

Frankenberger. Fest dismisses it as nonsense. Whenever there is obscurity in the origins of demonic personalities, someone is sure to resort to the mythology of the Jew . . . The SS were trained to see themselves as a close-knit élite, chosen supermen purged of the soft corruption of sentiment and harder than steel. The SS took care of its own. Did you know," the doctor suddenly recalled, "that every single member of the organization had his blood group tattooed under his arm?"

They looked at one another in excitement.

"Let's go!" exclaimed Shomron, racing for his car.

Dr. Buchner arrived at the Pathology Institute ahead of him. They entered the dark building and went straight down to the morgue. The sterile, blue-white light of neon tubes gleamed on tiled walls. A place drained of color, smelling faintly of formaldehyde, chilling the heart.

"This is it," said the doctor, pausing at one of the refrigerated body cabinets. There was a rasp of metal runners as he drew the shrouded figure out. Shomron experienced a tightening in the chest, an abrupt onset of panic. Did he really want to know?

Dr. Buchner folded back the shroud. A shattered human face; a frozen waxy-grey corpse resembling congealed lard; shrunken genitals; gnarled feet like the roots of a tree torn from the earth. Whatever had been Avram Benamir, whoever he was, had gone leaving nothing but carrion.

"Well, here goes," said Dr. Buchner. He moved

one dead arm and peered, replaced it and lifted the other. His gaze became fixed.

"Look," he said in a hushed voice.

Just below the armpit hair, about an inch-and-a-half in width, was an old scar.

As Jewish funerals go, it was a subdued and hurried ceremony, fixed for a time before the city was properly awake as if to smuggle the corpse away from the sight of men. The small group of mourners, their shadows elongated in the dawn sunshine, huddled around the grave as a tall, bearded rabbi intoned the burial service.

Here and there at strategic points intent young men scanned the perimeter of the cemetery with the eyes of sharpshooters.

Yisgadal veyiskadash shmai raboh . . . The widow, supported by her son and daughter, wept and wept with inconsolable desolation. Shomron intercepted the burning gaze of Yael Benamir. If he had been her father's murderer she could not have stared at him with greater malevolence. She seemed to be reading his thoughts and warning him not to utter them.

The rabbi completed the ceremony by placing a blue velvet bag containing phylacteries and a Hebrew prayer book on the coffin lid at the relatives' request. A shudder passed through Shomron's spine. A copy of *Mein Kampf* might have been more appropriate. Or was his mind diseased by its hideous suspicions? A few centimeters of scar tissue. Are not all men grazed by life's misad-

151

ventures? His own body bore scars it would carry to the grave even without the whips and scourges of Dachau.

And yet the morbid possibility remained. So little was known about Benamir—a man who emerged from the chaos of war, reticent about his origins, secretive of his past, pages, whole chapters, torn from the history of his life. That a man could be shocked into silence was understandable, but indefinitely? Not unless he had something to hide, something so appalling that it locked his tongue forever.

Yuval, the scientist, Jewish son of the mysterious corpse, shoveled the first spadeful of consecrated soil onto the coffin. Shomron watched with sombre concentration until the gaping hole was filled.

The funeral was over but it had not laid the ghost.

And the houses of Jerusalem, and the houses of the kings of Judah, shall be defiled . . .

Was it really possible that a Nazi was being interred in Jewish earth with Jewish prayers?

6

L IPKIN WHISPERED through swathes of surgical gauze: "They made a mess of me, eh, Amos?"

"You're tough as old boots," Shomron gruffly insisted. "You're going to be all right—better than ever, the doctor told me."

Something like an ironical gurgle emerged from the mummified wrappings. Almost too faintly to be heard, Lipkin said: "They're only keeping me alive ... because ... they want my kidneys ... for a transplant."

Shomron squeezed his hand and smiled ruefully. The old villain could still crack a joke. Thank God for that: it was a hopeful sign. His resilience had already been noted in the hospital.

"The first thing he asked was if his diamonds were safe," said the doctor on duty, a small brisk young woman with lively dark eyes. "I can't offer any prognosis, but he doesn't seem to see any profit in dying."

She evidently understood her patient; they drew their humor from the same well.

Shomron bent down and brought his lips close to Lipkin's bandaged ear. "Who did it to you, Louis? Do you know?"

There was no answer: Lipkin appeared to be drifting into unconsciousness.

"Louis, please! Try to think. Did you see the driver?"

The yellow eyes struggled open, drowning in fatigue, then crinkled at the corners.

"You're the detective," shrugged the wispy voice. It contained a silent vocabulary of reproach. They had shaken hands on a deal, a trust had been betrayed. And theirs was not a cold and cynical transaction. Lipkin had been his father's comrade, shared his danger. Together the two men had smuggled Jews out of the Soviet prison house. You were like my own flesh and blood, so where was the protection you promised when they ran me down like a dog and mangled my body?

A nurse appeared at the door. "The doctor allowed you only a few minutes," she said firmly.

Shomron nodded. "Give me some help, Louis," he pleaded. "Anything. The make of the car, the color. Did you speak to anybody before it happened? An eyewitness, maybe?"

"Ask . . . Rivka . . ."

Rivka, a common enough name, but the photo-file in Shomron's brain turned up an affably smiling lady of warmth and charm, Rivka Kloster. They'd met at Sheba's Cave in Jaffa's nightclub district. She had given him her card and invited him and Deborah to call, an invitation he had not intended to take up. Mrs. Kloster was also in diamonds, the top end of the market, with shares in De Beers. And, according to certain information, in heroin. There was also Sydney, "in movies," but by the look of him in anything that turned a smart penny.

As Shomron was about to leave he saw that Lipkin was struggling to speak. "Amos . . ."

"I'm here, Louis."

"If . . . if anything should go wrong . . . my diamonds . . . they are for the Yanovsky Yeshiva. In Mea Shearim."

Yanov was his birthplace, the home town in far-off Russia he'd left as a boy of fifteen to wander the world and live by his wits. But it came as a surprise that he wished to make a religious school in the ultra-orthodox enclave of Jerusalem the heir to his modest patrimony. That was not such a good sign.

"Nothing will go wrong. Don't even think about it," Shomron angrily declared, but Lipkin no longer reacted. The effort of speech had exhausted him. Only the shallow blips on the cardiac machine showed that his heart was still stubbornly alive.

Something in his voice must have alerted her to trouble, but Mrs. Kloster countered it with the strategy of charm.

157

"Well, if there's anything I can do to help you I shall be only too glad. Look, I'm having some friends over on Friday evening. Why don't you come? We can talk about it then. And bring your wife. I so enjoyed meeting her the other day."

Shomron would have preferred not to involve Deborah but the woman's friendly insistence brooked no denial. "I'll expect you at nine," she said, ringing off. The invitation had become a command.

Only the address had prepared him for Rivka Kloster's stylish opulence. Mishkenot Sha'anim, the "Dwellings of tranquillity," had been the first Jewish suburb to be built outside the Old City for the artisan poor. Reclaimed from dereliction after the Six Day War, it was expensively restored and landscaped by a more sophisticated generation of Israeli administrators who recognized that the area offered the choicest panoramic view of history, mythology and the sacred in all the world, an ideal source of inspiration to musicians, writers, artists and scholars of suitably international renown for whom government guest apartments were provided. The rich were close behind. Architects of genius designed millionaire dwellings to blend with the city of gold on their doorstep.

The lady lived in a good neighborhood.

Music blew out like a gust of warm air when the door opened and they were admitted by an elderly Arab manservant. The house was built on several levels. One passed through an inner arbor where an ornamental fountain surrounded by palms,

158

rubber plants and lush, green foliage gave off a moist, woodland smell. Garden fragrances drifted from clusters of blue flowers on yellow stone, blood-red geraniums, purple bougainvillaea, camellia and other blooms. Two steps up, the marble hall was guarded by Etruscan statues as in a Roman villa during the reign of Pontius Pilate.

While Deborah went off to attend to her face in the bathroom, Shomron's snooper's eye peeped through a half-opened door into a library stacked to the ceiling with volumes in tooled leather, an antique geographer's globe and a huge illuminated vellum bible open on a reading stand. As he did so he became aware of being observed. He looked up slowly. Standing at the top of a spiral staircase was someone who could be mistaken at first glance for a Spanish dancer, a slim dark man in a tight black suit with wide satin lapels and a red cummerbund. Descending the stairs with a kind of negligent arrogance, the man said: "I heard you were coming. A social visit, I hope?"

Shomron gave him a non-committal stare. "Sydney, isn't it? I don't know your other name."

"Abarbanel. Where's that pretty wife of yours?"

"She's here."

"Great, I'll see you both inside."

Sydney smiled thinly and disappeared into the noise of the party just as Deborah emerged from the bathroom in a daze of wonder.

"It's got everything but solid gold taps flowing with asses' milk," she whispered. "How can anybody be so rich?"

159

"The wages of sin, usually," he said. "Come on, let's make an entrance."

They paused in the doorway looking around at the gathering, each making a different assessment. Deborah said: "My God, they're all famous. I'm going to enjoy this." Shomron, his mind filled with nasty suspicions, noted the costly works of art and valuable furnishings that filled the cool white spaces of the enormous room. Reckoned in fields of opium poppies, it added up to a lot of juice. It also attracted some spectacular butterflies. A single glance netted two cabinet ministers, one of Israel's most glamorous and controversial generals, writers, theater producers, actresses, the South African ambassador, and an American Jewish tycoon whose donations had built university wings, hospitals, immigrant reception centers and whose name was commemorated in a forest of one hundred thousand trees.

Their hostess came towards them, diamonds sparkling on her outstretched hands. Classically elegant in an embroidered white silk caftan set off by a gold necklet, she was smaller than Shomron remembered, tiny almost, yet lively and vigorous like many small people of character.

"Ah, there you are at last!" she exclaimed, just as though they were the principal guests of the evening whose arrival had been eagerly awaited, but within minutes she skillfully contrived for them to be swallowed up in the crowd. Shomron was introduced to a woman with short grey hair and the weather-beaten face of a veteran kibbutznik. "I'm nobody," she shrugged, "only invited in the capacity of a somebody's wife. But if like me you're not too keen on parties, we can stand here drinking champagne and watch the others making fools of themselves." He relished the astringency, and far from being a nobody she was one of those who'd gone out as a young girl to make the desert bloom until the man she had married became too important to stay down on the farm. She had also raised two sons, one a paratroop commander, the other an expert in solar energy. They were permitted to remain together long enough for Shomron to get slightly tipsy, then she was called away and the evening went steadily downhill. "Are you in art or politics?" demanded a short, bald man with glistening fat cheeks and protuberant eyes. "A tax inspector," he answered loudly. "What may be your line of business?" Several of those in his neighborhood moved quickly away. Seizing a fresh drink from a passing waitress, he looked around for Deborah. She stood in the midst of a group of admirers, the odious Sydney fondling her bare arm, and laughed at something the general said, their heads close together. Once again, seeing her with an onlooker's eyes, he was struck by the way she had ripened into full beauty, glowingly alive; all that exercise on the bedroom floor, attention to diet, the compulsive swimming sessions had not been wasted. Her glance passed absently over him. He turned away, stabbed by jealousy, and wandered into the dining room where a number of the beautiful people were voraciously tucking into a luscious array of food. Morosely and without appetite, he picked at smoked salmon and swallowed a glass of chilled white wine. An odd feeling of disequilibrium came over him. "I've been drinking too much," he thought, carefully replacing the glass. Then, with frightening suddenness, he was rocked by a wave of giddiness. The room pulsated, voices became blurred and distant. Clutching the back of a chair to stop himself from falling, he waited for the attack to pass but instead was overcome by nausea. He staggered to the bathroom and vomited into the lavatory bowl. Undermined by self-disgust, he mopped up traces of the mess that had splashed on to the deep pile carpet and flushed the toilet several times. The reek of vomit still lingered. Rinsing his clammy face under the cold tap, he could not bear to look at the haggard stranger in the tinted mirror.

Needless to say, his absence had gone unnoticed. Under the mellowing influence of music, drink and feasting, the party had loosened up, started to swing. A high decibel of merriment prevailed, but underneath there was no neglect of serious purpose. Careers were being advanced, profitable horse-trading both political and commercial went on, tentative flirtations hardened into arranged liaisons. The only interests not being served, from Shomron's point of view, were those of justice. Still feeling shaky, in desperate need of air and solitude, he steered towards the terrace. But solitude there was not easily come by, not when the view that gave Mishkenot Sha'anim its priceless value, the floodlit domes, minarets and spires clustered in the shadow of the Mount of Olives, was spread out there before the wondering eyes of beholders.

Romantic couples nuzzled each other's cheeks and leaned against the balustrade drinking in the stars. A government minister, his arm extended like an ancient prophet pointing the way, picked out for an American guest the Dome of the Rock, the Temple Wall, the gilded onion-domes of the Russian Orthodox Church of Saint Mary Magdalene, the Basilica of the Holy Sepulchre and other objects of beauty and revelation. There was pride of ownership in his tone. An illusion; it was not something you could ever possess, that glittering wonder, no matter how much blood and treasure was expended to do so.

And seated alone in a corner in what appeared to be a trance of meditation was the Mossad's tall English-looking Colonel David Lester, his aristocratic profile half obscured by shadow. He glanced up reluctantly as Shomron asked permission to join him. The response was polite but not exactly cordial. "I didn't see you at the funeral," Shomron said, dropping into a chair by his side.

"No."

"It went off without incident, very quiet and decorous. No fuss, no publicity . . . Cigarette?"

"Thanks, I don't smoke," Lester replied, gazing

absently around as if he was being unwillingly engaged in conversation by a stranger encountered on a train.

Bitterness crept into Shomron's tone. "I suppose as far as you're concerned that settles it. The matter is closed. It isn't closed for me." He lit his cigarette with a brooding expression and watched the match burn. "I'm left with a question. Who was the man they buried? All we know for certain about him is that he was killed by a bullet in the brain and his arm bore two indelible marks—one a six-digit number, the other a scar left by the removal of a piece of skin."

David Lester discontinued his silence to remark mildly: "There's rather more than that. We can account for nearly forty years of his life in Israel. That's a great deal."

"Not enough. Twenty-eight years remain unaccounted for. Those could be the most significant."

"One must accept that we may never know."

The cigarette was beginning to revive Shomron's nausea. He flung it away in disgust and said tersely: "Not while you hold his killer incommunicado. What bothers me is that certain people may decide we can't afford to know."

"Sitting out here is pleasant," Lester mused, "but I think it's time to rejoin the party."

For all the softness of voice, Shomron detected the steel of a military command. He was trespassing on forbidden territory. Even worse doing so in public.

"Yes," he said. "Besides, I'm not here entirely

164

on pleasure. There's something I want to discuss with our hostess. Are you a friend? I've only met her once before."

The answer was carefully phrased. "A long time ago, when I served as a second secretary in our Dutch Embassy, Mrs. Kloster was very helpful to me. She still is."

That, Shomron decided as they walked together into the convivial room, could also be read as a warning.

Deborah came up to him, flushed and smiling, a hot-eyed suitor in close pursuit, and exclaimed: "Amos, where have you been? Rivka's been looking for you."

So it was Rivka already.

She peered at him with concern. "Darling, you look awful, aren't you feeling well?"

"Too much booze."

"Oh, God! You never could drink," she said. "By the way, this is Jack. I don't remember his other name. Will you be all right?"

Jack, an overweight, balding sixty or so, obviously represented no threat. His breath stank of chopped liver and onion on a sour stomach. Taking Shomron's hand in his own moist palm, he confided: "I've been telling your charming lady we ought to get together. D'you like sailing? I keep a motor cruiser in Caesaria. Got a villa there just by the golf course."

"Sorry, I also get seasick," said Shomron, turning away. "Listen, love, I'll get my business over and we'll go home."

She looked disappointed. "Barenboim's here. He's going to play some Schumann. Let's at least stay for that."

"We can hear him on the radio."

Over on the far side of the room he saw Mrs. Kloster in conversation with David Lester. By the time he reached her Lester had gone.

"Well, now let's go and have that little chat," she said, linking his arm. In the hall they encountered her Arab butler. "Ahmed, we're going into the library. See we're not disturbed," she ordered.

"Certainly, Madame."

The butler bowed with oriental dignity and closed the door noiselessly behind them. It was like being instantly transported to a mellow chamber of the past, a bibliophilic age of calm, silence and the leisurely enjoyment of scholarship. The portrait of a bearded, dark-visaged dignitary in a sable robe, one hand resting on an open book, gazed broodingly from the wall above the antique rosewood desk. His glance appeared to encompass the library's large geographer's globe which represented the world as men had seen it three hundred years before.

Noticing that the picture had attracted his attention, Mrs. Kloster said: "My late husband claimed him as an ancestor. It was painted by Jacob Adriaenz Backer in 1648. The other paintings here are all of the same period. My husband's speciality was collecting minor seventeenth century Dutch masters. Both our families settled in Holland when the Jews were expelled from

Spain." She smiled. "I hope you're suitably impressed." On this disarming note, Mrs. Kloster sank into the depths of a leather club chair and gave a sigh of relief. "Parties are fun but exhausting." She pointed to a neighboring armchair. "Make yourself comfortable, Amos, and tell me what all this is about."

He shifted uneasily. Now that the moment had come it seemed absurd. Could this urbane, gracious and self-assured woman really be connected with the criminal underworld?

"This is a tentative enquiry," he said.

Her clever eyes crinkled in amusement. "About what?"

There was a sort of seduction in progress, he told himself. Money, influence, aesthetic refinement, even the dazzling white gown of purity so effective in the masculine atmosphere of the sombre, book-lined room. But villainy does not advertise. An odd coincidence that poor old Louis should meet with a sudden accident after whispering Rivka Kloster's name.

"Something very unpleasant," he said. "Did you ever hear of a man called Lipkin?"

"Louis Lipkin? Yes, of course. An eccentric old gentleman, rather endearing."

"How did you get to know him?"

"'Know' would be an overstatement." She reversed the question. "Does he say he knows me?"

At least by sight, Shomron recalled. "A handsome woman," Louis had said. "If she was younger, a beauty queen." She might be flattered to hear

167

it. On the other hand the circumstances would require more explanation than he was prepared to give.

"I thought perhaps you'd done business with him. He deals in diamonds."

"Shares in de Beers don't make me a diamond merchant. I also have investments in Marks & Spencers but I don't sell underwear. Please get to the point," she said crisply. "Has Mr. Lipkin got himself into trouble? Is he under arrest? Why exactly do you want my assistance?"

"Two days ago he was knocked down by a hit-and-run driver."

She seemed genuinely shocked. "How dreadful! Is he badly hurt?"

"The hospital is not optimistic."

"I'm sorry." Mrs. Kloster could see that his involvement was more than professional. There was a questioning look in her eyes. Kind eyes, but very shrewd. She spread out her well-kept hands. "If there's anything I can do . . ."

Shomron said bleakly: "I'm convinced it was deliberate. Someone intended to kill him."

The shapely hands withdrew. "That's appalling!" she said. "A pathetic old man, why should anybody want to do it?"

"I wondered if you could think of a reason."

In the long, calculating silence that followed he fixed her with a hard, unrelenting stare. Mrs. Kloster got up and circled the room in indecision. Absently, she spun the geographer's globe, her ringed fingers traversing continents. Instead of returning to the chair, she settled behind the desk as if to place a barrier between them.

"Perhaps," she said, "he got mixed up with dangerous people. The way he lived it's not impossible."

"How do you know?"

Again she hesitated. "Because he once did something for me."

"Are you dangerous?" he asked.

"Only to my enemies," she said quietly. Her gaze was very direct. "If I seem evasive, it's because I'm having difficulty in deciding whether I have the right to tell you."

Shomron leaned forward. "I'm good at keeping secrets."

"Yes," she conceded, "I believe you are. Besides, it all happened a long time ago and perhaps it doesn't matter any more. I told you that my family were Jews who fled to Holland from Spain. What I didn't mention is that this applies only to my mother's side. My father came from a long line of Dutch Catholic farmers. As a young girl I was an eager daughter of the Church. Willem, my husband, was also brought up a Christian. A small boy during the Nazi occupation, he was sheltered by a Dutch family who raised him as their own son. His father, mother and all his relatives except for an uncle who settled in South Africa were deported to Auschwitz. One of the things we did after we were married was to make a pilgrimage there."

Mrs. Kloster was now looking beyond him, into

the tormented past. A wry smile touched her lips. "An unusual experience for a girl on her honeymoon," she reflected. "I was nineteen. I filed with other sightseers past the piles of women's hair, the heaps of children's shoes, the twisted tangle of thousands upon thousands of eye-glasses, cripples' crutches, surgical boots, artificial limbs. I stood in front of the ovens, stared and stared at endless passport photographs of people, many of whom I seemed to recognize, yet only a small fraction of those consumed by the crematorium. And one thought that before death came every cell of brain and body in each of them was forced through a sieve of horror.

"It might be strange to put it this way, but that visit to Auschwitz was a profound spiritual experience, a conversion. I became fiercely Jewish." Pausing in frowning concentration as though to marshal her thoughts into a coherent sequence, she said: "When I say I became Jewish, you are not to understand that I hurried away to take instruction in Judaism or to pack my bags for Israel. I might have done so had it not been for a certain conversation with someone whose name I'd rather not reveal. Life appeared to go on much as before. My friends still saw me as a Dutch girl from a wealthy family married to a rising young corporation lawyer. We had a house in the Prinzengracht, we entertained a great deal, through Willem's business activities we got to know people of influence in many countries. It doesn't surprise you to know, I'm sure, that some transactions conducted over brandy and cigars after dinner can be very curious indeed."

"It doesn't surprise me at all," said Shomron. The connection with David Lester was emerging. An attractive, intelligent young woman, well-placed, affluent, burning to be of service—what a windfall for an enterprising young intelligence officer.

"Before the Second World War, Willem's parents were friendly with a man named Albert Behar, an Egyptian Jew married to a Dutch woman. They had a son, several years older than Willem himself, a good-natured boy who was very nice to him and taught him to play chess. The war and all that intervened, then one evening in a London restaurant Willem saw him at a nearby table in the company of another man. His name was no longer Behar but Blake. His companion was an Egyptian about thirty years old. They were both charming, George Blake especially. A few years later he was exposed as an agent working for the Russians in the British secret service."

Mrs. Kloster smiled to herself. Long-kept secrets. Uncorseted of restriction, she was beginning to relish her indiscretion. "We've now reached the brandy and cigars stage, Amos," she said. "Would you like a drink?"

"It doesn't agree with me," he admitted ruefully. Besides, the conversation needed a clear head.

She went to a small cabinet and poured a measure of brandy into a balloon glass from a crystal decanter, lit a slim, brown, gold-tipped cigarette and returned to her original chair as if to indicate that a residue of mistrust had been overcome.

"I daresay you can guess what followed," she continued. "George Blake's Egyptian was a junior diplomat in his country's London embassy. Cards were exchanged. On Willem's next trip to London I also came along. Musa, as I shall call him, dined and night-clubbed with us. One of those swift, well-lubricated friendships developed. He visited us in Amsterdam on occasional weekends. At one of our parties there a guest who pretended to be drunk hinted that I had links with Dutch intelligence. That didn't shock him, so we were in business. He passed on one or two confidential economic reports, some political analyses. After all, we were not mixed up with Israelis or Americans and the information could be got from other sources. I'd like to say that Musa was a good-time guy, a compulsive gambler, fond of women and fast cars. In these situations they always are, aren't they? In fact he was diffident, rather lonely, wore thick-lensed glasses. When he realized we had records showing that he'd taken payment for passing on information and was hopelessly compromised, he was very frightened and talked of committing suicide. Eventually, after much persuasion, he agreed to do something big for us.

"This is the part that I shouldn't really tell you," Mrs. Kloster had begun, when an unexpected knock came at the door. They both swung around with the reflex of conspirators. Mrs. Kloster put down her brandy glass and disposed of her cigarettes. "Yes, what is it?" she called. The Arab butler cautiously inserted his head into the room and murmured: "I'm sorry, Madame, Mr. Abarbanel insists he has to see you."

"Excuse me, I shall only be a minute," she told Shomron, rising hurriedly.

Her absence took considerably longer than a minute. He accepted that it probably would; there was no reason to believe that his was the only transaction in progress that evening. He passed the time perusing the bookshelves. They revealed little about the taste and personality of their mistress other than that she had a collector's passion for rarity, excellence, the classic and encyclopaedic. More transient literature must obviously be relegated to another room.

Mrs. Kloster's absence also gave him time for reflection. The script she'd outlined was a routine one—the recruitment of a foreign diplomat by a skillful mixture of blackmail and bribery. But why blurt it out like this? He dismissed the notion that she was motivated by vainglory, boastfulness, a desire to make herself seem more interesting. Rivka Kloster was not that kind of woman. No, he was reasonably certain that the leak had been authorized, no doubt carefully edited to conceal as much as it revealed. He was deliberately being notified that his gracious hostess belonged to the shadowy brotherhood that guarded national security. "She has been very helpful to me. She still is," Lester had said. In other words, don't meddle. It occasionally happened that police investigation stumbled upon something—a burglary, an assassination, a mysterious disappearance—pointing to a skirmish in the secret war between rival intelligence networks. The police sheered off. The game was for other players, with different rules. Shomron was not prepared to resign from the game. Not on this occasion. He had his own rules, and one was the obligation he owed to those friends he put in danger.

When Mrs. Kloster returned she found him apparently immersed in a book. He placed it back on the shelf and resumed his seat.

"I'm sorry I took so long, but one does have obligations to one's guests," she apologized. "Now, about Mr. Lipkin, did you know that he acted as a courier for the Jewish underground in Europe after the war?"

"Yes, he worked with my father."

"Ah, that explains why you're so upset about what happened."

"It's one of the reasons."

She nodded understandingly. "He was very good at it. I'd arranged with Musa to pay over a rather substantial sum in return for certain information. Payment was to be made in diamonds. Mr. Lipkin had suitable contacts in Hatton Garden, so that eliminated the problem of smuggling the jewels through British customs. The rest was simple. At a pre-arranged time he arrived at the Regents Palace Hotel near Piccadilly Circus carrying a leather briefcase, took the lift to the sixth floor, was admitted to a room and, after giving a code word, exchanged it for an identical briefcase and left the hotel."

"Was that all?"

"All!" Mrs. Kloster raised an eyebrow. "It was a good deal."

"I mean, did he carry out any more assignments for you?"

"No." She busied herself lighting another of her slim, gold-tipped cigarettes. "But he may have done for others."

"Intelligence?"

"I doubt it," she replied judiciously. "He's a born wheeler-dealer. There are certain rumors . . . But I'm sure you'd know more about that than me."

Shomron stared grimly. With brutal directness, he said: "I've also heard rumors about you, Mrs. Kloster. That you're involved in drug trafficking."

Her eyes narrowed at the tone. "I see you're now a policeman, not a friend. Do you think it possible?"

"Speaking as a policeman, anything is possible."

"I suppose that's true," she said, laughing. Leaning back in the chair, she gazed thoughtfully at the ceiling then lowered her glance to meet his. "Let me put it this way, not all my friends are what conventional society would call respectable. Some are positively *louche*. I like it that way. It amuses me. It can also in certain circumstances be useful. Of course, infamy rubs off, one is judged by

175

the company one keeps. I daresay that's how the rumors you hear come about."

"In what circumstances," asked Shomron, "can your underworld associations prove useful?"

Mrs. Kloster answered: "I'm not sure *you need to know*." Her use of the secret service formula was not lost on him. "However," she added, "in this particular instance it may help me to find out who deliberately ran down poor Louis Lipkin—if, indeed, it was deliberate."

Shomron considered. For the time being that would have to do. As he was about to leave the room he paused, struck by a sudden thought.

"I'd like to ask you something else," he said. "You went to Auschwitz. You saw things there. Do you think it possible that anybody who took part in those atrocities could subsequently be accepted as a decent person and be forgiven?"

"The atrocities can never be forgiven," Mrs. Kloster said.

"And the person?"

She shrugged. "I would never forgive."

"In no circumstances?"

"Never."

On that at least, Shomron concluded, they were both in agreement.

Over the car radio came the strains of an old Beatles number. Deborah hummed along. She broke off to say: "I could do with a party like that at least once a week."

"I know."

"Have you got over feeling sick?"

"More or less."

"A pity we couldn't stay to listen to Barenboim. Just because you had one drink too many."

"It wasn't only the drink."

"Naturally not, your gastric morality was upset. All that overconsumption of expensive food and wine. Why must you be such a puritan? There's nothing in the Torah that says eating a *felafel* at a street kiosk is morally superior to roast duck and champagne."

"Did they have roast duck? I missed out on that."

Deborah snorted in a most unladylike way. The song came to an end. Prattling cheerfully, the disc jockey announced that the next number, *Nowhere Man,* was being played for a Corporal Yossi Cohen at the request of Miss Zippora Saskevich. It seemed an odd choice.

"It's very difficult sometimes," Deborah soliloquized. "I enjoy company, I love things to be happening, to be with people gossiping and laughing and having fun. I need the stimulation. You don't want to see anybody, go anywhere or do anything. If you had your way you'd be an absolute recluse."

Shomron kept his gaze on the line of cats' eyes glowing along the dark curve of the road.

"No, I wouldn't," he said. "If I was a recluse, what would I do about sex?"

"Are you busy? Can you spare a moment?"

Shomron peered over the edge of *Yediot Akhra-*

not at Sergeant Kogan, hovering in the office doorway as if uncertain of her welcome, and removed his feet from the desk. First thing in the morning, even before opening the mail and going through case reports, he spent a good half-hour skimming the newspapers. It gave him his daily fix on the world. However bad it was here, someone somewhere was getting it worse.

"Come in, Zina," he said, female company providing a more welcome form of procrastination. Symptoms of discontent showed in the downturn of her firm, determined lips and unhappy eyes.

Without preliminary, she said: "I've been put back on duty in the juvenile section. Did you know?"

"No, I didn't."

"I don't understand why. Do you?"

"Well, I suppose it's because you were attached to Homicide only for the Benamir case. Now that's been taken out of our hands."

"That's not a good enough reason," she insisted doggedly. "There are other cases. You yourself complimented me for being thorough and said I was a good investigator."

"You definitely are," Shomron hastened to reassure her. "I don't think you should be upset. Career prospects in the juvenile branch are very good."

"I didn't join the police force to become a uniformed social worker." She looked challengingly at him. "It wouldn't be because I'm a woman?"

"As far as I'm concerned it's an asset," he replied, holding her gaze. Sergeant Kogan, who had so far remained standing, slowly lowered her firm round bottom into the chair across the desk. "I'm not only thinking of my career," she said in a softer tone. "I've really enjoyed working with you. We've got on so well together."

"Yes, I know."

He spoke regretfully. Zina Kogan was no seductress. She looked right in uniform, a sturdy, capable, well-put-together young woman, too direct in her manner to play the coquette. She'd picked up the fact that he fancied her and had shown reciprocal interest. They'd been, he felt, on the brink of an understanding. The sex she offered would be a comradely fuck. You'd come out of it, he imagined, tired and exhilarated as from a good game of squash, no strings, no emotional demands, no threat to your marriage. Shomron had long given up trying to reconcile the indiscriminate persistence of his lust with his love for Deborah. He hadn't married for sex. Shulamit Fenster, a fellow law student, was giving it to him two or three times a week, the two of them repairing for a romp in bed after studying together. There had been a long period of celibate misery trying to get over the break up of his affair in London with black-haired Aileen, his lame little Irish ballerina. That was love and sex rapturously together and the loss of it pre-empted his heart. Shulamit Fenster was the cure for love: theirs was an incestuous kind of coupling, jolly and unromantic. She'd grown up in the children's house of a Marxist kibbutz and went from splashing about with boys in the shower to more sophisticated horseplay long before she'd guided his almost virginal penis into her steaming pussy. In contrast, Deborah was destiny, imprinted on his future from the moment of birth. And everything had been so right. They made good love, shared a common sense of humor, were close but not overpossessive, and the honeymoon of their early marriage had never entirely waned. Yet even standing under the canopy at his wedding beside his own lovely bride his eye had roved lustfully over certain of the younger female guests. He'd married with the seven-year itch. And now he was at it again, staring at the robust Zina Kogan and imagining her naked, on all fours, her plump rear raised in lewd invitation.

"You really do think I'd be good in the Investigation Department?" she was saying.

"Very good indeed," he sighed.

"Supposing I put in for a transfer, will you support the application."

"I'll do my best."

On that promising note, they parted.

It took a while, smoking a cigarette and staring absently out of the window at the clamorous traffic in Dizengoff Street, for the erotic feeling to disperse. Then the telephone went and the message it brought gave him something entirely different to think about.

"Captain Shomron," said the switchboard, "I have the Station Commander for you." The connection was made and Gillon's warm brown voice sprang a laconic surprise. "Amos, you're to get ready to leave for England."

"England!" He could not have sounded more astonished if he'd just been told he was going by rocket to the moon. "When?"

"The day after tomorrow. I've just had a call from the Attorney-General's office."

His immediate conclusion was that it must be connected with Frank Sinclair. At the hearing in Jerusalem, Attorney-General Halevi had decided to conduct his own enquiries into the Benamir affair. To do so necessarily involved investigating the background and circumstances of the assassin, Interpol's information being scant and of little use. And they were sending him! He was not, after all, dismissed from the case.

"I'm delighted, Gillon, but what about our police representative in Bonn? Since when can Israel afford to send an investigator to Europe on a homicide enquiry?"

"Who's talking about homicide? You're to attend an international conference on terrorism."

"I don't follow."

"There's a three-day conference in a place called Abingdon, near Oxford. You'll take part in discussions on the role of the civil police."

"Why me? I'm not a specialist. And at such short notice."

"A last minute decision, I suppose. Besides, you have had counter-terrorist training." While Shomron digested this information with growing suspicion, Gillon cheerfully rumbled on: "It's a nice windfall. Look, you're just about due for leave. Why not stay on after the meeting's over? Summer in England, plenty of nice cool rain. Maybe Deborah can join you."

"We do have kids, you know," Shomron growled. A doodle was appearing on his note pad—black and white chessboard squares, the name Lester.

"Gillon," he murmured into the phone, "am I by chance being got out of the way?"

"Look, kid," said Gillon, and the big gravelly voice resonated with friendly concern, "consider it possible you're taking yourself too seriously. It's just a job. This one is in the nature of perks. Do me a favor and leave crusades to the goyim. By the way, what news of Lipkin?"

"No change. So far he's holding his own."

"Good. I'll see he's kept an eye on while you're abroad."

Shomron rang off. He stared at his chessboard doodle as though pondering a strategy to counter an opponent's game plan, played with vague thoughts of resignation. Not that he'd ever voluntarily abandon the morbid fascination he derived from the study of crime, or sacrifice the sense of power and achievement derived from bringing some hard, violent underworld figure to justice; or abandon what Gillon was pleased to call his little crusade.

"England," he wrote on the margin of his note pad, and a plan began to form. What difference did it make why he was being sent? He had his own idea what to do when he got there. Not being clairvoyant, he did not foresee that he was about to embark on a journey that would bring him not only to another country, but also into another's past. He would not return home from it unchanged.

7

THE TEL AVIV flight touched down at Charles de Gaulle shortly after seven p.m. It gave him a three-and-a-half hour stopover, long enough to fulfill his big brother role before the plane left for London. But when he passed through Immigration and Customs there was no sign of Berl. Instead a message awaited him at the El Al desk. There had been an unavoidable hold up. It asked him to come to a restaurant at an address in the neighborhood of St.-Germain des Près. Fuming, he checked his luggage through for the London flight and hurried out to get a taxi.

Delayed by the inevitable traffic jams, the best part of an hour was lost before they edged into a narrow, rubbish-strewn street made almost impassable by the congestion of parked cars. A swarthy man in tight jeans and leather donkey jacket leaning against the doorway of the restaurant took the butt of a cigar from between his fleshy, mauve lips and spat with precision at the pavement. Shomron paid off the taxi and entered. Dim lighting, plastic table tops, the pungent smell of kebabs turning on charcoal spits, the ululation of a North African female singer issuing from a radio. The place was full of Arabs.

Except, it seemed, for his brother-in-law, so awkwardly Jewish with his large shy ears, studious glasses and round-shouldered timidity, who sat amid a noisy group of men crouched over a card game. They all stopped playing and watched in silence as Berl rose with swift excitement and hurried over to him.

"Sorry I couldn't meet your plane, Amos," he said after they had embraced and exchanged greetings. "A last-minute arrangement to see somebody. Very important, I couldn't let it pass."

"I've got an hour," Shomron muttered, glancing impatiently at his wristwatch. "Can't we go somewhere else to talk?"

"Oh, this place is all right. These people are friends. Let's eat something and we'll go to my hotel room just around the corner."

The solid opaque stares that followed them to an empty table struck Shomron as far from friendly. And Berl had pointedly greeted him in English, as though he feared that the use of Hebrew in the volatile atmosphere might set off an explosion.

"What would you like? They serve a very good couscous of lamb."

"I'll stick to coffee," Shomron said. "Berl, Leah wants you home. She's getting pretty desperate."

Berl responded with a sigh of contrition and turned to give their order to a snail-like waiter of elderly vintage.

"Deux café. C'est tout?" the latter grumbled.

"C'est tout, noir."

The old man meditatively scratched his head with the stub of a pencil, licked the point and slowly wrote it down before shuffling away. Shomron had visions of his suitcase travelling unaccompanied to London, lost among heaps of unclaimed baggage in the entrails of Heathrow.

"I've brought you this letter," he said, taking it out from an inside pocket and passing it across the table. Berl tore open the envelope and drew out the single sheet of paper. After reading it, he shook his head in comical dismay and said ironically: "Thanks for the good news."

"Why, what does she say?"

"She's threatening divorce again. It happens whenever I go on one of these trips."

"This time she means it."

Berl's large ears glowed red with emotion. "I don't believe that!" he declared passionately. "You know as well as I do what the trouble is. Leah doesn't really object to my political activities. Every time she has a period she goes into mourning."

Coffee arrived, slopped into the saucers, and he fell silent. The restaurant had begun to fill with

189

newcomers. One of them dropped into a chair at their table and entered into a bantering conversation with Berl, speaking the incendiary language of Hebrew with the accent of an Arab graduate of the Hebrew University. A fair, blue-eyed, pleasantly smiling man in his late twenties, casual in jeans and an open-necked shirt, his European appearance made nonsense of the theories of race.

"Are you also Israeli?" he asked Shomron with a twinkle of mischief.

"Yes."

"What rank do you hold in your army?"

There was a distinct note of provocation in this exchange and Shomron could not afford to be goaded. Replying quietly, in English, he said: "I'm in the reserves."

"A sabra?"

"Born in Jerusalem."

The newcomer's smile broadened. "You were born in Jerusalem but your true home is Bialystok. I was born in a refugee camp but my home is an eight-roomed house in Haifa presently occupied by an Israeli who is also from Bialystok."

"According to Samih, all Israelis come from Bialystok," Berl said, laughing uneasily.

Shomron carefully pushed his coffee aside and stood up. "I think we'd better go," he said. Giggles of merriment followed them.

"You mustn't take Samih seriously," Berl explained. "He's a moderate, not an extremist, but he has to cover his flanks."

"No doubt." Shomron waved down a passing

taxi. "Look we'll skip going to your hotel, it's getting late. Drive with me to the airport. There are still things to discuss."

"Do you really think Leah is serious?" Berl worriedly resumed when they were on the way.

"About the divorce? Yes, I'm afraid so."

"But all I need is a few days, a week at the most. There's a new spirit among the Palestinians I know, a genuine desire for a political solution. I really believe we're going to get something started this time. Even Leah will be pleased when I tell her."

Leah would of course be nothing of the kind. She studied fertility manuals, calculated her monthly thermometer readings, in the hope of starting something that would fill a cradle. Berl was optimistic about that too. He had an incurable innocence bordering on naivety in both politics and love that filled Shomron with exasperated affection.

"You talk about important contacts," he said sharply. "Who are they? Most likely intelligence agents out to use you in some way. Arabs who have been involved in secret peace discussions with Israel are targeted for assassination. It's a dangerous game and the players have to calculate that it's worthwhile. You don't represent a party, or speak for a government, or have access to influential sources of public opinion. Why should the PLO take you seriously?"

Berl was taken aback by this onslaught. He muttered defensively that many thousands of Israelis shared his views, there were people of goodwill on both sides, but Shomron dismissed goodwill with a contemptuous wave of the hand.

"Peace," he declared in a grim metaphor, "is negotiated by men of mistrust, armed to the teeth and ready to kill one another if their haggling is unproductive. What the Palestinians want is impossible for us to give. Your friend Samih dreams of sending us all to Bialystok so that he can have his Palestine back. It doesn't exist any more. It's become another archaeological layer of history. We are there and will stay until our cities and settlements also sink in ruins under the earth. We have nowhere else to go."

"So according to you there is no solution."

Shomron shrugged. "Time, maybe. Or the doomsday explosion everyone fears and expects, in which case we'll all be buried together."

The pessimism was suddenly that of a stranger. He was talking out of tiredness. Had he not often argued that if within a single generation of Auschwitz a reconciliation had become possible with Germans then surely the enmity of Arabs could also be overcome? But then reconciliation did not mean forgetting. It relegated a grievance to the past, not the memory of it. Why else had he become obsessed with the mystery of Benamir's true identity and the motives of his killer while others dreaded the traumatic effect of what he might discover? And what were Israel's aerial armadas, tank squadrons and guns but the terrible armory of a nation that could not forget?

Berl sat crouched in his seat staring out of the

192

taxi window, streaks of city lights whipping across his ruminating face. Turning to Shomron he said with some bitterness: "You sound like your namesake, the prophet Amos. How does it go? 'And it shall come to pass in that day, said the Lord God, that I will cause the sun to go down at noon, and I will darken the earth in the clear day.' There are too many gloomy prophets."

Shomron conceded defeat: there was no point in prolonging an argument he had lost. When they arrived at the airport and the moment of farewell had come, gazing into Berl's vulnerable yet stubborn eyes, he was pierced by a sharp misgiving.

"Look after yourself," he said, embracing him and hurrying away.

But up in the sky, the glittering map of the city fast dwindling into darkness, his brief visit to Paris became unreal, jumbled images of a fading dream. And as the earth dropped away so did his responsibilities, the links with family, home and career. He was on his own. After the Abingdon conference, he would be free. It was a good feeling and he intended to make the most of it.

The international conference on terrorism was held in a large country house alongside a curve of the river, green and gold in cool morning sunshine. Oaks three centuries old fringed the clipped perfection of aristocratic lawns. During breaks in the discussion, delegates strolled in the rose garden or wandered to the water's edge to gaze at swans and ducks and slow-moving river craft. It set a mood in which talk of violence took on the abstract air of theological discourse. This was heightened by the ecclesiastical platitudes of the British Minister of State for Foreign Affairs, a tall, mistrustful individual whose voice seemed to emerge not from his primly compressed lips but from the narrow cavities of his high-bridged nose. Deploring the use of violence for political ends (the tone implying that it was both lacking in sportsmanship and un-British), he hoped that good sense and international cooperation would put an end to such anarchy. The Minister then repaired to the room set aside as a temporary television studio to repeat this unexceptional message before being driven back to Whitehall in a black, bullet-proof Rolls Royce. The theme was amplified in different languages and accents by several other speakers and the conference adjourned for a buffet lunch in the refectory served by policemen dressed as waiters. Various experts were squeezed into the afternoon session before tea, then there were more speeches until the proceedings ended with a sit-down dinner in the long dining-room brought by catering van from the Trust House hotel in Abingdon's Thames Street. So it went, although in subsequent sessions there was a tendency among some to tire of the human voice and go absent.

Shomron dutifully put in a full attendance, his notepad sprouting intricate doodles as he listened to lectures on the motives, the methods, the transnational ramifications of terror networks and their increasing use of murderous technology. By the third and last day, when he delivered his own modest paper to a subcommittee on the role of the civil police, he was left with the fearful impression that the world was fast becoming ungovernable, subverted by irrepressible coalitions of the power-crazed, the fanatics of religion and politics, the nobodies cancerous with envy, frustration and hate.

Being the sort of man who cannot read a book of popular medicine without discerning in himself the symptoms of all its described diseases, the conference left Shomron with this vision of bleak apocalypse. Then he closed the book. As delegates drove off to eat, drink, bed their lovers or otherwise amuse themselves, he went to the railway station and caught the first available train to London.

The *coq au vin* was perhaps a little overcooked, but no unpalatable. He wiped a trace of grease from his mouth, inwardly amused by the irony. In Paris all he'd managed was a few sips of bitter black coffee, yet here he was dining in a French bistro, guttering candles, wine cellar decor, Gallic waiters in striped aprons: on High Street Kensington.

Uzzi, an old friend, Counsellor at the Israeli Embassy, grinned at him across the table.

"You're almost famous. I caught a glimpse of you on the TV news. You were holding a drink and chatting up a pretty woman."

195

"She was doing the chatting up. Mistook me for a Moosadnik. A voluptuous girl, very sexy. They pick them well, the SID."

"What on earth is that?"

"Italian secret service."

"At what stage did she discover that you were the wrong man?"

"She didn't, but don't jump to the wrong conclusions. I lost her to an Argentinian colonel."

The arrival of the dessert interrupted this conversation.

"The English do these things in style," Shomron resumed when the trolley left. "Nice country house, lawns sloping down to the Thames, tree-shaded walks, afternoon tea on the terrace. A very gentlemanly occasion considering that it was mostly a gathering of cut-throats."

"And the business side?"

Shomron took a thoughtful sip of wine. "A mini United Nations. First a disgreement over the differences between guerrillas, terrorists and freedom fighters. Black delegates walked out when a South African got up to speak, Arabs boycotted Israelis, East Germans only there to watch the West Germans. At least half the world was not represented. The Russians, who got rid of their terrorists a long time ago, only sent an observer, so that spared the Czechs, Poles, Hungarians and Bulgars the need to send anyone at all. Any real business was done by men who never raised their voices in public. They were either sizing up the opposition or slipping away in pairs to conclude secret arrangements. You know the sort of thing."

Uzzi did know the sort of thing.

"So you learned nothing."

"Only that in global terms it's a losing war. An American expert predicts that before very long some Baader-Meinhof group or Red Brigade working in some back room will have the technology to assemble an explosive device powerful enough to destroy a city. On that cheerful note, people smiled, shook hands and said goodbye."

They strolled back to the Embassy in Kensington's "Millionaire's Row" talking of other things. Uzzi pressed the door buzzer and submitted to scrutiny by the closed-circuit TV camera. A chauffeur-driven limousine stood waiting in the drive. "I won't come in," Shomron told his friend. He handed over a sealed envelope. "I'd be grateful if you could send this through the Dip." Strictly speaking, the envelope did not qualify for inclusion in the diplomatic mailbag. It contained a letter to his sister Leah urging her to go in person to Paris and persuade Berl to return to Israel. According to information that came his way in Abingdon, the lethal rivalry between competing groups of Palestinians was intensifying. Peacemaking, always dangerous, had even more become the occupation of brave but foolhardy men and he wanted Berl out of it.

He was walking toward Kensington High Street when the Embassy gate opened electronically and the limousine emerged from the drive. It slowed down by his side.

"Can I give you a lift?" enquired a woman's voice.

He turned in surprise. Rivka Kloster rested a white-gloved hand on the open window and smiled quizzically. Stylishly dressed in a light blue suit of masculine cut set off by a silk shirt and tie, she looked rakishly sophisticated, almost dissolute, and much younger than her years, with that mysterious chameleon ability of women to change personality along with appearance and setting.

"Where are you going?" he asked.

"I'm on my way to the St. Ermin's Hotel in Westminster. I have a suite there. It's convenient for my political friends because it has a division bell and they can dash over to Parliament if a vote is called."

Shomron shook his head. "Mine is in the opposite direction."

"I'll be happy to take you."

"It's really not necessary. I'll go by cab."

"You are independent, aren't you?" Mrs. Kloster said in mock reproach. "If you're going to be in London for a week or so, you must come and dine. You might find it interesting." She signalled the chauffeur to drive on.

Odd, thought Shomron, that the lady had shown no curiosity about the purpose of his presence in England. He had a strong suspicion that it was not due to lack of interest, nor to an innate delicacy about prying into other people's affairs. Mrs. Kloster was either observing the principle of secrecy, or she knew. But she could not know his next destination.

Number 157 Belsize Close was one of a row of

tall crumbling houses fronted by small areas of unruly vegetation, immediately recognizable to him as typical London NW3 bed-sitters of the kind in which he himself had once roomed. Passing along the street, he had noticed other familiar landmarks—a girl in the glow of a table-lamp tapping the keys of a typewriter, orchestral music reverberating from the open uncurtained window of a large room whose walls were decorated with faded Modigliani reproductions and Bal Tabarin posters by Toulouse-Lautrec, rows of empty milk bottles awaiting doorstep collection, a whiff of damp and dry rot, the sedimental odor of stagnating time.

Late twilight had deepened to dusk. He mounted the steep flight of steps to the entrance and struck a series of matches to read the names on several bell-pushes. Gummed strips of paper, yellowed pieces of cardboard, offered complicated instructions. "Howell Jones—ring three times." "Kofi Mustapha—one long ring, one short." "Polly Kemsley—bell out of order, knock hard twice," and so on. There was no "Frank Sinclair"—157a would, of course, have a separate entrance. Retracing his steps, he walked around the side of the house past a row of dustbins. Yellow eyes gleamed in the dim light of a street-lamp that filtered through tree branches; there was a blur of black fur and a tremendous clatter as the galvanized lid fell off one bin. Shomron froze, more startled than the cat, but the noise seemed to have attracted no attention. Proceeding stealthily, his feet sinking into mud along the broken pathway, he reached a door and again struck a match. There it was, a neat white slip in a rusted metal holder above the letterbox reticently inscribed "F Sinclair." Nothing else, no invitation to knock or ring, not even the means to do so. A small window, barred and prison-like, occupied space between two drainpipes. It was too dark to see inside.

Shomron ventured further and passed through a dilapidated door into the green wilderness of an overgrown garden. The back of Sinclair's semi-basement was separated from the weed-infested grass by a cement pathway about two feet below ground. There appeared to be no way of entering it except by the window. Concealed in the shadow of a tree, Shomron gazed speculatively over the rambling exterior of the house. An iron staircase led to the curtained French window of a first floor flat and music drifted into the garden accompanied by voices interrupted by laughter. Other lighted interiors shone out from the dark facade and on an upper floor someone picked slowly at the keys of a typewriter. A poet in the throes of composition, perhaps. People in rented rooms living their separate lives. How well he remembered all that, strangers who came together by chance through some notice in a shop window or a newspaper advertisement to endure the daily frictions of communal toilet and bathroom, the intrusive noises of altercation, love-making and music machines, tenacious in defense of their small areas of privacy. Weeks could sometimes pass before they recognized one another in the passage.

Hesitating no longer, he went to Sinclair's window and examined the catch: it was broken. In a few moments the bottom half had been levered open. Darkness crouched in the stale-smelling, unoccupied room. His heart thudding against his eardrums, he swung his feet over the ledge and dropped noiselessly to the floor.

He was now in the country of the blind, reconnoitring by touch, cautiously navigating from one vague object to another, fingertips exploring the smooth textures of wood, leather, the cold of metal. Something fell and splintered; his shin collided against some hard-edged piece of furniture; there was the soft scatter of spilled papers. At last, searching the abrasive surface of the wall, his hand encountered a light-switch. Once more he hesitated, then, with as much trepidation as if about to detonate an explosive, he flicked the switch.

Sinclair's empty room gazed back at him, awaiting the arrival of its absent owner: the large scarred desk and ancient typewriter, the worn leather sofa, sagging armchair, low table ladden with books, newspapers, periodicals; the chest of drawers covered by a layer of dust, filing cabinets, reading lamp, books spilling from over-crowded shelves, the threadbare carpet. No pictures, not a single photograph. But in all that outdated shabbiness, one technological intruder from the late twentieth century—a powerful Japanese radio receiver, its chromium dials glittering with robot menace.

More than a room was suddenly revealed. It was the shape and texture, the indelible imprint, of an individual human life. Whereas at first the place had seemed empty, waiting, now it began to fill with an invisible presence as though Sinclair's ectoplasm was seeping in. The armchair hollowed by the nervous pressures of his body, the hole worn in the carpet under the desk by the friction of his restless feet, the frayed covers of his much-thumbed books, his old woolen robe hanging on the door: Shomron could almost hear him breathing.

Shaking off a weird feeling that his own personality was being infiltrated by alien influences, he pulled the dusty green cloth that served as a curtain across the window and settled down to investigate the contents of the desk. First he collected the sheets of paper dislodged by his blind progress through the room and found that they were written in German. They appeared to be part of a political commentary on literary censorship in the German Democratic Republic. On closer inspection, the pages proved to be disconnected—some fragments drawn from a review of the British press, a sheet dealing with a crisis in the British labor movement that stopped in mid-sentence, another reflecting the views of the British government on agriculture in the European Economic Community. Shomron then realized they were random extracts from BBC broadcasts in German presumably collected by Sinclair for use as scrap. He put them aside and pulled open a desk drawer.

Chaos. Crammed to bursting with faded newspaper cuttings in Czech, Polish, German, Russian, Dutch and other languages, letters of a similar polyglottal complexity from individuals, governments and academic institutions, domestic bills ancient and withered as autumn leaves. Each drawer revealed a similar disorder, although some obscure system of classification was indicated by the presence in one of sheets filled with statistics, which also contained an expired passport, two calcified rubber erasers, a loose assortment of paper clips and elastic bands, an outdated certificate of vaccination, and a variety of visiting cards, one belonging to a Professor Dr. Friedrich Schumacher which had been neatly annotated *"Tot,"* dead, "December 19, 1963." In addition to this abundant confusion, cardboard boxes had been used to accommodate the overflow.

The newspaper cuttings, letters and statistics were all concerned with the manifold aspects of Nazi inhumanity. When Shomron turned his attention to the bookshelves he encountered the same obsession—an almost exclusive concentration on records of German massacres of Jews, Gypsies, homosexuals, mental invalids and civilian hostages in occupied countries. There were volumes of war crimes trials, histories of liquidated ghettoes and concentration camps, documentary accounts of medical experiments on human guinea pigs, of Jewish girls subjected to sexual abuse in German army brothels before being gassed, memoirs of survivors, the autobiographies of Speer and other rehabilitated Nazi criminals, commentaries and analyses produced by the vast academic industry that sifted the charred bones and pestilential dust of mankind's greatest evil in the vain and desperate search for understanding. The phone rang. Preoccupied, forgetting for a moment that he was an intruder, he took up the receiver and held it absent-mindedly to his ear.

"Allo, allo! Franz is that you?" Accent German, voice gutteral yet feminine. The tone sharpened, demanding a response, "Allo! is anybody zere?"

"No, it's not Franz," Shomron said, adding with careful deliberation: "I'm—a friend."

"Oh!" The inflection was one of surprise. A pause followed. "Are you expecting him?"

"He's away."

"Aha! So never mind, I'll ring again. When is he back?"

Shomron settled for dissimulation. "I'm not sure. Do you wish to leave a message?"

"Just say Friedl phoned."

"Friedl?"

"Zussman. It's not important. Tell me just one sing, is Franz all right?"

"When I saw him," was the evasive reply, "he seemed in good health."

"Zo! Then is good. I had a feeling. Wiss Franz you neffer know. From one year to the next you don't hear."

On this brusque note the caller rang off. Shomron was left wondering. Did he detect suspicion that a stranger had answered the phone? The woman knew the assassin well enough to feel concern for him, to have an intuition that he might be in trouble: she sounded peeved that he failed to keep in touch. It added up to a relationship, maybe one of long standing. Friedl Zussman. He made a mental note of the name.

Once again, more thoroughly, he began to search the desk. Among the chaotic mass of papers there must surely be notebooks, a diary perhaps, some map to guide him through the labyrinthine collection of documents, press-cuttings, correspondence. Many of the letters were replies to queries about people. "No, we regret we have no record of X." "There is nothing in our files relating to Y." "The last information we have about Z is that he was included in a batch of repatriates to Slovakia."

Why was Sinclair so preoccupied with tracing missing persons? Perhaps he had ambitions to emulate Simon Wiesenthal, searching out Nazis who had escaped justice. Considering that possibility, Shomron was gripped by a macabre thought. In the last weeks of the war a small number of young Jewish partisans, boys and girls who had escaped from the Vilna ghetto by crawling through the sewers to fight from the shelter of Polish forests, had carried out swift and silent acts of vengeance against Germans. Sinclair was a concentration camp survivor. Could he have elected himself a one-man executioner, hunting down individual Nazis or their collaborators? Shomron recalled how Detective Sergeant Motti Rubin of the narcotics squad, lying in a cell of the Abu Kabir remand prison, had overheard Sinclair's soliloquy: "Not murder, but an act of justice." Was it conceivable that Avram Benamir was not his only victim?

An hour or more passed. So absorbed had Shomron become that he'd lost all sense of time. He left the desk and rummaged about in boxes, peered into cupboards, walked into the adjoining bedroom annexe that gave off the stale odor of a hermit's cell, overcome by a queer sense of familiarity. The place had eerie echoes of home, so that he almost forgot he had forcibly entered the apartment and had no legal right to be there. It was as though he was revisiting a forgotten corner of his past, returning to the scene of a recurring dream.

The knock therefore caught him unprepared. "Frank, are you in?" someone called. Shomron moved irresolutely towards the window. Flight would foreclose his opportunity to continue the investigation. It would be assumed that the caller had interrupted a burglary. Extra precautions would be taken to prevent a repetition. No, he'd have to take a chance on bluff. Assuming an innocent smile, he opened the door.

A big blonde woman stood on the threshold cuddling four bottles of wine to her generous bosom. "Who are you?" she demanded, opening her round, blue eyes in astonishment.

"I'm a friend of Frank's," he said. "The name's Shomron, Amos Shomron."

She peered over his shoulder. "Where is he?"

"In Israel, actually. Won't you come in?"

The woman looked him over with a kind of Rabelaisian slyness. Apparently her assessment was not unfavorable, for she stumped into the room still clutching her bottles and deposited her broad hips in Sinclair's armchair. The springs gave out a rusty groan.

"I saw the light under the door and thought old Frank was back from one of those trips of his. Mind, I didn't hear anyone come in. I'm the landlord here, Betty Purves. I say 'lord' because otherwise people think you're one of these bed-and-breakfast landladies." She glanced up shrewdly. "It's not like Frank to have anyone staying in his place."

"I'm doing some research. Frank's letting me consult his library."

Betty Purves chuckled. "He must be getting more amiable in his old age. What are you, a historian?"

"A lawyer. Post-graduate study in war crimes."

"Oh, dear! Morbid stuff. Rather you than me. Well, I only came down to get some more booze." Heaving herself out of the chair, she said: "Why don't you come upstairs? A few of us are in having drinks."

"Are you sure I won't be intruding?"

"Not in this house, we're sociable," she declared comfortably. "Next time you can bring a bottle."

Shomron could hardly believe his luck. He had already been accepted into the community.

"Look what I found lurking in the basement,"

Mrs. Purves announced to several somnolent people distributed in semi-darkness around a large, high-ceilinged drawing-room. She deposited the wine bottles among a collection of empties on a low table and introduced him to various individuals whose names registered vaguely and were promptly forgotten. "Betty, to you," Mrs. Purves admonished him, passing over a tumbler half-filled with vinegary Beaujolais. A bearded old man, all wrinkles and hair, in faded corduroy and a check shirt, whom everyone referred to as "Bill," asked where he was from. "How interesting," he remarked when Shomron told him, exposing long yellow fangs in an amiable but vulpine smile before gazing long and contemplatively into his glass. An eminent poet and critic knighted for services to literature, Shomron later discovered. He got to know them all, more or less, before the evening ended. The light-skinned, Caribbean actor, Claude, crossing and recrossing his long tapering legs, confided that he was usually employed as the token black in TV melodramas, but needed the bread, man. Sad, brown-eyed Mary from Cork, a lapsed nun, with Irish eloquence softly declared herself to be a pilgrim soul presently taking a course in social science in preparation for work among juvenile delinquents. The rest of the company remained shadowy, a low soporific murmur of voices, profiles glimmering and vanishing in the darkened room.

Betty Purves joined him on the sofa for a tête-à-tête, smelling of wine and garlic.

208

"How well do you know Frank?" she asked, her warm, perspiring flesh pressing against his side.

Some prevarication was called for. "Only slightly. He's staying with some friends of mine. How well do you know him?"

She gave a low gurgle of laughter. "Twenty years he's lived in this house and all you get is good morning, good night and a chat about the weather. All right, that's an exaggeration, but not much. When he does his talking it's to himself. I've heard him through the door muttering and carrying on as if he's wrestling with the devil. Specially in German. Quite scaring if you're not used to it. Of course, most of the time he's very soft-spoken, very quiet. I don't think I've ever heard him laugh."

"Perhaps he hasn't got much to laugh about."

"Oh, come on! There's a funny side to everything, even a funeral. I had a suicide here once, Steinberg, a middle-aged bachelor up on the third floor, pouches under his eyes, wheezing with asthma. He told jokes all the time. Put his head in the gas-oven but didn't lose his sense of humor."

"An interesting paradox," murmured Shomron, slowly nodding his head.

"Well, he's a haunted man, isn't he?" Betty Purves said in a confiding undertone. "Not mad, but very peculiar. He keeps sniffing himself, have you noticed? I watch him in the garden from my kitchen window pacing up and down. Suddenly he'll stop, slip his hand down the front of his trousers then bring it up to his nose and go sniff-

sniff. You know what he lives on? Cornflakes and tins of Campbell's soup, although I expect he eats canteen lunches at the BBC. That's what Mrs. Zussman thinks, anyway."

The husky voice on the telephone. Skillfully, Shomron began to probe. It wasn't difficult: Betty Purves' lubricated tongue gossiped freely, imparting more than he needed to know. One thing became clear: Friedl Zussman was well worth a visit.

Descending into the semi-basement around midnight, he reentered Sinclair's apartment and closed the door on neighborliness. The spirit of its absent owner grew more imminent as other doors banged above and the nighttime silence settled on the house. Switching on the desk lamp, he began to read at random among documents laconic and terrible, until his eyelids grew weary and words blurred on the pages. It was time to go. A bed awaited him in the Holiday Inn Hotel, a few minutes walk away. Japanese and German businessmen, American tourists, cocktail bar gossip, air-conditioned bedrooms; no, the transition would be too abrupt, incongruous.

Returning the room to darkness, he went into Sinclair's sleeping annexe, slowly undressed and slipped into the unfamiliar bed. At first he shifted about uncomfortably, then his body settled into the mattress as if the hollow of its worn springs was made for him. Spectral faces, disembodied eyes, floated through his mind as consciousness

210

receded and soon he was trapped in a labyrinth of loss and confusion.

Frank Sinatra crooned *Come Fly With Me* and women of assorted shapes and sizes clad in leotards dipped and swayed in time to the music. Standing in front of the class, the lithe instructress beat time with flowing gestures of her dancer's arms. "*Up* and down, and *up* and down, and *up* and down," she chanted, rhythmically nodding her glossy black head. Her disciplined figure was small, slender and perfectly shaped; curved hips, supple waist, firm round buttocks and proportionately long legs in black net tights had a balletic power and grace. Now and then she darted among her pupils to improve their coordination. "Don't strain yourself, dahling, you are vasting energy. Bend like a tree in the vind." A change of musical tempo and the class began a different exercise designed to tighten the pelvic muscles. The movements were frankly libidinous, accompanied by ribald exhortations from the instructress and giggling from the ladies, a grinding of groins and clenching of thighs as if practicing to macerate anything that came between them.

"We have an audience," one of the class remarked, pausing in her pelvic rotations.

"It's a man,' said another, following the direction of the woman's glance, and Shomron became an object of collective hostility.

Edging further out of sight behind the door, a peeping Tom caught in the act, Shomron's embarrassment was compounded by a vague disquiet. Deborah performed similar gymnastics on the bedroom floor at home. It hadn't brought any difference to the way they made love. He'd been given to understand that it was a cure for a subcutaneous condition known as cellulite. But if it had to do with sex, why the deception?

The tape-recorder went abruptly silent. Hurriedly, he took up a position by the window pretending an interest in the weather prospects of the sky.

"Yes, young man, what can I do for you?"

Shomron turned and his carefully composed smile became dislodged. He stared in disbelief. The girl he'd glimpsed from behind and imagined to be a seductive wench in her twenties had the ravaged face of an old woman. Youthfulness stopped at the sinewy neck. Triangular black eyes thick with mascara and surrounded by a crosshatch of wrinkles, a wide red gash of a mouth and rouged cheekbones; the dense, crow-black of her dyed, short-cut hair gave her the appearance of an aged harlequin—with gorgeous breasts. The effect was chimerical like that of a breasted Sphinx crouching in the sands of Egypt on lion haunches.

His glance was irresistibly drawn to the agile pelvis and the firm rounded thighs so assertively displayed by her black net tights, reluctantly returning to the mask of flesh and bone no exercise of will could rescue from the disrepair of time.

212

"You are Friedl Zussman?" he enquired uncertainly.

"Yes," she drawled in a husky, weather-beaten voice. "But who are you?"

"We spoke on the telephone last night. I'm staying in Franz's flat."

"Ach, so! And your name?"

"Amos. From Israel." Instinct prompted him to withhold further information.

Friedl Zussman subjected him to a cool, appraising stare. "Very goot, Amos from Israel. Please to wait in my office. Zis class is soon finished."

She piroutted away, miraculously restored to youthfulness, firmly closing the studio door against further trespass.

The music resumed. Feeling like a schoolboy guilty of a misdemeanor and ordered to the headmistress's study to await punishment, Shomron obediently did as he was told.

The office was designed to make visitors aware of their need for self-improvement, inescapably conscious of being too fat, too thin, too clumsy and unfit compared to an attainable ideal. It contained a weighing machine, mirrors strategically placed to trap the body at unflattering angles, blown-up action photographs of superbly sculptured gymnasts of both sexes flying with the grace of birds, glossy magazines of beautiful people beautifully young and beautifully nude. A vase of daffodils adorned the elegant desk and geraniums stood on the sill of a window that overlooked the converted stables of an eighteenth century cobbled mews.

213

Glancing around, his eye was caught by a somewhat faded picture of a ballerina. He examined it more closely. The portrait was unmistakably that of Friedl Zussman, aged about eighteen, and bore the embossed legend "Studio Dührkoop, Unter den Linden 27." One detail, in the context of history, was remarkable. The young dancer wore a pendant Star of David on her breast. If every picture tells a story, as it does, then this one also revealed a character. Judging from her present age, Shomron was looking at a girl posing in a Berlin photographer's studio sometime during the menacing years of 1938 or 1939. Hitler had marched triumphantly into Vienna and signed the Munich Pact with Neville Chamberlain. The whole of Berlin was hung with Nazi flags; jack-booted stormtroopers looted Jewish shops, set fire to synagogues, despatched thousands to the concentration camp at Buchenwald. Those Jews who could fled, the others waited in terror for the tramp of boots on the stairs. Yet in this nightmarish atmosphere young Friedl Zussman, little more than a child, had chosen to be photographed wearing the symbol of persecution.

To recreate the gallantry of that moment, Shomron tried to imagine the circumstances more fully. Friedl would of course not have been permitted to perform in Germany's Aryanised theaters. Perhaps she danced with her reflection before the mirror in a locked apartment, curtains down against the spying eyes of vigilant neighbors. Perhaps the evanescent image, vanishing so quickly in the shrouded room, left an unassuaged hunger, a fierce sense of injustice. She was a ballerina and a Jew and could proclaim it. There can be occasions when to deliberately subject oneself to the camera's eye is an act of heroism. Did she have to disregard parental anguish? Shomron saw her packing ballet shoes and costume in a small bag, concealing the Star of David in her pocket, slipping out of the apartment. She enters the dangerous streets, trembling inside but pretending unconcern, not looking at shop windows on which the word *Jude* has been scrawled in whitewash, not looking at the truncheon-swinging men in brown uniforms and swastika armbands, trying not to run at the sound of following footsteps, until at last she has reached Berlin's most fashionable street thronged by the élite of Germany's Third Reich and enters Studio Dührkoop. Quickly she changes into her dancer's costume, fastens the Jewish star around her thin arched neck and the camera clicks, capturing the moment, if not forever, long enough to retain its fading image on a London wall almost forty-five years later.

Preoccupied with these imaginings, Shomron failed to observe Madame Zussman's silent arrival until he glimpsed her still form poised in one of the mirrors. She had slipped on a woolen cardigan, leaving only her magnificent legs uncovered to exert a hypnotic fascination as they walked the elderly person to her chair behind the desk. Opening a drawer, she took out a box of slim cigars and lit one from the flame of a jeweled lighter, deeply

215

inhaling the smoke with little apparent concern for the state of her lungs.

"Do you bring me some news of Franz?" she opened in a far from friendly tone and Shomron saw that he was going to have problems. The requirements of secrecy, for one, and concealing his own true identity.

"I believe you've known him a long time," he parried.

"Since he was fifteen years old. And you?"

"A very short time. We met in Tel Aviv." She maintained a skeptical silence, waiting for him to elaborate. In his own profession, the technique was deliberately employed to induce self-incrimination. "I'm hoping you can tell me something about him."

"For what reason are you asking?"

The question had been anticipated and his cover story prepared. He was conducting research into the way concentration camp survivors had adjusted to post-war society. Some spoke freely, others like Sinclair found it difficult to talk about their experiences. With casual deliberation, he cited the case of a former inmate of Dachau who remained mute about the past, refusing to discuss it even with his grown-up children. Deftly, he dropped the name Bindermann into her silence and watched for a ripple of interest. "The man is known in Israel as Avram Benamir," he added.

It elicited no reaction. Friedl Zussman crossed her slender ankles and swivelled from side to side in the revolving chair, puffing her cigar and regarding him with a frown.

"Franz is in trouble," she said.

"What makes you say that?"

She tapped the center of her wrinkled forehead with a sapphire-ringed finger. "I am looking wiz my third eye. Do you believe in the occult? Since all my life I haf zis gift."

"Can you see what kind of trouble?"

"Young man, don't play wiz me games!" she snapped, black eyes aglitter. "Just tell me if it's true."

The woman was worried. An unexpected idea came to Shomron. The impetuous girl in the photograph: smooth out the ravages and how much had she changed? The poignancy of aging is that the heart remains no less vulnerable than in youth. There was that discreet X entered every other Friday in the small green diary he'd found among Sinclair's possessions in Tel Aviv. According to Betty Purves, Madame Zussman was one of his very few friends, his sole comforter.

"What exactly is your relationship with Franz?" he said, risking a rebuff.

"You want to know if he is my lover! Shame on you!" She gave a coarse chuckle: no poignancy there. "He is much too old—and not enough beautiful. You men are too sentimental. I'm his muzzer."

"His *mother*!"

"It shocks you, I see. After all, I am only eight years older. Don't misunderstand, he is only a foster-son."

An element of playfulness had suddenly been introduced. She sprawled out in the swivel chair,

217

her cigar smouldering in the ashtray, net-stock-inged legs spread wide in blatant invitation. But a glance at the cynical droop of her painted lips and the wrinkles of amusement around her eyes told him that sex was being mocked and so was he. Friedl Zussman did not have much of an opinion of men.

"So," she said, "tell me please about my little boy."

Shomron realized that to get any further he must permit himself a partial indiscretion. Choosing his words carefully, he said: "Yes, he is in trouble. A gun was found in his possession. It seems that he planned revenge against an Israeli he believes did him an injury in Dachau."

"A gun!" She sat bolt upright and stared incredulously. "He wouldn't know even to hold it! Have ze police arrested him?"

"He's being detained."

Friedl Zussman threw out her hands in consternation. She went on at length, guttural with emotion, pleading Sinclair's innocence of violence with angry gestures of her hands, her shoulders, her whole expressive body. Shomron had difficulty calming her down.

"Listen to me!" he urged. "No harm has come to him. There has to be an investigation. If his grievance proves justified, he will receive sympathy in any Israeli court. The case may even not come to trial."

"You talk like a policeman," she said bitterly.

"I'm not a policeman now. Like any Jew, I'm only a survivor by the accident of geography.

Luckily for me, I'm a member of a generation raised in the principle of self-defense, but it's not difficult for an Israeli to step into the shoes of a Jew who suffered in Dachau. If only Franz would understand that instead of keeping silent and refusing to cooperate."

She shook her head violently. "You are asking ze impossible. He has always been ze same."

"Is there nobody he confides in?"

"If such a person exists, I don't know it," she answered in a voice that held the sour, resentful tone of rejected love.

Shomron probed further. "How did you become his foster-mother? You must have been very young to take on such responsibility?"

Streaks of black trickled through the spiky lashes of her brimming eyes. The question had touched a nerve. Angrily plucking some tissues from a Kleenex carton on the desk, she wiped away the tears, muttering furiously under her breath at the ruin of her make-up.

"You were looking at the photograph of zat silly girl," she said sniffing. "It was made a few days before I left Berlin in spring, 1939 to smuggle myself into Switzerland. After six weeks I arrived in London, sixteen years old and wizout a penny. I ran away from Germany not because I am a Jew but because I was a Young Communist. You see, my muzzer was *echt Deutsch,* more Aryan zan Adolf Hitler."

The thought made her laugh. Lighting a fresh cigar, she sat for a few moments tuning into her memories then told the following story:

Her father broke away from his orthodox Jewish family, married out of the faith and in time became a prominent member of the German Communist Party. He wrote film scenarios. The German cinema was then at its most innovative, playground of radical intellectuals who declared war on petit-bourgeois values in a series of so-called "street films," *die strasse* of brothels, and it was while making one of these that he met a young actress playing a prostitute's role and married her. Born into this artistic milieu, Friedl studied music and dance in preparation for what seemed an inevitable career in the theater. The advent of the Third Reich put an end to that.

On March 23, 1933, Richard Zussman was one of sixty *politische Haftlinge,* or political opponents of the regime, brought to a once-derelict munitions factory on the fringe of the country town of Dachau, some fifteen kilometers north-west of Munich. This was the chosen site of Nazi Germany's first concentration camp. After some weeks he was released but, convinced that the good, sturdy German *volk* would sooner or later send Hitler and his Brownshirts packing, he did not take the opportunity to emigrate while the going was good. It was of course a catastrophic mistake. Very soon it became later, then too late. Richard Zussman returned to Dachau never to leave it.

Friedl and her mother, who reverted to her maiden name of Ottmer, went to live with the mother's spinster sister and Friedl's grandmother in a huge gloomy apartment, one room occupied by a retired schoolmaster who had spent years trying to build a machine that would type musical scores and make his fortune. Constant failure had made him cantankerous, the spinster aunt was embittered, grandmama inhabited a remote past of well-drilled servants, country estates and aristocratic idleness, Friedl's mother grew morose as her youth wasted away. There were edgy silences, festering grievances, sudden outbursts of hysteria. They lived behind drawn blinds while outside the whole of Germany seemed to be goose-stepping to the stirring strains of martial music.

With feverish longing, Friedl dreamed of plunging into the dangerous world of the streets and taking up the role of conspirator. Half-Jewish but forbidden to mention it, fiercely communist, she made contact with Otto, a boy of her own age, the son of one of her father's friends, and the two of them began to put handwritten leaflets in letterboxes. Her mother found out and panic was let loose in the house. Did she want to put the whole family in prison? They would come and take her away to a place from which mad people never emerged alive. It had happened to the inventor's sister, whose ashes were mailed to him in a small black box. The women peered constantly through the window in terror of the imminent arrival of a Gestapo van. At every unexpected knock on the door they locked Friedl in the linen cupboard. Early one morning while everyone still slept she crept out of the apartment and fled to Otto. When his father heard of their escapade, he too became alarmed and arranged through one of his contacts for an escape network to smuggle them into Switzerland. There they obtained visas for England.

"For little Friedl ze war was fun," Madame Zussman wryly recalled, and recalled it at greater length than was necessary, for Shomron had seen so many movies, newsreels and documentaries that it was just as though he'd gone through it all himself. Also the First World War, Korea, Vietnam. His own experience of battle seemed more unreal, phantasmagoric orgies of violence as vivid and fragmentary as nightmare. He consumed three or four cigarettes waiting for her to deal directly with his question, but her clairvoyant powers did not extend to the detection of boredom.

"You want to know about Franz Slonimsky? Now I will tell you," she said at last. His interest quickened. Just hearing Sinclair described as Slonimsky gave the far-off prisoner a reality his shadowy presence had lacked, if only because it fitted him into an East European background that was part of his own inheritance, for his own family name had once been Ziskovits, Ziskovits from Czernovits until his grandfather went off to become a socialist farmer in Palestine. It was a kind of kinship.

"When ze Americans liberated Dachau, zey found a small number of children—orphans—still living. One was Franz, fifteen years old. The Jewish Rescue Committee brought him to England. Already I had a few such youngsters. You see, when Otto was demobbed from ze British Army we started a kind of commune and took in child refugees, teenagers. It was difficult to deal wiz some of zem at such an age, but for us, being good communists"—the tone of irony indicated political deviation—"we had ze example of Russia's orphaned *bezprizhorni* after ze Revolution. If Uncle Stalin could tame such savages, so could we. Support money came from Jewish welfare organizations. Very respectable bourgeoisie, so first we had to get married.

"I collected Franz from an office in ze East End. He was a tall, skinny boy who looked much older, wearing a navy-blue suit zat hung on his poor thin shoulders like he was a coathanger. The day was sunny and warm as we went in ze bombed streets. He never lifted his eyes from ze ground. When I tried to make conversation he answered wiz one word, *'Ja' oder 'Nein.'* Traveling by Underground, a terrible thing happened. At Moorgate Station hundreds of people pushed and struggled to get on ze train, everyone packed together so you couldn't move. Franz became white like he was going to faint. It was hot and almost impossible to breathe. He started to scream and struggle just like an animal who smells death in ze slaughterhouse. Somebody pulled ze alarm cord. At ze next station came in ze guard and zis frightened boy struggled even more. The uniform, you see. He ran away, but everywhere people were coming, more and more, from every direction, and here I was running after him and crying: 'It's all right, it's all

223

right! Nobody will hurt you!' All of a sudden he gives up and makes a small bundle of himself on ze floor, putting his head between his knees and protecting it wiz his hands, whimpering. A policeman came. 'Don't lay a finger on him!' I screamed. 'This child is from a Nazi camp. Can't you see he has a crippled mind?' Zat poor policeman, a big man like a tree, he stood so helpless."

Shuddering at the memory, a clownish grimace on her smeared, painted face, she relit the cold stump of her cigar, more than ever an old androgynous head balanced on the body of a seductive young woman. Somewhere or other, Shomron had read of an African kingdom in which it was customary for the spirit of a dead king to take possession of a young medium, entering by the head which underwent a paroxysm that left it aged and wrinkled.

"He had some terrible secret, ze boy, which he vas afraid for someone to find out," she went on in her resonant tobacco-stained voice. Unlike her other wards who conspired amongst themselves, quarrelled, flew into rages, played out in deadly earnest parodies of the cruelties that had been commonplace in their lives, Franz padlocked himself behind impenetrable barriers of silence. Records compiled by the Jewish Rescue Committee showed that his father, mother and small sister had perished in the camps, but he himself never referred to it nor to the circumstances by which he had escaped their fate. How the family had lived previously was also unknown. Dachau records

224

indicated that they had been brought to the camp late in 1944 in a transport mainly composed of Russian prisoners, suggesting that they may have succeeded in finding a hiding place for themselves when the Germans invaded Czechoslovakia. This seemed borne out by Franz's uncanny skill in concealment. He knew every crevice of the rambling house in which their apartment was situated, from cellar to attic, and could vanish without trace for hours on end without leaving the building while food to nourish him mysteriously disappeared from the larder.

"'Why don't you talk to me?' I used to say to him. 'Why always brooding on ze past? It's over, it's finished! Once and for all let it come out and forget it.' He would look at me so puzzled like I am speaking in an idiot language. It gave me pain—" Friedl Zussman banged her temples with small clenched fists—"I felt like I wanted to shake him and shake him until he came alive."

Yet sitting alone with him when he worked at his schoolbooks in peaceful silence, she could feel a closeness, an understanding that communicated without words, and it was then she became aware of a rare human quality buried deep under his reticence.

At school Franz Slonimsky was brilliant, hungrily absorbing all that his teachers could give. The paradox in one so wilfully mute was that he particularly excelled in languages, perhaps because prisoners from many different countries passed through the gates of Dachau. At the early age of seventeen he passed his university entrance exams and was offered an Oxford scholarship: then he did something totally unexpected—he went back to Germany.

Friedl Zussman said: "Because he never explained anysing, it vas a bombshell. One day, very quietly, he told me, 'I am going to work for ze Allied Control Commission in Berlin' and pouf! He vas gone more zan two years. Sometimes a postcard came. He always remembered my birsday. The *Manchester Guardian* newspaper published a few articles from him. Once I heard a man speaking on ze BBC about Nazis who still had leading positions in Germany. Afterwards ze announcer said it was a talk by Frank Sinclair. I didn't recognize ze voice, I didn't recognize ze name, but it vas still ze same Franz Slonimsky only older who came through ze door to ask please can he have his old room back. He vas beginning a new job in ze German Service of ze BBC. It couldn't be. All my foster-children had grown up and moved away. Otto had also returned to Germany, even more strong a Communist, to join ze Party in East Berlin. I had started a dance studio in my apartment and taken a new lover. Franz never showed nothing on his face, but I could tell he vas disappointed. You know what he said, zis silent man? 'Many times when I stayed here I thought of committing suicide. If not for you, I would have done it.' I asked him if he still thought such things. He gave a strange reply. 'Now I have anuzzer reason not to do it.'"

226

"Too busy doing what?" Shomron asked himself and the answer seemed obvious. Franz Slonimsky was driven to go to Germany to confront the thing he most feared and could not forget. He had emerged from hiding to confront his torturers. It must have been a quest for rediscovery, undertaken with dread. In doing so he had reached a decision that gave meaning to his continued existence—to stop running and become the pursuer. And for this purpose Franz Slonimsky assumed the identity of Frank Sinclair, undercover agent of retribution.

Friedl Zussman said: "Does it help, what I tell you?"

"Yes," he said, "I think it does."

The route to assassination was beginning to appear on the map.

"Well, I hope so." She sounded unconvinced. Shrugging, she went over to a washbasin in the corner of the room and began to remove her makeup. "Please go now, I have anuzzer class beginning."

Her fierce black eyes in the mirror observed his retreating reflection with melancholy and sudden mistrust.

8

CLOSING YET another file of documents, Shomron crammed it back into the drawer and went into the tiny kitchen-ette. He poured some boiling water over a teabag and sipped the scalding brew from a tannin encrusted cup. There were times when he wished he had more of a stomach for alcohol. His brain was slogged out by the pedestrian trudge through the accumulated, repetitive records of brutality that choked the desk, overflowed into cardboard boxes and stagnated in airless cupboards. And still no luck: not a single scrap of paper had turned up that could provide a clue to the workings of Sinclair's mind. Yet he was convinced that such a document existed, hidden somewhere in the apartment.

Returning to the living room, he lit a cigarette

231

and abstractedly switched on the powerful Japanese radio. Instantly the smooth voice of a German invaded the silent room bringing news of strife from all corners of a warring globe. Because of all he'd read these past few hours, the language jarred. A flick of the wrist cut it off in midsentence.

Apart from the wireless, Sinclair appeared to inhabit a world without music—no television, no hi-fi, no casette recorder, nothing but an old-fashioned gramophone standing in a corner dusty from disuse. The dowdy object merged unnoticed with the faded wallpaper. In his investigation of the apartment, delving behind bookshelves, looking under the mattress, climbing on chairs to peer into cupboards or scrutinize the assortment of neglected objects on top of the wardrobe, doing almost everything except prize up the floorboards, he had paid only cursory attention to the old gramophone. A plugless lead trailed from the motor and its turntable had long rusted into immobility. It had not seemed worth the space it occupied.

Then why keep it?

Impelled by curiosity, he went over and tried the cabinet door: it was locked. Still only mildly intrigued, he got a knife and attempted to force the catch. The task was more difficult than expected. Someone had inserted a steel bolt to reinforce the lock, an excessive device to safeguard a collection of records. Shomron was now thoroughly aroused. He attacked the lock with hammer and screwdriver, digging out splinters of wood until at last the violated cabinet swung open. Inside was a pile of obsolete vulcanized twelve-inch gramophone records in torn paper sleeves weighed down by a boxed set of the *Readers' Digest Treasury of Great Music*. Having removed these, he studied the empty cabinet and noticed a disparity in size between its interior and exterior. He gripped the plywood base and pulled. The false bottom slid out easily—and there, incredibly, they were, black covered, neatly numbered from one to six, the secret notebooks of Franz Slonimsky.

A ghostly echo of that momentous awe experienced by those who disinterred from the rubble of the Warsaw Ghetto the sealed archives of the murdered historian Emmanuel Ringelblum sounded in Shomron's heart. *Shema Yisrael*. Hands trembling, he carried the notebooks over to the desk and spread them out. He was about to commit a transgression. Turning page after page at random, the minute writing blurred before his eyes. Then, with a feeling of trepidation as if plunging into the unknown, he opened the first notebook and began to read.

My grandfather, who came from Poland, used to call me Itzikle, his little Isaac. It made my father cross. The old man's Yiddish embarrassed him even more than grandfather's habit of taking out his false teeth to eat. Father was a dental surgeon and the set of dentures he provided for grandfather was the best you could get, yet grandfather only wore them when visitors called and as soon as food was served to him, out they came." Itzikle, who will say Kaddish for me when I die?" he would ask. My father was also embarrassed by Judaism. He believed in humanism. Grandfather became senile and went to live in a Jewish old people's home. The Germans took them all away when we were already in hiding.

These are pictures that come out of the dark, fading around the edges, as unrelated to me as the name the International Tracing Service gave me when the Red Cross took me from the camp: Franz Slonimsky.

The Voice has been going on in my head for longer than I can recall. Sometimes the voice in my head sounds like my father's, soft and irritable; sometimes like Herr Doktor Gutermann, the headmaster of my gymnasium in Prague, who always spoke in a loud, clear, sarcastic tone. It keeps on and on telling me things I can see with my own eyes, commenting on everything. "A man is coming down the street riding a bicycle. He has red hair. Now he's turning the corner. It's beginning to rain, didn't you feel a spot of it on your face? Stop, fool! Don't run across the road, there's too much traffic. If you fell in front of that truck all that would be left would be a greasy smear of pulverized flesh and blood." When I read a book it insists on speaking the words aloud. I am looking at the letters of Heinrich Heine. "You can't expect me to send you my heart's blood in an envelope," the Voice shouts. Blood, blood, blood, the Voice remembers things I would prefer to forget. The time when we were hiding in the farmhouse just outside Frydek in the Carpathians and a German patrol was searching

234

the district. *Father and Mother were taken to the mountain cave, Zofia and I hid in the place our farmer made under the floor of the barn. It was narrow and dark. We lay side by side, afraid to make a sound. Zofia touched something wrapped in a sack. When we looked it was a dead piglet. Blood came from its nostrils and it had the white skin of a baby. The tiny eyes held a frozen look of agony. I stopped my sister's scream with my hand.*

A priest prisoner in Dachau once told me that the world is illusion and only the soul is real. Life on earth is the soul's tribulation. He had a job in the potato kommando and when he told me about God he gave me a handful of potato peelings. Could it be that the Earth and all its people are God's nightmare?

We believe what we choose to believe. Friedl sits opposite me reading a magazine. She looks up and smiles, convinced I need her companionship, while I hide behind my books. In the camps, to go unnoticed, to be invisible, to avoid the eye of an SS guard, to take on the camouflage of the grey anonymous mass, may make the difference between death and survival. But how can anyone understand who has not with his own eyes seen the emaciated dead hanging naked from gibbets in the Bunker yard or lying in their own excrement waiting to be thrown into the crematorium?

Friedl scolds me for not trying to be happy, for "burying myself," as she puts it, "in the past." She arranges a party in the house, wine and cheese on little sticks and gramophone music. I watch her dance and with every movement she is saying: "See

235

how wonderful it is to be alive, to be full of fire and tenderness." When she looks around I am gone, not because her dancing arouses feelings I cannot bear but because even the sensuous beauty of women's bodies evokes the worst of human degradation. Friedl reminds me of the sad, dark-eyed, lustrous girls selected from the women's camp at Ravensbrück for service in Dachau's brothel. I recall my relief that my sister Zofia, being skinny and underdeveloped and only eleven years old, was at least spared the bestialities of Block 31 before she was taken to be gassed.

No, Friedl Zussman, it is not for want of trying that happiness remains unattainable. I have striven towards life in panic and hopelessness. The terror is mute: it cannot be described: it has no common language with the living. What you do not understand is that the disease is incurable: Dachau is locked inside my brain. Starvation, cold, exhaustion, the crematoria stench that impregnated the rags we wore, the filth we ate, our scrofulous hair and ulcered skin—these do not vanish. Dachau is not the past, it is the reality. What we see now is illusion.

Every other Friday evening I travel down to a street off the Commercial Road in East London to sit with a group of old men in a bare room above a synagogue. There are not many of us—fifteen at the most—but each is a survivor: of Auschwitz, or Sobibor, or Majdanek, or Buchenwald, Dachau, Bergen-Belsen and so forth. It is possible to view us in different ways. We are fifteen winners of a fantastic lottery, the lucky numbers of a miraculous survival tattooed on our arms. We are also a strange League of Nations, drawn from every country of Central and Eastern Europe, elected by chance to represent the multitudes disenfranchised of life, the living tombstones of those lying in unmarked graves, or those whose ashes were dispersed by the howling darkness of the German wind that swept through Europe. Sitting there on hard wooden chairs in a small lighted room of an impersonal city, it seems to me that we are adrift on a raft, the last survivors of an engulfed civilization clinging to one another. Our humor is macabre, corrosive. In the camps laughter was the exclusive property of the SS; we would have been crucified for it. We come together because we cannot be grafted on to the living, our roots are too entangled with death.

I first came to the group in search of someone who has come to embody for me all the executioners. To my new friends I put the question. "Did you ever meet an SS Oberleutnant Ulrich Walther Kampfmann?" No. "Did you hear about such a man?" No. "Do you know if he is alive or dead?" They shake their tired heads. No. Each has a Kampfmann of his own, a Müller, a Kaltenbrunner, a Hoess, but not the one I seek. The years pass. One by one, unobtrusively, we slip away, drowned in the sea of forgetfulness.

I see people, hear them, move aside to avoid the space they occupy. I see grass and trees, and leaves drifting down, changes of light and dark, a world of objects. My body experiences heat, cold, hunger, the *pressures of bowels and bladder, the smell and taste of food. If the evidence of these appearances are to be trusted then I am not dead. Yet I am haunted by the distinct impression of having been dead more than once. The suffocation in the cattle truck of the train that carries us to Dachau, the long delirium of pain and loss of consciousness: was I among the many dead on arrival? Did I really escape the net in those endless "special actions" when we were rounded up for consignment to extermination camps in the East? I have hurled myself to electrocution on the barbed wire fence of the camp perimeter and seen my own face lying among a heap of corpses. I swear there were days when reveille sounded in the frigid darkness of a winter dawn and only a ghost rose from my lifeless body. "You trained yourself to become stone," I tell myself, "not to see or hear or feel, but you remember. Do the dead remember?"*

He read the diaries during sleep, lying in the hollow of Sinclair's bed, dreaming Sinclair's dreams and sinking deeper and deeper into the morass of horror. Sometime during the night came the false awakening. The sound of splashing water made him open his eyes. With a wild and joyous relief, he saw that he was back at home. Morning sunshine crept through the white slats of the window blind and music of deceptive geniality played on the radio. Deborah came out of the shower wrapped in a bath towel, tendrils of wet hair clinging to her cheeks. Everything was in sharp focus as though he had emerged from a long dim tunnel into the brightness of day. Then an oddness intruded. Old Louis Lipkin, the man who knew his father, materialized beside him in the bed weighing glittering crystals of time on a pocket balance. His mother turned a young face to smile at him over the whirring sewing machine, stitching a black shroud. Dread settled on his heart. A harsh voice barked: *"Block zweiundzwanzig! Mut-zen-ab!"*

He was standing with many shadowy figures in a bleak railway shed. Outside, a moonless sky hung low over the jagged darkness of a deserted battlefield. Panic surged up in him to the roots of his hair. Where was Deborah? Her white form glimmered from afar, floated nearer. She had the face of Friedl Zussman.

Another metamorphosis. The setting had become a theater, the floodlit stage floating on an ocean of darkness. A multitudinous murmur rose from the auditorium like the restless noise of waves breaking on the shore. He stood in line with the others, stripped naked and cringing in the merciless glare of a battery of spotlights. Slow drumbeats that may have been the thudding of his heart signalled the arrival of a tall black-clad figure, pacing with ceremonious precision along the length of the stage. The narrow, impassive, coldly handsome face was that of a bronze medallion. The figure halted: its ice-blue eyes glittered beneath the peak of its military hat. *"Komm, Frau!"* it commanded in a quiet deadly voice, lifting a thick beckoning finger and pointing at Orit. Shomron found he could not move. The scream in his throat emerged soundlessly. "You can't take my daughter!" he pleaded. "She's only eleven!" A prurient smile passed across the clean-cut, sinister features. Stiffening its gross finger, the black presence pushed it up between the legs of the small girl. "A woman," it said, displaying the stain of menstrual blood.

Shomron struggled like a drowning man to free himself from engulfing horror and woke in a tangle of bed-clothes. Evil crouched in the darkness of the room. From outside came the cheerless sound of incessant rain dripping from the eaves. The night seemed interminable. He put on the light, afraid of the dark and afraid of sleep, but the drab bedroom brought no relief and a morbid, self-punishing obsession drove him back to Sinclair's desk, to the harrowing contemplation of another man's pain.

My dear father,

I am condemned to relive that moment when you turned to look for me and found me gone. The prison train had arrived in Dachau, a hellish journey was over. With relief, our stifled lungs drank in the cool, fresh air of that October dawn. We were pushed and whipped into a straggling formation five lines deep by SS men wearing the Death's Head badge on their helmets and accompanied by snarling dogs straining against their leashes. They jostled me to the rear. An SS officer walked through the lines, glancing at each prisoner and directing some to go to the left, others to the right. He pointed his finger at Mother and Zofia, ordering them to the left. You stepped forward to join them then turned and looked for me. I saw the panic in your eyes. You kept glancing over your shoulder, still searching, as the guards drove you all aboard the trucks with whiplash and blows of their fists. Zofia screamed and clung to Mother. I tried to call out but a man clapped his hand over my mouth and stopped me from following. The three of you disappeared into a mass of writhing bodies. There was a dense trail of smoke as the transport drove off, carrying you out of my life forever.

It brings back the terror of the mechanical doll. I was five years old, out shopping with Frau Lützen, the housekeeper we had in Prague. The grinning doll was dressed in clown's costume. It turned its head from side to side and moved its legs and arms in a jerking dance. I stared in fascination. When I looked around for Frau Lützen she was gone, vanished in the bewildering street of hurrying crowds and tumultuous traffic. You will recall that a kind stranger found me crying outside the church of St. Vits and brought me to a police station. Not until late in the night did you find me there asleep on a chair. That premonitory experience of loss and despair reminds me of the terror that made me unable to divulge my name to the police. I was afraid to be punished for being bad.

"Don't believe a word of it. Your son is lying," the Voice interrupts, speaking in the sour, contemptuous tone of Herr Gutermann. He enters the class stealthily, as is his habit, and stands listening at the back of *the room withholding his shafts of ridicule until a suitable victim presents himself. I watch his advance through the rows of desks, hands clasped behind his back, to take up a position beside nervously smiling Jaroslav Hajek, our teacher. No-one can appear more kind and benevolent than Headmaster Doktor Gutermann when he has cornered his prey. The eyes with their thick, blonde lashes smile in the plump, rosy face and the girlish mouth has a mischievous smirk. He looks at you affectionately and you suddenly realize that it is the expression of a gourmet contemplating an appetizing morsel. In a loud, clear, carefully enunciated voice, he declares: "Everything you have just said is a lie. When the selection was taking place, you saw that those being sent to the left were women and children, the old, the feeble, the lame. It was evident that those poor wretches were doomed. In cowardly panic you concealed yourself behind a large Russian prisoner, terrified that your mother and father would claim you. You stopped your ears against their cries. Did it occur to you at that craven moment of desertion that, at the very edge of annihilation, your father looked for you to send you an agonizing message of love: 'Goodbye, my son. Preserve yourself, cling on to life. You are all we have left in the world.' They were swept away by the iron broom, your own flesh and blood, and all you could think of in the turmoil of your heart was that you must pretend to be tall and strong to evade the pointing finger of death."*

How can I deny my primitive craving for survival, the stealth, cunning and greed I employed to ensure it. Yes, I was afraid. But I did not recognize the appalling implications of weeding out the strong from the weak at that dawn selection. I thought that those unfit for work were to be placed in separate barracks. Only later one of the Ehrenhäftlinge, *the privileged prisoners, a Catholic priest of high rank, explained that Dachau was not classified as an extermination camp. "Pray for the souls of your loved ones, my son," he said. "They were sent to the East and you will never see them again." A day or so later I saw the SS officer who had carried out the selection crossing the parade ground. He was a man of unmilitary appearance, about thirty, dark-haired, studious-looking. His eyebrows were crooked, his nose thin and pinched at the nostrils, his manner preoccupied. He seemed only vaguely aware of his surroundings. Quite deliberately, I stood in his path watching him come nearer and nearer until I held his face in close-up, every fold of the skin, the dark flecks in his eyes. He passed me like a sleepwalker. From his collar markings he was an SS Oberleutnant. It took me three weeks to find out his name.*

I committed him to memory.

You may wonder how I survived. Six months still remained before the Americans liberated the camp and in Dachau a life could run its unnatural course in weeks if not days. On arrival in the quarantine block, I made the mistake of asking an SS guard which bunk I should take. Without expression, he kicked me in the balls. Stampeding prisoners trampled as I writhed in agony on the floor. The journey

243

to extinction had begun. Battered, insulted, in a stupor of pain and baffled by the maze of regulations, it seemed that I would soon be added to the piles of corpses that fed the ovens of the crematoria. At five a.m. reveille on the fifth or sixth day I failed to rise from my bunk. The kapo cursed. "Don't fuck me about!" he snarled. "I'll get twenty-five or thirty fucking strokes if you don't make it for roll call." He was a small, gnarled, scowling Sudeten German with a criminal record. I cringed away from the expected blow. Instead, he said in a disgruntled voice: "How old are you, kid?" I answered that I was eighteen. "You'll croak before you see it," he grunted. The hint of kindness in his tone was so unexpected that it made me cry. I told him I was fourteen and ten months old. Sighing, he looked at me indecisively then squared his shoulders. "In that case, you've got typhus. They won't come near you to check in case a louse crawls into their pubic hair." For the time being I was saved. I lay for a week on the stinking floor of a hut in the segregated east wing where death by infectious diseases raged with the virulence of fire. I staggered out at the end of this period to begin a new season in hell.

My kapo benefactor had been put in charge of the disinfection kommando. "First class job," he told me, having wangled my enlistment. We met the trains transporting prisoners from other camps about to be overrun by the advancing Allies—Jews, Gypsies, Poles, Russians in thousands. When the sealed trucks were opened, the reek of decaying corpses was as suffocating as poison gas. Our kom-

244

mando plunged through the mist to unload the bodies. We stank of dead men's vomit, excreta and rotting flesh. It clung to our fingers when we chewed our crusts of bread. Scientists today talk gloomily about something they call "the greenhouse effect." The massive discharge of carbon dioxide from motor vehicles throughout the world is increasing the temperature of the earth. In time the polar caps will melt, raising the sea level by two hundred feet and drowning entire cities. Is there not also a greenhouse effect of evil, an overflow from the murderous orgies of our twentieth century inundating continents with riot, cruelty, terror and massacre?

My dear father, you may wonder what point there was in continuing this existence. Better to invite a quick bullet by trying to escape. Yet the closer I drew to death the more desperate my determination to live. It wiped out my grief so completely that mother, Zofia, you and all our life together were obliterated. And there was a flicker of hope, rumors that Germans were falling back on all fronts. Far away in Berlin, in the Fuerherbunker, a decision had been made to prolong the misery of the Jews by slowing down the slaughter and setting the vermin to work. I was attached to a transport brought from Auschwitz and sent to join the Jewish kommando engaged in building underground Messerschmidt factories in the forests of Kaufering to replace those bombed by the Royal Air Force. Here was the lowest region of Dachau's hell. Winter had come. Men and women, tottering skeletons clad in rags, toiled in sub-zero weather until they died of exhaustion and hunger.

We slept on rotten planks in huts consisting only of a roof, queued to defecate at two latrines allocated for the use of several thousand Jews, staggered out for four-thirty a.m. reveille to stand for hours in darkness, snow and drenching rain. Even more than beatings and starvation, filth was the death of us, clogging the air we breathed, rotting our intestines, polluting the blood to the very depths of our shrunken hearts.

And it was there in Kaufering IV that I again set eyes on your murderer. The working party had returned from the catacombs carrying three who had collapsed and died. A guard turns the lifeless bodies over with the toe of his jackboot. He does it with massive indifference, for he has long ceased to be a man. For him it is a matter of simple arithmetic, one hundred and fifty stück, "pieces," minus three goners. He will have to make the numbers up. Beside me, Schafler is muttering a Hebrew prayer, teeth chattering in the freezing cold. He, too, looks as if he will not last much longer—shuffling along in his wooden clogs, the rags flapping on his emaciated body, the flesh of his face so wasted that his nostrils, the cavities of his lustreless eyes, his gristly ears, all seem enormous.

There is the sound of an approaching engine. A staff-car churns through the mud, headlights gleaming, and stops at the far end of the assembly yard. Two figures alight and approach at leisure. One of them is SS officer Kampfmann. My immediate thought is: "A selectsia." There has been another intake of Jews from the East and people are clamber-

ing over each other like stupefied ants. Room must be made, so we are to take part in the lottery of death. The same idea occurs to many of us. Will it be done here or in the open hut after we have been ordered to strip naked and expose the tell-tale sores, the skin rashes, swollen ankles and other ravages of malnutrition that mark out those no longer worth the feeding? We straighten our weary bodies, push out our ribs, glance covertly at our neighbors, competitively measuring our own chances of survival. But some are too sunk in apathy to make the effort, drowning men going down for the third and last time.

Schafler, beside me, does not interrupt his prayers. Rocking slightly, eyes half-closed, he seems to have gone into trance. Or a spark has ignited his soul and he is choosing martyrdom by keeping his head covered to conform to Jewish tradition in defiance of orders.

I am ashamed to remember that I shifted a fraction away, the cringe of a slave.

The guard's plump jowels clamp like a bulldog's. "Shitbag! Think this is a synagogue?" he growls. He lifts a threatening fist and is about to smash it into Schaffler's chattering teeth when, to my amazement, Kampfmann steps forward. Immaculate in his highly-polished jackboots and warm, well-tailored, black leather coat, the swastika armband of the Master Race on his left sleeve, he listens attentively to the Semitic liturgical chant intoned by the scarecrow. His face is so close to mine he must surely feel the scorching breath of my hatred, but I do not exist for him. His attention remains focused on Schafler: and from the alert, receptive look in his eyes it would almost seem that he is able to follow the meaning of each word.

"Are you reciting your Jewish burial service?" he asks in a deceptively mild voice.

Schafler's eyes were tightly shut and he continues to rock backwards and forwards.

A terrible hush grips the assembled Jews. We are witnessing an apocalypse. This is Kaufering IV, more dreadful than Gehenna, and Israel's God, if he exists, has gone into hiding. The only uncertainty is the manner of our martyr's death—a pistol bullet between the eyes, a ceremonial flogging until the skin hangs in strips from his back, snarling dogs tearing at his genitals.

Still dangerously quiet, Kampfmann asks: "Are you a rabbi?"

"Amen," *says Schaffler, having finished praying, and takes his cap off. He moistens his dry lips and replies almost inaudibly:* "I am the rabbi of a small congregation in Galicia. We no longer exist."

Kampfmann greets this information with a sagacious nod and bends closer. "Tell me, rabbi, do you see in all this—" *he gestures towards the three dead Jews, the frozen congregation of prisoners and the noisome darkness hovering above the camp*—"in all this . . . travail, a metaphysical drama of sacrifice and redemption?"

Schafler follows the direction of his hand, gazes at the corpses. "Oberleutnant, sir, these people died because their boots were stolen. A man who loses his boots here does not have long to live."

248

A threatening growl sounds in the guard's throat. Straining at the leash like a well-trained blood-hound, he waits for the command to make his murderous leap, but the SS officer wishes to play his own amusing game.

"And it is written thus," he murmurs with refined mockery, "the Lord will have mercy on Jacob, and will yet choose Israel, and set them in their own land. And the strangers shall be joined with them, and they shall cleave to the house of Jacob."

Later that night, when Kampfmann had gone, Schafler was dragged from his sleep and, as we used to say, they crossed out his number.

This is one of the few episodes I can now recall in detail. We schemed and struggled each day to remain alive; men fought with desperation over a few crumbs, a rag to cover them at night, rotted boots; everybody underwent the terror of imminent selection and the wild relief of reprieve. Yet in the concentration camp world existence becomes a grey blur in which only the sensations of cold, hunger, the tedium of pain, remain vivid. Time passes like the drip of a leaking tap. There is no future beyond the next bowl of watery soup and crust of bread, the plunge into exhausted oblivion. For me, the months I endured in Kaufering IV have become the dream of one long tormented night.

War, our deliverer, was coming closer. But would it come in time? For as the Third Reich crumbled, tremors of panic began to shake our jailers. Their eyes moved uneasily, the harsh assurance of their voices turned to bluster. They watched us warily, with misgiving, vigilant for unguarded signals of revenge. More and more derelict Dreckjude, *Jewish shit, was being shovelled in from overrun camps and it was going to be a problem to get rid of so much vermin. For get rid of them they must. It had begun to dawn on Himmler's Nordic élite, these Aryans of purest blood, that it might go hard on them when the Allied troops arrived and set eyes on these diseased and tottering skeletons.*

A mood of indiscipline spread amongst the SS. Our numbers had dwindled and conflicting orders left them undecided about what to do with the rest of us. Drilled to strict obedience, the slackening of leadership confused and frightened them. A few disappeared. One heard that they had shed their uniforms and deserted. There were random killings. Food went unsupervised and the sick and dying were no longer segregated. At last we began to hear approaching gunfire.

One night towards the end of April, as I lay sleepless in the hut, Kravits, a Belgian Jew, crawled over and whispered: "Slip out to the bog, I want to ask you something." Kravits was a veteran survivor, a graduate of Auschwitz who knew every trick in the lager *repertoire.*

The usual queue of dysentery sufferers was lined up at the two latrines. "Listen," said Kravits, drawing me aside, "they're going to finish us all off. Today, tomorrow, any moment. They want to see to it that no Jew gets out of here alive. There's only one chance. We have to make a break for it."

250

"Why are you telling me this?" The suddenness of his proposition was as frightening as the fate he predicted.

"Because it needs two of us. Will you join me?"

I turned my head away. What Kravits offered was a choice between the hangsman and the axe and I continued to cling to the minimal hope of survival the Nazis exploited to ensure the cooperation of their victims until the very last. There are those who reproach the dead for not having fought back even with bare hands and enfeebled bodies, a suicidal mass uprising like that of the Warsaw Ghetto. Ask them if they can truly believe in the reality of their own death. A myth has arisen that only the Jews meekly submitted to extermination. Yet battle-tried Red Army soldiers brought to Dachau as prisoners undressed on command, neatly piled up their clothing and knelt naked on the SS firing range offering their defenseless necks to the bullet. No matter how starved, tortured and humiliated, when nothing but a thread links us to life, we still shrink from the loneliness and terror of our own moment of death.

The silhouettes of the guards brooded menacingly behind the watchtower searchlight. We shuffled along in the latrine queue and stood together ankle-deep in sewage.

"So you prefer to die lying in this shit," Kravits hissed savagely. He began to walk away. I seized his arm. "Supposing I agree, how will we do it?"

"There's a gap under the electrified fence just this side of the SS barracks. It hasn't been spotted yet. We can crawl through it."

251

"I'll let you know tomorrow," I said.

The marauding glare of the searchlight cut a swathe through the dark. Kravits winced. "There is no tomorrow, kid, it's a fighting chance!" he urged. "Better to cop a bullet or burn on the wire than go like a zombie."

Returning to the hut, he adopted the posture of a broken prisoner, feet dragging, head drooping between bowed shoulders, but his eyes were watchful. "Now!" he muttered, running forward and throwing himself to the ground. Without being aware of a conscious decision, I found myself beside him. We crawled a few yards, froze. The searchlight passed and we moved again, keeping to the shadow afforded by the huts. The groans of sleepers filled the night, crowded in suffocating intimacy, lying in a tangle of limbs. Then we left them behind, nothing but an open stretch of ground between ourselves and the perimeter. Kravits pointed to a slight hollow where the wire fence did not quite meet the earth. A sickening dread settled on my stomach. The gap was barely deep enough to allow a cat to squeeze through. I felt like crying.

"We've got to dig a bit," he whispered.

Kravits took a metal spoon from inside his striped prisoner's jacket. "Keep watch, I'll go first," he said. Wriggling forward inch by inch, he began to gouge at the rain-softened soil. When the searchlight lit up the fence his flattened, motionless form looked like a muddy heap of rags or a decomposing corpse. The sound of scraping sawed at my nerves. I was terrified that it would set the dogs barking and bring the guards running out of their barracks.

The leaden minutes passed. Kravits wormed his way back to where I lay and handed me the spoon. "Now your turn, it's going fine," he panted. Crossing those few yards of open ground in peril of a sudden burst of machine-gun fire was a taut yet liberating experience. Kravits' exhilaration was contagious: the fear had suddenly gone. We were fighting back and it tasted sweet. Huddling away from the high-voltage wire, I set to work. The hole grew deeper. When my energy flagged Kravits again took over. An hour passed, perhaps two. Still we remained undiscovered.

In the east darkness was beginning to fade from the sky. I struggled against exhaustion, against the renewed encroachment of despair. Dawn would destroy us.

"O.K., one more go then over to the other side," Kravits decided. He wished me luck. I dug and dug in frantic haste, clawing at the soil with spoon and hands until my fingers bled. Then, closing my eyes, pressing my face into the damp earth, I slid slowly, oh, so slowly, under the lethal fence. The effort almost did for me. I lay on my back staring in a daze at the reeling stars. "Come on," said Kravits, dragging me upright. In a stumbling run, he led me behind the sleeping guards' barracks, bounded by barbed wire. Clambering through at a place where the coils were thinned, scratched and bleeding from iron thorns, we drew our first deep breath in the miraculous open country of fox and rabbit, and did not stop running until we reached the shelter of Kaufering's forests. When the world woke up it found us buried in the sleep of the dead. I opened my

eyes to what sounded like the approaching reverberations of thunder, but sunlight filtered through the leaves and birds flew in a blue sky.

The Americans had finally arrived.

They found Kaufering IV in smoking ruins. The SS had set the camp on fire before they fled. Lying heaped in two ditches were nearly 5,000 Jewish corpses and another 268 scattered around the compound. There were no survivors.

9

"**H**E'S ALMOST as bad as Frank, shutting himself away with his history," Betty Purves chided, earth-mothering Shomron into her usual circle of acquaintances, each clutching the mandatory glass of Beaujolais. "I almost had to drag him from his gloomy books, he was in such a daze," she explained, her jolly laugh reverberating in the cavernous room.

Shomron was still in a daze. Grinning half-heartedly, he handed her two bottles of super-market wine he'd rushed out to buy, plucking them at random from racks stacked with a bewildering selection of vintages.

"Spanish claret, how fascinating! I haven't sampled this label before." Mrs. Purves deftly unpeeled the price stickers he had forgotten to remove. She filled a glass for him and invitingly patted the sofa at her side. "Sit here and tell us how you're getting on with your research. Are you going to write a terribly deep book?"

"I hope it's biography. I adore biography," said a middle-aged lady the others called Emily, who sat stroking a large cat on her lap. "I'm reading such a fascinating book about Mary, Queen of Scots. I got it from the library. It's written by that very clever authoress who is always on the television. You know, the beautiful one."

Betty Purves said: "Ah, yes, what's-her-name. Now there's a brainy girl." Nudging Shomron, she asked: "Do you like brainy women, Amos?"

Out on the fringe of the circle, Bill, the aged recipient of a literary knighthood, lifted his seamed and hairy face from his glass to ambiguously pronounce that the history of the world, according to Carlyle, was but the biography of great men.

"Yes, and haven't they made a mess of it," Betty Purves tartly observed.

Shomron smiled and nodded politely, unable to dispel an oppressive sense of unreality. His mind was out of focus. It was as though he sat in a theater so preoccupied by an inner turbulence that words spoken on the lighted stage, gestures, facial expressions, laughter, were drained of meaning, disappearing in the spectral visions that had arisen from Sinclair's notebooks. There he was, absently sipping his wine, turning his face from

258

one speaker to another, vaguely noting the noise of a passing car, the shadow of branches through the windows, whilst his dislocated mind still stumbled amidst scenes of horror and mutilation.

"I'm sorry, what was that?" he enquired, blinking up at a sandy-haired man of about thirty leaning against the mantelpiece of the empty fireplace, hands thrust into the pockets of a black leather donkey jacket worn over a sweatshirt reading "Psychiatry Kills."

"I said my name's Trevor. We haven't been introduced. I teach sociology at the Central Polytechnic." The accent was northern, the manner combative. Hitching up the knees of his skin-tight jeans and squatting on his haunches, the man said challengingly: "What's your definition of history?"

"Oh, Trevor, you only want to start an argument," Betty Purves said, laughing. "Everybody knows what history is."

"That's where you're wrong, Betty. Bill just quoted Carlyle. His history is the biography of great men, it's not mine, it's not yours, it's not the working classes." I shouldn't be surprised if for our friend here it's the Bible."

"Why do you say that?" Shomron asked, puzzled.

Betty Purves squeezed his arm. "Take no notice. He's just being provocative."

"Och, history is no good to anyone," came the soft Irish brogue of Mary, the lapsed nun, who perched herself on the arm of the sofa so that her leg rubbed against Trevor's shoulder. "You get nothing from it except wars and bloodshed and the martyrdom of saints. Would there be the trouble in Ireland today if we paid no mind to history and only thought of the present?"

The pout of her full lips and the abrasive tenderness of her stealthy caress caused Trevor to pause while he considered the proposition. His thoughtful gaze lingered on her parted knees. "I've got a radical solution for the Irish problem," he declared huskily. "Let's go into it later, eh?" Their glances clung and for a moment or so his intellectual aggression was deflected. Then he cleared his throat for action.

"What I wanted to ask you is this," he said to Shomron. "You're an Israeli, right?"

"Yes."

"An Israeli Jew."

His voice cut through the low murmur of conversation. A hushed stillness settled on the room as everyone glanced at Shomron, some quickly averting their eyes in embarrassment. A solecism had apparently been perpetrated. To call someone a Jew to his face was considered tactless, if not worse.

Shomron experienced the discomfort of a buried neurosis. His generation of Israelis prided themselves on being free of Jewish insecurity, the oversensitivity to Gentile opinion and the fear of being held in contempt summed up in the disparaging phrase "ghetto complex." They had cultivated self-reliance, physical courage, the open manner of

260

a free people who did not need to authenticate their existence by seeking outside approval. A thin-skinned chill penetrated the marrow of his being. This must have been what his grandfather had felt as a young man in Tsarist Russia before he'd shaken the dust of centuries from his feet and gone off to become a farmer in Turkish Palestine.

"Yes, I'm a Jew," he said.

Trevor nodded. "That's what I mean about the Bible. For most of us the Bible is a collection of myths and legends, for you it's history. And on that basis you commandeered a country no Jews had lived in for two thousand years. You said you owned the deeds. Jehovah had promised you could have it."

"If that's your historical truth, this discussion is over," Shomron said curtly, putting down his glass and rising to leave.

Mrs. Purves restrained him. "No, don't go, Amos. We were having such a pleasant evening." Rounding on Trevor, her plump good-natured face flushing, she snapped: "Why do you have to bring politics into everything?"

Trevor got to his feet, smiling indulgently. "Politics, my dear Betty, *is* in everything."

"Not in my house," she retorted. "Now, then, anybody for more wine?"

The bottle circulated and an uneasy truce was established. Bill the poet, recalled his wartime experiences in Cairo where he was attached to the Intelligence branch of Army HQ. On one occasion, flying low over the Gobi desert in an RAF recon-

261

naissance plane, he had seen what appeared to be a dinosaur, and the conversation meandered whimsically to the mysteries still contained in remote regions of the planet, to the possibility that extra-terrestrial beings were keeping the Earth under observation and other paranormal topics safely removed from politics. For his part, Trevor seemed preoccupied in continuing the game of seduction initiated by Mary and Shomron reckoned that he'd soon be able to make an unobtrusive departure.

But the evening's drama was merely dormant, not ended. It resumed when Trevor took the Irish girl by the hand and led her over to the sofa. Seating himself beside Shomron, he said in a conciliatory tone: "Look, don't get me wrong, I know that lots of the people who came to your country were refugees who had nowhere else to go. It landed them in a typical colonial situation and they were right to fight for freedom from the imperial yoke."

The blue, fair-lashed eyes held a deceptive candor, an expression of earnest concern, of honest perplexity.

"What worries me," he went on in a soft, sincere voice, "is the racist attitude Israelis have developed towards the Palestinians. You've turned them into the Jews of the Jews, have you thought of that? I mean, you treat them like the Nazis treated your own people."

Shomron absorbed the shock. It was by no

means the first time the outrageous comparison had been made. Arab spokesmen and supporters, the ultra-left, communist representatives at the United Nations—in recent years their voices had become clamorous with the accusation. Zionism equals Fascism: Israel is the successor to Nazi Germany.

Auschwitz, Belsen, Treblinka, Babi Yar; Riga, Vilna, the Warsaw Ghetto. A procession of names made infamous in the history of mankind. Street by street, the cities of Europe were emptied of Jews, the young, the old, the maimed and sick, occupants of orphanages, babes in arms, ancients too feeble to walk unaided—a vast migration of multitudes to annihilation, each sentenced to a monstrous and individual death in agony, loneliness and terror.

Statistics are faceless. These were the women weighing groceries in a corner shop, the doctor in his surgery, young girls walking home from school swinging their satchels of books and dreaming of future love, tailors sitting cross-legged on their work-benches, the rabbi, the schoolteacher, the visionary whose genius would have enriched music, poetry, science or philosophy, the mother wheeling in her pram some infant Aristotle, Pythagoras, Newton or Einstein whose marvellous brain was destined to be smashed by the fist of a Nazi. These were Everyman, various, singular, unique and collectively doomed only because each contained what the deranged prophets of Aryanism considered the ineradicable taint of a loathsome racial inheritance.

"Do you really think we're as bad as that, like the Nazis?" he murmured in response to Trevor's accusation.

"Well, to put it bluntly, in some ways, yes."

Shomron could feel the heavy thud of blood against his eardrums. There was really no way of putting into words his sense of injustice. What could be said to someone who drew no distinction between those who set out to exterminate an entire people they had designated as human cockroaches and a small nation of three million, overburdened with an intolerable history, rootless for two millennia, defending its survival against the hurricanes of violence raging through the century? And yet there were acts of cruelty, there was arrogance, hatred, prejudice and corruption that left the sour after-taste of shame. There was even, God help them, the glib tendency to justify excesses in the name of the Holocaust. That sickness, too.

Shomron was inheriting the embittered eloquence of Frank Sinclair's silence.

Having prepared himself for an angry response, Trevor mistook his opponent's reticence for an admission of guilt. The ease of his victory was disconcerting: it spoiled the fun. Say things like that back at the Polytechnic and you'd get the Zionist students jumping up and down in fury, giving you the satisfaction of shooting down their protestations with deadly accurate political marksmanship. He'd deliberately staked out an extreme position to make the argument more interesting, but if it failed to provoke . . .

"O.K., maybe I've gone a bit over the top," he magnanimously conceded, "but the fact is we had a right to expect better of the Jews."

The subject thus disposed of, he resumed his attention to Mary, unaware that he had ignited a fuse. For he had raised for Shomron the anachronistic spectre of Jewish meekness, the passive sufferance of generations inured to the harsh winds of hatred that swept through their ghettoes bringing rapine and slaughter. Shaken by a sudden detonation of rage, Shomron leaned over and seized him by the lapels of his black leather jacket.

"What gives you the right?" he ground out, staring into the other's startled eyes.

Trevor, his face pale, tore himself free, sending the drinks flying off the low table, and jumped up ready to fight.

"If that's how you want to settle an argument, O.K., I'm ready," he said jerkily.

The counter-belligerence was a mistake. Shomron's diffidence, his somewhat abstracted and studious appearance, could be misleading. For three months every year he went back to the army to do his reserve training. His reflexes were fast, tuned to instant action. There was a blur of movement as he sprang from the sofa and Trevor lay stunned on the frayed carpet.

An appalled silence followed. Shomron clasped

his closed fist and held it against his chest as though he wished he could withdraw the blow. He gazed at the spreading stain of spilled wine, the scattered cigarette ash, the shocked, astounded expressions of Betty Purves and her friends. Mary stared at him in horror with the wounded eyes of a violated nun.

"I'm sorry," he muttered and slouched out of the room.

Downstairs, in Sinclair's apartment, he stood in the darkness overcome by mortification. It hadn't been worth it. He should have shown more self-control. And yet, undeniably, the brief spasm of violence had provided an atavistic satisfaction.

Footsteps sounded on the stairs and a knock came at the door, sharp, peremptory. He opened it to find Betty Purves, not smiling now, looking as if she'd come to order him to pack and leave.

"I'm dreadfully upset about this, Amos," she said severely, then added: "I shall insist that Trevor apologizes. At the moment he's still too shaken."

"Oh!" Shomron was taken aback. "I shouldn't have lost my temper, Betty."

"That's why I won't have politics, or religion. It makes people so quarrelsome. And we were having such a nice evening."

"Yes, I'm sorry."

"And Trevor's nice, too. Just argumentative. But I won't have my house turned into a debating society—or a saloon bar."

Quite cleverly, Shomron realized, she had succeeded in administering a diplomatic reprimand. Closing the door on the incident, he went to the desk ånd switched on the light.

Immediately he was with Sinclair in Berlin.

10

THE SHOCK OF arrival at Templehof airport on a cold grimy February afternoon was indescribable. It had been the first flight of my eighteen-year-old life, a trauma of unnatural suspension in space, and I had vomited into a paper bag after gazing through a porthole at the huge, bright sun flying alongside the fragile metal cylinder while far below shone peaks and valleys of snow-white clouds. The upheaval in my stomach was not air-sickness alone, I was traveling in search of myself and dreaded what I might find.

The taxi that took me into the torn and divided city passed through acres of desolation. Berlin had been hung, drawn and quartered in the final frenzy of war and each of the four victorious powers presided over a share of the ruins. Entire districts had been obliterated, smashed into mounds of rubble, with here and there gaunt skeletons of twisted girders, gaping structures of brick, stone and rusted iron rearing towards a sullen sky. Shabby men and women, their faces pinched, trudged past with heads bent against the bleak wind blowing hard from the east. Entire families lived like troglodytes in cellars or huddled for shelter in the remains of bomb-scarred tenements, and old men pushing wooden carts on perambulator wheels or carrying sacks scavenged in the rubble of the once-imperial German capital for serviceable scraps of wood and metal.

But already the outline of the post-war city was beginning to emerge in the Western zones of military occupation—strings of lights marking out future centers of prosperity, the scaffolding of theaters, churches and new apartment blocks, renovated shop fronts throwing a bright dazzle of neon red, green, blue and silver on the wet pavements, all spreading a thin yet glowing promise that stopped abruptly at the darkness of the Soviet zone east of the Brandenburg Gate and the charred remains of the old Reichstag.

Gazing numbly out of the car window, I experienced none of the gratification I might have expected at the misery brought upon the land of my persecutors. I could not summon up the energy required by hatred. I had the odd sensation that I was dreaming myself, sitting at my desk in London within the circle of light cast by my reading lamp, that in a moment I would be awakened by Friedl Zussman's husky voice calling me in to tea and hot buttered toast before the glowing coal fire of the communal living room.

The taxi turned into the neat graveled drive of a large suburban villa in the Grunewald, requisitioned for use as one of its offices by the Investigation Department of the Allied Military Government. It had escaped shellfire and aerial bombardment, every pane of glass in its windows intact. Put a Mercedes-Benz instead of the camouflaged jeep in the driveway and it could have been the home of a prosperous German family, some privileged Nazi functionary circa 1938 perhaps, happy in his blonde wife and children, his dogs and his future of Strength through Joy promised by the Fuehrer. Defeat had taken the shine out of it. An American GI wearing steel-rimmed glasses sprawled behind a desk in the scuffed hall reading a copy of the army newspaper Stars and Stripes. Phones rang, typewriters rattled, heavy boots clumped along an upper corridor, a woman soldier carrying a sheaf of papers stopped to pin a typewritten list of names on the green baize notice board.

"See Captain Garfunkel, upstairs, first door on the right," said the GI.

"He's on the telephone," said a trimly uniformed girl, giving me a blue appraising stare that made me go hot with embarrassment.

The information was unnecessary. Through an open door leading to the adjoining room, a sallow, harassed looking man about thirty was both visible and audible. "I don't give a damn what his yarn is!"

273

he shouted. *"The guy commanded a unit of the SS Schutzaffel and personally supervised the massacre of civilians. We've got the evidence!"* Captain Garfunkel, a cigarette stuck to his lower lip, held the phone with one hand and gesticulated with the other. *"Yes, Jack, I'm sure he's got witnesses to prove he's an officer and gentleman. They'll also tell you he loves Mozart, little kiddies and the beauty of nature. The sun shines out of his ass, Jack, but there's sworn testimony that he hanged a group of Lithuanian villagers in April 1944 in reprisal for a partisan raid and there's a lot worse than that where he made sure of no survivors."*

Wandering into the reception office after the call was concluded, he said: *"An epidemic of innocence is sweeping this whole country, Sue. Eighty million Germans struck blind, deaf and dumb. They didn't see a thing. They were always somewhere else. They kept Jews hidden in the linen closet."*

"Yes, Captain," the girl said demurely. *"This is Mr. Slonimsky, the interpreter you've been expecting."*

"Great! Come on in," said Garfunkel, shaking my hand. He unpeeled the smouldering stub from his lip and lit another cigarette from it. Ash dribbled down the front of his Ike jacket. Eyes screwed up against the smoke, he regarded me narrowly and remarked: *"I thought you'd be older. According to your curriculum vitae you're a graduate of Dachau. That's some education. What brings you here, revenge?"*

"Perhaps. I'm not sure."

274

"Forget it, it'll only get you frustrated. And forget justice. This is some mess. Where d'you start and where d'you stop? Hell, when we first arrived and got a look at the camps and put it all together it looked like murder was Germany's biggest industry. When the trials started the grizzly details became so damn commonplace that it took things like lampshades made out of skin or Jews made into soap to get a reaction. Some of the big ones flew the coop to South America and a lot of others reinvented themselves or got fixed up with false papers and disappeared into the crowd. The lucky ones got picked to keep the new Germany running. One quick dry cleaning put a lot of them back in service."

Garfunkel spread his hands helplessly. *"What amazes me is the power of self-deception. They not only proclaim their innocence, some of them, they believe it. Paradoxically, it's the truly innocent who are most bothered by guilt, those who found ways of resisting but are tormented by the thought that they should have done more. There are thousands of them too. Germany has its heroes. Ultimately, it becomes a question of degrees of responsibility. Leaving aside those who directly participated in the mass killings, how culpable are the rest? Hitler did not advertise the existence of his death camps. When people here say they did not know there was such a place as Auschwitz they are not lying, but pieces of the monstrous jigsaw were turning up everywhere and if they did not put them together it was because they avoided doing so. Millions sleep-walked through horror, succumbed to moral paralysis, surrendered to inertia.*

275

Others were too young, too old, too feeble or too frightened. To condemn an entire nation is to set out on a road marked by bloody footprints. The Nazis did it and cut the throat of humanity."

Captain Garfunkel pinched the bridge of his nose as if to stifle a pain. "What I suppose I'm really saying," he muttered almost as if speaking to himself, "is that justice is unattainable. For a lawyer, that's a crippling conclusion."

Disclosing nothing of what I myself felt, I said: "When can I start work?"

Sometime in the middle of that first night I awoke from a fretful sleep, shivering, unable to recall where I was or how I'd arrived there. The piercing cold brought an illusion that I was still in Kaufering IV, the whole of my existence in London nothing but a dream of desperate longing. Laughter, mindless and derisive, came from nearby. Once again I inhabited the geography of desolation. Then came the awareness that my limbs were not constricted by the crush of other sleepers, there was space to move and air to breathe, and once again I experienced the massive, liberating shock of reprieve. The place was Berlin, the date February 1949. I lay in a rented room of Pension Eberth in Bleibtreu Strasse. The tiled stove had gone cold and my feather duvet had slipped off the lumpy bed. Next door my neighbor was having a party. Time resumed its normal sequence.

Captain Garfunkel had recommended the place. It was cheap, clean and within walking distance of the office. I found it gloomy, ponderous and oppressive. Herr Eberth, the small wrinkled proprietor, held out a swollen arthritic hand, politely bobbing his speckled, bald cranium, and this, the first handshake with a German, had made me feel unclean. "You must take coffee with us," Herr Eberth insisted, leading me into a parlor crowded with heavy mahogany furniture, the windows muffled by claustrophobic curtains of faded red velvet. An odor of decay, sickly and sweetish, hung in the room like breath from the mouth of a diabetic. To add to my discomfort, presiding above a row of photographs on the mantelpiece was a framed oleograph of a side-whiskered old German, his chest adorned with medals, wearing an expression of Prussian haughtiness.

Coffee and cakes were served by Herr Eberth's middle-aged daughter, a gaunt, silent woman, her grey-blonde hair screwed into a tight bun, who avoided looking at me and after a perfunctory greeting left me alone with her father. Garfunkel had told me the woman's story. She'd been married to an officer on General von Paulus' staff who was killed at Stalingrad. A fourteen-year-old son drafted into the Werewolves was killed in the fighting for Berlin. The woman herself had been subjected to an orgy of rape by a group of drunken Russian soldiers. In retailing this harrowing catalogue, I suspected that Garfunkel intended it as an object lesson to the effect that there had been victims on both sides, that a brutal and indiscriminate revenge had already been

277

exacted on those Germans least able to protect themselves.

My principal reaction was one of resentment. Garfunkel had no right to preach at me about good and bad Germans. How could I feel anything about the sufferings of Herr Eberth's daughter? I'd seen my father, mother and sister taken away to be gassed. I'd shoveled corpses, watched people dying slowly of torture and starvation, seen hanged men jerking in their death-throes like the mechanical doll in the Prague toyshop window. My mind was a charnel house. There were times when I touched myself to convince myself I was really alive, because inside I carried the experience of my own death, because my feelings remained numb, because an impenetrable barrier stood between me and the world's reality.

Herr Eberth, picking crumbs from his plate, matched my silence with a silence of his own. Having drunk the coffee to the last drop, he filled the charred bowl of a pipe with some dry grains of tobacco and lit it from a paper spill.

"If you will excuse me, I think I'll go to my room now," I said.

Just as I was about to leave, the front door slammed. "Ah, that will be Herr Krantz," Herr Eberth observed with relief. "He lives in Room Number Four, next door to you. I am sure he will wish to greet you." In a reedy, ingratiating voice, he called out: "Herr Krantz, can you spare a minute?"

The newcomer, a large obese man in a baggy suit, entered the parlor carrying a shopping bag filled with bottles of liquor. The stub of an unlit cigar protruded

278

from the corner of his loose, wet mouth and his flabby cheeks were flushed.

"What is it, Willibald?" he grunted.

Herr Eberth, a dwarfish figure in comparison, stood up and formally declared: "I would like to introduce our new guest, your neighbor, Herr Franz Slonimsky, from London."

"Wilkommen," said the man, sizing me up shrewdly. "The name's Hugo Krantz."

His moist handshake was even more repulsive than Willibald Eberth's. Krantz was the caricature of a coarse German, a gross, beer-swilling, sausage-stuffer with something brutal about his fleshy jaw, a middle-aged stormtrooper run to seed.

"What are you doing here in Berlin?" he asked.

"I'm an interpreter with the Allied Military Government."

Krantz looked at me through narrowed eyes. "You don't speak German with a British accent."

"I was born in Prague."

"Aha, Prague! I spent some months there in thirty-eight. Not a good time for anyone. An unlucky people, the Czechs. That's why they practice a subversive humor."

The remark was pitched like a fisherman casting a line, but the fish refused to rise. "Thank you for the coffee, Herr Eberth," I said, backing out of the room.

I had not long finished unpacking when my next door neighbor called, bringing a bottle of whisky and two glasses. Wasting no time on preliminaries, he poured out the drinks and settled expansively into a chair.

"You didn't choose the best time to arrive," he said, "Are you a sound sleeper? I'm having friends in tonight and it may get rather noisy."

I left my glass untouched, hoping he would soon leave.

"Join us if you like. It will be a stag party, no ladies. Are you fond of the theater? Otto Glenk is coming, a producer at Theater am Zoo. There will also be two young fellows—about your own age."

"You are most kind, but I am tired from traveling and must go early to bed."

"Ach, so! Well, drink up. It will make you sleep better."

To avoid discussion, I lifted the glass and touched it to my lips.

"Gezuntheit," Krantz said with a malicious smile, "and mazel tov. I see you are surprised that I wish you luck in Yiddish."

I averted my eyes the way I'd learned to do in Dachau. Hate rose in my throat as sour as vomit.

"It's not a language I speak very well, but I know a few good curses and the whole of Rozhinkas mit Mandlen. Raisins and Almonds, a beautiful cradle song. My Polish mother used to sing it."

Rocking backwards and forwards, eyes closed, the gross German hummed the tender melody with much feeling in a surprisingly tuneful voice. Incredulously, I exclaimed: "Are you half-Jewish?"

Laughing sardonically, Krantz replied: "On my father's side I can claim descent from a long line of rabbis. Until 1933 I preferred not to. My dear young friend, we are two Jews here in the Berlin pension of

280

Willibald Eberth. This is such a rare phenomenon that he could open a booking office and charge admission to view us."

"Have you lived here, in Germany, through— everything?"

Krantz leveled a threatening forefinger at me, scowling. "Now, look here, sonny, you better not give me that shit about how can a self-respecting Jew bear to live among a lot of murderous ex-Nazis. I'm a Berliner, born and bred. I came back last summer. This is my home town. The best years of my life were spent here—and a few of the worst. Now here I am again. For the present, it's just a reconnaissance, spying out the lie of the land. I have to return to England to settle up a few things, then I'll be back for good. Are you going to raise a moral objection?"

"What you choose to do is not my affair," I muttered.

"Maybe not, but now we've started I want to talk about it. You can be my little rabbi. I haven't unburdened my soul for a long time. It would choke me to do so even to those here who call themselves my friends. I couldn't stand their Schadenfreude.*" The heat of emotion was making Krantz sweat. "Phew! it's warm in here," he said, pulling out a silk hand-kerchief and mopping his face. "D'you mind if I open the window?"*

Lumbering to his feet, he wrenched open the dou-ble glazing and let in a gust of cold air. Then he lit a long cigar and puffed reflectively, staring over the rooftops towards the electric glow thrown up at the sky from the neon-lit Kurfürstendamm. *For a*

281

while, his back to the room, he talked aimlessly about Berlin in its pre-war heyday, the doomed, feverish, pleasure-loving, cosmopolitan city of his youthful follies and excesses, its beer cellars, dance halls, spiel-casinos, the brittle vitality of its theaters and caba-rets. The orgy of nostalgia promised to continue when he closed the window again to shut out the draught and settled his big, clumsy body back in the chair.

"You may find it hard to believe," he said with a crooked smile, "but I once weighed in at 160 pounds and was famous for my dazzling smile and boyish good looks. You could almost describe me as pretty. If it survived air raids and artillery fire, somewhere in the archives is a pile of faded newspaper clippings noting the rise of Hugo Krantz from juvenile lead to celebrity writer of satirical revues. Then, of course, Hugo Krantz became a degenerate Yid splattering filth over German culture. It got so bad, in 1935 I moved to Vienna. Chancellor Dollfus put up with my jokes, even if they didn't go down too well on the Ringstrasse, *but when he choked in his own blood I hurriedly packed a suitcase and fled to Prague from the shadow of the swastika. By the time it became necessary to move to London my hair was falling out, I'd lost my smile and I was coughing my way through three packs of cigarettes a day."*

As he talked on, refilling his glass and drinking the whisky as recklessly as water, Krantz's personal-ity underwent a curious transformation. His eyes became moist and childlike and his bluster was dis-rupted by pain. The mask that had seemed to belong to a brutal, unregenerate oppressor dissolved into the face of the victim.

"You remind me of my London psychiatrist, the way you sit there listening and saying nothing," he observed peevishly. "Joseph Emanuel Feldenkreis. He practices in Canfield Gardens. Very eclectic, combines the methods of Adler, Freud and Jung and prefers to be known as an alienist. Tufts of grey hair grow from his ears and nostrils and he sits there in his consulting room, tugging at his wing collar and staring out at the scabby patch of grass that passes for a garden. To pay his fees, I sacrificed my 22-carat gold cigarette case from Sy & Wagner in Unter den Linden given to me by a very dear friend on my thirtieth birthday. I used to lie on the couch tracing the pattern of damp on the ceiling and talk about my writer's block. After six months, Feldenkreis asked: 'If you hate women so much, why don't you find yourself a different job?'

"I was the press officer for a Zionist women's organization—seven pounds sterling a week and free meals of boiled salmon at fund-raising banquets. More than half my wages went on cigarettes and rent for my furnished room. To keep warm in cold weather, I would sit a whole evening over a cup of coffee in Swiss Cottage restaurants. The women were awesome. Our President, who had been Colonel-in-Chief of a regiment of female soldiers, was the wife of an Anglo-Jewish earl, and the honorary officers were ladies in mink and pearls from Mayfair and the wealthy ghettoes of London suburbia. One day the honorary secretary of the Functions Committee summoned me to her house on Wimbledon Common to discuss publicity for the Annual Ball at Grosvenor House. 'Dear Mister Krantz, why have you never married?' she tenderly enquired, bending over me in her low-cut dress. A little too skittish for fifty, I thought. If such was to be my fate, it should be possible to find a more suitable bidder. To be fair to Feldenkreis, he had never suggested anything as drastic as marriage. Perhaps he thought no woman would have me, but I'd just brought out a rather malicious little book on Central European literary politics which the Manchester Guardian was kind enough to find amusing and Hampstead intellectuals were inviting me to dinner parties. They'd all discovered Kafka and Robert Musil. Koestler, of course, had published Darkness at Noon. A few specks of this glitter drifted on to my shoulders. In any case, I had to make the most of my modest possibilities. Taking orders from bossy philanthropic widows and sitting over the gas fire in my shabby bed-sitter at the age of forty-five was proving too dispiriting. I had reached the point of playing Russian roulette with a bottle of sleeping pills, so although I'm a bachelor at heart I compromised and took a wife.''

Krantz stubbed out his half-smoked cigar, overcome by despondency. It required the stimulus of another glass of whisky before he felt able to continue. "Servitude to one woman can be a worse hell than domination by a committee," he reflected. "Marion is rich, ambitious and emotionally demanding but not the best judge of character. She mistook my des-

284

tructive sense of humor for wit instead of something that grew out of the compost of despair. When I was gloomy and locked myself in the study, she concluded that I was concocting some tragic masterpiece. Instead I took steadily to the bottle. I was disappointing on all counts: not a pretty sight in the bedroom, either. Sex with Marion required a faculty for erotic fantasy and soon my imagination couldn't rise to it. We had a season in hell. One night she walked into the bathroom and there was blood all over the place. Old Feldenkreis, who had a talent for the obvious, wouldn't have been surprised. 'Clinical depression,' he used to say, 'is a symptom of ego deathwish,' Marion snatched the razor from me and threw it into the bath. 'I could have you committed for that!' she screamed.

"The truth is I'm too much of a coward to kill myself. I had no recollection of slashing my wrist. It scared the shit out of me. There are two things that bring me back to Berlin and that was one of them."

Unable to stifle my curiosity, I asked: "What is the other thing?"

Hugo Krantz gave me a melancholy smile. "If you haven't already guessed, I congratulate you on your innocence."

Every weekday after breakfasting on coffee and rolls brought on a tray by Herr Eberth's taciturn daughter, I left the pension for my desk in the Grunewald villa, a walk of twenty minutes. Lights from shop windows shone out on the early morning wintry dusk along the Kurfürstendamm. And there was always the smell, the charred odor that hung over the burned and devastated acres of Berlin, a clinging memory of fire—storm and carnage. People stared out of crowded buses, jostled on the busy pavements, a city hurrying to work. It filled me with vague panic. My eyes darted from face to face, driven by a compulsion to scrutinize everybody. Their ordinariness baffled me: they merged indistinguishably into anonymity. Outwardly they could pass for a crowd in Prague, London or any western city. Where was the mark of the Beast? Sometimes I singled out an approaching figure and imagined it in uniform— long, black leather coat, peaked hat with Death's Head insignia, polished jackboots, swastika armlet.

I was looking for someone to hate.

The search continued when I arrived in the small backroom office shared with two other civilian interpreters. They came and went on different assignments, returning to write up their reports. All day long, except for an interval for lunch, I read through Fragebogen, *the 131-paragraph questionnaires the Allied Military Government had served on all Germans suspected of having been criminally involved in the Nazi regime. Originally there had been many thousands of* Fragebogen. *My responsibility was to check through the files marked "Cases for Re-Examination," noting points of contradiction, misstatements and evasions that may have slipped past the original examiners. The task was confusing. In most cases, all I could conclude was that some suspects were good at filling in forms, others hopeless. Those who had most skill strove to be interesting and* give an impression of candor. Answering Questions 19 to 23 which concerned religion, they were ready to confess everything, baring their souls as if at the Last Judgment, but when it came to Question 29—"Give a chronological history of your employment and military service"—and Questions 41 to 96—"Indicate on the following chart whether or not you were a member of, and what offices you held in the organizations listed below"—reticence or evasion prevailed. Membership of the National Socialist Party, the SS and SA were briefly acknowledged when denial was impossible, but the paragraphs containing such other loaded implications as membership of the Institute for the Jewish Question or the State Academy of Racial and Health Service were invariably marked "Nein." "Nicht schuldig," shrugged the Fragebogen. "Yes, perhaps we put on the wrong uniform and joined the march of healthy young men in brown-shirted columns, but we are guilty of nothing. When certain unfortunate things were happening we were at the front-line engaged in honorable warfare, defending our country."

It amazed me later when I recalled that weeks had gone by methodically working through the alphabet before it occurred to me to take down the "K" file. All because of a stranger who attracted my attention in the cafe where I took lunch. The man sat in a corner, half-concealed by the steaming espresso machine, the tabloid newspaper BT spread before his face. It was an ideal place for someone who shunned company yet wished to keep the cafe under observation.

I also sat apart, at a table near the coat-stand,

immured in my own solitude. An uneasy sensation of being watched stole over me. I felt the gravitational pull of danger. The stranger was staring at me over the top of his paper—a grey, mournful, suspicious gaze. Our eyes interlocked and my heart gave a lurch of recognition.

The arrival of a boisterous party of American GI's and their girl-friends blocked my line of sight. Throwing off their great-coats, rushing to feed coins into the juke-box and jostling one another playfully over seats at the bar, the soldiers created a turbulence that generated a sullen resentment among the German civilians. It took a while for the invasion to settle. When I looked again, the stranger's place was empty.

I hurried out, leaving my meal unfinished. It was a raw, damp afternoon, as cold as misery. A despondent flow of people swirled and eddied along the congested sidewalk. I looked frantically up and down the street. The search was hopeless: I knew the face of my enemy, but could not single out his retreating form in the fast-changing crowd. A chance in a thousand, a million, had been lost. Yet wildly, insanely, I set out at random, almost at a run, turning to peer into the faces of men as I passed them by.

The stranger had not gone far. He walked slowly, aimlessly, a man with nowhere to go. The height was the same, the eyes. There were vestiges of a military bearing under the shabbiness of defeat. The collar of his worn overcoat was turned up, concealing his mouth. He looked at me with a smouldering bitterness.

288

"Guten Tag," *he said indistinctly.*

The man had no lips. His teeth were made of metal. The flesh of his cheeks was pink and waxen like a celluloid doll's.

"Wurden Sie mit mir eine Tasse Kaffee trinken? *Would you care to join me for coffee?" The mutilated mouth appeared to be smiling. There was a desperate appeal in the haunted eyes, loneliness imploring friendship, perhaps, horribly, sex.*

I fought down an impulse to flee. "Wie is Ihr Name?" *I asked.*

"Otto," *answered the stranger. He had detected my foreign accent and spoke in English.* "You may call me Otto."

"Were you—ever—in Dachau?"

The man flinched. "You insult me," *he said gratingly.* "In ze war I was a submariner. Look at my face—burns from petroleum!"

I turned away. "I'm sorry, I mistook you for somebody else."

Back at work, I went straight to the shelves where the Fragebogen *box-files were kept and took down one marked* "Ka-Kl." *Three of those who had filled in questionnaires shared the hated name. Although no Ulrich Walther was among them, and none held the rank of SS Oberleutnant, I read through each case carefully. Not a single detail fitted, but now the hunt was on. Returning the file to its shelf, I went to the Archive Department.*

"Would you please let me have the transcripts of the two Dachau trials," *I told the woman in charge.*

My sudden lack of diffidence surprised her. "Why do you need them?"

289

"Cross-checking. You'll have them back before the day's over."

The self-assurance was precarious. Back again at my desk, staring at the stiffly bound volumes, a fit of shivering overcame me. Already, before I opened the pages, the dormant shadows rose up and gathered in my mind. I covered my face with my hands.

"What is it, Slonimsky, aren't you well?" asked Gruner, the senior of the two interpreters who shared the office, a stocky middle-aged Israeli who had left Germany in his teens to join a kibbutz. He came across and picked up one of the two volumes. "This stuff's not for you," he remarked shrewdly. "The more you brood over it, the worse you'll feel. Tell me what you're looking for and I'll check it out."

"I prefer to do it myself," I said.

Gruner chewed contemplatively at the stem of an unlit pipe. A strongly-built, fair-complexioned man who conveyed an impression of quiet resolve, it was rumored in the department that he had connections with a branch of Israeli intelligence engaged in tracking down Nazi criminals who were in hiding.

He said: "I understand your commitment, but remember you're not on your own. If there's anything you can't find, perhaps I can be of help."

I waited until he withdrew. On this appalling journey I needed to travel only in the company of my dead. Silence crowded in on me, Berlin and the present retreating as I entered the tunnel that descended into the darkness of anti-life. Once again the transport shook and rattled through the suffocating night carrying its cargo of 1,564 prisoners, but

290

added to the nightmare of fear was now the terror of certitude. My father, mother and sister Zofia were separated from me, struggling for breath in the crush of bodies. Now I knew they were being dragged away from me forever. The trial transcript supplied one new detail of their fate. They had not been sent "to the East," as I had been told by a prisoner priest. On the very day of their arrival, when SS officer Kampfmann selected them for death, a trainload of "invalids" was sent to Linz in Austria to be gassed. They died anonymously. From 1942 onwards the SS no longer thought it necessary to record the names of Jewish victims. Knowing that it was their final destination, Linz joined the cities of damnation in my mind.

The American tribunal sat in judgment from November 15 to December 14, 1945. There were forty accused and one hundred and twenty witnesses. Seventy former prisoners appeared for the prosecution, thirty-six accused were sentenced to death by hanging, many later reprieved, and four to imprisonment. SS Oberleutnant Kampfmann did not stand trial, his name did not appear in the testimonies. For among the many witnesses, one was missing—Franz Slonimsky. Kampfmann, I told myself, is my war criminal and I should have been there to accuse him. And yet another anger: how little the recital of atrocities conveyed the anguish of reality!

Four men could be hanged at the same time on the hooks outside the ovens and business con-

tinued whether the ovens operated or not . . .
Often the rope broke: if that happened Bongartz
would double it and the man was hanged again.
Bongartz and Mahl were a perfect killing team.

Of the murder of ninety-two Russian officers:
"The Gestapo Russian interpreter ordered the
first fifteen prisoners to undress completely. He
then told them to walk some thirty meters away
from the place where they left their shoes and
clothes on the ground. There they had to kneel
down in a line by a small heap of earth with
their backs towards us. The SS who executed
them went up to them and shot them in the back
of the neck, each one executing several men.
When the first fifteen had been killed, prisoners
working at the crematorium removed their
bodies and took them inside the crematorium.
The next fifteen who had undressed at the same
time as the first fifteen were then executed in the
same way . . . Between eleven o'clock and eleven-
thirty the whole execution was over."

Statement by Dr. Muthig, Chief Camp Doctor at Dachau (given at the Doctors' Trial in
1947): "In the autumn of 1941, on the occasions of a duty inspection of my Revier by Dr.
Lolling, he told me that a commission of four
doctors led by Professor Heyde would shortly be
visiting Dachau camp. The commission's duty
was to select prisoners unfit for work to be subjected to euthanasia and transferred to Mauthausen concentration camp to be gassed. Shortly after my conversation with Dr. Lolling the

292

commission duly arrived. It consisted of four psychiatrists and was led by Professor Heyde, who was also present. I and the other camp doctors had nothing to do with the commission and its work. But I saw that the doctors had sat down between two huts and that several hundreds of prisoners were being paraded before them ... I know that this commission spent only a few days in Dachau and that it was impossible to give so many prisoners a medical examination in so short a time ... A few weeks after the commission had left Dachau in December 1941 the first trainload of several hundred prisoners selected by the commission left for Mauthausen to be gassed. Another trainload of prisoners chosen by the commission and also containing several hundred prisoners left in January 1942 for Mauthausen ... The operation for selecting those unfit for work and for euthanasia was known in Dachau as "Aktion Heyde."

Mass murder, sanitized, without agony, without stench, without the shrieks of mortal terror and the quaking of soil as those buried in mass graves while still alive writhed and suffocated in quick-lime.

In another dimension of time, telephones rang, voices spoke, typewriters clicked busily, people came and went, daylight turned into night. I remained oblivious. My journey into the past had brought me to the seven-month Dachau Doctors' Trial of December 9, 1946 to July 19, 1947. German medical science found itself in the unique position of being *able to dispense with rats, mice, guinea pigs, dogs and monkeys in favor of human experimental material. The seventy-four-year-old Professor Klaus Schilling, an international expert on tropical diseases who had received grants from the Rockefeller Foundation and the Kahn Foundation in Paris, arranged for large batches of prisoners to be bitten by malarial mosquitoes—for the good of mankind, he had told the judges at the earlier Dachau trial, but was nevertheless executed. Other SS doctors tried experimental treatments on tuberculous patients who were afterwards gassed. Then there were high altitude and freezing experiments designed to discover if Luftwaffe airmen exposed to subnormally low pressure, lack of oxygen or deathly extremes of cold could be resuscitated. Luftwaffe SS Major Dr. Rascher was authorized by Reichsführer SS Himmler and Air Marshal Milch to make experimental use of human subjects because monkeys were unsuitable. One report on a prisoner who died stated: "This was a prolonged oxygen-less experiment at an altitude of seven and a half miles on a thirty-seven-year-old Jew whose general condition was good. Respiration continued for thirty minutes. After four minutes the subject began to perspire and wag his head. After five minutes, cramp set in; between six and seven minutes, respiration quickened, the subject lost consciousness; between eleven and thirty minutes, respiration slowed to three per minute and then stopped completely. In the meantime a strong cyanosis set in and the subject began to foam at the mouth."*

Medical students were also able to benefit from the ample supply of guinea pigs by practicing surgery on healthy prisoners.

I continued reading to the bitter end. It was self-punishing. It set me throbbing with the phantom pain of my amputated life. It led me nowhere, least of all to understanding. A devout Jew in the camp once described Dachau as a terrible mystery. "We are experiencing the absence of God." I did not understand about God, either. My own experiences and the endemic cruelties of the world bore witness to an evil destructive force whose agents were human. Men, not God, must be judged and condemned.

Wearily pushing the trial volumes aside, I said to Gruner: "Have you read these?"

"Yes." The Israeli replaced the cover on his typewriter and took down his shabby anorak from the coat hook. "I've also put in homework on Nuremberg and a few other trials," he added dryly.

"Do you think enough is being done?"

"It depends by whom. Russians, Poles, Czechs and other East Europeans have their hearts in it. The Germans did it to them, in their own towns and villages. The Western Allies, especially the British, are in a hurry to forget. There are more Nazi criminals walking free in the British Zone of Occupation than anywhere else. Gestapo officers are back in police uniform, Hitler's judges preside over courts and industrialists who worked slave laborers to death are busily reconstructing German prosperity with Marshall Plan aid. Do you know what I was told by a senior British official?" Gruner mimicked a supercilious upper-class English accent. "'My dear chap, don't you think that Old Testament eye for an eye and tooth for a tooth stuff is rather primitive? We have to be generous enough to forgive. After all, most Germans are basically decent fellows.' I pointed out that it must have taken quite a lot of bad fellows to organize the cold-blooded murder of more than twelve million innocent men, women and children and, given the will, they were not difficult to identify. Yes, well, that was a complex question, but he was already overdue at a luncheon appointment."

Thinking of the quiet civilities of London, of England's bombed cities and of the courage of Britain when she stood alone in conquered Europe, thinking also of its hospitality to hundreds of thousands of refugees, I told him I liked the English. I was sure the official was not representative."

"The English," Gruner said diplomatically, "are wonderful people in their own country. Tell me, what exactly were you looking for in these trial records?"

"The name of an SS officer."

"Did you find it?"

"No."

Gruner fastened the pegs of his anorak and pulled up the hood. Framed by the cowl, his face had the austere and dedicated look of a votary of some secret order. "That's too bad," he remarked.

"Write it down. I'll check in one or two other places."

The authoritative tone commanded obedience and I unwillingly complied. It was like surrendering a piece of myself. My hatred, like love, craves an exclusive gratification.

"Let's hope we'll have some luck," the Israeli said, folding the piece of paper and slipping it into his pocket. "It's not difficult for a determined man to arrange his disappearance, but he can't hide forever."

11

S HOMRON RUBBED his smarting eyes and reluctantly opened another notebook. He wanted to stop; he'd had enough. But reading Frank Sinclair's diary was no longer a voluntary act. The diary was reading him.

I woke up sweating in the middle of one night a week or so later, Sinclair wrote. *Standing at the foot of the bed was my little sister, Zofia. She looked exactly as though she'd stepped out of a photograph taken when she was six years old, gravely posed against a painted garden background in a white, frilled dress, her long, brown hair tied with a silk bow. Then the hallucination vanished. By morning I had a raging temperature.*

The fever lasted several days. There'd been a turn

in the weather bringing drenching rain and an early spring mildness, and as my cotton mac was designed only to give protection from light showers I'd got repeatedly soaked and contracted a bad chill. My illness aroused sympathy. Herr Eberth insisted on keeping the stove in my room well stoked up regardless of expense and Hugo Krantz, embarrassingly solicitous, doctored me with brandy and lemon, brought gifts of fruit and magazines, and supplied his own sardonic brand of wit to relieve what he regarded as the tedium of the sickroom.

But the person who most overwhelmed me with attentions was Herr Eberth's daughter. This gaunt woman, usually so reticent and withdrawn, became a constant presence at my bedside. In lucid moments between bouts of delirium I would find her there ready to spoon soup into my mouth or offer a glass of warm milk. She changed the bed-linen, washed and ironed my sweat-soaked pyjamas, emptied the chamberpot when I was too weak to journey to the lavatory and brought in soap and bowls of hot water for washing, hovering around with a kind of frustrated tenderness as if she ached to bathe me herself.

"Can I do anything else? Would you like me to boil you an egg or bring some bread and milk? Is it too stuffy in here, shall I open the window a little?"

The exorbitance of her need to lavish care and affection, the way she smoothed my pillow, the yearning touch of her hand quickly withdrawn, irritated and embarrassed me. She must have been no more than thirty five but premature widowhood, suffering and loneliness made her look much older, and I reckoned that nursing me was an outlet for her stifled maternal instinct.

Then it came out in a rush, an agonized confession. Hugo Krantz had told them I was a Dachau survivor whose entire family had died in the gas chamber. Her voice shook: she clasped and unclasped her big raw-boned hands. The most terrible thing was that she herself had been a member of the League of German Maidens, the girls' section of the Hitler Youth. Summer camps and keep fit classes, Winter-hilfe collections and stirring youth parades: at fifteen how could she have even dreamed of the monstrous wickedness it would come to in the end? Once late in the war a wounded soldier on leave from the Russian front showed a number of his friends some snapshots of hundreds of corpses lying in a ditch. He said they were Jews taken from a ghetto in Lithuania and murdered by the Gestapo. "We refused to believe that Germans could commit such an atrocity. The Bolsheviks must have done it. We were angry that he showed us such communist propaganda.

"But God punished us," she went on in a low voice, describing the retribution visited on Berlin's civilian population when by land and air the full fury of war closed in and the city became a vast slaughterhouse. Continual bombardment, cellars crowded with the wounded and dying, dysentery, typhus, starvation. On one occasion a dead horse was found in the street. Men and women rushed out of cellars under shellfire to hack pieces of flesh from the animal's carcass. And the destruction! She urged me to imagine New York with the whole of Manhattan a *smoking ruin, London, Paris, Rome devastated by earthquake, unburied corpses in the rubble of Piccadilly and Regent Street, burnt-out tanks rusting among the splintered trees of Central Park. Hitler was dead in the* Fuehrer-Bunker, *the war was over and the world had come to an end.*

"It was a dreadful time to be alive," she said, shuddering. For swarming into Berlin in tanks and lorries, by motorcycle and on foot came the avenging barbarians. Schnapps, watches and women were the spoils of victory and anyone who resisted risked being shot out of hand. I stopped listening. Almost everybody in Berlin at the time had stories of women subjected to savage and repeated rape by bands of Russian soldiers, so-called "Mongolians." Herr Eberth's daughter was reaching out for reconciliation. If I have sinned, I have been punished, she was saying. I felt neither pity nor indifference. Our lives revolved in different circles of hell.

"You are wanted on the telephone," Herr Eberth told me early one evening, his wrinkled monkey face showing surprise. Calls came for other guests, never for me. Mistrusting the unexpected, I put down my book and went into the hall. The old German left the door of his small overcrowded parlor slightly ajar preparing to eavesdrop behind an outspread copy of the Berlinger Morgenpost.

"Gruner here," the caller said. "I hear you've been ill. There's something I have to tell you. I'm at the Old Vienna in the Ku'damm. *Can you come?"*

Herr Eberth's armchair creaked and the shuffle of his slippered feet approached. The false teeth hung loose on his shrunken gums reminding me of my

304

Yiddish-speaking grandfather and the way he couldn't get along with the finest set of dentures in all of Prague. "You want to catch pneumonia, going out in this weather?" he scolded. "If I can't stop you, at least put on a scarf."

Entering the street after a week of confinement in the claustrophobic atmosphere of a sickroom made me dizzy. Night life in Berlin, the spurious gaiety that masked the grim pursuit of pleasure, held the menace of the unpredictable. The Kurfürstendamm glittered and throbbed amid desolation like a traveling fairground erected in the margins of chaos for a brief season of revelry, soon to be dismantled. The Old Vienna was already crowded and noisy, jazz pumping out from the huge American juke-box surrounded by a group of girls and Allied soldiers. Gruner waved from a table near the window.

"You've got news about Kampfmann," I said.

He nodded and beckoned a waitress. "Two cognacs, Fraulein."

"What is it? Have you found him?"

"Take it easy," he said, laying a hand on my arm. "Even good news can come as a shock . . . You can give up your search, the man is dead."

An abrupt sense of dislocation set my mind spinning on emptiness, blurred reality drowned out the noise, the music, the low rumble of conversation at adjoining tables. "Drink up," said Gruner in an authoritative voice. Hypnotically, I sipped the fierce liquid and slowly came back to life.

"Are you sure?" I muttered. "Are you certain there's no mistake?"

He shrugged. "The evidence is fairly conclusive.

305

Just before Dachau was liberated a skirmish took place between some SS camp personnel and the Americans. Kampfmann's papers were found on one of the bodies." Gruner took out his pipe, thoughtfully stuffing it with tobacco from a worn leather pouch. He lit a match and stared at the flame. *"You're not very pleased, are you?"*

"I don't know."

"He died too easily. It's almost as if he escaped you. You wanted to kill him yourself, slowly, in agony. You wanted to see him die before your eyes."

"Perhaps," I said.

Gruner threw the spent match away and said curtly: *"Forget it. Put it behind you. Waste no more time and start to live."*

All that night I struggled in asphyxiating dreams —my father hurtling into the dark, my mother naked under the hissing gas-jets, Zofia melting like wax in the flames of the crematorium, dead in her white frilled dress.

Next morning my mouth was full of blood.

Spring advanced. Flowering weeds sprang up among the rubble, daffodils blossomed in the Grunewald and people ventured out to picnic on the grassy banks of the Spree. A mood of optimism was setting in. No longer an enemy capital, Berlin had become the front-line city of the Free World, rapidly being transformed into a glittering advertisement that flaunted the superiority of Western democracy.

All this increased my estrangement. Sunk in the lethargy of failure, I slept late, stumbled unwillingly out of bed and stared with dislike at the white, drawn face reflected in the bathroom mirror. "Why are you still here? What do you think you are going to achieve?" said the loud sarcastic voice of Dr. Gutermann, a question I'd repeatedly asked myself and to which I had no answer. It seemed to matter little what I did or where I went.

Early in May I was sent to Frankfurt on special assignment. Three ex-prison guards of a concentration camp in Magdeburg were appealing against ten-year jail sentences imposed by an Allied military court. My task was to produce documentary evidence of their war crimes at the appeal hearing.

I'd long got over my disbelief at the transformation wrought by civilian dress in the appearance of SS men and Gestapo officials. Stripped of the dreaded black uniforms, wearing shabby ill-fitting suits and expressions of puzzled innocence, most of them could have been chosen at random from any group of ordinary citizens. The three men in court had all been convicted of brutal killings. Weber, the oldest, resembled a bluff countryman—a lined, weather-beaten man with wrinkles of humor around the eyes. Gerd Hoffman was fresh-faced, boyish and a ready smiler. The third, Adolf Becker, lugubrious and sallow, sat throughout the proceedings in slack-mouthed stupefaction as if lobotomized, yet he'd been production supervisor of the concentration camp arms factory.

Krupp, the lawyer who led the appeal, was a lean, long, languid aristocrat more English than German in manner. He did not disguise the abhorrence with *which he viewed his clients. Their atrocious deeds merited the moral indignation of all civilized men. However, he pointed out in quiet, conversational tones, justice was not an exercise in moral indignation. What it must determine is the measure of responsibility borne by the appellants, to what degree if at all they had operated through freedom of choice. Not that Krupp was basing his plea on the doctrine of* respondent superior *as outlined in Oppenheimer's* Treatise on International Law: *namely that violation of the laws of war in obedience to a government order was a valid defense against charges of war crime, or that if a war crime was actually committed, exclusive responsibility lay on the shoulders of the commander and his subordinate should be absolved of guilt. Instead he referred the Court to the* Agreement for the Prosecution and Punishment of Major War Criminals of the European Axis *signed in London on August 8, 1945 by representatives of the United States, the Soviet Union, the United Kingdom and France. Article Eight of that Agreement stated: "The fact that the defendant acted pursuant to the order of a superior or to Government Sanction shall not free him from responsibility but may be considered in mitigation of punishment if the Tribunal determines that justice so requires."*

Skillfully, lawyer Krupp developed his argument. He analyzed the structure of the Nazi state, its doctrine of absolute obedience to the Fuehrerprinzip, *the severity with which it punished the flouting of orders. With drawling contempt, glancing at them down the length of his thin patrician nose, he spoke of* his clients as depraved and cowardly bullies not worth a good man's spit. They were grovelers at the feet of brutish leaders, the lowest of the low, clinging to self-preservation at all costs and richly deserving of punishment. But the integrity of justice required that it be extended even to the ignominious. They were conditioned to unquestioning obedience. They were gutless. It was a proven fact that SS execution squads stupefied themselves with drink and drugs to carry out the work of killing. In a notorious speech to his followers, Himmler had declared: "When somebody comes to me and says, 'I cannot dig the anti-tank ditch with women and children, it is inhuman, for it would kill them,' then I have to say, 'You are the murderer of your own blood, because if the anti-tank ditch is not dug German soldiers will die, and they are the sons of German mothers. They are our own blood . . .'" Himmler's threat was explicit. When these men said they feared it would place their own lives at risk if they did not blindly carry out orders, it did not exculpate their guilt nor lessen the loathing they arouse, but at least to some extent their crimes were committed under duress. That should count towards mitigation of their sentences.

There was a curious absence of drama in the courtroom. International authorities on law were cited—Kelsen's Acts of State, Lauterpacht's War Crimes, Schwartzenburger's The Judgment of Nuremburg and his definition of crimes against humanity, etc. Spectators drifted in and out of the public benches. During recessions, lawyers on both sides mingled in the lobby, laughing, handing one

309

another cigarettes, then composing their features into suitable masks of decorum when the hearing resumed. The prisoners scratched themselves, stifled yawns. It defied the imagination to see them as monsters. In all probability, once released they would settle into grooves of respectability to work at humdrum occupations, accompany their wives on shopping expeditions, play with their children. It was as though they had passed through a virulent phase of madness and emerged unscathed.

There and then the assassin was born in my soul.

I returned to Berlin cold with rage. That evening when quiet had settled on the pension I opened an exercise book and wrote the following sentence:

"Three ordinary-looking mass murderers left a court of justice in Frankfurt on a sunny day in May to mingle in the everyday crowds and disappear into freedom."

The sounds of the city grew faint, lights were extinguished in all the windows of the street. I wrote steadily through the night using the trial as a prism reflecting the futility of justice in post-war Germany. When dawn arrived and the task was finished, I had the definite impression that something strange had happened to me. It can best be described as a kind of bifurcation of personality. Franz Slonimsky moved like a shadow into the background. Emerging into the spotlight from the wings of my mind, the stranger said: "My name is Frank Sinclair."

Hugo Krantz called on me later in the morning. "What were you up to last night?" he asked. "I went out to piss twice and your light was still burning."

He picked up the pages I'd written. "You're blowing the gaff on the new Germany," he grinned when he'd finished reading. "Good stuff! Do you mind if I show it to a pal of mine here, a correspondent for the BBC?"

A short while afterwards his friend telephoned and invited me to the studio. Seated before a microphone and speaking with practiced skill, he said: "Is denazification a failure? Are too many former members of Hitler's National Socialist Party finding their way back into public life? These are questions that cause much heart-searching among people concerned for the future of democracy in the Federal Republic of Germany. Here in Berlin to discuss this topic is Frank Sinclair, who has studied the case histories of ex-Nazis absolved of responsibility for war crimes."

A red light flickered. "Three ordinary-looking mass murderers left a court of justice in Frankfurt," I began in a trembling voice, but soon I was speaking confidently, with an edge of harshness, and I recognized that the voice of Frank Sinclair had taken over.

12

SO THAT'S HOW it was.

Shomron closed the notebook and pushed himself away from the desk. Like someone waking from a heavy sleep and still dazed, he went into the kitchenette, absently boiled some water, poured it into a chipped cup and infused a tea-bag. A slice of processed cheese between two hunks of bread made a meal of it. Supper, he noted, staring through the grimy window at the garden's tangle of darkness. Time flew.

Franz Slonimsky's abrupt metamorphosis into Frank Sinclair had caught him by surprise. He shook his head in silent amazement. The intrusion of that grey presence reminded him that he'd been reading the history of an incurable illness. So intensely had he followed the experiences described that they'd become part of his own life, he'd come to think of Slonimsky almost as a younger version of himself. For a while he'd actually allowed himself to hope things would turn out right in the end, forgetting that the unhappy, mistrustful youngster in Berlin was fated to grow into a dry twig of a man without ever knowing ripeness.

Depressed, he returned to the living room and made an effort to be professional, to think of it as just another case. What were the facts?

If Walther Ulrich Kampfmann really met his death in Dachau in the spring of 1945 he couldn't be the elderly Avram Benamir killed by Sinclair in Blumenthal Street, Tel Aviv. There was, after all, enough evidence to make it seem improbable—concentration camp number, circumcision, marriage in a DP camp to a young Jewish widow and illegal emigration to Palestine, thirty-five years devoted service to the Jewish state, a fine Israeli family. Yet a man does not travel more than two thousand miles to one particular house in a particular street and shoot dead a preselected victim unless he is convinced of the victim's identity. He could have made a terrible mistake, chosen the wrong man, but there must have been a compelling reason why he pursued and hunted down precisely that one unlikely individual among millions.

There was only one possible conclusion. Sinclair had discovered—at least to his own satisfaction—that the body of the SS officer found in Dachau was not Kampfmann's.

How and when?

He still knew very little about Sinclair. Living in the man's apartment, sleeping in his bed, prying among his papers, he constantly had the feeling of an imminent presence. Sinclair's personality clung to the place like a persistent smell. For twenty years, in self-imposed solitude, he'd occupied these rooms surrounded by his library of the numerous dead, turning brittle and yellow at the edges. This reclusive existence was interrupted by mysterious journeys abroad. He hoarded press-cuttings and memorabilia of the Holocaust with a collector's obsession, traced the movements and careers of former Nazis, but he was no Simon Wiesenthal intent on bringing war criminals to justice. His yearning for vengeance was concentrated on a single enemy. There must have been a period after Berlin when he was more unsettled, moving from one drab furnished apartment to another. If only someone had been able then to break through the crust of his loneliness. Friedl Zussman refused him his old room, the one place he'd known as home. Was it conceivable that if she had not rejected him then he might have taken that one crucial step into the future and moved away from his ghosts?

Given enough time, Shomron thought, it would of course be possible to trace Sinclair's movements through the years—electoral rolls, income tax returns, bureaucratic registrations of all kinds. Blank pages usually turn out not to be blank at all. But time was a commodity he did not have. Absence is perilous. Fate has a way of dealing crippling blows when one's back is turned. For almost two weeks he'd left his home, his family, job and friends to conduct this investigation in defiance of orders. He had stumbled into a nightmare. It wrought changes in him he had not reckoned with, undermined his sense of security in some unexpected way. Intimations of jealousy and loss had begun to haunt him, dreams like thickets of barbed wire, dreams of trains traveling endlessly into mist.

The sensible thing would be to turn his back on it and go home, but the case had come to mean more to him than any he'd been engaged in in his entire career. He could not leave it unfinished. The hook was in his soul.

A rumpled, silver-haired gentleman in a baggy, brown tweed suit appeared in the lobby of Bush House and glanced enquiringly around at the persons waiting there. Tentatively approaching Shomron, he asked: "Are you the visitor from the Israeli Radio? Ah, good!" He shook hands vigorously. "Bill Ackerman, German Service. Shall we go to the canteen? Atrocious coffee, but a good place to talk."

The canteen was as filthy as a British Rail buffet—greasy smell of factory produced food and plastic trays. Used cups and saucers, filled ash-trays, sticky plates waited to be cleared away by a turbanned Sikh who swept the empties into a trolley and wiped tables with a wet cloth. Yet the most civilized broadcasting voice in the world, Shomron reflected, cool, literate and objective. He'd read somewhere that Orwell amused himself by using Bush House as a model for the Ministry of Truth in *1984*, and he thought how strange it was that the book had sent shivers through the spine of a generation which grew up alongside Auschwitz, Hiroshima and the Stalin prison colonies.

Mr. Ackerman brought the coffees. Breaking open the paper-wrapped sugar and stirring it into his cup, he said: "I'm not quite sure from our telephone conversation exactly what you have in mind."

Shomron was not surprised. Impersonating an official of the Israeli Radio had been a despairing improvization. In normal circumstances, if Sinclair's arrest could be made public, he might have found an easier way to ask for information. As it was, he'd have to work around to it.

"There are many listeners to your broadcasts in my country," he said. "German is their mother tongue and some of them are still not comfortable with Hebrew."

"Yes, we get letters. The numbers are dwindling though, aren't they? After nearly half a century, they're dying off." Mr. Ackerman smiled wistfully. "The same generation as my parents, people in their seventies and eighties. We came over from Vienna when I was ten years old."

"That's precisely what I find so interesting, the historical dimension. I'd like to do a feature programme on the BBC German Service, a retrospective. You must have some amazing recordings of broadcasts made during the Hitler period, the war, the war crimes trials and the Berlin airlift."

Mr. Ackerman politely acknowledged that they did have. He turned briefly to wave at an acquaintance.

"It would also be very interesting to talk about some of the people who made your programmes," Shomron struggled on. "One example who comes to mind is Frank Sinclair. He's made quite an impression in Israel."

"Really?" The other elevated his bushy, silver eyebrows. "Do listeners there still remember him?"

"Oh! Well, yes. Most of them are, as you say, rather old. Isn't he with you any more?"

"Not on the staff. Three or four years ago he decided to become an outside contributor. His main work now consists of translations for the Oxford University Press and other publishers."

"Why did he leave?"

"Well," Mr. Ackerman said judiciously, "I always thought he was more suited to the academic life. His speciality is the Holocaust and, frankly, today well . . . it's a different Germany altogether, isn't it?"

The tone was tolerant, wryly amused, just a

trifle patronizing. His careful enunciation, too precise to be truly native, became even more pronounced. Apart from the faintest hint of Viennese *gemütlichkeit,* Bill Ackerman in his rumpled tweeds was almost as English as the Cotswolds.

"Of course, he writes extremely well on his subject. We expected that he'd one day produce an important book. I daresay it's not too late."

"Is he a friend of yours?"

"As a colleague, yes. But he's—how shall I put it? Introverted, self-absorbed." Mr. Ackerman smiled benignly yet not without a certain cunning. "You know, you're the second person in a week or so to express an interest in Frank."

"Am I?".

"Yes, there was a certain lady, Dutch, she said. Very charming and most persistent."

The description was vague, but Shomron immediately guessed whom it fitted.

"She gave the name van Goudt. Perhaps you know her."

"I'm afraid not."

Mr. Ackerman smiled again. He glanced at his wristwatch. "I shall have to let you know about your feature programme. In principle, I can't see why not. Perhaps you'll leave me your card."

"Unfortunately, I don't have one with me. I'll call you tomorrow, shall I?"

"That will be fine," Mr. Ackerman said cordially. "Now, if you'll excuse me, I'm expected in the studio. I'm recording a book programme."

They shook hands and parted. There was no doubt in Shomron's mind what the affable Mr.

Ackerman would do next. Mr. Ackerman would go straight to the telephone.

"A friend's called to see you," Betty Purves said when he arrived at the house. "He said you were expecting him, so I let him into the flat. He's been waiting more than an hour."

A friend it couldn't be: no one had the address. But he'd given Ackerman his real name, and Ackerman of course would know where Sinclair lived.

"Are you sure he didn't ask for Frank?"

"Nobody ever asks for Frank," Mrs. Purves said. "A nice-looking boy," she added, a lubricous gleam in her eye. "I'm just having some tea. Why don't you both join me, the pot's still fresh."

"Not this time, Betty," he said. "He won't be staying."

The noise of pop music was coming from the apartment. To cover the shifting of furniture? A skilled policeman could turn the place inside out in an hour. Shomron meditated a hurried retreat, but there was a small difficulty: his passport, return air-ticket, clothes and suitcase were in the back bedroom. Steeling himself, he quietly opened the door.

A fair-haired, powerfully built man of about thirty who could pass for a blonde Russian or Pole got up slowly from a chair, hands thrust into his jacket pockets in an attitude that spelled confrontation.

"*Shalom, ma shlomkha,*" he said in Hebrew.

Shomron switched off the radio. "Who are you?" he demanded.

"Goren. Embassy chief of security." The stranger walked to the window and drew the curtains shut. He re-started the radio. "What are you up to, Captain Shomron?"

"I don't know what you mean. Do we need that racket?"

"We don't want this conversation overheard, do we? If you prefer, we'll get something classical." He twiddled the knobs, raking the airwaves of Europe until Vienna responded with a Bruckner symphony.

"How did you find me?" asked Shomron. "I didn't realize the Embassy knew where I was staying."

"That's another thing," Goren said severely. "You should have let us know your address. It would have saved a lot of trouble. Unless of course you're here as a private citizen. In which case certain things need explaining."

"In due course they will be." Shomron broke off the discussion and went into the kitchenette. "How about some refreshment? I can offer you instant coffee or a tea-bag."

Goren grimaced with distaste. "Nothing, thanks. How could you be so bloody stupid?" he said in sharp reprimand. "Snooping around the BBC Overseas Service, acting suspiciously. They've got people there on the wanted list of half the world's most ruthless police states. Don't you remember the case of the poisoned umbrella?"

"I didn't see the movie," Shomron laconically replied.

Goren was not amused. "You put the Embassy

in the position of having to lie to save an embarrassing situation. I've been asked to cable a full report."

"I'm sorry, I can't help you."

"Why not? You seem to be breaking all the rules."

"Rules," said Shomron, emerging from the kitchenette carrying a cup of tea-flavored hot water, "are broken by policemen every day. But there's one rule I was trained never to break. The rule limiting access to classified information on the basis of 'need to know.'"

"Are you telling me you're on a secret investigation?"

"You must draw your own conclusions."

A look of uncertainty entered Goren's face. No Israeli involved in security would be so foolish as to underestimate the complex and mysterious ramifications of his country's secret intelligence operations, nor fail to be awed by the glamour and heroism of its agents. To enquire too closely was as dangerous as stepping into a minefield.

"I don't understand," he said frowning. "I spoke to your own chief in Tel Aviv. He insists that you're not here on duty, just on a short vacation."

"He would, wouldn't he?"

"But he ordered your immediate return. We've booked you a seat on the next El Al plane."

"You'd better check that. I think you'll find that the order's been countermanded."

"I must ask you to return with me to the Embassy while I make enquiries."

"No, that's impossible. I have something very important to do."

Goren looked undecided. "You won't leave this flat until you hear from me?" he asked suspiciously.

Shomron promised.

As soon as he was alone he switched off the radio and dialed Gillon Romm's private number in Tel Aviv, by-passing the station switchboard. The deep, rumbling voice, so clear it could have come from the next room, brought a stab of homesickness. Late afternoon sunshine, the smell of petrol mixed with orange blossom, warm Mediterranean breezes blowing a fine drift of sand along the city pavements. Deborah, fresh and tingling from her afternoon swim, her slim brown arms bare, would be getting supper for the kids while they goggled at the children's TV programme *Ritch-Ratch*.

"Amos, what the hell's going on?" growled Gillon.

"I need a little more time, Gillon. Please!"

"Nothing doing. I want you back tomorrow. Bad enough almost causing an international incident without starting a civil war here. You were told not to meddle. Fuck up your own career if you want, but it's my skin too. Get on that plane and don't argue." Click.

Shomron replaced the receiver. He felt as though he'd suffered an intimate betrayal. The thought of all he was putting at risk gave him a moment of vertigo. Grimly, he began packing. Sinclair's notebooks lay on the desk. One of them he'd only glanced through; it appeared to contain random jottings, little of interest. After brief hesitation, he put them into the case.

Slanting sunlight shone on the disordered garden. The great cadenza from Liszt's *Concerto for Piano and Orchestra in E flat major* soared out from Betty Purves' open window above. He thought of her drinking her tea alone. She had good taste in music, and not only in that. He debated whether or not to leave her a note, and decided not; a pity. Wherever one experiences an intensity of feeling a part of oneself is left behind.

One last look at the shabby, cluttered reclusive room and Shomron climbed stealthily out of the window with his suitcase. He'd arrived like a thief and like a thief he departed.

Later the telephone began ringing. It went on a long time, then stopped. After an interval it began again, ringing and ringing in the deserted apartment.

Rivka Kloster, bare shoulders wrapped in a lacy black stole, her small neat ears sparkling with diamonds, came into the St. Ermin's Hotel on the arm of a tall thin Englishman whose face Shomron recognized as famous although he couldn't put a name to it. She collected her room key and a sheaf of messages from the desk. Shomron watched from behind his newspaper as jealously as a lover. It would be infuriating if the two of them were spending the night together: there were questions that wanted answering and he was too impatient to wait.

Mrs. Kloster turned to her escort and said something, smiling. The man smiled in return, stooped a long way down and kissed her. It was not an amorous kiss: he was saying goodnight.

"Goodnight, Sir Hugh," the hall porter called out deferentially as the tall Englishman left, and Shomron placed him at last. He was in fact a Scotsman, the brother of an earl, a leading Conservative politician who had a long-standing friendship with Israel.

Instead of confronting Mrs. Kloster, who might well have put him off with the excuse of being too tired to talk that evening, Shomron took the parallel lift and arrived at the top floor just as she was unlocking her door.

"Amos, good heavens! What are you doing here?" she exclaimed, taken aback.

"I've been waiting to see you."

"You didn't have to pounce, there is the house phone," she remarked dryly, leading the way into what must have been St. Ermin's VIP suite, spacious, discreetly luxurious and dignified enough for a visiting head of state. "Fix yourself a drink, I've just got to go into the bathroom a minute."

Standing by the huge window, sipping a brandy well-diluted with soda and gazing over Westminster's rooftops at the amber glow of the London skyline, the tension in him began to dissolve. After the frugalities of Sinclair's semi-basement in Belsize Close, his senses were agreeably soothed by the expensive furniture, soft carpet, shaded lights gleaming on glass and polished wood, the vases of flowers scenting the air-conditioned room.

327

Rivka Kloster was away for considerably longer than a minute. When she returned she had changed into a green silk kimono that suited her fresh, Dutch coloring and silvery blonde hair.

"I took the opportunity to slip into something comfortable," she grinned, flopping into an armchair with the tired relief of a middle-aged housewife rather than the abandon of a seductress. "It's been an exhausting evening. Dinner at the Army and Navy Club and a socially significant experience at the theater. Still, I suppose it's worth it. Hugh's one of our few political friends who isn't flirting with the PLO." She reached for a slim, gold-tipped cigarette and lit it from a Ronson tablelighter, blowing out a mouthful of smoke and giving him the shrewd appraisal of a hard-bitten gambler.

"Your vacation hasn't done you much good," she commented. "What's the matter? Not sleeping too well?"

"That reminds me of a dream," he said. "I was walking in Jerusalem amidst the ruins of the Temple. Hebrew letters set in the mosaic floor spelt the name of God backwards and whoever saw it was struck with blindness."

Ringing for room service, she said: "Please send up a selection of sandwiches and coffee for two . . . What does it mean?"

Shomron regarded her quizzically. "You didn't have much of a Jewish education, did you, Rivka?"

"In my Catholic girls' school?"

"*Khillul Ha'Shem,* the desecration of the Name. The rabbis would say I have a blasphemous imag-

328

ination. What a psychiatrist would make of it, I'm not sure. But the dream had an element of prophecy. I've been warned to turn away and not look at the forbidden. Or else."

"Sometimes it's tactful to look away, or a necessary expedient."

"A certain *Mevrouw* van Goudt seemed to think otherwise."

"Ah, so you know about that."

Mrs. Kloster crushed out her cigarette and spent some moments examining her manicured fingernails. Rehearsing a glib evasion, Shomron thought cynically, but when she looked up her glance was open and direct.

"You're extraordinarily obsessed with this case, aren't you?"

"Yes, but what's *Mevrouw* van Goudt's excuse? Instructions from the Mossad?"

"If it was, you wouldn't expect me to tell you," she flashed back, her candid green eyes hardening. "Isabella van Goudt was never an obedient creature and never did anything unless she wanted to. I think I told you about her. Her Jewish education began when she spent part of her honeymoon visiting Auschwitz, an island in hell instead of the Aegean. Until then she was a rich little Dutch girl with a remote Spanish-Hebraic strain through the maternal line of her family. When she came back she was Rivka Kloster, Rivka being the name of a nineteen-year-old girl whose picture she saw among the photographs of victims displayed in the Auschwitz museum. We had the same birthday, except that I was seven

329

years old when they killed her. There is something profound in the idea of *Khillul Ha'Shem*. I believe in the power of names. When I became Rivka something of Rivka became me."

"Does that mean you're on my side?" he asked.

"In wanting to find out the truth, yes. But . . . you seem to want to turn it into a public debate. That would cause bitterness and pain."

"You sound as though you're already convinced that the man Sinclair shot really was a Nazi war criminal."

"No, but the mere possibility appalls me. What it would do to his innocent family, to Israelis generally, makes me shudder. Our people are too exhausted to be made to go through it all again. The inquest has gone on too long. We keep tearing our hearts on the barbed wire of the past."

Mrs. Kloster clenched her shapely hands, her eyes flashing like the diamonds on her fingers. The animation and the warmth of color that flooded into her cheeks transformed her into a vividly handsome woman.

"Nothing makes me angrier than philosophical speculations of the Hannah Arendt kind that the men, women and children who died in the Holocaust were in some way accomplices in their own destruction." She glared at Shomron as though he too subscribed to this view. "There they are, ten, twenty, thirty years on, looking back in anguish from their university chairs and explaining how, if only this, that and the other, it could have been different. That really is a desecration of the Name.

I have all the books in my library. It took 2,500 heavily armed SS troops with tanks, artillery and demolition squads thirty-three days to put down an uprising by eight hundred starved and ill-armed Jewish boys and girls in the Warsaw Ghetto, and the Germans lost a thousand men. The revolt of prisoners in the Treblinka death camp killed and wounded more than a hundred Nazi soldiers in a matter of minutes. Acts of resistance took place in scores of ghettoes. There was nothing like it on the battlefield; not only physical bravery, but the courage to remain human shown by thousands upon thousands of anonymous people in the face of helplessness and certain massacre."

The wound festers, Shomron thought. He'd said it all himself, an antidote to despair. It didn't help or give consolation. How different it was in battle when you could go out to meet your enemy with weapons in your hands. You incurred losses, you carried back your dead and wounded, heavy-hearted you counted the cost. But your homes had been defended and your people survived.

She was lighting another cigarette. The rush of adrenalin made her hand shake. Leaning forward, he took the Ronson from her and held out the flame. There was a fullness in his heart, the welling up of tenderness, almost like falling in love.

"That was quite an outburst. I'm sorry," she said gruffly, as if to forestall the danger. A knock announced the arrival of a waiter with the food. "The sandwiches are for you," she said. "I'm sticking to black coffee. I have to think of my figure. The Dutch side of my family tends to expand like old Queen Wilhelmina."

He laughed. "I have the same trouble in my family, only Deborah calls it cellulite. Of course, she works for a woman's magazine and in that world they don't call fat fat."

"Your Deborah is beautiful, slender and young. I hope you appreciate her."

"Oh, I'm mad about the girl," he confessed cheerfully, biting into a smoked salmon sandwich. He hadn't realized he was so hungry. The stimulation of an attractive woman's company almost returned him to his normal self.

"What made you go to Bush House?" he switched abruptly, using his old technique of interrogation.

"Just a minute," Mrs. Kloster said. Looking very pleased with herself, she went into the bedroom and returned with a businesslike briefcase. Opening the combination lock, she produced a document. "This is a transcript of a broadcast Sinclair made, originally in German then translated into English for the general Overseas Service of the BBC. Just glance through it."

Shomron took it from her. It was the review of a book and from the first line it gripped his attention.

Perhaps nothing has exasperated anti-Semites more than the astonishing talent for Jewish survival. Through more than two millenia one man-made cataclysm after another has swept over this small, gifted, provocative, and obstinate people. They have been conquered, dispersed, expelled, forcibly converted, massacred; fear and contempt have pursued them in all their wanderings; but each decimation strengthened their will to live, and soon they were as ubiquitous and venturesome as ever. Small wonder that men have believed them protected by a divine, or evil destiny: a people whom dispersion could not divide, and who could regard two thousand years of exile as but a temporary divorce from their homeland.

But in this, the worst century in Jewish history, the myth of the indestructible Jew was almost broken. Exterminated in Europe, ground by the millstone of the Russian Revolution, fleeing from an Arabia they had inhabited since the days of Babylon, even submitting to the gentle suicide of assimilation in the kindly West, it seemed that soon—within a century or so—they would have virtually disappeared except for the isolated ghetto of Israel, and that only waiting for a modern Saladin to sweep it into the sea. But if this had been the worst century for the Jews, it has also been a time when the Jewish technique for survival has been seen magnificently at work, and something of this story is told by Herbert Agar in *The Saving Remnant*.

Mr. Agar tells the story through the activities of the American relief and rescue organization, the Joint Distribution Committee, better known as the "Joint," which collected the money of American Jews, combined it with the courage, intelligence and selflessness of Jewish volunteers, and in forty-seven years helped to save up to two million people from death. Is it not a commentary upon the times that the great powers of the world, when they did not actually obstruct, stood by and left the rescue of survivors of the worst holocaust in Jewish history to a few voluntary Jewish organizations and a handful of resolute men? It is not altogether surprising that when the last Jewish survivors left a DP camp to begin the illegal, hazardous journey to Palestine, they wrote in the final issue of their mimeographed camp newspaper: "We have given the world the will and testament of those who perished: 'Do not put your faith into European civilization. In the Stygian chambers of inhuman persecution we signed the divorce. We are handing the divorce papers over to you. Return to the sources of Jewish morality!'"

The Saving Remnant is not an easy book: it stings the nerves again and again. But it is an encouraging book. It should sweep away once and for all the idea that Jewish survival is an enactment of some supernatural providence. It shows that Jews have survived because of sheer human solidarity; because in a national disaster, wherever it may occur, the Jews remember that they are brothers. The rich give their money, the poor their shelter, the young their strength, even their lives. It shows that love can take a creature broken by cruelty and turn him into a farmer in Galilee. There is surely a lesson in that, and not for the Jews alone.

So that was her passport. Clever. Shomron handed the document back to her. He recognized the voice of Franz Slonimsky, but harder, more assured. It did not fit the image of the man he had seen in the cells of Abu Kabir except, he recalled, for the latter's sudden tirade against Israel—"You call it a state, I call it a ghetto." He was not alone in fearing a modern Saladin, but the broadcast expressed an optimism that the ravaged prisoner appeared to have lost.

"A friend in the Dutch Embassy here arranged an introduction to a nice BBC man named Ackerman," she said. "We lunched in the Savoy Grill. I used my connections with the Anne Frank museum in Amsterdam and explained that I'd come across the text of this broadcast in its archives. It would give me so much pleasure to meet the author."

"And so you discovered that Sinclair was no longer with the BBC."

"Well, not as abruptly as that," she replied, amused. "We were drinking some very good claret which made for a rather discursive conversation.

Bill Ackerman was more interested in talking about himself. He's writing a book on German Romanticism which is over my head, but then he talked about his childhood. His father was a Viennese urologist. They came to England as refugees in 1938. Bill went to Westminster School as a boy of ten speaking hardly a word of English. I rather like the story he told about his return to Vienna on a visit in 1949. He went to see his dear old nanny. They were sitting in the old lady's parlor. She was describing indignantly how, when his family were hurriedly forced to leave, their neighbors descended on their apartment and seized the furniture, silver, paintings and carpets. 'And all the time,' he told me, 'I sat there in frozen silence gazing at my mother's best china displayed in the china cabinet.' By the way, have you seen the psychiatrist's report?"

Shomron frowned. Their own conversation was becoming discursive. "Which psychiatrist's report?"

"The one on Sinclair, of course."

"We were never allowed to get that far," he grumbled. "I suppose the Mossad has produced proof that he's mad."

Mrs. Kloster raised an eyebrow. "Isn't that obvious? It's one reason why it might do no harm to let him appear in court, as he insists. The judge would surely find him unfit to plead."

"I'd enter a strong objection. Listen!" He leaned forward as though already arguing the case at a public trial and checked off point by point on his fingers. "These are the symptoms: one, difficulty in forming close relationships; two, an obsession with the past; three, guilt at having survived; four, severe anxiety manifested in depression, hypochondria, insomnia, possibly excessive micturition. The clinical name is K-2 syndrome, derived from the fact that it's commonly found in concentration camp survivors. Serious cases can be highly incapacitating and last a lifetime. I come across it all the time in my job. It's not insanity."

"And five? You've got another finger."

"You've seen the report," he shrugged. "I haven't."

"Delusions of a messianic nature. Would that tip the balance?"

"Trust a Jewish psychiatrist to come up with that one," Shomron said with a derisive laugh.

"Well, it is borne out by one or two of the things I heard from Ackerman. For example, the reason Sinclair was fired by the BBC."

"I thought he resigned."

"That's the polite way of putting it. Do you remember the agitation for the release of Rudolf Hess from Spandau on his eightieth birthday? Sinclair was broadcasting a commentary. Suddenly he committed the unpardonable. He departed from the script and launched into a tirade about the thousands of war criminals left unpunished. They cut him off but not before Kampfmann and Dachau and goodness knows what other ad-libs were loosed on to the airwaves."

"Innermost secrets, eh?" he remarked sourly.

She gave a demure smile. "Bill Ackerman hasn't got the best head for drink and we were into the third bottle of claret."

Mrs. Kloster was a very skillful operator, he reflected with wry admiration. She was tough, intelligent, unsentimental yet dedicated, carried a formidable charge of sex and would never be taken for Jewish. The Mossad knew how to pick them. He recalled a tall, beautiful South American girl, also half-Jewish, who after fighting a deadly secret war against the assassins of the Israeli athletes at the Munich Olympics had landed up in a European prison but emerged, bright-eyed, without regrets, to finish her doctoral thesis at the Hebrew University. And there was the legendary half-German "champagne spy," a blonde, blue-eyed Wagnerian "superman" who operated for years in Nasser's Egypt entertaining top generals and politicians and coolly radioing vital military intelligence back to Israel from his luxurious Ismailian villa.

"I'm a simple policeman," he said dryly. "When one person deliberately kills another, the first thing I look for is motive. The higher metaphysics may decide that Sinclair fired a messianic bullet. I see it as revenge."

"Ah," said Mrs. Kloster, "you may be a simple policeman but Sinclair is not a simple man."

"And what's that supposed to mean?"

"He denies his motive was revenge. Had he found Kampfmann hiding in some other country he would have denounced him to the authorities,

338

been the principal witness at his trial, let justice take it's course. He needed justice far, far more than revenge, he said. But how could a Jewish state harbor a Nazi and confer its citizenship on him? How could he pass unrecognized unless he could merge with people who were not unlike himself? You would not bring him to trial because it would expose the scandal of his unquestioned existence among you. The virus of Nazism had infected the bloodstream of Israel and the only way he could focus attention on it was by putting himself on trial and forcing a public examination of Israel's conscience."

Shomron drew in his breath. A sharp pain had pierced his heart.

"It's all in the report," she added quietly. "Signed not by one but by two psychiatrists. You know there was that claim by a splinter PLO group that Benamir, the victim, was assassinated on its orders. Of course that had to be checked out because of his son's importance in the defense industry. It would have been so much simpler than coping with the enemy within."

The enemy within. Shomron groped with the enormity of it. After the sympathy, the sense of solidarity, he'd come to feel for Sinclair, it was a treacherous blow; scar tissue stripped from wounds constantly being reopened. There was the lacerating debate over German reparations he remembered from the time when he was a boy, not only in Israel but throughout the Jewish world, the anguished rhetoric about blood-money and shaking the hands of the murderers of six million. *Dayenu.* There was the assassination of Hungarian Jewish leader Rudolf Kastner on a Tel Aviv street after he fought a libel case and was denounced by the presiding district court judge as a willing collaborator of the Nazis who had "sold his soul to the devil." That renewed the inquest into the tormented role allocated by the Nazis to Jewish communal leaders in the ghettoes, forcing them to deliver quotas of victims for extermination. *Dayenu.* The wound began to heal when Israeli Nazi-hunters spirited Adolf Eichmann, fugitive architect of mass-murder, from his Argentine hiding place and the drama in a Jerusalem court performed the catharsis of justice; only for the fragile membrane to again be torn when Hannah Arendt in *The Banality of Evil* magisterially pronounced her own retroactive judgment on those who went quietly into the flames.

In the turbulence of his mind, Shomron imagined himself storming into the prisoner's cell and shaking him until the teeth rattled in his head. "Is that what you're after?" Or was it something more? A defensive mood prevailed among Israelis, worried, self-questioning, veering from agony to defiance. Decades of military struggle, harshness in the occupied territories, the arrest of stone-throwing Arab schoolchildren, long detention without trial, the punitive destruction of people's homes, the stupidities of army censorship: there were times, after a bombing raid on PLO targets in which innocent civilians were killed or maimed, or a general strutted like a warlord, or religious bully boys planted the banner of Jehovah on Arab land, when the fearful question arose: have we won our wars at the cost of moral defeat?

"I must be mad, not Sinclair," he said wearily. "This whole business has stopped me thinking straight. And if I'm not on the El Al plane tomorrow I may have to find myself another job."

"Then you must go," she said. "What's the point of delaying?"

He jerked his shoulders. "The way I feel at the moment, I'd like to prove he shot the wrong man."

Mrs. Kloster thoughtfully blew a smoke ring with a fresh cigarette and watched it float toward the ceiling. "It's not going to be easy," she murmured.

"Any special reason why?"

"Pour yourself a brandy—and one for me," she said. "This will be quite a shock."

"I'm getting used to them," Shomron shrugged. He moved his chair closer.

The direction of his gaze made her pull the flaps of her kimono together.

"Bad Godesberg," she said.

He looked up, puzzled.

"Sinclair got a telegram from Bad Godesberg."

"I don't follow."

"You will if you pay attention. That unauthorized broadcast of his touched a nerve. Letters poured in. Listener reaction ranged from indignation and abuse to self-justification, expressions of remorse and distress at the raking over of past grievances. A neo-Nazi group sent a death threat, and a man named Tadeusz Rodowicz sent a telegram. It said that he was a former inmate of Dachau and had important information about Kampfmann."

The unexpected jolt this gave him deflated his libido. "What kind of information?"

"Bill Ackerman didn't know. It was most frustrating. This could have been the breakthrough."

"Well, we can find it!" Shomron exclaimed. "Do you have an address, a telephone number?"

"Calm down!" she said and gave a complacent smile. "It's been taken care of. I saw Mr. Rodowicz last Tuesday."

"You never cease to amaze me, Rivka. Going to all that trouble."

"Not at all. I had family business in Amsterdam, Bad Godesberg is only an hour's drive from the Dutch border, I'm shamefully self-indulgent when it comes to satisfying my curiosity—"

"And," Shomron inserted, "you were acting in obedience to orders."

"Hasn't it occurred to you," she murmured, "that in telling you all this I may be acting in disobedience to orders?"

The thought had occurred to him. On the other hand, he didn't believe it. Mrs. Kloster was not, he judged, an indiscreet woman. She knew exactly what she was permitted to disclose and why.

"Do please, go on."

And so she told him.

International directory enquiries in Amsterdam located a T. Rodowicz, Osteopath, at 16 Munster-strasse, Bad Godesberg. She had decided against making a telephone call: the unexpected was usually more effective. Not that she hoped for much, but the drive at least should be pleasant. And so it turned out, travelling in the open Maserati through the flat Dutch countryside with the sun on her face, stopping at a farmhouse inn near Venlo for lunch, and following the winding road along the Rhine in almost a holiday mood to arrive in leisurely style at Bad Godesberg soon after four in the afternoon.

Munsterstrasse was a small, neat street of red-roofed houses in a new suburb on the edge of town built around a bustling supermarket as, in a more devout age, it would have clustered about a church. Young women zipped around the district in the latest Volkswagens ferrying children from school or making for smart boutiques in the shopping arcade. Long hair, tight jeans, the liberated assurance of 1980s Common Market Europe. And sun, summer flowers in tidy green gardens, colored streamers flying from pleasure boats on the Rhine—a long, long way from the pestilential past.

"Do you have an appointment?" asked the woman who opened the door. She left her in a tiny waiting room furnished with hard chairs and a low table for magazines mostly specializing in homeopathic medicine, vegetarianism and nature cures. Groans and gasps came from the surgery. "My husband is treating a patient. He will see you soon," the woman said on her return, immediately disappearing into the domestic part of the house. Sounds of therapeutic agony continued, then sighs of relief, a rumble of guttural voices. A stout man, smooth-faced and baby-pink in complexion, waddled from the surgery rotating his short fat neck as though he'd just discovered he could do it. After another interval a buzzer sounded.

Tadeusz Rodowicz, a small man with large powerful hands smelling pungently of embrocation, sat at a desk in white, short-sleeved overalls that exposed his sinewy forearms. Behind him were charts illustrating the bones and musculature of the human frame. Blue periwinkle eyes observed her keenly from under thorny eyebrows and his narrow Polish face was as trenched as a battlefield.

"Please sit down," he said, indicating the chair opposite. "Can I have your name?"

"I haven't come as a patient," she hastened to explain.

The osteopath laid down his pen. His hands looked disappointed. Yes, he recalled sending the telegram to the BBC. A Jewish gentleman came from London to speak to him about it, a Mr. Sinclair. Mr. Sinclair was particularly interested in a certain SS officer because he knew about him from a former Dachau prisoner, Franz Slonimsky. He himself couldn't say he remembered this prisoner, there were so many thousands . . . If the *gnädige Frau* could forgive him for being personal, what was the nature of her interest? Ah, the Anne Frank Foundation. Such institutions did good work; people were in too much of a hurry to forget."

"The SS officer," she prompted.

"Ah, yes, Kampfmann. When I heard his name on the radio a ghost walked through my head. A most unusual concentration camp official."

"Did you know him well?"

Rodowicz gave her a look of mild reproach. "How could I? We were the dirt under their feet. Twice, three times, he spoke to me. I'll never forget how terrified I was the first time. You see—" a tiny hesitation—"they put me on orderly duties in Experimental Medical Block 7. Kampfmann came in one night to check the drugs storeroom. As he left he came to me and stared for a long time, me stiff with fright. "*Häftling,* are you a Christian?" My heart stopped. He thinks I'm a Jew, I thought. "*Herr Oberleutnant,* I'm a baptized Catholic of the Polish race. It's in my papers," I said. He waved his hand in the air. "As a Christian, what meaning do you see in all this?" I wasn't so stupid as to answer. One wrong word . . . Another time, a Monday—Monday was the day of the week when the German nurses liquidated prisoners by injecting benzine or evipan into their hearts—I was swabbing the floor, cleaning the vomit, and he said: 'Did Christ vomit on the road to Golgotha?'"

"Do you think this Kampfmann was secretly a Christian?" she asked the osteopath.

Rodowicz's leathery face creased in a smile of derision. "Secretly dirtying his pants, more likely. The guns of Judgment Day were getting closer. Some of the swine were beginning to wish they were Jews, I reckon. I wasn't—" he admitted gruffly—"to much at peace with my own conscience."

Avoiding her glance, he stood up and walked to the window. Outside, children released from school played on the grass, wove patterns of movement as they wheeled on chromium-plated bicycles and raced in the sun; old men smoked and cackled on a wooden bench; women talked in the leafy shade of plane trees: the laughter of a suburban afternoon.

"The things I saw that I wasn't supposed to see," he went on with his back to her, staring out at the street. "They had a secret dissecting room in the Block. When they finished experimenting on a prisoner, used him up, they moved him in there and, while the poor wretch was still alive, cut out the organs of his body to be sent to Munich for clinical examination. That's in the records of the Nuremberg Trial. But Dachau was given a special research job. Air Marshal Milch wanted to find a way to revive aviators who'd been exposed to extreme cold. A Luftwaffe medical officer, Major Rascher, was put in charge. He set up an experiment in freezing human subjects and then trying to restore them to normal. Healthy young prisoners were selected and immersed naked or in flying suits in water of thirty-seven degrees Fahrenheit. Tubes were inserted into the rectum and stomach attached to a thermometer to measure the fall of body temperature from its average level of between ninety-seven and ninety-nine degrees Fahrenheit. Blood, urine and respiration tests were also carried out. They hauled them out blue as corpses and set out to warm them back to life by radiation or electrical heat or stimulants. One way was to get naked women to try to bring the frozen prisoner to a state capable of coition. Leading Nazis used to come and watch. Himmler brought along his special guests. In my opinion," said Rodowicz, facing her and clenching his powerful hands, "nothing they did was more hideous and disgusting than the use they made of those terrified women. Raise the dead and you'll go free. As though they'd let a single witness get out alive."

"How did you manage to do so?" she asked quietly.

"I knew you'd say that." He gave a despondent shrug. "I never thought I would. In the last few days conditions were chaotic. I'd got hold of some potassium cyanide to do it myself if it came to the worst. In the meantime I carried on. We still had some of Professor Schilling's malaria subjects. The old man was completely barmy, very proud of his scientific work. Must have thought they'd give him the Nobel Prize for services to humanity. I made a hiding place in the storeroom, behind the oxygen cylinders. When the battle got really close I crept inside ready to sweat it out until the end."

The little Pole returned to the desk and swiftly drew a diagram.

"This is me, here. I could watch what was going on through a gap between the cylinders. In the early hours of April 28, the day before the liberation, I heard someone come into the storeroom. All I could see was a pair of legs in jackboots. Now, this is the extraordinary thing." He bent closer, his bright blue eyes hypnotically fixed on hers. "One of the prisoners infected with malaria was a Jew named Bindermann. After waiting a bit— about half-an-hour—I crept out and had a look in the ward. A man was at the filing cabinet searching among the papers with a flashlight. He wore the striped uniform of a Jewish prisoner. What is he up to, I wondered. Then I caught a glimpse of his face. Do you know who it was? Oberleutnant Kampfmann. He found what he looked for, switched off the torch and left.

"Bindermann's bed was empty."

Mrs. Kloster picked up her brandy and absently swirled the dregs in the glass. "It wasn't until I started to drive back to Holland that the full implications occurred to me. Bindermann was Avram Benamir's name before he adopted a Hebrew one."

"It's not that uncommon," Shomron said. "We had a Bindermann in my class at school." A skinny boy in glasses, mad about music, he remembered. Killed on the Golan Heights in seventy-three. He felt queerly dislocated by what she had told him. It brought home how deeply he feared the consequences of the investigation into which he had become obsessively drawn. Perhaps the others were right. The truth may be too hideous to be exhumed.

"So the word of a Polish osteopath in a suburb of Bad Godesberg spelled death to some unsuspecting old fellow in Tel Aviv," he said bitterly, arguing with her that the connection was still tenuous, stretching coincidence to the point of incredulity. "Among the millions swept into the camps and ghettoes by the iron broom there was likely to be a fair number of people named Bindermann. Let us concede the possibility that Sinclair combed the records of DP camps and found some Bindermanns among the survivors. Let us even concede that he may have traced their subsequent movements, a task of enormous difficulty. What distinctive factor did he find to convince him that the Bindermann he eventually chose for retribution was the very man he'd sworn to track down? The color of his hair, the shape of his features? What? In nearly forty years appearances can change beyond recognition. As long as this vital piece of information is missing, we are no nearer a solution of this mystery than when he began."

"For which many of us may be truly thankful," Mrs. Kloster said. She lit another of her black, gold-tipped cigarettes and leaned back in her chair smiling a green-eyed cat-like smile. "All the same, it's intriguing to speculate. Let's play a macabre game," she suggested provocatively. "Imagine for a moment that Herr Kampfmann, the filthiest kind of Nazi, a vile concentration camp murderer, does indeed lie buried in a Jewish cemetery in Holon. What brought him there in the first place? Why did he choose to marry a young Jewish widow and raise his children to love and serve the Jewish state? How did he acquire his knowledge of· Hebrew and Judaism? A Nazi father and a son who dies fighting for Israel—how can one make sense of it?"

"One can't," Shomron said. "The idea is an abomination!"

"The Jewish half of me agrees with you. The Catholic part isn't so sure. Listening to our Polish friend Rodowicz I started to wonder. Did Christ vomit on the road to Golgotha? An extraordinary thing for a Nazi to say. It raises the possibility that for Kampfmann an analogy existed between what was being done to the Jews in Dachau and the Crucifixion. Can it be that he was a secret Christian?"

"In the SS?"

"He could have deliberately joined the organization to work against it from within. If so, he'd have to do things that were abhorrent to him."

Shomron grimaced. "Such as selecting people for gassing? You made a pilgrimage to Auschwitz, you saw what they did. Enough to shrivel the soul of any Christian, I would have thought."

"A year or so ago," she went on after considering his point, "a French professor of literature, Faurisson, defended in court his claim that the genocide of the Jews was, to use his own words, 'a huge historical lie' because there were no Hitler gas chambers. He denounced Leon Poliakov, the French historian of the Holocaust as 'a fabricator and a manipulator' for citing the evidence of Kurt Gerstein and the Auschwitz SS doctor Johann Paul Kremer, both of whom testified that they witnessed the gassing of Jews. Gerstein and Kremer are now dead but Professor Poliakov was fortunate in being able to produce a living witness, seventy-four-year old Baron von Otter, a retired Swedish diplomat. The Baron's evidence was riveting.

"On the night of August 22, 1942 he was traveling through occupied Poland on the Warsaw–Berlin express returning to the Swedish embassy in Berlin, where he was then a junior consul. His attention was attracted by the strange behavior of a young SS officer, Kurt Gerstein, who desperately signaled that he wished to speak with him. The Baron joined the man in the corridor of a sleeping compartment and offered him a cigarette to establish an acquaintanceship. They talked for twelve hours as the blacked-out train traveled through the night. Gerstein had just returned from the Belzec extermination camp near Lublin where he witnessed Jews being herded into gas chambers. He had seen the gold teeth extracted from their corpses. These things were still shrouded in a conspiracy of silence and von Otter was horrified. The SS officer showed him documents from the Belzec camp commandant requisitioning supplies of the hydro-cyanide acid used to gas the Jews. He implored the Baron as a neutral diplomat to bring the news to the outside world. This nightmarish conversation, reported to Stockholm, was the first eyewitness account of Operation Final Solution from a German to reach the West. During the rest of the war Gerstein made other efforts to smuggle the information out of Occupied Europe, yet Gerstein died a war criminal in a Paris prison in 1945. We don't know how or why he joined the SS or how it happened that he was present at an extermination, only that he was a brave and honest human being."

Shomron said somberly: "I honor him. He's truly one in a million. Apart from the fact that Kampfmann also held junior rank in the SS, what is the analogy?"

"That Kampfmann may also have become overwhelmed by remorse. He may have been driven by a need to punish himself by becoming a flagellant. Turning himself into a displaced Jew could be a remarkable act of penitence."

With a violence that brought an answering flush to Mrs. Kloster's cheeks, Shomron, who seldom swore, uttered an explosive obscenity. Glaring at her, he said: "You're not serious about all this, are you? It's not something that will end up in a report on the Attorney-General's desk?"

"Pour me a little more brandy," she said. "I'm

about to make an even more outrageous suggestion and I need to fortify myself against your displeasure. And have another yourself, you're far too tense."

"I can do without the stuff," was his surly reply. He brought the drink over and stood looking down at her with an exasperated mixture of reluctant admiration, resentment, erotic arousal and suspicion that he was being guilefully manipulated.

"I didn't grow up liking Jews," said Mrs. Kloster. "The sisters in our convent spoke to us of the agony of Jesus and we all know whose fault that's supposed to be. It didn't have a lasting effect. Anti-semitism of the authentic kind requires a religious intensity: you need to have a vocation for it. But supposing I had—pert nose, Dutch coloring, a sound Christian lineage through the paternal side of my family that can be traced back to a seventeenth century member of the Cloth Drapers' Guild who features in a Rembrandt painting: I could have concealed my Sephardic origins and crossed the line. If there'd been a Dutch Hitler, it wouldn't have been difficult for me to have joined his League of Aryan Maidens."

"You would have been put to stud and awarded the Rosette First Class for breeding," Shomron said, having recovered his humor. "So far you're not being at all outrageous."

"Supposing Kampfmann was a Jew all the time—or, as the cynics have it, Jew-ish?"

He took the suggestion calmly. "And joined the

353

Nazis because he hated his father—or mother, as the case maybe?"

"Not necessarily out of self-hate. If a really dangerous Nazi movement existed today you know as well as I do that we'd infiltrate the organization with our agents. After a couple of thousand years of hybrid dispersion we're better at the game than anyone." She mentioned a few foxy examples. "It wasn't unknown for blonde young Jewesses to pass themselves off as *shiksas* during the German occupation of East Europe and act as spies for Jewish partisan groups. Had I been old enough, brave enough and suitably Germanic, I like to think I might have done something of the sort myself."

"During the Nuremberg Trials," Shomron observed, "the Nazi Governor-General of Poland made the malevolent suggestion that Adolf Hitler's grandfather was the illegitimate son of a Graz Jewish merchant named Frankenberger by Maria Ann Schicklegruber, a servant in Frankenberger's house. It's part of a putative tradition. Moses is said to be the bastard of an Egyptian princess, Samson of a Philistine, and it is forbidden for a Jew to speak the Name of Him Christians claim to be the true Father of Jesus."

He was sitting on the arm of her chair. She smelled of brandy and expensive French perfume. The scent came from between her breasts, the cleft just visible through the V-neck of her kimono. Temptation and opportunity. They were alone together in a luxurious hotel suite, in the glittering anonymity of a foreign city. Nothing discouraged Eros, the incorrigible; that was how the world constantly renewed itself.

"You're not impressed by my speculations," she said, glancing up at hom.

"Of course I am. Game, set and match to you," he answered and kissed her full on the mouth.

Mrs. Kloster savored the kiss for a moment, then detached herself. "I haven't been playing that game," she said discouragingly. "In fact, I've been deadly serious. We have been asking who is, or was, Avram Benamir. The question is wrong. It should start from the other end. Who is, or was, Ulrich Walther Kampfmann? If we can find out that then we'll know if the two can be fitted together." She consulted the tiny watch set into her gold bracelet. "It's after one a.m. You have to catch the plane later today. Shouldn't you be getting a good night's rest?"

"I'm not sleepy. Besides, I had to leave my lodgings in a hurry. My suitcase is in the left luggage office at Victoria Station and it's a bit late to look for a hotel room."

"You didn't, by any chance, plan to be homeless tonight before you came this evening?" she asked, elevating a smooth eyebrow.

"No," he grinned, "but I was trained to show initiative."

"Hm!" She looked frowningly at him, then laughed and said briskly: "Well, I won't throw you out. Make yourself at home, I'm going to take a bath."

The waiting was tantalizing. He smoked, walked about restlessly, stood gazing out of the window at the dark skyline of London. Down below, the siren of a police car or ambulance gave out its urgent warning. He was experiencing his own signals of urgency. Unable to contain his impatience, he ventured into the bedroom. Late night music came from a radio beside the wide soft double bed, invitingly turned down. The bathroom door was open.

Mrs. Kloster, handsome and comfortably fleshed, rose like a ripe Aphrodite from the foam and stepped on to the bath mat. He took the large towel from the rail and spread it wide, inviting her into his embrace.

"Amos, there's just one thing I'd like to get straight," she murmured as his hands took possession of her breasts. "Infidelity in a foreign country far from home can be treated as though it never really happened. This is not the beginning of a romantic affair."

13

THEIR BODIES grew slippery in the sweat of their love-making. It was as though they were in the grip of honeymoon fever, the first taste of strangeness and delight. The eagerness of her response amazed him. She cried out, shuddering, and her sharp teeth bit into his shoulder. A moment later, riding his own dark ecstasy, his body released the primal explosion of seed.

Deborah lay back on the pillow, limbs outflung in abandon. The pink tip of her tongue licked the salt moisture on her lips. Her breath came in gasps as if she'd just completed a racing circuit of the pool.

"God, Amos!" she panted and gave a throaty laugh. "After twelve years of wedlock. Scandalous. I only hope the kids didn't hear."

"They'll think you're doing your exercises. When I was a kid and we were living in that rickety house in Yemin Moshe, I could hear the Yarmolinskys' bed creaking next door and these terrible groans, 'Oy, Moishe! Oy, Rivkele!' My mother said they were crying in Yiddish over the destruction of the Temple. It was good enough for me."

"Innocent little Amos. How old were you?"

"An unprecocious seven. After all, ancient grey-beards crowded in front of the Temple Wall beating their breasts and wailing. Reb Yarmolinsky had a red beard and sold fish, his wife was round as a barrel, wore a ritual wig and bred a lot of little Yarmolinskys. If anybody had told me that was because he put his thing inside Sheindele I'd have thought they were very silly."

"You said Rivkele," Deborah pointed out.

"Oh, did I?" Shomron laughed guiltily. "I didn't."

"Yes, you did," she insisted and imitated his imitation of Reb Yarmolinsky's "Oy, Rivkele!"

He shrugged. "Sheindele, Rivkele, what's the difference?" and, rolling over, shook a cigarette out of the pack beside the bed and lit up.

Deborah's nose twitched. "Is that a Rothman's? Let me have a puff," she said, taking the cigarette from him and inhaling avidly, with a sigh of relief. "I'm still giving it up," she said. "I'm using a new method. We had an article about it in the magazine. You keep a chart in which you put down the time of each cigarette (twelve minutes to midnight), why you smoked it (for relief after exhausting sex with uxorious husband), if it was enjoyable or not (naughty but nice)."

"Now I feel I'm really at home," he said, lightly kissing her and turning on his falling asleep side. Yet even with his arm resting on the curve of Deborah's warm, resilient hip, the dreams awaiting him on the other side of darkness were filled with images of desolation.

Far below, tiny vessels cut flecks of white in the luminous deep blue sea. The shore line approached. Excitement, as always when on the point of arrival in Israel, spread through the aircraft. A party of youngsters exuberantly struck up a Hebrew song. "Look at it down there, a golden city," said an elderly tourist to his stout wife in a tone of awe, peering through the window at the panoramic spread of Tel Aviv lit by the glow of declining sunshine.

Shomron felt a tightening around the heart as if returning after a long absence. As in a fast-run film, he saw the vanishing line of tall hotels edging the coast along Hayarkon Street, the marina with its gaudy pleasure craft, the rectangular blue of the Gordon pool where Deborah, it being her swimming hour, may at that moment have caught a glimpse of the plane on its sweeping descent to Ben-Gurion Airport.

"I'll expect you about six, then," she'd said when he called her office from Heathrow. Across the 2,200 miles of space, her voice arching through

361

the stratosphere from another continent, she sounded constrained. "Yes, of course I'm all right. Perhaps you've forgotten how I sound." Her laughter turned the reprimand into a jest, but he detected resentment at his unexplained silence, and experienced an answering resentment. She could at least have offered to drive out to the airport and meet him. Jealousy briefly ran riot as he sipped lukewarm British coffee in the cafeteria waiting to board the plane. What had she been doing with her liberty while he was away? There was that hairy magazine photographer Noah, belly hanging over his belt, whom she found so amusing. And Benno Rizkin offering the sleazy diversions of Sheba's Cave and scheming a booze and marijuana seduction. Only hours away from his own extra-marital romp in the bed of Rivka Kloster, he brooded over his wife's imagined adulteries with gnawing anxiety.

But this was an overflow of deeper misgivings. He was flying into trouble, a man divided against himself, unprepared. Whenever he got a really bad attack of doubt and despondency, or confronted failure, whenever it seemed to him that his life was slipping out of control, he was overcome by an irrational fear of losing Deborah, that one day he would come home to find her and the children gone. He traced it back to having grown up fatherless, in the sheltering protection of a large-hearted mother who sometimes had to go away and leave him and his sister Leah in the care of strangers. The findings of sociologists that men were more prone than women to break down under the stress of divorce did not surprise him. The notion that Eve was Adam's thirteenth rib struck him as absurd even as a child. Men were the children of women, so how could it be? And as he had grown older he'd come to the conclusion that the myth of Creation should be rewritten with Eve, the first great mother of the human hive, as the prime beginner.

Yes, he was returning to the ordeals of uncertainty, unsure of his role, his judgment, his duty, not knowing whether he had the inner resources to resolve these doubts. Strapped into his seat, the warning lights on, he prepared for the jolt of landing.

Things· began to happen quickly: the sudden oppressive heat, the noise and bustle of the arrivals lounge, jostling crowds craning for a sight of relatives and friends, security formalities. He shuffled forward in the queue for passport clearance.

"*Mar* Shomron, will you please go to the arrivals desk," boomed the public address system.

He was momentarily confused. A message from Deborah? But their arrangement had already been settled. Who else knew he was on the London plane? Gillon Romm had ordered his return in no uncertain terms but could be less certain of his obedience, particularly after he had defied the Embassy security officer by decamping from Sinclair's flat in Belsize Close. Only one person in London could have reported his departure for Tel

Aviv. After their late breakfast in her hotel suite, it was she who ordered his taxi. Warm heart but ice-cool brain, he reflected wryly.

The girl at the desk said: "A gentleman is waiting for you in Room Five of the Administration Section. I'll get someone to show you where it is."

"I know the way," he said. He could even hazard a guess at the identity of the gentleman—tall, Anglo-Saxon, diffidently charming, dangerous.

Room Five stood at the end of a row of busy offices humming with electric typewriters, word processors, cybernetic thinking machines, teleprinters. Through the glass of one door he saw an acquaintance chatting up a pretty secretary and looked in to say hello. He entered Room Five without knocking. Colonel David Lester turned from the window with a deprecating English smile and held out a welcoming hand. "Hi, Amos," he said. "Did you have a good trip?"

"Not as good as I had hoped, as you probably know . . . but, interesting."

"I'd like you to tell me about it." Lester's voice was eager, devoid of irony. "We can leave for Jerusalem immediately, the car is waiting. I'll arrange to have your baggage cleared through customs."

"Immediately!" Shomron stared in anger. "Look, I've just got back, I'm tired, my wife is expecting me, and there's nothing I can tell you that you don't already know."

"Perhaps, but we must make sure. Why not telephone and say you'll be a little late? A short debriefing. It shouldn't take long and we'll run you home as soon as it's over."

How skillfully he played down his authority, leaning gracefully against the window frame, boyishly smiling, his manner almost apologetic. The art of understatement: he brought it off perfectly. But Shomron was undeceived. He was receiving the treatment of a recalcitrant subordinate, placed under orders, a degree or so less severe than disciplinary arrest.

Traveling in the car, Lester kept the atmosphere from congealing into silence with pleasantries and small talk. Had he seen any interesting plays? What was the mood of the British public on this, that and the other? Dinner table conversation on culture, politics and social trends at best. The speed and abruptness of air travel made it all unreal, a blurring of time, landscape and sensation that produced the elusive quality of dream. Only on reflection did Shomron realize that his replies when put together revealed much of the deliberate withdrawal into solitude that immersed him in a macabre meditation on the recent experience of Jewish suffering.

And this is where he began when they arrived at the Kirya in Jerusalem, sitting in a comfortable room more like a scholar's study than a government office. It all came out in an impassioned burst of eloquence that seemed beyond his control, a disgorging of the bitterness and grief that had accumulated in his soul during the reading of the "black notebooks," as he now considered them.

365

The timber of his voice sounded thin and unrecognizable, oddly distant, as if it emerged from the throat of the past, as if indeed he had become the voice of Franz Slonimsky.

David Lester listened without interruption, his expression sympathetic but professionally detached. He could have been a doctor observing the symptoms of a rather agitated patient.

"I'd like to see those notebooks," he said. "You have them, of course."

Shomron hesitated. The notebooks were vital documentary evidence, yet taking them had somehow been like robbing the dead, an act of sacrilege. "Yes, they're in my luggage," he replied reluctantly.

"Fine, I'll ask my secretary to have your suitcase brought in." Lester lifted the phone and gave the order. "If you have anything else that might be relevant to this investigation, notes of conversations with people who know Sinclair, I'm sure you'll let me have them too."

"I kept no notes."

It could have been interpreted as an admission of incompetence but was received without comment. Instead the questioning became brisk.

"I understand you broke into his flat and made yourself at home there. Wasn't that risky?"

"People came and went. It was that sort of house."

"How did you explain your presence there to other residents?"

"I said he'd given me permission."

366

"They believed you?"

"If not, they were too polite to say so."

"Did you learn anything about him from them?"

"Not much. He lived quietly, he appeared to have no close friends, he was uncommunicative, he went on journeys but they didn't know where."

"Nothing more explicit? No gossip about his private life?"

"The English," Shomron said, smiling thinly, "have a great respect for privacy." The interrogation was beginning to annoy him.

"What about his foster mother, Friedl Zussman, surely she must have had a good deal to tell you?"

"She spoke more freely."

"I see. And how did you explain yourself to her?"

Shomron winced. The loaded question was slipped in neatly, a knife between the ribs. He had a sudden vision of the cigar-smoking Mrs. Zussman tapping her wrinkled forehead and pronouncing: "My little boy is in trouble. I see zis wiz my third eye." In his eagerness to get her to talk he'd divulged that Sinclair was under arrest, a calculated indiscretion. At the time the risk had seemed worthwhile, now he was not sure. He was not sure at all. *Never divulge classified information to an unauthorized person.*

Evasively, he said: "I still have to sort things out in my mind. You'll have my full report in a day or so."

David Lester subjected him to a long, deliberate stare. "When you write out your report," he said at last, his voice ominously quiet, "perhaps you can explain a telephone call Mrs. Zussman made to the Israeli ambassador in London. She said she had been visited by a police official from Israel. He told her that Sinclair was arrested for being in possession of a gun and threatening the life of an Israeli citizen. She intends to ask the British Foreign Office to take up the case."

"The British Embassy here has already been notified. We also contacted Interpol for a report on Sinclair. These things are on file."

The reply was ignored. An inflexible rule had been broken: there were no excuses. "Even if you hadn't been taken off this case, it would be necessary to remove you now," Lester said. "I can sympathize with your emotional involvement, but it's reached the point where it impairs your judgment."

"All I'm concerned with is to get at the truth," Shomron insisted.

"Impossible. No matter how deeply you probe, the truth will never be established. What we have is rumor, conjecture and suspicion—a poisonous brew in this country given the circumstances. And not only here. That's why the lid has to be nailed down tight."

Shomron thought of the mysterious corpse hurriedly interred in the Holon cemetery. The coffin analogy was appropriate. Yet the ghost refused to be laid.

"The Mossad," he said, "wishes to protect a

368

valuable scientist. I understand that, but I'm not convinced you can keep the matter secret, or that it's right to do so."

"Then there's something you'd better hear." Taking out a bunch of keys, David Lester went over and unlocked a heavy steel filing cabinet, returning with a casette. He fitted it into a tape-recorder on a low table beside the desk and switched on the machine. There were faint noises, indecipherable crepitations, irregular footsteps, the clang of what sounded like a metal door.

"Good morning, Mr. Sinclair, how are you today?" came a gruff, jovial voice. The reply was inaudible. "You didn't eat your breakfast. Why, you don't like? Tomatoes, cucumber, olives, cottage cheese, fish—healthy food. You want something else, I bring it."

Another voice, edged with mistrust. "When can I see the prison governor?"

"Yes, I will ask him."

"You say that every day. I want to know if the date of my trial has been fixed."

"Mr. Sinclair, they will tell it you. For sure. You want more law books, I bring. Also writing papers."

"No, you would wait until I slept and steal what I wrote."

David Lester pressed the button to wind the tape faster. When the twittering stopped, Sinclair was caught in the middle of a monologue. Poor devil, the very thoughts in his head were being stolen.

"... Dr. Mengele, who used Jewish children like

369

laboratory rats in his Auschwitz vivisection experiments. If they are sane, I choose madness, Elie Wiesel wrote. In this court and in this country it is only too familiar, but please be patient. What I have to say is bitter, you may hate me for saying it but it is necessary. We no longer gouge out eyes with red-hot pokers, tear out the tongues of the world's torturers. Our humanity makes it impossible. Millions can be slaughtered but the murderers escape with the payment of only their single lives. Justice is feeble, at best a poultice to ease a psychic wound, but the palace of justice is a place where the injured can cry out in protest and be heard by all men. It is a court of morals or it is nothing." Sinclair paused to cough up some phlegm. There were sounds of shuffling movement, the groans of labored urination, a water-closet being flushed. Once the listener's ears adjusted to the hidden microphone, the aural signals opened up visions of the subterranean prison world—hollow echoes of distant voices, footsteps pacing a stone corridor, the faint ringing of a phone, desolation. The voice resumed. "I devoted many years to the search for Ulrich Walter Kampfmann who by a mere flick of his finger condemned every member of my family to annihilation. Israel tried and executed Adolf Eichmann, but there are many Eichmanns and he was mine. You can imagine the incredulity and horror I felt when I found him, wearing the identity of a victim he had murdered, masquerading as a respectable citizen of a state founded on the martyrdom of the

Jewish people. I am approaching the moment of vertigo. My throat gags on what I am about to say. Looking back over the past forty years, we must ask ourselves: 'Has Nazism triumphed?' I can see that you already know the answer. It spreads its cancerous spores in continent after continent. Do I need to list the atrocities country by country? Innocent people, the weak, the old, the helpless, are tortured and massacred in the brutal exercise of power by those who invoke religion, socialism, patriotic duty, tribal loyalties, honor. Yes, you will say, but thank God not here, not in Israel, not among us who know what it is to be spurned, insulted and abused, who have taken up arms only in self-defense, a nation mourning its recent dead yet vigorous in building a humane society that provides refuge for its persecuted brethren. Are you sure? No gratuitous cruelty, no slaughter of innocents, no racist arrogance, no alliances with regimes that practice torture . . . ?"

David Lester stopped the machine. "The speech goes on for more than an hour. I can summarize the rest," he said. "Roughly, it goes as follows. History has turned us into a world nation, universal spreaders of ideas, among the most highly educated and sophisticated people anywhere, more an intellectual milieu than an ethnic category. Yet in Israel we have regressed into tribal atavism. So did the Germans. Education and militant nationalism, a dangerous combination in their case and ours. In short, we're turning into Nazis. Can you imagine what our enemies will make of it if we give him the platform of a court of law? The *J'accuse* of a concentration camp survivor!"

Shomron moved his shoulders as though chafing under a burden. Listening to the tape had revived the painful ambiguities of his feeling for Sinclair, the pity and revulsion. The hardest thing about being born into the covenant of Abraham was the history you dragged around with you. You couldn't just live out your ordinary life. Jewish kids in the diaspòrà came running home with bloody noses because they killed Jesus, and in the synagogue when you were thirteen you took upon yourself not merely the responsibility of being a man but the whole sackful of all it was supposed to mean to be a Jew. And anyone felt free to lecture you on how you should discharge it.

"You're reading too much into what Sinclair says," he argued. "The man's in solitary confinement. He's emotionally disturbed and can't sleep. He broods aloud. A bugging device picks up a fantasy drama played out in the privacy of his mind. Paranoid night thoughts. We all have them but they're not put on tape."

"Most of us don't shoot people," Lester commented dryly. "For my part I take him seriously. He sounds as if he's rehearsing his lines." Consulting his wristwatch as though reminded of an urgent appointment, he said: "I've kept you long enough. The driver's waiting to run you home. Don't forget those notebooks before you leave."

Morosely, Shomron unstrapped his suitcase and rummaged among the accumulation of soiled shirts and underwear to find them. A faded sepia photograph slipped out of one. Sixteen-year-old Franz Slonimsky shortly after his arrival in Britain, the charity suit he wore bagging on his skinny body.

David Lester picked it up and studied it thoughtfully. Sombre accusing eyes stared out of the narrow etiolated face. "It reminds me," he said, "of another Czech Jew. He also had a fantasy about being put on trial."

"One is the prophecy of the other," Shomron, who considered the remark apt, said as he walked out of the door.

He climbed the four flights of stairs, weighed down by his luggage, and stood hesitating outside the apartment like a traveling salesman unsure of his welcome. He could hear the children laughing. Returning from a prolonged absence, the anticipation of their boisterous greeting usually gave him a feeling of elation. Now his despondency made him feel an intruder. Quietly, he unlocked the door and stepped into the lighted hallway.

"It's *abba*!" screamed Orit, rushing to meet him, long hair and spindly legs flying. Noam, second in the race, exuberantly clambered on his back.

"Hey, give me a chance," he pleaded, staggering with them into the living room and collapsing on to the couch. The screech and zoom-zoom of a TV car chase in the switchback streets of San Francisco contributed its safe, synthetic violence to the excitement.

"Imma! Imma! he's here," the children yelled in chorus.

Tan, beautiful and heart-stoppingly flesh and blood, Deborah appeared from the kitchen completing the family and he was irradiated by a burst of gladness and relief. He was home again and everything was exactly as he had left it. A long, disordered, hideously vivid nightmare had erased reality. A good night's dreamless sleep, the children's breakfast chatter, Deborah at her morning exercises. He could regain perspective.

He kissed them all. "I've got presents, lots of them. Wait here and I'll bring them."

"They must get themselves ready for bed first," Deborah said firmly. "I only allowed them to stay up until you came."

She switched off the TV and chivvied the protesting youngsters into the bathroom while he wandered from room to room getting the feel of the place again like a dog sniffing out its territory. In his study even the calendar stood at the date he had left. The intervening period could indeed have been a dream.

But once he and Deborah were alone there was the usual moment of awkwardness: separation had to be reconciled. She stood irresolutely, then joined him on the sofa. Their conversation circled warily, almost that of polite strangers, and he saw her with the novelty of a stranger's eye—her lean,

374

superbly fit, sinuous body; the erect, arrogant poise of her shapely head; her firm wide mouth and close-set myopic hazel eyes which, at that particular instant, gazed at him with frowning concern.

"You've been ill, haven't you?" she declared accusingly.

"Why do you say that?"

"You look it. Pale, harassed and undernourished. Even worse than when you went away and you were in a pretty bad shape then."

"It isn't anything serious, I'm just bushed," he said evasively. "It's been a very tiring trip."

"Doing what? All I know is that you went to a conference. The rest is hush-hush. Whatever it was it's left you looking half-dead and I have a right to know why."

As they went on talking he began to experience a weird hallucination. It was a late July evening in Tel Aviv. He sat with his wife in their bright modern apartment with its blonde Danish-style furniture, its neat bookshelves with built-in Hitachi record-player and speakers, its reproductions of Klee, Mondrian, Magritte and Chagall, its potted plants, framed family snapshots, silver candlesticks. Yet the physical sensations of place and time blurred and receded. His mind escaped the anchorage of his body, returning him so vividly to the basement of Belsize Close that he could see the cracked plaster of the kitchen wall and, through the small window, rain dripping from the leaves in the dank back garden.

The children calling from their bedroom brought him back to the present. "I'll go in and say goodnight to them," he said, grateful for the interruption.

Noam and Orit were greedily awaiting their presents, hoping as children always do that each had been brought a miracle. Heathrow Duty-Free had been a bit short of the kind of miracles he could afford, instead he'd gone for color and variety—a snow storm in a plastic globe, paints, space adventure books, a model racing car, a bracelet of beads and scented toilet soap for Orit, for Noam, the precocious mathematician, a stupendous pocket calculator. Then the stories, insatiably demanded.

"I'm too excited to sleep," said Noam, falling asleep. And Orit, her face drowsily upturned for the goodnight kiss, said: "Will you take us with you next time you go to London? You went away for *ages* and *ages* and didn't send me a picture postcard," an adult hurt in the limpid hazel eyes she inherited from her mother.

Eleven years old, the same age as Zofia Slonimsky. And was the world any less dangerous?

Huskily, he said: "I promise, *boobele*. We'll go to lots of wonderful places together."

Deborah had laid out a supper of chilled avocado soup, cold chicken, salad and white wine. "I'm not very hungry," he apologized.

"You've got to eat it whether you're hungry or not. The soup's a special recipe to make you talk." She leaned her chin on her hand and gazed steadily at him across the table. "So tell me, what's the trouble?"

"Well," he grinned feebly, "here's a provisional list. The nuclear arms race, smoking and lung cancer, the weakness of the shekel."

"I'm not asking you to editorialize," she said acidly. "Let's be specific. What were you doing in London?"

Did she suspect his infidelity? Deborah had once been very jealous. On one disastrous occasion, at a summer beach party, she'd caught him in horny entanglement with a seventeen-year-old American girl. For a whole week afterwards she stormed and raged and wept, for another week bitter silence. She took revenge by flirting blatantly with other men. It ruined a season of their marriage. But those were the honeymoon years when their mutual lust was exorbitant—sex before and after meals, whenever they could have it, but in time they'd stopped leaping into one another's arms and jealousy became intermittent, a touch of paprika to spice the familiar dish.

"What was I doing in London?" He shrugged. "That's a good question. I'm not allowed to say."

She frowned. "Oh, come on! I did my army service and got top marks for security. Besides, there's nothing in the rules that says you're absolutely forbidden to confide in your wife." She squeezed his hand and her voice softened. "Come on, Amos. You know the old saying. A trouble shared is a trouble halved."

The way she spoke brought a wry laugh. Firmness, sympathy and understanding—the technique of a skilled interrogator. Add love and the craving for confession becomes irresistible. To unburden oneself, to receive absolution, to be comforted, reassured, restored to grace. He was ready to tell her everything.

Pushing his plate away, he said: "Let's go on the balcony."

They went out interlinked, his arm around her waist. The night was sultry, deceptively peaceful. In lighted rooms behind open windows people could be glimpsed eating, talking, playing cards, languidly fanning themselves in the summer heat. Blue shadows flickered on television screens, there was music—then, suddenly, disruptively, came the sonic boom of a squadron of Israeli jets streaking through the blue-black starry sky towards Lebanon. There'd be headlines in the morning papers.

He waited until the reverberations died away. "There's this case," he began, speaking slowly and reflectively at first, then with a gutteral outpouring of bitterness and grief. Deborah sat motionless, her head averted, an unwilling listener.

"It's horrible, I know, but why does it affect you so badly?" she asked when he finished. "Why more than usual?"

He lit a cigarette and puffed morosely. "I'm not sure. Perhaps those of us born in Israel are more Jewish than we think, a peculiar people cursed by an inability to forget. History doesn't let us. Too often the past has been a mirror of the future. You

378

see, if I was Sinclair and a Nazi war criminal had come to live amongst us, I would not be able to forgive it, either."

"But you're still not convinced it's true."

"I'm not convinced."

"And it may be impossible to prove one way or the other?"

"Yes."

"There are Nazis everywhere," Deborah said. "We have our own Nazis."

He caught his breath at the outrageous statement. The glowing tip of his cigarette stabbed the darkness. It was some moments before he could trust himself to speak.

"No cause is entirely just," he said in a harsh voice. "We have our fanatics. We are capable of cruelty. We have committed outrages. There are murderers among us, but even among murderers there are gradations of evil. We do not have Nazis."

"God! This is the kind of conversation in which I need a cigarette," Deborah exploded. "Let me have a puff of yours." She inhaled deeply, brushing away the lock of hair that always fell into her eyes when she became excited. "I know about our struggle to survive. I know what they've done to us and what we've done to them. It's been going on all the thirty-one years of my life and there's no end in sight. It's a terrible price. You remember the depression I had after Noam was born. The doctor called it post-natal blues and put me on Valium. How do you tranquillize a mother who looks at her three-week old baby and is already a quivering jelly at the thought that at eighteen he'll be driving a tank or making parachute jumps in yet another war with the Arabs? It wasn't long after the Yom Kippur bloodshed. Whenever one of my friends gives birth to a girl she feels reprieved. Isn't that appalling?"

They were covering old ground. Shomron was about to make his customary placating reply when the doorbell rang. "Are you expecting anybody?" he asked her.

"No. It's probably Leah and Berl. I told them you were coming home this evening. Berl is full of his peace mission in Paris. He has plans for publishing a joint Arab-Israeli magazine."

Shomron growled: "In that case I'll go to bed. I'm in no mood to discuss obstetrics with my little sister or listen to Berl telling me how beastly we are to Yasir Arafat."

But when he opened the door he was confronted by the magazine photographer, Noah. "Yes?" he enquired, not immediately recognizing the burly stranger. Noah had evidently not expected to see him either. "Hi!" he said, grinning uneasily. His thick, wiry, grey-black hair shone greasily and he reeked of pungent aftershave. "I brought the pix for an article we're doing, me and Deb." Deborah appeared from the balcony and his swarthy ribald face broke into a sweat. "I know you need the stuff first thing in the morning and I'm gonna be out on location," he told her.

Shomron eyed him with disfavor. "You must come in for a drink."

380

"You haven't got time, have you, Noah?" Deborah pointedly and inhospitably suggested.

"Well." He gave an expansive shrug. "Just a coffee." Settling himself on the living room couch, short arms folded over his belly, he entered into an affable discussion about Shomron's trip.

"You knew I was away then?" Shomron asked, narrow-eyed. The fellow seemed altogether too much at home.

"Deborah said something. You know, we sometimes swim together." He made it sound lecherous. "Besides, what's secret in Israel? You went to talk about the PLO. I heard it on the radio." He bared his big yellow teeth in a grin of savage innocence. "Did you tell our critics we make no deals with the bastards? A good hack in the guts. We showed how at Entebbe, and in Lebanon."

Deborah returned from the kitchen with coffee and a plate of cinnamon cakes. Seating herself beside Noah, she shook the photographs from the envelope and spread them out on the low table. "I'm working on a feature about an immigrant family from Samarkand," she explained to Shomron. There were pictures of stout, bewildered women and children bundled up like Russian dolls; a gnarled old man with long drooping moustaches supported by two husky young Asiatic Jews; weeping relatives greeting them at the airport; the immigrant reception center; the box-like apartment in a new development town. The end of a pilgrimage across centuries of exile, a staple of the national press: Shomron had seen the like too often to be distracted.

Instead, gnawed by mistrust, he watched the two of them discussing technicalities, her long brown hair almost brushing Noah's coarse, pitted face. Was he justified in being suspicious? Surely she didn't find the gross, ungainly, fifty-year-old Iraqi Jew attractive? A bull of a man. Some women went for that, but Deborah?

"How often has he been dropping in while I've not been around?" he demanded when the photographer left, the odor of his body lotion lingering in the air.

"Once," Deborah said shortly. She carried the crockery to the sink and began washing up.

Shomron pursued her in a daze of fury. "He didn't come to show you photographs, did he?"

"No," she retorted. "He came to seduce me. If you knew Noah as well as I do you'd know he was bound to try."

"Did he succeed?" He was too far gone to stop himself saying it. Deborah gave him a hard stare. "Why don't you answer?" he yelled.

"Because it's ridiculous!" she yelled in reply, wiping her hands on a kitchen towel and stalking away.

"Well, you can't blame me for being suspicious, the way he turned up."

She swung around glaring. "What do you think I am? If I'm ever tempted to be unfaithful to you, I won't choose an over-sexed grandfather who leers over every shapely bum parading down Dizengoff Street."

The absurdity of it suddenly struck him. He

began to laugh, not without pain. Deborah joined in. "God knows, we've got more important things to quarrel about," she said, and added: "Don't jeopardize your whole career over this horrid case, Amos. Be a bit cynical. You know, Leah's right about Berl. Too much idealism is tough on human relations. We owe something to our private lives, too."

Shomron tried to smile. He felt a stinging in the back of his eyes.

"Let's go to bed," he said simply.

14

"WAIT here, I'll see if he's awake." The young nurse disappeared behind the screen. Lipkin was not making progress. Nothing had actually been put into words but headshakes and shrugs said it all. Also the screen round his bed in a far corner of the ward, so often the beginning of final isolation from the living.

"How are you, Mr. Lipkin? You're looking well this morning," said the girl in the brisk, cheerful hospital voice used to humor the sick. "I've brought you a visitor."

"What time is it, Shoshana?" came the faint reply.

"Seven o'clock."

"So early? Then I must be dying."

"If you are the doctor will be furious. You promised to be a guest at her wedding."

Lipkin gave a low groaning laugh. "Her wedding, my funeral. We'll make it a double affair."

Even gallows humor requires a residue of vitality and Shomron took comfort from that. But he was shocked at the way the flesh of the old man's face had shrunk to its skeleton, the corpse-like tinge of his skin. A catheter ran from under the bedclothes into a plastic urine bottle and he was connected to a cardiac machine. Shomron put the fruit he'd brought into a bowl and drew a stool close to the bed.

"Hallo, Louis," he said.

Lipkin peered through the swollen slits of his eyes and turned away when he saw who it was. "So why didn't you come?"

"I had to go abroad at short notice, but I asked the office to see that you were well looked after."

"Ach! strangers."

"I know. It just wasn't possible for me to visit you before I left. There was no time."

"Excuses! Your father, God rest his soul, would go through fire and water. In the underground nothing was more important than a comrade."

"For me, too, Louis. Honest."

The sick man brought a sigh out of his broken body, still punishing Shomron for his neglect. "Water, I'm thirsty," he groaned and sucked noisily from the spout of the invalid cup held to his lips. The drink refreshed him. Drawing on his meager reserves of energy, he boasted again of his exploits in the great migration of Jewish survivors across the shifting frontiers of war-torn Europe to the safety of Palestine; how he and Shomron's father had outwitted Polish frontier guards, British generals and Russian secret police, assembling their charges by daring and subterfuge, finding secret routes through forests and across mountains, forging documents, commandeering trucks, performing miracles of diplomacy. Until an unlucky Russian bullet robbed him of a friend and Shomron of a father.

Listening to this familiar story, Shomron had the melancholy thought that Lipkin was making a special effort to repeat it, that these precious reminiscences were being presented to him as a dying bequest. But the telling of it restored Lipkin's philosophical humor.

"The best years of life," he said fondly. "The rest? . . . Ach! I had too much of an education to become a successful man. You know the story of the little Polish Jew who came to America and became a multi-millionaire? I'll tell you in Yiddish." Laughter crinkled the corners of his eyes. "Friends asked him how he managed to get so rich. So he answers, 'Because I never learned to read and write.' The people threw their hands up. 'But how is it possible?' The little Jew explains. 'I came to New York without a penny. Someone told me a synagogue in Brooklyn was looking for a beadle, fifteen dollars a week, so I went. The synagogue president looks me over from top to toe. Are you a good Jew? he asks. Yes, I try, Mr. President. Do you keep all the commandments? Every one to the last. The president, a master tailor, is pleased. Naturally, you can also read and write, he says. When I answer him no, he looks at me like I'm *meshugga*. You can't read and write and you expect fifteen dollars a week to be a beadle? So I borrow a few dollars from a *landsman* and sell fruit from a push-barrow. Then I open one restaurant, two, then five, ten, fifteen, and I buy a few hotels. This is how I became rich. But if I could read and write I would still be the beadle in a Brooklyn synagogue.'"

A pleased expression entered Lipkin's wasted features at Shomron's appreciative laughter. Closeness was re-established. "You know, Amos," he said after a brief silence, "my life is nothing to be proud of, not since I was young. Wheeling and dealing in the diamond market, a bit of smuggling, picking up a few dollars from American tourists. But I never cheated a poor man and in all my life I didn't eat pork."

This reminded him of the joke about the Catholic priest and the rabbi who met on a train. Everything reminded Lipkin of a joke, but his garrulity had reached exhaustion.

"I'll tell you next time, now I'm too tired. By the way, I had a visit from Motti Rubin—the boy who plays drums in a jazz band. Is he a policeman?"

"Why do you ask?" Shomron parried.

"He brought me some photographs. The driver who ran over me."

"Motti found him!" Shomron was delighted. It

was the best news since his return. "Did you recognize the bastard, Louis? I'll have him for attempted murder."

"Don't bother. A boy, nineteen, driving a stolen Renault. Nobody. And I thought I had enemies." A dry rattle of laughter at the ironies of chance came from Lipkin's throat. "Come tomorrow, Amos," he said, wearily closing his eyes.

"Your visit seems to have done him good," commented the nurse as he was leaving the ward.

"I hope so. Certainly it's done me good," he answered in a tone of wonder. The guilt and despondency was eased, a minor miracle: healing flowing from the sick. "Ask him to tell you the joke about the priest and the rabbi."

She laughed. "Oh, he's already told me that one."

He stepped out of the hospital into the white glare of sunshine and the resinous odor of pine that drifted in the air of Tel Aviv. It was going to be very hot. Gusting up from the south, the fierce desert breath drew vapor from the Mediterranean and early morning weather reports forecast a *sharav,* an ordeal of oppressive humidity, listlessness, sudden explosions of anger. Driving to the office to face the day, he felt keyed up and ready to cope.

It was good to be back at work. Reading through the accumulation of incident reports, case records and departmental memoranda, taking up the phone to verify a detail, respond to a call or request his secretary to bring in a file, his mind slipped into gear and picked up speed, doing what it was trained to do. He made an appointment at the District Attorney's office to discuss a bank embezzlement. There'd been an art robbery in an Allenby Street gallery he needed time to investigate. An arms cache of stolen weapons found in a Jaffa slum house must urgently be checked out to see if there was a terrorist connection. Absorption became total—the amnesia of work; he might never have been away. So that when Gaby Cohen, his deputy, dropped in at mid-morning to drink a glass of tea with him and mentioned the Blumenthal Street affair, the connection momentarily eluded him. Blumenthal Street? He glanced at the map on the wall behind the desk. No pin marked the street. It must be something that had happened in his absence.

"I haven't seen anything in the reports," he said, frowning. "Fill me in on the details."

Gaby stared, unmistakably aggrieved. "You're asking me! All I know is what I read in the papers. You were too busy to discuss the case with me before you left."

The blankness dispersed. So that was what it was called, the Blumenthal Street Affair. If only it could remain so parochial.

"I'm still too busy, Gaby. Look at this desk."

"Well, at the risk of sounding insubordinate I think you should spend a few minutes considering the facts. A man is shot dead. A terrorist group claims responsibility. The victim's son is a *wun-*

derkind scientist in the defense industry. The killer is detained but his identity, his nationality, his motive remains undisclosed. It's a sensational package and the press keeps asking questions. When I went to check the file I found it had been removed. What are we hiding and why?"

"Who said we're hiding anything?"

"O.K., message received. It's secret. What's the classification? Does it exclude even me?"

"You're taking it too personally," Shomron gruffly protested.

"So I'm sensitive," said Gaby with mock resignation. "But I've no intention of imposing my weakness on you, I'm here to warn you. The rumor mills are grinding. There's a deafening whisper in the undergrowth that our scientist is perfecting a revolutionary anti-missile device, that he's kept under day and night guard to forestall a kidnap or assassination attempt by Middle Eastern agents of the KGB. It's even been put to me that your attendance at a conference in England was a cloak for a secret mission." Gaby gave him a sidelong glance. "I won't ask if it's true."

"I like it," Shomron announced judiciously, "but I hope it doesn't get into print and blow my cover."

"The press is so frustrated there's no telling what will get into print. Dov Yudkin's already carrying on about unconstitutional withholding of information by the police. He's threatening to have a question on press freedom raised in the Knesset."

"Good, it might bring down the government."

"For God's sake, leave the funny stuff to Kishon, Amos. Unless we make some kind of statement this thing's going to get out of hand. Can't we deny the rumors, release a few details . . ."

Shomron put down his glass of tea with unnecessary violence. "Don't press me, Gaby," he snapped. A new anxiety had begun to gnaw. Instead of rumor and speculation being frustrated, it was spreading in a dangerous direction. And with disturbing accuracy. Who could have leaked the information about an anti-missile device? Shomron had the disquieting feeling that when all possible sources had been eliminated, the finger of suspicion would point to him. He rang the switchboard and tersely left instructions that calls from the press were not to be put through.

"You won't keep the hounds at bay for long," remarked Gaby with satisfied gloom, and the prophecy had no sooner been uttered when the phone went again.

"Captain Shomron, I have the Station Commander for you," said the operator.

This was one call he couldn't refuse. The line clicked as he reached nervously for a cigarette.

"So you're back at last, you rascal," boomed the deep chuckling voice of Gillon Romm. "Not a minute too soon. Get your ass over here first thing tomorrow."

"Can't it wait until the afternoon, I've got a meeting."

The rejoinder was grim. "Cancel it. We have to figure out how to save your skin—if it's not already too late."

Before he could react the connection was cut off leaving a ringing in his head as if his ears had been boxed. Slowly, in confusion and disbelief, he replaced the receiver. Things were even worse than he feared. They'd gone so far as to consider wiping out his whole career. The possibility had occurred to him but he'd dismissed it: the penalty was too drastic. He'd put in fifteen years of service, earned commendations, chances of promotion had been high. In Israel state officials were guaranteed life-long security as long as they refrained from plundering the public purse and avoided other gross misbehavior. Soon he'd be forty, he recalled with a sinking heart. A bit late to brush up on his old text books and join the jostle of lawyers in private practice. And who'd be fool enough to hire an ex-police investigator dismissed from the service in disgrace?

He pushed the thought aside: it hadn't come to that yet. For a while he tried to resume work but the residue of panic remained. He felt hot and sticky and unable to concentrate. Seeking relief by standing in the cool stream of air blowing from the ventilator, he glanced through the window and saw Sergeant Zina Kogan talking to another police girl in the forecourt. Either by intuition or coincidence, at that moment she looked up at him, held his gaze and, breaking off her conversation, hurried into the building. It came as no surprise when shortly afterwards she knocked and entered the room.

"Excuse me for bursting in," she said breathlessly, "but I've been waiting for you to come back."

Shomron fiddled with the papers on his desk, pretending to be busy. "Only got in yesterday," he grunted. Zina Kogan was a voluptuous young woman and normally he would have been glad of the distraction, but she'd chosen a bad time. She was also a girl of determination, not easily put off.

"Can you spare me a few minutes, I won't keep you long?"

"A few minutes," he agreed, sighing. "How's the Juvenile Department?"

"Much the same. I've just come from giving evidence in the case of a thirteen-year-old picked up soliciting tourists on the beach in front of the Dan Hotel. It practically makes me a social worker."

"And you're still keen on homicide."

"More than ever."

Irrelevantly, Shomron said: "My grandmother always refused to believe that there were Jewish prostitutes. Or homosexuals. Maybe in the Diaspora, but never in Israel."

Zina Kogan was in no mood to fritter away the precious minutes in idle chat. She came straight to the point. She wanted a transfer to his department. She was eager to get back on the case they'd been investigating together. Her eagerness brought a flush to her smooth olive skin and a bulging brightness to her licorice eyes.

"You said you were pleased at the way I worked. It was my first homicide and you told me my assistance was invaluable. I questioned the dead man's relatives, his cleaning woman and neighbors. You praised my reports. You said they were brilliant."

Shomron could not recall being quite so fulsome, but her youthful vehemence touched him. He was also suddenly curious. The difference in their ages was ten, perhaps twelve, years. She represented a generation for whom the events of the Holocaust were a dwindling perspective, atrocities of the distant past, the stuff of history books. Their experience of violence began with the tanks of the Six Day War rumbling by their schoolrooms. Each generation confronts its own terrors. What had the spectre of the Benamir case meant to her? Did she find it shocking—even frightening?

Sergeant Kogan gave the matter earnest consideration. And missed the point. "I suppose it always is when somebody's killed," she declared judiciously. "But one gets used to it. After all, I went through the war in Lebanon. Nothing's more horrible than seeing bits of people shovelled into plastic bags like butcher's leavings."

Shomron, who'd also seen it in other wars, winced. Briefly, his mind churned up a chaos of images, hallucinatory glimpses of disaster, memories of grief, anger and shame that time would never expunge. New holocausts, the recurring rhetoric of patriotism, hatred and revenge: the need to sift one's conscience made more urgent than ever.

"I was referring," he said with an effort, "to Sinclair's claim that his victim was an SS officer."

"Oh, I didn't believe a word of it. What a ridiculous idea! A Nazi hiding in Israel."

"Would it upset you if it was true?"

Her eyes dilated in astonishment. "Surely you don't think so?"

"It does seem the height of improbability," he conceded, the migraine of anxiety throbbing unrelieved. Day after day, exhaustingly, he'd gone over the same ground. Often he awoke with the bruised feeling that competing voices had quarrelled throughout his dreams. "Listen, Zina," he drove on, questioning himself as much as her, "imagine a scenario like this. A war criminal is on the run, not a specially important Nazi, one of thousands. He asks himself: 'Where is the last place they will think of searching for me? A DP camp.' He strips a dead Jew of his concentration camp rags, has a number tattooed on his arm, mingles with the survivors. They come from all over Europe, they speak different languages, no one gives him a second glance. In the camp he meets a Jewish girl and falls in love. They marry. Now the Mossad has begun to organize illegal emigration to Palestine. No doubt he would prefer to remain in

Europe but his wife recoils from it. For her the place has become a graveyard—"

"But Mrs. Benamir said she came to Palestine because her husband insisted on it," Zina Kogan pointed out.

The interruption grated: he stared at her as though she were a recalcitrant witness. "It's nearly forty years. How reliable can her memory be?"

"She would never forget something like that," she firmly insisted. "You're suggesting he came to Israel because of his love for a Jewish woman." She considered the proposition with half-closed eyes, then emphatically shook her head. "I don't buy it. It would be too horrible to think of a Jewish woman loving a Nazi murderer, having his children. The idea makes me feel sick!"

The shudder in her voice stripped away the thin membrane of rationality. Shomron's grandmother had a tale of a dybbuk who came in the guise of a student to a Russian Jewish village and violated an innocent maiden in her sleep. The seed of evil germinated and produced a boy child, outwardly perfect except for a cloven left foot like the hoof of a beast. He hid this deformity by wearing high boots of the finest leather and grew handsome, tall and strong, his hair black as night, an unearthly glow in the golden iris of his eyes. And he brought upon the village a ruinous plague of drunkenness, debauchery and violence. Primitive superstitions of whorish couplings between humans and creatures of demonology paled beside Zina Kogan's image or moral miscegenation, her instinctive revulsion. If she could feel like that, it boded ill for those with starker, more immediate memories.

"Okay, Zina," he said in tired dismissal, rising to escort her to the door. "I'll do what I can about your transfer. I have to sort out a few problems first, but don't fret about it. You'll win. You've got what it takes. Nothing can stop you." Walking back to the desk, preoccupied, he wished he could say the same about himself.

Strange hieroglyphs had appeared on his writing pad, faces in obverse, symbols of the enigma of identity. Was one a summary of one's behavior? Is a man defined by the roles he plays—and, if so, can he change himself by adopting a different role? Shomron had read somewhere that no man can ever be entirely what he is: he creates himself out of his imagination. Then can he not recreate himself? But like handwriting individual traits of personality are inextinguishable, no matter how one tries to disguise them: as unique as fingerprints. How useful it would have been if he had fingerprint samples of both the ambiguous Avram Benamir and SS Oberleutnant Kampfmann. A single glance would settle uncertainty once and for all.

The intercom buzzed. Absently, he pressed down the switch. "Yes?"

"There's someone here who says he wants to see you," announced the receptionist.

"Who is it and what's his business?"

"He won't say. He won't tell me anything except that he's here on a personal matter. There's a woman, too. His wife, I think."

Cranks arrived unannounced, public nuisances complaining of infringements of their citizen's rights—persecution by neighbors, too much noise in adjoining apartments, vandalism, unjust parking tickets. On the other hand, one could never tell: valuable information came in unexpected guises.

"Ask them to wait, I'll come out and look them over," he said, lighting up yet another cigarette and continuing to review different methods of establishing identity—blood group, dental records, hair, scar formations, voice prints, innate mannerisms. How often had it been tried: a new name, a new persona. But the body was intransigent. He thought of the tell-tale scar under Avram Benamir's armpit in the exact spot of an SS blood group tattoo. A baffling coincidence that settled nothing. Sighing with frustration, he went into the outer office.

The visitors sat patiently waiting—a diffident man about thirty-five with thinning dark hair and deep-set fugitive eyes and a plain, heavy-bosomed woman of the same age. The man rose to confront him and Shomron experienced a sensation close to fear. No wonder he refused to give his name. He could not afford to be noticed. His dress, his movements, his guarded expression, strove for anonymity. Yet there was something naked and defenseless in the lean, ascetic face, a transparency of feeling as though the nerves ran too close to the skin. And the man was suffering.

It was Yuval Benamir.

"See that we're not disturbed," Shomron told his secretary. He motioned them into the room and closed the door. The next half hour was not going to be pleasant. With exaggerated politeness he arranged two chairs in front of the desk, invited them to be seated and retreated to his own chair. The sun streamed through the window behind him, leaving his face in shadow. He preferred it that way.

"Did you come without your bodyguard?" he asked, breaking a difficult silence.

Yuval sketched a smile. "They're downstairs in the car. I persuaded them it was safe to leave me in police custody." The fleeting humor faded. Nervously clasping his hands, he said: "We've come straight from my mother's house. She's still in a severe state of shock. This tragedy has brought back bitter memories."

"Yes, indeed," Shomron murmured. "It's most unfortunate." The scientist's wife was looking at him strangely. "Do I know you?" she enquired in a tone of suspicion.

He shook his head. "I don't think so."

Mrs. Benamir continued to stare. At last it came to her. "Kibbutz Telem, 1963. You were one of a volunteer group helping with the harvest. So was I."

The summer of his eighteenth year, faded snapshots in the album of lost time. His life had been going awry, squandered in days of sullen idleness, aching in the dark of cinemas in a swelter of unsatisfied lust, dreaming vengefully of his own heroic death. Kibbutz Telem was an armed youth settlement on the Jordanian border. Six weeks vacation there filled with work and sex and song had infused him with the oxygen of optimism.

"I was in charge of the orchards," said Mrs. Benamir. "Yael Fishman."

The name meant nothing to him.

"You were going to join the paratroops. You wanted to do something dangerous. Our group leader told you off for being reckless."

"I must have been boasting," he shrugged, nostalgic for the vanished bravado of inexperience. He remembered her now, a broad-hipped, forthright girl with strong arms and bare tanned thighs who smelled of clean sweat and ripe apples. Other faces came crowding in, recalling the joys of youthful comradeship. The kinship troubled him. It made him feel he owed her protection he was not in a position to give. They'd been like one big family, buoyant and idealistic, children of the lost Zionist dream. How long ago it all was.

And how macabre the irony if Yael Fishman, daughter of Zion, had indeed become the mother of a Nazi officer's grandchildren . . .

Yuval Benamir remained withdrawn during this brief exchange, his eyes fixed in brooding concentration. Not until they became silent did he

403

speak. "Please tell me what you've found out about my father," he said, coming straight to the point.

Although prepared for it, the directness of the question threw Shomron into disarray. The allegations against Avram Benamir were quite literally unspeakable. When he had first encountered the scientist on the latter's arrival at the airport from America, he'd had in mind the possibility that the dead Benamir may have performed the ugly function of a kapo, a Jewish camp policeman. It was an appalling thing to have to tell a man stunned by grief and he'd refrained from doing so. How then could he break the news to an Israeli born and bred that he may have been fathered by a German concentration camp officer who'd been engaged in the slaughter of Jews?

"There's really nothing I can say that you don't already know," he lied. "Besides," he added hastily, "I'm no longer working on the case. Colonel Lester of the Massad has taken over."

Yuval plucked nervously at the loose skin of his cheek. "David is my friend. He refuses to do more than hint at unpleasant rumors." His voice rose. "Why the secrecy? It's as though something shameful is being kept from me. Is it?"

"I'm sure when Colonel Lester has something definite to tell you he'll do so."

"You're the one who's been digging into my father-in-law's past," intervened Mrs. Benamir angrily. "My husband can't understand why. It's torture for him."

404

"Shush, Yael! Let me speak," said Yuval, controlling his own agitation. "As I understand it, Captain Shomron, the murder was committed by a man who says my father did him an injury in Dachau. Well, perhaps. We have no right to judge. Things happened in concentration camps which don't bear thinking about. A survivor's behavior should not be scrutinized through a moral magnifying glass. Not even that of my father's killer. For a real or imaginary grievance to fester for nearly forty years, the man must be mentally deranged. But I want to know what he believes was done to him, however unpleasant it may be."

"I've no authority to discuss it," Shomron obstinately replied.

"In regard to the victim's family, I think you have." The scientist spoke with quiet insistence. He turned to his wife. "Yael, please wait outside."

She looked at him in dismay. "But, why?"

"I have a feeling that Captain Shomron finds it difficult to talk in your presence."

"Anything that concerns you also concerns me. I want to hear it," she protested.

"You will, later," he said.

Mrs. Benamir bit her lip and stared at him in indecision. "This is ruining our lives," she said in a low voice. "Even the children are affected."

He nodded, struggling for composure. "I know."

Watching this subdued domestic drama of grief and trepidation, Shomron experienced a sour gush of shame at having in any way contributed to their misery. It came to him that however one looked at

405

it Yuval, Yael and all their family belonged with the victims of the vast explosion of evil which had released deadly clouds of hatred over the lives of succeeding generations. For Jews it created a mutation in their humane history; a nation that once took pride in being the People of the Book sprouting iron teeth and claws. It brought plague to the Middle East, scattering the Arabs of Palestine like the Jews of ancient times. Death rained upon their innocent and helpless refugees as Israeli pilots swept through the skies destroying PLO strongholds planted in the midst of their hovels. "Never again" became overkill, yet another episode in the age of Auschwitz. Sinclair, dreaming of retribution, also brought catastrophe upon the innocents.

Yuval returned from escorting his wife to the door. "I asked her to leave so that we can both speak freely," he said. "I'll begin by saying that if you've learned anything about my father's past then I am more anxious than anyone to hear it."

"Did he tell you nothing about his early life?"

"Nothing. He behaved like a man suffering from willful amnesia. All I know is that he was the only survivor of his family. There are Holocaust survivors who have an obsessive need to remember, others wish to blot out all memory of it. He was one of those. If he referred to it at all he did so in apocalyptic terms."

"How do you mean?"

"Oh, as a kind of holy martrydom. The Holocaust was the sacrifice, the Crucifixion of the

Jewish people, Israel is the Redemption. We used to quarrel about it sometimes. I'd get angry and he'd quote Isaiah at me—my father knew the Bible almost word for word." Yuval gave an agonized laugh. "You'd be surprised how many signs he found that the Kingdom of God was just around the corner of the year. When we took Jerusalem in the Six Day War, I think he expected to see the Messiah descend by parachute. It was a tremendous consolation for him that my brother, Itzhak, was killed fighting for the city."

Shomron listened with strained concentration, his pen absently doodling on the pad at his elbow. The blasphemous notion that six million were horribly slaughtered as part of a divine plan drove the blood from his heart. Israel could never redeem that loss. Glancing down, he saw the outline of a figure on a cross. Over it spelled out in Hebrew letters was Elohim, the Name of God, written backwards. With slight variation the letters now read: "He Who Is Not." An occult evil hovered on the edge of his consciousness. SS Oberleutnant Kampfmann rose from the spectral gloom of Experimental Medical Block 7 to confront the Polish orderly. *"Did Christ vomit on the road to Golgotha?"*

Covering the sheet with his hand, he said: "I really meant it when I told you I've found out nothing you don't already know. The barest of facts. Your father came to Palestine as a Displaced Person, served in the War of Independence, started a business, raised a family. One morning he got

407

into his car to drive to work and a man shot him dead. Naturally, we assume there must be something that links them in the past, but we haven't established what it is and we may be wrong."

"And the killer has given you no explanation?"

"We're dealing with a strange and morbid personality," said Shomron, deliberately ambiguous. The description could equally be applied to both the victim and his executioner. "Highly articulate yet very secretive, he exists in a twilight world and thinks of himself as dead. In a sense he is. Your father's life begins at the age of thirty: his effectively ends in boyhood, at fifteen, buried among the corpses whose ashes fertilize the countryside of a small German town. When he looks in a mirror the face that stares back at him is the ghost of his father."

"I'm not interested in a report on his mental condition," Yuval interrupted with brusque impatience. "What did he tell you?"

"That Avram Benamir was not who he pretended to be."

"In what way?"

"He claims he wasn't a Jew."

Yuval's eyes widened in shocked disbelief. For a moment he was too overcome to speak, then with a gasp of ironical laughter, he said: "I've heard of people who feel strongly about who is or isn't a Jew. It's a subject of debate in the Knesset. But there must have been a more compelling reason why the man felt justified in taking my father's life. I'm here to find out what it is and I don't intend to leave until I do."

408

Shomron shifted his chair further into the shadow, groping for some evasive formula. He could plead sub-judice, but it would be useless. They had reached the point of naked confrontation; there was no possible justification for turning back. The throb of traffic vibrated against the window panes, a distant ambulance wailed. Heat filled the room like the moist and foetid breath of an invisible predator.

"Your refusal to speak frightens me," Yuval said tightly. Sweat glistened on his drawn face. "It's as though there's a bomb under my feet ticking towards the moment of detonation. It can only be defused if I understand the mechanism. The worst thing is indecision." He stared haggardly. "I know my father was in a concentration camp. The killer says they were together in Dachau. He denies that my father was a Jew. What nationality did he have then? French, Polish, Russian?"

"None of those."

"Were they fellow prisoners?"

Almost imperceptibly, Shomron shook his head.

"Is my father accused of being a German?" Yuval asked in a low tense voice. "I insist on a direct reply."

It came in a single syllable.

"Yes."

The scientist flinched but held himself rigidly under control. He had located the detonator. Now, desperately mastering his fear, he concentrated on the next move.

"What," he enquired carefully, "is he supposed to have been doing in the camp?"

Invaded by dread, experiencing an unnerving distortion of reality, Shomron had the brief illusion that he was struggling to wake from a suffocating dream. Even his voice sounded disembodied.

"There was an SS officer named Kampfmann," it said. "According to the records, he was killed when the Americans liberated Dachau. An eyewitness reports that he assumed the identity of a Jewish prisoner, Bindermann. That's all I know."

Yuval sat with clenched eyelids. He covered his face with his hands and remained motionless. When he withdrew them, it was as though every drop of blood had drained from him.

Shomron took out the hip flask he kept for emergencies, methodically unscrewed the cap and filled it to the brim.

"Here, drink this," he said, forcing a tone of briskness. The scientist neither saw nor heard. His eyes were those of a stunned animal. "Come on, it'll do you good," Shomron urged, holding the metal cap to his dry lips. With hypnotic obedience, Yuval swallowed the brandy. It caught in his throat and made him splutter. Tears streamed from his eyes and the pain of consciousness returned.

Shomron said: "Shall I call your wife?"

"For God's sake, no! Please!" The afflicted man stared wildly at him. "It isn't true! You can't possibly believe it!"

"There's absolutely no proof," said Shomron.

Yuval gulped back his tears. "Have you got a cigarette?" he asked shakily.

410

Shomron broke open a pack of Sheraton and placed one between the other's lips as tenderly as if consoling a wounded soldier. Yuval puffed inexpertly, holding the cigarette between thumb and forefinger like a boy experimenting with his first smoke. A strange brief calm overcame him, the false tranquillity that appears when the mind is numbed by shock.

Almost inaudibly, he said: "The killing of my father is a wicked injustice. He was given no chance to answer this accusation. How can a dead man prove his innocence? Israel has a law for the punishment of Nazis and their collaborators. If the assassin had denounced him, he could at least have defended himself in court."

In a gesture of fellowship, Shomron brought a chair close to him and sat astride it, crossing the bureaucratic barrier represented by the desk. Talk is therapy. He had an instinctive feeling that it was necessary to show that they were on the same side.

"He didn't trust us to prosecute. He was afraid the case would be hushed up. But there's more to it than that. Earlier you said he must have had a more compelling reason for his action. You're right. There are occasions when a defendant in a court of law turns the tables on his judges and becomes the prosecutor. In Berlin after the burning of the Reichstag in February 1933 the Bulgarian communist Dimitrov used the prisoner's dock as a platform from which to denounce the Nazis. Blacks have done it in the civil rights struggle in America. Acts of terror often have the same

411

motive. Sinclair killed your father in order to put Israel on trial."

Yuval was too engrossed in his own misery to recognize the implications. Cigarette ash dribbled down the front of his shirt. He brushed it absently and said in a broken voice: "If this . . . slur is allowed to remain . . . I can see nothing but . . . utter ruin for my family. How can my children..." He paused to control a spasm of grief. "This Kampfmann, the Nazi you referred to," he resumed, speaking the name with loathing, "what do you know of his background?"

"Nothing at all."

Yuval stared incredulously. "But it's vital! You should have found out everything about him—where he was born, when, if he was married, who his relatives were, every available detail. Don't you see," he exclaimed agonizingly, "there could be something about the man that makes this allegation impossible. My father was sixty-five, the other may have been ten, fifteen years older, shorter or taller, entirely different physically. You may even be able to find him. The man may still be alive.

On the other hand, Shomron reflected, if they were the same person, it would be like fitting together the two halves of a torn photograph.

"The investigation is still not complete," he offered. "It's only two-and-a-half weeks since the homicide occurred."

"Eighteen days," Yuval corrected with bitter accuracy. "And every minute of it is unbearable.

You owe it to us to bring this torment to an end as quickly as possible."

"Yes, indeed," agreed Shomron. Guilt throbbed in him like a diseased nerve. He owed it to them to act with surgical swiftness, but deep in his heart he feared the operation could prove fatal.

That evening he said to Deborah: "Tomorrow morning I have an appointment with Gillon Romm. I won't be there."

She looked concerned. "Why not?"

"I'm about to have forty-eight hours' diplomatic illness."

"Is it as serious as that?"

"I'll let you know when I get back."

Deborah threw up her hands in exasperation. "Good heavens, Amos! You've only just come home. You're not going away again?"

"Got to, love. The only cure for this exists abroad," he said, going into the bedroom to pack an overnight case. She followed him. "What shall I tell Gillon you're suffering from—severe inflammation of the conscience?"

15

"WELCOME to Berlin," said the fresh-faced young man at Passport Control in English, glancing at the Hebrew lettering of his Israeli passport. The military stiffness of the old-fashioned stereotype was absent; pale gold hair curled over the back of his collar like the locks of a German World Cup footballer and a disarming candor shone in his bright cerulean eyes. "How do you say it? *Shalom, L'hitraot,*" he added, grinning, handing the document back duly stamped.

"Danke. Auf Wiedersehen," Shomron reciprocated. It was a good beginning. He hurried through customs having nothing to declare but haste. Due to a delay in changing planes at Frankfurt he was running over fifty minutes late. The tight sched-

ule he'd set required that he go straight to the Berlin Documentation Center from the airport, consult the available records, stay overnight and leave by the 7:30 a.m. plane the following morning.

"How long will it take to get to Zehlendorf?" he asked the taxi-driver. "Can I make it before six?"

"Not possible," the man shrugged.

"Couldn't you try? It's very important."

The driver shrugged again. Shomron bit his lip in vexed indecision. It meant the loss of a day. The very vagueness of his quest induced a panicky sense of urgency. To come so far, to risk so much so recklessly . . . And what should he do with the unwanted time on his hands?

"Take me to the synagogue," he said on impulse.

A momentary wariness entered the taxi-driver's eyes. *"Gewiss,"* he said. He was old enough to remember.

The late afternoon was overcast, with a northern nip in the air that made Shomron shiver after the sultry summer heat of Tel Aviv. This was his first visit to Berlin. Gazing out of the taxi as it maneuvered into the sleek stream of city-bound traffic, he wondered if the flavor of the past would set his teeth on edge. To arrive in a strange city was to feel poised on the brink of adventure. It had something of the stimulation of aloof and unfamiliar women cloaked in the mystery of taboo. But Berlin was different. A friend had once described his sojourn there as an exhilarating yet frightening experience, like being under fire. Terse messages crackled over the taxi's short-wave radio like command orders to an embattled tank. The driver switched to music. Simon and Garfunkel sang *Bridge Over Troubled Waters* and the hallucination vanished, replaced by an unwinding panorama of suburban dwellings, shopping arcades, a children's playground, glimpses of flowered gardens and distant fields of green. Then the affluent streets of the new city closed in, congested with traffic, crowded buses, people hurrying into subway stations and jostling along pavements, as in the homeward rush-hour of any European metropolis.

The effect was one of unreality, a suspension of belief. Jews who came here saw people turn into stormtroopers before their eyes. The sound of the language brought a shudder of revulsion. They could forgive the young but shrank from contact with older Germans as though their hands still reeked of Jewish corpses. It wasn't happening to Shomron. Turning into the *Kurfürstendamm* at the tall phallic cathedral erected near the ruined *Gedächtniskirche,* dazzled by a Broadway glitter of flaunting electric signs, a fairground noise of carousel, the Berlin of swastikas could have been an invention of a bad movie. In a collective determination to expunge the memory of its shame, Germany had rebuilt itself as though the past had never existed, an amnesia of soaring modern buildings, commercial gloss, the material comforts of enterprise and prosperity. It had found a merit in being rich.

The taxi drew up outside the great *Fasanenstrasse* synagogue. He got out slowly, paid off the driver, and stared up at the imposing facade before entering. Here, at least, history rustled in the shadows. The original building had been destroyed in the orgiastic pogroms of 1938 that followed the assassination of a German diplomat in Paris by a seventeen-year-old Jewish youth. There were those who thought it should have been left in ruins like the neighboring *Gedächtniskirche*; instead Restitution funds had restored it anew—the Ark of the Holy Scroll, the rabbi's podium, the great chandeliers and handsome benches, the women's gallery—grandeur and emptiness: nothing could bring back the vanished congregation.

As he sat in sombre meditation, his bare head covered by a folded handkerchief, he became aware of heavy breathing. *"Guten Abend, mein Herr,"* said an asthmatic voice in a tone that meant: "Who are you, and what are you doing here?" It came from a large perspiring face surmounted by a black homburg. Small eyes cushioned in fat subjected him to a melancholy scrutiny that had learned not to expect too much of human nature.

"I'm staying in Berlin overnight. I would like to join you for the evening service," said Shomron.

The man gave a ponderous nod and handed him

420

a black skullcap. "We are honored, but it is too early. The service will not be for another hour. Where are you from, friend?"

"Israel."

"Ah, Israel!" The tone was perceptively warmer. My name is Wolfenstein, Secretary of the synagogue. May I offer you a coffee in my office?"

"You're very kind."

Herr Wolfenstein waved the formal compliment away. Weighed down by age and obesity, he plodded ahead of Shomron, leading him through a door, along a corridor, past a lecture hall into a suite of administrative offices, deserted except for a well-groomed, handsome woman of about sixty who turned her aquiline profile to stare with undisguised interest at the Secretary's visitor.

"Frau Doktor Fischer, this is a young man from Israel," said Herr Wolfenstein.

Shomron pressed the thin, heavily-ringed hand the lady extended. "Shomron," he said.

"What brings you to Berlin?"

"I'm just passing through."

She smiled with withered lips and inclined her head regally. "Many Israelis," she said, "have come here to live. They feel quite at home." A gleam of malice shone in her large amber eyes but he chose to ignore the provocation, sensing the self-justifying neurosis behind it.

"Helena, would you be so kind as to bring us some coffee?" Herr Wolfenstein intervened, having difficulty with his breathing.

"With pleasure," she answered, still gazing at Shomron. "It's a pity you cannot stay for a while. You would find it interesting."

"Frau Doktor Fischer is the widow of a magistrate," Herr Wolfenstein said when he had settled Shomron into a comfortable chair in his own room. "She has lived in Israel for a while, but she had difficulties. The climate and the language . . . Everyone has his own reasons . . ." He gestured helplessly and his voice trailed into silence.

They went on to fill the conversational gap with generalities until Helena Fischer brought in two cups of instant coffee, a plate of almond rings and a gadfly determination to draw social blood.

"If you are looking for ways to amuse yourself this evening, let me know what your tastes are and I'll be happy to advise," she offered. "Berlin is a wickedly amusing city if you know where to go. Who knows, you might not be in a hurry to leave when you see what is available."

Shomron received the impression of a truncated life. The woman had once been beautiful. She had enjoyed admiration, status and prosperity in a society that prided itself on its refinement, culture and durability. Then, brutally, everything came to an end. Her roots were torn and it had left her lonely and embittered—Frau Doktor Fischer, eking out the pension of a magistrate's widow with secretarial work at the synagogue.

"I'm grateful for the offer," he said. "Unfortunately, I have to make an early start in the morning. I'll have to come back some other time."

She bowed ironically. "In that case I shall say goodnight, gentlemen."

"Goodnight, Helena," said Herr Wolfenstein to her stiff retreating back, sighing. He stroked his vast stomach as if in pain, then cheered up. "I'm going to defy my doctor and smoke a cigar. Would you care for one?"

"I prefer cigarettes," said Shomron, lighting one. "My doctor also forbids it."

Laughter rattled in the old man's throat. "I died even before you were born, I tell him. For him a figure of speech but, allowing for a slight exaggeration, it's true. Would you care to hear the story?"

"Very much."

Herr Wolfenstein clipped his cigar, ignited it lovingly, and tipped his homburg to the back of his head. He was about to enjoy himself.

"In October 1934 I shared a small flat in the suburb of Friedenau with Amsler, a painter. We lived together because of poverty. I was twenty-seven and had been dismissed from the advertising department of the *Berliner Zeitung am Mittag* because Jews were not allowed to work in the newspaper. I earned a little by selling books from my collection of first editions, also rare stamps. The night of Yom Kippur, Amsler didn't come home. For a long time I couldn't sleep, worrying. Then I dozed. Just before dawn there was a terrible banging on the door and I thought it's him, he's drunk. It sometimes happened. Three ugly, big Brownshirts burst into the apartment led by a dapper little fellow, something like Goebbels, wearing a black leather coat and a wide-brimmed hat pulled down over his eyes. 'Is this the Jew-sty of the Communist pig Amsler?' he asked. He said it in a soft voice, very politely. 'Amsler is not a Communist,' I told him. The SA men turned the place upside down. They shouted at me to tell them where the guns were hidden. I was very frightened. The little fellow started to look through my books. He picked one up between his fingertips as if it was filth and my heart stopped. I should never have kept it. It was the 1867 edition of *Das Kapital* autographed by Karl Marx himself with an inscription that read "To my dear friend and collaborator, Friedrich Engels." To make things worse, I also had a copy of the Paris edition of *The Protocols of the Elders of Zion*. He said, 'Quite a library of Bolshevism, Wolfenstein,' When I tried to explain, he became angry and shouted, 'I'm not stupid, Jew. I can recognize Russian when I see it. Get dressed, I'm taking you in.' Aie! Aie! Aie! The absurdity of it almost made me laugh.''

Herr Wolfenstein swallowed a mouthful of cigar smoke and fell into an alarming fit of wheezing and spluttering. The veins in his short neck swelled and tears ran from his bloodshot eyes.

"The doctor is right," he panted, tearing a tissue out of a box on his desk and mopping his face. He crushed the cigar into an ashtray. "He also warns me to avoid excitement. An asthmatic attack can be brought on by the sight of a beautiful woman. But even when I was young, I never smoked and made love at the same time."

424

The old man's recourse to humor was a relief. "Perhaps it's not good for you to dwell on such unpleasant memories," Shomron suggested.

"When you have lived to my age, young man, life becomes just a series of anecdotes. The pain goes, the reality goes. Sometimes you feel you have invented yourself. Besides, it gives me satisfaction to sit here in Berlin drinking a cup of coffee and talking about my experience of death when Hitler has long vanished from the face of the earth. That day in 1934 when I was pushed violently trembling onto the floor of a black limousine I could not have dreamt to be so lucky. The SA men rested their feet on me, one had a boot in my face. To be frank, I'm a terrible coward. I was already half dead of fright at the thought of being tortured. We drove very fast, the klaxon screaming, and stopped in Bülow Platz outside the old Communist Party headquarters which they had renamed the Horst Wessel Building. The Brownshirts shoved me into a small courtyard through an iron door, snarling, 'Get a move on, shit-face.' They took me up a twisting staircase. I caught a glimpse of a neat secretary with blonde plaits walking along a carpeted corridor carrying a box-file, such a wholesome-looking, fresh-faced girl, and somehow I was reassured. Except that I was a Jew, what did they have against me? Now it seems stupid, but at the time many of us believed things would get better. Exercising the responsibilities of government, the National Socialists would control their hooligans and become more civilized. I was taken into a room where ten or twelve men sat on a long wooden bench guarded by a youth of about eighteen in uniform. There I saw my friend Amsler. They'd given him a real pasting. His lips were split and swollen, there was a large bruise under one eye and his nose looked broken. Amsler was hot-tempered and I guessed he'd put up a fight. All we could do was stare at each other: no one was allowed to speak. For hours and hours nothing happened. The guard was changed twice. They refused us permission to relieve ourselves, so you can imagine the agony. At last, one by one, we were called out of the room. When Amsler went, he winked at me with his bruised eye. I never saw him again."

Sighing noisily, Herr Wolfenstein dipped an almond ring in his lukewarm coffee and masticated it with absorbed concentration. A damp crumb clung to the corner of his mouth and moisture oozed from between his puffy eyelids.

"Amsler left a painting on the easel the day he disappeared, a green and yellow picture of a man looking at himself in a mirror. There was no reflection. He hadn't decided what the glass would show. When I think of that unfinished picture it becomes for me a symbol of all that was lost in those unfinished lives ... Ach! You must be tired of such reminiscences. Living in the past is a disease of the old."

"I'd like to hear the rest of the story," Shomron said.

Herr Wolfenstein consulted an old-fashioned pocket watch. "Very well, we still have time," he said, his voice turning somnolent like a subject under hypnosis. "I was brought into a room. My little Goebbels sat next to a tall, thin officer who wore an Iron Cross attached to the collar of his tunic. 'Give me the names of all your Jew Bolshevik accomplices,' he said. Every time he asked a question he smiled: his teeth were very white. I had trouble holding my bladder in. All I could think of was that I mustn't disgrace myself by wetting my pants. 'Please let me go to the toilet, I'm not a Communist,' I begged. The officer went on smiling and asking the same questions. Eventually he wrote something on a piece of paper and called the guard. 'You want us to do it now, chief?' the man asked, glancing at the paper. 'First of all let him pray for his sins. It's the yid holy day Yom Kippur,' the officer answered, flashing his white teeth. I didn't understand. What sins, what prayers, what were they going to do? The guard took out a pistol and said: 'Put your hands up and walk.' I stumbled down the stairs. When we passed the guard room, my escort glanced in and beckoned to some SA men playing cards. 'We got to do a quick job on this yid,' he told them. They threw down the cards, grumbling, and got up noisily." Reliving this episode, the old man began to breathe in gasps, his throat guttural. "They pushed me into the yard. I couldn't believe it was happening. They were going to kill me. The men drew their guns and started to put the cartridges in. *'Warum? Warum?'* I shouted and began to cry. 'All right,

427

Jew, get praying,' growled the guard. Urine poured down my legs: I could hear myself sobbing. Looking back, I cannot remember if I heard the guns explode but I was pierced in heart and brain by the pure terror of the instant of death . . . The next thing I knew I was lying in my own excrement on a stone floor. There were others there, vague shapes huddled in darkness. I felt an enormous apathy. Was I really dead? How is one to know, perhaps it is like that? Even today I sometimes wonder. People, places, things: do they really exist? At such moments I share the pessimism of Schopenhauer." Herr Wolfenstein gave a dry laugh. "Have you read our great German philosopher?"

"No," said Shomron, although he was inclined to accept that Herr Wolfenstein's skepticism about his existence was justified. At least in terms of futility. "What happened to you afterwards?"

"I spent a few weeks in a concentration camp, then I was permitted to emigrate. In those days it was possible. For twelve years I stayed in Zurich working as a book salesman."

"After such experiences, why did you come back to Germany?"

The answer was slow in coming. Herr Wolfenstein raised his eyes to the ceiling and sighed. He retracted his short neck and sighed again. He held out his palms, then folded his hands over his swollen belly. At last, gazing sadly into Shomron's eyes, he translated these dumb gestures of bewilderment into words and said:

"Many times I've been asked the same question

428

—I ask it myself—and I don't have a satisfactory explanation. During the war we used to say the history of Jews in Europe is coming to an end. The continent is our graveyard: our blood watered the seeds of a new exodus. I'm a Jew of the diaspora. Over the centuries my family moved slowly west from Poland. About two hundred years ago they were timber merchants in Danzig. Another century brought us here to Berlin. There are second and third cousins who were born into the Prussian aristocracy. For me, the Nazis were interlopers: I belong here." A ruminative expression entered the old man's face and he smiled crookedly. "I once saw a TV programme about wild-life in New York, nothing to do with drugs and debauchery. It showed how untamed animals adapt themselves to life in the big city. What I most remember is the sparrows who have learned to live in the cracks between skyscrapers. They nest there, raise their young, fly up and down the narrow spaces like people travelling in escalators. When the buildings are torn down they nest in the cracks of other Manhattan skyscrapers. It's the only way they know how to live."

Shomron shook his head. "The analogy doesn't fit," he argued. "They are living with their own kind, not among their murderers. There are no Nazi sparrows."

"My dear young man," Herr Wolfenstein said wryly, "it may shock you to hear this, but the Nazis are not birds of a different feather. They have existed everywhere, in all times, and they are like us. This is what is appalling."

429

"I can't accept that," Shomron harshly retorted.

The old man shrugged. "Nor can I. The notion is intolerable. Well," he said, lumbering to his feet, "I think it is now time for us to go and pray."

A group of about twenty men shrouded in prayer shawls were gathered in the synagogue. Swaying rhythmically, the black-robed rabbi intoned the immemorial liturgy and a subdued murmur echoing with melancholy drifted over the empty pews. *Blessed art thou, O Lord our God, King of the universe, who maketh twilight merge into evening . . .*

Shomron struggled against a bleak sense of desolation. His voice with its resonant Israeli accent sounded different from the others, for he alone of the congregation was speaking his mother tongue, a language roughened by the friction of bustling streets and crowded buses, of farmers yelling above the noise of tractors and children chanting rhyming games, the tense, laconic language of soldiers responding to battle orders. As the service proceeded, his initial despondency was replaced by a mood of sombre dedication. *Thou shalt not fear the terror by night, nor the arrow that flies by day, Neither the pestilence that walks in the darkness, nor the destruction that ravages at noon. A thousand may fall by thy side, even ten thousand at thy right, but it shall not come near to thee, Indeed, with thine eyes shall thou behold and see the retribution of the wicked . . .* So they continued through to the great prayer of Israel's faith, the *Shema*, reaf-

430

irming the Covenant in the fallen capital of the cruelest enemy the Jewish people had ever known. Poetic justice.

The evening pursuit of pleasure was at full tide when he took his leave of Herr Wolfenstein and the small group of worshippers and voyeuristically inspected the abundant choice of music, food, theater and other hedonist diversions. The syncopated drum-beat of approaching night stirred in his pulse. It intensified his solitude and sharpened his hunger: he thought inevitably, wolfishly, of women, staring at laughing girls, their breasts swinging free under thin summer blouses. The urgency of his lust dismayed and depressed him. It could only lead to joining other transient strangers in some garish bar, playing slot-machine games of electronic star wars to the noise of a juke box only to end up with some joyless pick-up or depart into the night lonelier than ever.

Having conjured up this bleak prospect, he denied himself a decent meal and instead ate a hamburger charred from the sizzling stove of an American-style fast-food restaurant before setting out in search of a cheap hotel. Just as he was passing the corner of a street, something familiar about the name caused him to retrace his steps. *Bleibtreu Strasse.* For a moment he couldn't place it, then it came to him. The Black Notebooks. With quickening excitement, he left the dazzle of the *Kurfürstendamm* and hurried along the street peering closely into doorways. After traversing the length of one side and part way up the other, his attention was drawn to a large neglected building. A jumble of nameplates inside the recessed entrance advertised a chiropodist, a firm of literary agents, an artificial eye-maker (human), and the *Mitteleuropäisches Reisebureau* written in gothic script. And there in chipped, faded letters of gilt was the legend "Pension Eberth, Proprietor: Willibald Friedrich Eberth." It looked defunct—they all did—relics of a bygone time overlooked by the property developers, but he decided to explore further. A creaking lift brought him to the third floor, to a scuffed mahogany door with tarnished brass fittings. The bell gave out a disused ring as if breaking a century of silence. After an interval, shuffling feet approached. He had the uncanny feeling that he was about to step into a dream.

An elderly bent woman opened the door and stared up at him through a mass of wrinkles. The small hairy animal at her side suspiciously sniffed his shoes.

"Do you have a room for the night?" he enquired.

"Wie bitte?"

"A room. For one night," he repeated loudly.

She looked him over, her glance lingering on his week-end case, a Gucci extravagance bought for his birthday by Deborah, and came to a favorable conclusion. "A single room?"

"Yes."

"Jawohl."

With a vague sense of *déjà vu*, he followed her through the frugally lit hall into an overcrowded parlor, noting the clutter of heavy mahogany furniture, the framed picture of a whiskered, dewlapped German with a resemblance to old Marshal Hindenberg, rows of ancient family photos on a velvet-fringed mantelpiece, the brass fire-irons in an empty grate, the crucifix, bulky leather armchair and plush, green chaise-longue worn bare in patches. The room had a frowsty warmth, a hibernating coziness that had withstood the siege of history. It was here, Shomron reflected, that the young Franz Slonimsky reluctantly endured his first German handshake: from this apartment he set out on the patient, obsessive pursuit of his shadowy enemy, drawing loneliness around himself like a cloak of invisibility.

The woman opened a roll-top desk. She put on a pair of wire-framed spectacles to write his name and address in an old leather-bound guest book, forming the letters in fine copperplate. He sat and stared at the funereal assembly of dead relatives arrayed on the mantelpiece—stiffly brocaded women, men with Kaiser Wilhelm waxed moustaches, solemn over-dressed children who grew proud in uniform or inherited the solid dignity of Prussian womenkind. The world can be read in particularities of manner, expression and dress, and it seemed to him that frozen in these poses of rectitude was the doom that overtook an empire.

"Will you please sign," the woman said, handing him her pen. "For one night, the charge will be Deutschmarks forty-five including breakfast."

He paid in advance. The hairy little dog licked his hand with its rough tongue as if in gratitude, and all three went in procession to inspect the rented room. An odor of sweetish disinfectant clung to the antiquated brass bedstead as though to dispel the smell of a recent death, the washstand tap had left a yellow crust on the porcelain basin, the light from a ceiling fitting was crepuscular. It would do.

"Frau Eberth, before you go, may I ask you something?" Shomron said.

"Frau Mehring," she corrected him primly. "My maiden name was Eberth."

"Yes, of course. I wonder if you remember a guest who once stayed here. Franz Slonimsky?"

The wrinkles around her eyes deepened. "Slonimsky . . . When was the gentleman here?"

"A long time ago. 1949 or 1950."

"Ah, so long ago. My father would know. He remembered every single person. For him everyone was a friend. I have a box full on condolences from people, former guests. They read the announcement in the *Allgemeine Zeitung*."

"You once nursed him when he was ill," Shomron prompted. "He was very young, Jewish, a survivor of Dachau."

A flicker of recall entered Frau Mehring's troubled grey eyes, then the shutters came down, leaving them blank and expressionless.

"Those terrible days, we don't think of them any more," she muttered hurriedly. *"Entschuldigen Sie bitte,* I have to get on. Sleep well, *mein herr."*

But Shomron found it difficult to sleep at all. It was still quite early. Lying fully dressed on the bed, trying to read a copy of *Newsweek,* he caught a glimpse of his reflection in the wardrobe mirror. It stared back at him like a stranger. The growl of the city vibrated against the glass of the window. A radio played in a nearby room, bringing news of the violent world. He felt marooned, trapped in an intersection of time between past and future, a limbo of ghosts. Was this how Franz Slonimsky had felt, lying perhaps in this very same bed?

During the long insomniac night, listening to a distant clock chiming the slow passing of the hours, his mind conjured up visions of disaster—an accident to Deborah, the children held hostage by terrorists, cities in flames. His love for his family was an anguish of tenderness inextricably bound up with the hopes and fears he had for Israel. In his early youth he'd thought that nothing could go wrong, the marriage of land and people produced daily miracles. Before one's eyes, victims of persecution grew straight and tall and unafraid. There was joy in work, harvest festivals of song and dance. Then the wings of giant birds flew across the sun, casting swift black shadows. The nation went to war in self-defense and swiftly, brilliantly, with superb courage, overcame its enemies. Jews had shown that after their long and passive history of exile they had recovered the strength to shape their destiny with their own hands. But things were never to be the same.

Israel proved more proficient in the terrible skills of war than in the art of peace. Its strength was as the strength of ten and its soldiers guarded sullen captive populations. Too many obituaries, military funerals: the singing turned to mourning. The mood of many turned sour, their ideals crumbled, they worked as little as possible, for profit instead of joy.

Tormented by these thoughts, Shomron was unable to shake off a crippling feeling of personal responsibility, that somehow he had wandered from his destiny and become lost. He and his generation. Would they be able to find their way back?

He awaited the impending day with a sense of trepidation and foreboding.

"Yes, I expect we have his file. Our records are fairly complete," said the pleasant, grey-haired lady librarian glancing at the name written on the slip of paper. She added with a schoolmistressy hint of reproof: "It is usual to give advance notice so that the material can be got ready."

"I'll be glad to wait," said Shomron. He chose a vacant table near one of the tall windows. Outside, long shadows of trees cool on the smooth green lawn, a gardener tending rose bushes in the weak early morning sunshine. The atmosphere was that of a small university library. Several researchers were already busily engaged—scholars of atrocity, historians of genocide, fiction writers in search of authenticity. That's what it came to in the end, he thought with weary cynicism. Wars, revolutions, massacres, the sum total of human misery encapsulated in rows of volumes neatly catalogued and arranged on library shelves. And the darker thought: next time even the volumes might not be spared, nothing would remain but the embers of silence.

Irony abounded. The taxi-driver who brought him had recounted his hair-raising escape from the other side of the Wall and referred to the communist secret police as the Red Gestapo. Then, except for two smartly turned-out GIs guarding the fenced-in area, the U.S. Military Government's Berlin Documentation Center at Wassersteig I, Zehlendorf, could have been mistaken for a cluster of prosperous suburban villas. Instead it was the repository of captured National Socialist Party archives, detailed dossiers of Party members compiled with the meticulous administrative efficiency the Nazis had perverted to criminal ends. A strange paradox, Shomron reflected, that those who had murderously set fire to books as well as people had hesitated to put a match to their own incriminating records before they fell into the hands of their victorious enemies.

The librarian beckoned. She had not been gone long and he wondered briefly if his quest had been in vain; but then he saw the buff folder. He stood up and slowly crossed the quiet room. A small blue-enameled Star of David slipped from the V-neck of her dress as she bent forward to pass him the file.

"I think this is what you're looking for," she said, matter-of-factly, her slender, well-kept hand resting on the cover.

He glanced at the name-tag and an icy finger touched his spine. "Kampfmann, Ulrich Walther. Oberleutnant SS."

"Yes, it is," he said and signed the receipt slip.

Back at his table, he stared at the unopened dossier, prolonging the moment of suspense. Coming to Berlin had been an act of recklessness, a gamble. Gamblers were said to be driven by a craving to lose, not win. Burning with curiosity to turn up the next card, the thought that it might be a winning trick filled him with sick dread. He opened the thick folder as though handling something dangerous. Everything necessary for purposes of identification was there—fingerprints, blood group, dental chart, the passport photograph of a man in his twenties.

It had the starkness of a police mug-shot, the face startled by the white glare of a flash-bulb. Kampfmann gave an impression of immaturity. His eyes had the earnest sincerity of a young man showing eagerness to learn: the mouth hesitated between a smile and a grimace, as if the subject was uncertain of the look appropriate to the occasion. His hair was combed back flat from the narrow forehead and the collar of his uniform was too large for his thin neck. The total effect was one of bemusement. The young SS officer had the appearance of someone who did not quite know what to make of the world.

With intense absorption, Shomron began to read the curriculum vitae. The details were stated impersonally. Ulrich Walther Kampfmann was

438

born in the town of Oppeln, Upper Silesia, on September 4, 1917, only child of Captain Heinrich Kampfmann and Elfrida, née Mätsky, of mixed German and Polish Aryan origin. His father commanded an infantry company and was killed on August 5, 1918 during General Ludendorff's offensive at the second Battle of the Marne. His mother died in the great influenza epidemic that swept Europe after the war, leaving the orphaned infant to be raised by his maternal grandmother. When he was seven, she too died. Ulrich Walther was then taken into the guardianship of his maternal uncle, Fr. Arnold Mätsky, a Catholic priest and an officiant at the German Hospice of St. Giles Borromaes.

Shomron stared blankly out of the window at the play of sunlight and shadow in the garden, seeing only darkness. Papers rustled in the hushed room, a researcher scraped his chair, someone coughed: to these small disturbances he remained oblivious.

St. Giles German Hospice was in a street he knew well, Emek Refaim. The first link in the chain was revealed. Ulrich Walther Kampfmann had lived in the German Colony of Jerusalem.

A paragraph characterized by its brevity outlined the boy's upbringing in the Holy City. An average pupil, he received his education at a church school taught by priests and nuns, acquiring in addition to general subjects and theology a knowledge of Latin, some Greek and Hebrew. At the age of eighteen, persuaded by his uncle that he had a vocation for the priesthood, he entered the Jesuit college of St. Ignatius Loyola in Vienna. What had he felt, seen, done in the eleven intervening years? How had his development been affected living in a closed community separated by religion from the pullulating city where the faithful of Allah in crowded souks and mosques prayed towards Mecca, black-robed Orthodox Jews dreamed of their Messiah, and secular Zionists in the bustling new Jerusalem of bright lights, cafes and motor traffic maintained an embryo government, a city of lethargy, intrigue and sudden riot once described by a nervous observer as a bowl of scorpions? Not a word.

Nor did the curriculum vitae detail the novitiate's progress in ecclesiastical studies during the three years that preceded Hitler's triumphal entry into Vienna on March 14, 1938 and SS chief Himmler's Austrian purge of Jews, traitors and other enemies of the expanded Third Reich. Was he one of the ninety-nine per cent who voted by plebiscite for *"Ein Volk, Ein Reich, Ein Fuehrer"*? There was no mention of it. On July 19, four months after this expression of public rejoicing, the apprentice priest Ulrich Walther Kampfmann took the oath of loyalty to Adolf Hitler and was sworn in to membership of the SS.

Gaps in the narrative were filled in by the confidential report of a certain Otto Schlips, who held the rank of colonel in the SS investigative bureau. Because of special factors in UW Kampfmann's background that emerged during routine interrogation, his case had been referred to the colonel. The problem did not have to do with his breeding. Enquiries made into the Polish genealogy of Elfrida Mätsky ascertained that it derived from Polonized German stock and was therefore racially pure. As for his upbringing in Jerusalem, the German Colony had been founded by that curator of Teutonic warrior chivalry, the Order of Templars. Through no fault of his own, Kampfmann was deprived of the opportunity to take part in the National Socialist struggle to wrest Germany from the clutches of Jews and political degenerates. Family loyalty rather than conviction led him to enter the Catholic Church.

However, the colonel thought it proper to interrogate him in depth about his activities in Jerusalem. He discovered that UW Kampfmann had used the opportunity to make a close study of the habits, customs, religious practices and criminal psychology of the Jewish race. Adopting a Jew disguise and at great personal risk, he smuggled himself into synagogues to observe their secret rituals, infiltrated political meetings, eavesdropped on conspiratorial conversations in kosher restaurants. He read Hebrew and understood the jargon Yiddish. These qualifications, Schlips concluded, should be placed at the service of the Party. Kampfmann was invited to apply for membership in the SS. The young man pleaded unworthiness of the honor. The colonel assured him he would be given an opportunity to prove his mettle in the battle to eliminate "the eternal parasitic fungi of humanity—Jews," as the Fuehrer described them. Kampfmann was instructed to attend the crash course in National Socialism and racial anthropology at the University of Vienna. Schlips re-interviewed him after graduation and formed a favorable impression of his potentiality. He therefore recommended that the said Kampfmann, Ulrich Walther, be recruited into the SS and posted to Dept. 4T4 (Jewish Affairs Section) at the Reichsführing-SS, Berlin.

Now there were several links in the chain of circumstantial evidence. Shomron took a break to smoke a cigarette in the garden and think things over. The written texts lent themselves to reconstruction. A boy grows up in a cloistered Christian community within the city where Jesus lived and died and was resurrected. Many times he walks under the stone archways of the Via Dolorosa, retracing the nine Stations of the Cross. He relives the agony of Jesus as the nails are driven into His hands and feet. According to the testimony of the saintly eyewitnesses, Matthew, Mark and Luke, when Pontius Pilate asked the Jews, their chief priests and elders, should he release unto them the criminal Barabbas or Jesus who was called Christ, they chose Barabbas, and of Jesus cried out, "Let him be crucified." And the descendants of these murderers of God are all around. Curious and, yes, fearful the boy ventures among them. In the market of Mea Shearim he sees pale exotic Jews with hairy faces, in black satin coats reaching to their ankles and broad hats decorated by fur, haggling over dead chickens and fly-blown groceries. He mixes with the noisy, polyglot crowds in Zion Square, watches them gorge on sticky pastries in the cafés of Ben Yehuda Street, listens to the quarrelsome-sounding gabble of liturgical Hebrew in synagogues. Jews are thrusting and arrogant. The Church says they are accursed. They frighten yet fascinate him. The virus of a diseased obsession invades a young impressionable mind.

But reading between the lines of Colonel Schlips' smugly posturing report, it would appear that Kampfmann was less than eager to enlist in the SS. A bit of arm twisting seemed to have taken place. Himmler and the Gestapo had arrived in Vienna to root out the "one per cent" who voted "no" in the referendum. Not difficult to imagine the panic of a theological student remanded after "routine interrogation" for further investigation. The dossier photograph was far from being the sort of self-conscious picture of noble virility fledgling Nazi warriors sent home for display on the family sideboard.

With a vague feeling of astonishment and disquiet, Shomron realized that something in him was groping not merely for understanding but for mitigation of Kampfmann's guilt. The man's image had begun to merge with that of the dead Benamir. Did he therefore want to prove him better than the rest, a weakling intimidated into complicity with evil? He returned to the reading room sternly reminding himself that he was examining the case history of a mass-murderer.

Kampfmann's career at the Berlin SS headquarters as recorded in his dossier was that of a low-ranking bureaucrat. It must have been regarded as a cushy job. He killed at long range with lethal bits of paper, compiling Jewish population statistics so that the necessary quota of cattle trucks could be requisitioned to transport the victims to death camps, researching into communal records for prominent Jews to lead their fellows passively to annihilation, cataloguing the illustrious, writing brief monographs on Jewish religious festivals so that large-scale atrocities could be synchronized with the Days of Awe and Rejoicing. The SS Jewish section kept the account books of the Final Solution. Like managers of busy factories, camp commandants sent prompt and meticulous reports: how many "pieces" received, how many sorted out for work kommandos, the number of "pieces" fed into crematoria. Belsen, Auschwitz, Treblinka—day by day the figures poured in as the vast industrial process of turning millions into ash increased. Kampfmann was well-placed to measure the scale of the operation.

He was also apparently in the position to stretch out his hand and pluck a human insect from the fire. Included in his file was the report of an anonymous informer. It disclosed that among Catholic priests incarcerated in Dachau had been a certain Father Wertheim, subsequently released. This man's papers were falsified to conceal the fact that he was born a Jew. Investigations were set in motion but did not succeed in tracing Wertheim.

However, it was discovered that he had entered the priesthood in Vienna after graduating from the Jesuit college attended by Ulrich Walther Kampfmann. After being held for enquiries in the Alexanderplatz police headquarters, Kampfmann appeared before a Party disciplinary court. He must have defended himself skillfully. His superior at the Reichsführing-SS attested to his valuable services. The verdict of the court was that he needed an education in hardness, one of the basic requirements laid down by Heinrich Himmler for members of the SS, the others being loyalty, honesty, obedience, poverty and bravery. Announcing his verdict, the presiding officer quoted from the Reichsführer SS's famous speech:

Every Party member says, "We will liquidate the Jewish race. Naturally, it is in the Party programme. We will eliminate them, liquidate them. Easily done." Then your eighty million good German citizens turn up and each one has his decent Jew. Of course all the others are pigs, but this one is a splendid Jew. None of those who talked like this has watched, none of them has stuck it out. Most of you know what it means when a hundred corpses are lying side by side, or five hundred, or a thousand. To have stuck it out and at the same time—apart from exceptions caused by human weakness—to have remained decent fellows, that is what has made us hard. This is a page of glory in our history which has

445

never been written and is never to be written . . .

In the early autumn of 1944, SS Oberleutnant Ulrich Walther Kampfmann took up his duties in Dachau. Several weeks later while carrying out a routine selection of a fresh batch of victims for gassing he entered the black notebooks of Franz Slonimsky.

A single line entry added by the hand of an American military official closed the record. "Reported killed in the fighting to liberate Dachau Concentration Camp, 24 or 25 April, 1945." A military identity disc taken from the corpse was attached together with a Nazi Party membership card in a transparent plastic cover on which the holder's photograph was affixed. Shomron compared it to the earlier picture. The transformation was striking. Time had fleshed out the face under the Death's Head cap badge. The confusion and uncertainty had gone. There was a wary, secretive look in the unsmiling eyes. Kampfmann had lost his innocence and mastered the strategy of deception.

Returning the dossier, Shomron said to the librarian: "Can I have zeroxes made of these documents?"

"Certianly, I'll have it done right away," was her crisply efficient answer.

Shomron sat down and began to assess the consequences.

16

"**Y**OU WERE gone precisely sixty-four hours, thirty-five minutes," said Deborah, following him into the bathroom to continue the conversation. "By Israeli time that's long enough for a lot of people to be killed and maimed in another war. I've unplugged the radio and stopped reading newspapers, so for all I know it may already have happened. Excluding that there's nothing much to report and I hope your journey proved worthwhile."

"It was necessary," said Shomron. He stepped into the cold shower to clear his head from the daze of travel, lifting his face to the sharp stinging spray. "Did you phone the hospital to ask about my friend Lipkin?"

"I did better, I took him some fruit. He fell asleep in the middle of one of his jokes. They say he's very weak but still holding on."

"If he can still tell jokes, he'll live. Humor is the old rascal's survival kit. I'll call in and see him in the morning."

"You haven't given me a proper answer," Deborah insisted. "Did Berlin solve anything? Did you find what you were looking for?"

For some moments there was only the sound of splashing water. The question held existential undertones. The question bred more questions. Martin Buber once said a man must do what he can until he comes to a point he knows is the border. But what if he travels blindly, groping in mist? What if he suddenly finds he has blundered into forbidden territory?

"I'd rather not have found it," he said, turning the water off and taking the towel she held out to him.

She stroked his wet hair, moved as much by his nakedness as his obvious distress. "Poor Amos, I'll get you something to eat."

Shomron kissed her. "You're making me feel sexy. How long have we got before the children come home from school?"

Playing her seductress role and fluttering her eyelashes, Deborah answered: "How long do you need?"

Laughing, they entered the bedroom and were soon exchanging erotic caresses with the tenderness of married lovers when the telephone shat-

450

tered the afternoon's curtained peace. Cursing softly, Shomron rolled over on his side to answer it. Deborah heard a muffled voice speak briefly. There was silence. "When?" Shomron said in a strange tone. The voice spoke again. Deborah's heart was pierced by a needle-like intuition. Raising herself on her elbow, she gazed at his motionless back. He continued to hold the dumb telephone to his ear.

"Darling, what is it?" she asked in hushed alarm.

Blindly, he replaced the receiver and looked at her. His eyes were stunned.

"Louis," he said, "is dead . . . Two hours ago."

She put out her arms to embrace him but he broke away. Oddly, like a child hurt and disgraced, he stumbled to a corner of the shadowed room and stood with his bowed head leaning against the wall. Deborah went over, held him for a moment, then slipped on her robe and left him alone with his grief.

Dear Louis Lipkin, with his shapeless flapping coat, his wry philosophy and moralizing wit; Louis the *luftmensch,* his portable livelihood of flawed diamonds in a greasy wash-leather bag tied to a waistband underneath his baggy trousers; Lipkin bobbing like a cork on the turbulent sea of life, smelling of spiced herrings and garlic cucumber and small Jewish ghost towns of upturned gravestones and desolation . . .

His body shuddered as though something in him was breaking apart, then the tears he had

451

been too young to shed for his father, the scalding, exorbitant tears of irreparable loss, blinded his eyes.

Yisgadal ve'yiskadash shmai raboh . . .

After a while, Deborah brought him a glass of lemon tea, holding his hand and sitting quietly beside him while he drank it. A short while later, he dressed himself and left for the hospital.

Colonel David Lester of the Mossad, linguist and master of reticence, ignored the Berlin xeroxes Shomron had placed on the desk. Reflectively fingering the lobe of his left ear, he asked: "Have you prepared the report on your London visit? When we last met you promised to do so without delay."

Blue penetrating eyes regarded him with quizzical detachment, perhaps a remote compassion. Lipkin's black-bordered death notice had appeared in *Ha'arets.* The morning's newspapers were neatly piled at Lester's elbow. He probably knew the connection. He knew a great deal.

"I haven't had time," replied Shomron. "Aren't you going to read these documents?"

"There's nothing in them we don't already know."

"But you haven't even glanced at them!" Shomron vehemently protested. He shook out the contents of the envelope and thrust them under the Colonel's nose. "It's all here, the SS officer's complete dossier, and it makes a very convincing case for Sinclair's claim. Kampfmann spent eleven years in Jerusalem. He grew up in this city! He could have passed for a Jew anywhere!"

David Lester calmly moved the papers aside. "You went to a great deal of trouble and expense to get these documents. A waste of energy. While you've been carrying out your unauthorized investigation, we've not exactly been idle ourselves." Rising swiftly, he crossed over to a large safe and brought out a substantial file. Opening it, he began to lay out a number of exhibits.

"Item one: curriculum vitae of Kampfmann, Ulrich Walther. Two: blow-ups of subject's two passport photographs. Three: a report and character assessment by SS Investigator Colonel Otto Schlips. Four: an anonymous informer's report of certain irregularities in relation to the documents of a Catholic priest of Jewish origin. Five: proceedings of an SS disciplinary court. Six: account of subject's service in Dachau and presumed death. Etcetera."

Shormon nodded ruefully. He might have guessed that Israel's resourceful intelligence service, leaving nothing to chance, would have gathered every piece of information on Kampfmann by every means available. How much, he wondered, was contained in that cryptic "Etcetera"?

"Am I allowed to know what else you've discovered?"

"Not a great deal. A few small but revealing details omitted from his Party records. The Nazis were accustomed to reducing human beings to

453

generalities. Kampfmann fitted their stereotype—Nordic, German, racially pure. It was enough for them. Sinclair did the same. He came to think of Kampfmann as symbolic, an embodiment of evil, significant less for who he was than for what he represented. But who was he, really?"

Lester gathered up the documents and returned the file to the safe. Restlessly prowling the room and musing aloud, he said: "Given, as you say, that he knew enough to pass as a Jew, why should he wish to do so? And why here in Israel? Let's assume that he and Benamir were indeed the same person. Adopting the identity of a concentration camp victim, mixing with survivors, was a strategy of concealment. The murderer vanished in the crowd. Then he meets a woman: he could have fallen in love."

"But," Shomron pointed out, "the choice of coming to Palestine was his, not his wife's."

"True, so we move to another hypothesis—an act of penitence. His Catholic conscience is reawakened. Rivka Kloster, who herself grew up a Catholic, believes the answer may lie there. I find it as unconvincing as another metaphysical idea, that the Nazi creed is the mirror image of Judaism, its followers saw themselves as locked in combat with a cosmic enemy, and when Germany lost Kampfmann joined the winning side."

"Is there nothing in what you've found that provides a credible motive?"

"Credibility is precisely what is lacking. The man was an occultist dabbling in theories of imaginary and symbolic worlds. He believed that the Book of Revelations contains the key to the universe. We have this on the authority of a fellow seminarist, Wertheim, whose papers he helped to falsify and whom the SS were unable to trace. Wertheim is now a parish priest in Chicago. He and Kampfmann shared adjacent cubicles. Kampfmann was convinced the mysteries of Revelations could be unlocked by applying to the text the numerical equivalent of the Tetragrammaton, the name of God Jews are forbidden to speak. He stayed up whole nights covering sheets of paper with mysterious calculations."

Colonel Lester came to a halt by the window, tall, blond, English-looking, his cool-cut profile outlined against a shaft of sunlight. If he had not been a Jew he could never have passed for one, not even in Israel where a long-dispersed people had returned seeded with the racial characteristics of Slavs, Teutons, Latins, Vikings, Arabs and remote tribes from the mountains and valleys of Asia. In his secret career, David Lester had used various identities and passports, all of them Anglo-Saxon. But he always knew why: he was rational, deliberate, systematic and, above all, highly motivated.

And he knew exactly why he had chosen in this instance to be unusually talkative.

Sauntering back to the desk with a preoccupied look, he spoke to Shomron with donnish precision. "The reason for this arcane disquisition is that you place too much reliance on the various discoveries made about Kampfmann. As a study in human oddity he is no doubt interesting, but the obscurities remain impenetrable. Ultimately, his metamorphosis into a Jew named Avram Benamir is unprovable: and I'm not sure it matters."

"It does to Sinclair," Shomron retorted. "And to me."

"In Sinclair's case that is understandable." The note of asperity in Lester's voice was unmistakable. "It also matters to Benamir's innocent family. Why you should be obsessed by it is a question only you can answer."

"Great is truth, and mighty above all things," Shomron quoted. A morbid excitement set his heart beating fast. He had a famished need for a smoke and lit a cigarette with an agitated match. "The peculiarity of this case is its metaphysical character," he said intensely. "We're dealing not with a crime but a mystery. Everything connected with it is irrational, ambiguous, not least the assassin. He calls himself Frank Sinclair and wears the identity like a borrowed suit. He buries himself in silence yet craves a platform from which to address the world. Did he kill out of revenge and a desire for justice? Yes and no. Beyond that, he sees himself as a redeemer with a mission to purge Israel from the contamination of evil. The victim is another enigma and of him we know the least. He arrives on the scene without a past, as weird as a man who casts no shadow. For me this is the most convincing argument that he and Kampfmann are one, if not the same. For

456

Kampfmann *is* his shadow. The one is the obverse of the other. Let me remind you of some of the things Benamir is reported to have said," Shomron went on, fixing Colonel Lester with a glittering eye and waving away the smoke of his smouldering cigarette. "Mrs. Benamir told me that her husband believed very much in God. If proof of God's existence was needed one only has to look at the history of the Jews. It was God's will that the Jews should return to the Promised Land and, even though it's hard to understand, that was the meaning of the terrible events they had lived through. Benamir's daughter quoted her father as saying, 'Everything we were, everything we believed, is on the other side of the grave. We're not the same people. Palestine was a new beginning.' Perhaps the most revealing conversation of all took place between Benamir's son, the scientist, and myself a few days ago—I'm sure it's no secret to you that he came to visit me. Yuval explained that his father spoke of the Holocaust in apocalyptic terms. The way he did so was so appalling that every word is engraved on my memory. 'It was a holy martyrdom. The Holocaust was the Sacrifice, the Crucifixion of the Jewish people. Israel is the Redemption.'"

Once again Shomron experienced the revulsion these macabre sentiments had originally aroused. He stared broodingly at his glowing cigarette-end, then crushed out the stub.

"Can you begin to see what pattern emerges?" he demanded of David Lester, who listened intently, leaning back in his chair in an attitude of quiet deliberation. "Benamir was a man lacking a past, Kampfmann a man without a future. He was born a Catholic, underwent training for the priesthood, held eccentric, probably heretical, ideas, chief of them a belief in a divine plan the secrets of which were locked away in prophetical Bible texts. It can be inferred from the SS dossier that this idiosyncratic apprentice priest did not fling himself into the Nazi Party with any enthusiasm. In the Jewish section of the SS he performed the function of a civil servant in the administration of death. Tuned as he was to the Infinite, he may have retained only an abstract conception of the true significance of what was going on. It's more than possible. He dealt in numbers, supply sheets, paper information. Television had not been invented, the Nazis abstained from publishing pictures of extermination in their newspapers, atrocities were cloaked in euphemism, listening to foreign broadcasts required courage. It was a matter of knowing, yet not knowing. All this came to an abrupt end when the SS first lieutenant quitted his desk job for active service in the concentration camp. Paper deaths became mountains of real corpses, the stench of shit, vomit and roasting human flesh. How is a one-time priest, an avid reader of biblical prophecy, a would-be interpreter of the supernatural, to view such monstrosities? He fits them into his eschatology. Whatever happens is an expression of the will of God and here His terrifying mysteries are being enacted.

The novice priest is reminded of the Crucifixion: now there is the Crucifixion of an entire people. That is how God manifests his esoteric purpose. He makes a Sacrifice of those He has elected—the Son hanging on the Cross, the Chosen People choking in gas-chambers and incinerated in crematoria. Was it not written that God in His judgment of his own Children of Israel would invoke a Day of Wrath, a catastrophe of cosmic proportions to herald the advent of the Messiah, gathering together a saving remnant to dwell once more in the Land of Israel and the Holy City of Jerusalem?

"The question that arises," continued Shomron, "is how he sees his own role in this awful and majestic process. Butchery is filthy work for a sensitive, idealistic man. But did he choose it? No, step by step he was led to this task, and if God is the omnipotent dictator of each soul's destiny then He has laid this burden upon His servant. Not a stone falls or a blade of grass stirs except by Divine will. So Kampfmann submits. It will not exclude him from salvation. Where is it written that Pontius Pilate or the Roman soldiers who hammered the nails into the hands and feet of Christ were sentenced to eternal damnation? Only those who chose Barabbas and rejected Jesus, only those who refused to believe were damned."

A long, echoing silence followed this blasphemous tirade. Shomron sat with eyes closed, arms hanging limply over the sides of the chair in the attitude of a trance medium used and abandoned by the voices of the dead. Seated opposite, David

Lester's expression remained inscrutable. He had listened and watched and committed to memory, standing one pace behind himself as his profession trained him to do. Emotional turbulence interfered with judgment, and he allowed the silence to continue as one might open a window for smoke to disperse from a room.

"I agree with those who think we have overburdened ourselves by dwelling too much on the Holocaust," he pronounced crisply. "Like generals who always fight the last war, it has adversely influenced our actions and impaired our judgment. The Holocaust is a distorting shadow over Israel and its future. We must move out from under it."

"We still remember Haman. How can we forget Hitler so soon?" Shomron asked tiredly. The remark was rhetorical: he had a more immediate question on his mind. "Now that you have all the available evidence, what happens next?"

"What do *you* think should happen next?"

Shomron flinched at the challenge. A dead man lying behind the shattered windscreen of a car, a routine homicide, and the earth had opened over six million graves. He thought of the agony of Yuval Benamir and all his grieving kin, and how the past like a hidden mine could detonate an explosion that would shatter their lives . . . He wanted to say: let's forget it, it's been a bad dream. Instead, reluctantly, he said: "Sinclair has a right to a trial, in open court. Whatever the consequences. Will he get that?"

Colonel Lester stared at him and replied with cold severity: "The form of judicial process will be decided by the Attorney-General as the Government Legal Adviser. Because of the factors involved, he may consult the Prime Minister." His mouth twisted wryly. "He, as you know, also has a passionate commitment to the history of yesterday." Rising from his chair to signal that the meeting was terminated, he added: "As for you, Captain Shomron, I think it would be wise to give serious consideration to your future."

About three in the morning Deborah was awakened by the insomniac sound of a typewriter. The place at her side was empty. Getting up to investigate, she saw a light under the door of Shomron's study.

"Amos, what's going on," she asked sleepily.

"Darling, please go back to bed," he said. "I'll explain in the morning."

Her drowsiness vanished. They had been married more than twelve years. Long enough to finish one another's sentences, to communicate by sudden flashes of intuition.

"You're writing a letter of resignation," she said.

"How did you guess?"

"It's been coming. I've sensed it."

Deborah felt scared and oddly excited. The occasion called for strong nerves and coffee. She went into the kitchen to brew up.

"Don't tell me why, because I know," she said

on her return. "Tell me what you propose to do for a living."

"Can you support me on your salary?" he joked, as they always did in a crisis.

"Not with the present rate of inflation."

"I'll use my degree in law and go into private practice," he said, becoming serious.

Deborah drank her coffee reflectively. "We'll begin by discussing that," she said.

They were going to have to do a lot of talking and the dawn came early.

They had managed to keep things quiet, unobtrusively listing the case to give no indication of its traumatic importance. When Shomron arrived at the Tel Aviv District Court shortly after eleven the Yallin hearing was still in progress. Black-gowned lawyers had flocked to the courtroom, for the trial was a sensational one concerning a gang killing gruesomely performed in a meat cold-storage plant. The victim's body, expertly dismembered, had been buried in sand dunes. There were other colorful details. The chief defendant, a power in the Israeli underworld, enjoyed the life-style of a mafia godfather on the proceeds of prostitution, extortion, robbery and blackmail. Officers of the Tel Aviv police had cracked a bottle of champagne to celebrate his arrest: it marked the fall of a kingdom.

Shomron came in on a subdued titter of laughter. The principal judge, a matronly woman of late middle-age, leaned back in her thronelike chair under the state seal of Israel and exchanged amused glances with her two male colleagues. In the dock stood the mafia chief, a smooth dark Yemenite, nattily dressed, with a pencil-thin moustache and neatly trimmed sideboards, who turned his head from side to side smiling brilliantly as if acknowledging applause. The six rows of public benches were full and he was playing to the gallery. Smiles came from the prosecutor too, for when the laughter died away and the auditorium darkened, the comedian would be left with only the harsh judgment of his three magisterial critics. The same thought must have occurred to his co-defendants, who did not smile at all. The oldest of them, a full-bodied patriarchal figure wearing an embroidered skull cap, mournfully stroked his chest-length beard and gave the philosophical shrug of one who was a mere accessory after the fact and might yet end his days in a comfortable bed.

The press bench was also crowded. Ace crime reporter Dov Yudkin, sharp nose close to the pad, busily scribbled his fast-paced, thrillerish impression of the scene. "Gang killings should be classified with blood-sports, like duels to the death between Roman gladiators," he'd written in one of his columns. Crime as entertainment; the court of justice as theater. It outclassed fiction. But for Yudkin, who missed nothing, the main drama of the day was yet to begin.

An adjournment was called. Prosecutor Gottlieb, a spry, cheerful Ben-Gurion-like man with tufts of wiry grey hair fringing his ruddy bald patch, emerged from the courtroom rubbing his hands.

"Our friend is talking himself into a life sentence," he said to Shomron. "And, by the way, what is this I hear about you resigning from the police force?"

Other lawyers were equally curious. A few rungs of the ladder and he'd have been at the top. Shulamit Fenster, the old flame of his student days, was attorney for one of the lesser defendants. She came over, long blonde hair hanging down the back of her gown, green eyes avid with curiosity, and exclaimed: "Amos, is it true? I can't believe it!"

They stood in the corridor while he parried her cross-examination, then exchanged news about their respective children. Glancing idly through the window overlooking the rear entrance, he saw a blue police van describe a semi-circle and pull up at the door. Two armed guards alighted followed by a manacled prisoner. The man walked unsteadily, looking dazed and wincing from the sunlight like a nocturnal animal. Shomron stopped abruptly in the middle of a sentence and moved closer to the window.

"What is it, Amos?" Shulamit Fenster asked, following the direction of his eyes. She could see nothing out of the ordinary, just the stationary prison van and a police officer wearing a crash-helmet standing by his motor-cycle in a small patch of shade.

Shomron shook his head and muttered: "Nothing. Nothing at all . . ."

Frank Sinclair had arrived and he looked as if he'd been broken.

Within moments a black Chevrolet turned into the courtyard. Two men got out of the back seat. The first was David Lester, a packed briefcase tucked under his arm, his movements brisk and confident. He was joined by Yuval Benamir. Silently, they approached the building. As they did so a girl stepped from the doorway, her thin summer frock lifting in the warm breeze, and clicked a camera at their faces, smiling as though taking a holiday snapshot. Colonel Lester ignored her, but when he and Yuval had gone the motorcycle cop walked over, took the camera from the girl without a word and exposed the film to the sun.

"Shulamit, I have to go," Shomron said, the clock of his heart ticking fast. "I'm sitting in on my last case."

The stage of Number Two Court was deserted. On one of the public benches sat a man reading an early edition of the evening newspaper, *Ma'ariv*. The woman beside him had her arms around a plastic shopping bag. Shomron slipped into an inconspicuous seat at the back, hoping to remain unnoticed. Minutes passed: court officials took their places in readiness for the appearance of the principals: the duty policeman positioned himself at the door. David Lester's hopes for a small audience looked likely to be fulfilled.

But the trial could not hope to escape publicity. Lean and hungry Dov Yudkin came prowling in, glanced at the vacant press bench, and gave a satisfied nod. Secrecy had worked in his favor, with luck he'd have a world exclusive, on the preliminary hearing at least. They'd all come flocking in after that.

The funeral procession of Benamirs arrived, Yuval supporting his widowed mother, his handsome sister Yael searching the courtroom until her eyes, glaring tragically, settled on Shomron with an undying look of enmity. He shifted uneasily. The migraine of guilt throbbed in his temples; whatever the justification, he'd never get over that.

Quietly, without fuss, a sandy-haired man in a shabby lawyer's robe entered through the rear door and methodically laid out his papers. The State had chosen its prosecuting attorney well, one of Israel's most brilliant advocates, a deflator of rhetoric, a man of dry and astringent wit with a brain cold and sharp as a surgeon's scalpel. When he got to work on Sinclair's defense, it would be like watching a man being dissected alive.

The scent of expensive perfume distracted Shomron. Rivka Kloster slipped into the place beside him, elegantly dressed for a sombre occasion. Crumpling a lace handkerchief in her small ringed hands, she whispered: "God! this is going to be unbearable. I almost didn't come."

The usher called silence. Enter the magistrate. A brief bow to the assembled court before taking his seat and everyone settled down, gazing at the door through which the prisoner would appear.

Frank Sinclair stood for a moment in the doorway flanked by his escort, eyes closed as if in prayer. His head was covered by a black skull cap and he had grown a straggling grey-streaked beard. Cadaverous, moving with slow precarious steps, he mounted to the dock and stared out at the world with a severe and haunting gaze, rabbinical, terrifying and remote.

Quietly he took the oath. Then raising his voice in a vibrancy that resonated throughout the court, he announced:

"My name is Franz Slonimsky and I am here to speak for the dead."

Amos Shomron shuddered. The trial had begun and it would bring no good to anyone.

OTHER STEIN AND DAY BOOKS YOU'LL ENJOY:

OTHER STEIN AND DAY BOOKS

MILITARY BOOKS FROM STEIN AND DAY

			U.S.	Canada
	8035-8	**ALL THE DROWNED SAILORS** Raymond B. Lech	3.95	4.50
	8015-3	**DEATH OF A DIVISION** Charles Whiting	2.95	2.95
	8109-9	**THE GLORY OF THE SOLOMONS** Edwin Hoyt	3.95	4.95
	8100-1	**A HISTORY OF BLITZKREIG** Bryan Perrett	3.95	NCR
	8039-0	**HOW WE LOST THE VIETNAM WAR** Nguyen Cao Ky	3.50	3.95
	8027-7	**MASSACRE AT MALMEDY** Charles Whiting	2.95	3.50
	8045-5	**ROMMEL'S DESERT WAR** Samuel W. Mitcham, Jr.	3.50	3.95
	8105-2	**SALERNO** Eric Morris	3.95	4.95
	8033-1	**SECRETS OF THE SS** Glenn B. Infield	3.50	3.95
	8093-5	**SUBMARINES AT WAR** Edwin P. Hoyt	3.95	4.95
	8037-4	**THE WEEK FRANCE FELL** Noel Barber	3.95	4.50
	8057-9	**THE WORLD AT WAR** Mark Arnold-Forster	3.95	NCR

EATING TO WIN

Food Psyching for the Athlete

Frances Sheridan Goulart

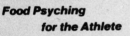

Whether you are a weekend athlete or a professional, whatever your age or sex, *Eating to Win*, the *original* book about sports nutrition, will teach you which foods increase your strength and stamina—and which do not. What you eat can determine whether you win or lose.

Eating to Win tells you how to win through food. It is sure to be the most indispensable piece of sports equipment you'll ever own.